PANDAEMONIUM

ST. MARTIN'S

PRESS

NEW YORK

PANDAEMONIUM

A NOVEL

LESLIE

EPSTEIN

PANDAEMONIUM. Copyright © 1997 by Leslie Epstein. All rights reserved. Printed in the United States of America. No part of this book may be used or reproduced in any manner whatsoever without written permission except in the case of brief quotations embodied in critical articles or reviews. For information, address St. Martin's Press, 175 Fifth Avenue, New York, N.Y. 10010.

Portions of this work first appeared, in slightly different form, in the *Boston Book Review*, *Georgia Review*, the *Partisan Review*, *Tikkun*, and *Bostonia*.

Book design by Gretchen Achilles

Library of Congress Cataloging-in-Publication Data

Epstein, Leslie.
     Pandaemonium / Leslie Epstein.
          p.   cm.
     ISBN 0-312-15622-7
     I. Title.
     PS3555.P655P36   1997
     813'.54—dc21   96-53874
                                                                                          CIP

First Edition: May 1997

10   9   8   7   6   5   4   3   2   1

The author would like to thank the Rockefeller Foundation for the opportunity to stay at the Bellagio Study and Conference Center, where some sunshine entered this book. Thanks, too, to the officials and staff of the Villa Serbelloni, whom he remembers with fondness.

The author happily acknowledges his debt to Alexander Granach and the wonderful account of his early life in *There Goes an Actor*.

THIS BOOK IS FOR PHILIP G. EPSTEIN, 1909–1952

AND FOR JULIUS J. EPSTEIN, 1909–

Gift of Gab, 1934
Love on a Bet, 1936
The Bride Walks Out, 1936
Grand Jury, 1936
New Faces of 1937, 1937
The Mad Miss Manton, 1938
There's That Woman Again, 1938
Daughters Courageous, 1939
Four Wives, 1939
Saturday's Children, 1940
No Time for Comedy, 1940
The Bride Came C.O.D., 1941
The Strawberry Blonde, 1941
Honeymoon for Three, 1941
The Man Who Came to Dinner, 1941
The Male Animal, 1942
Casablanca, 1942
Yankee Doodle Dandy, 1942
Mr. Skeffington, 1944
Arsenic and Old Lace, 1944
One More Tomorrow, 1946
Romance on the High Seas, 1948
My Foolish Heart, 1949
Take Care of My Little Girl, 1951
Forever Female, 1953
The Last Time I Saw Paris, 1954

Living on Velvet, 1935
In Caliente, 1935
Little Big Shot, 1935
I Live for Love, 1935
Star Over Broadway, 1935
Sons o' Guns, 1936
Confession, 1937
Four Daughters, 1938
Secrets of an Actress, 1938
Daughters Courageous, 1939
Four Wives, 1939
Saturday's Children, 1940
No Time for Comedy, 1940
The Bride Came C.O.D., 1941
The Strawberry Blonde, 1941
Honeymoon for Three, 1941
The Man Who Came to Dinner, 1941
The Male Animal, 1942
Casablanca, 1942
Yankee Doodle Dandy, 1942
Mr. Skeffington, 1944
Arsenic and Old Lace, 1944
One More Tomorrow, 1946
Romance on the High Seas, 1948
My Foolish Heart, 1949
Take Care of My Little Girl, 1951
Forever Female, 1953
The Last Time I Saw Paris, 1954
Young at Heart, 1954
The Tender Trap, 1955
Kiss Them for Me, 1957
Take a Giant Step, 1958
Tall Story, 1960
Fanny, 1960
Light in the Piazza, 1962
Send Me No Flowers, 1964
Return from the Ashes, 1965
Any Wednesday, 1966
Pete 'n Tillie, 1972
Once Is Not Enough, 1975
Cross of Iron, 1977
House Calls, 1978
Reuben, Reuben, 1982

CONTENTS

PART FIVE   DAYS OF INFAMY

At last as from a cloud his fulgent head
And shape star-bright appeared, or brighter, clad
With what permissive glory since his fall
Was left him, or false glitter.

—MILTON

Excuse, please. Explain later.

—MOTO

PART

ONE

FESTIVAL

February–April 1938

STORM CLOUDS

If this had been a movie and not real life, the stormclouds beyond my airplane window would be painted on canvas or constructed from papier-mâché. A couple of grips would be shaking our cut-out fuselage. That lightning, so near, so frightful, would be made by the arc lights, and the roar of the thunder would come from a piece of tin. Alas, I had only to look through my own familiar reflection—that round face, the bulging eyes, lips set in an idiot's perpetual grin—to know that this was no motion picture. Down below: that was the Wiesbachhorn, and that the Reichenspitze; and there, practically under the seat of my pants, loomed the Grossglockner, king of the Alps. I pressed my face to the glass, to stare at the riveted wing. The propeller was a blur. The engine howled like an animate being.

Here was the bedeviling question: why was a Jew, a Hungarian, not to mention a coward like me, making such sickening circles in the sky? In one sense the answer was easy. Our DC-3 had been chartered from Air France by the Austrian government. Everyone on board was flying from Paris to Salzburg in order to mount a new production of *Antigone*. This was the play that would open that city's festival for 1938. For some reason having to do with politics, with Herr Hitler, only a Rudolph Von Beckmann production would do. Rumor had it that Von Schuschnigg, the Austrian chancellor, had fallen onto his knees before the director. He wanted this great impresario to save his nation from being swallowed up by its neighbor to the north.

Just then, as I was pondering the reasons for hurtling at such fantastic speed through the air, a sudden blaze of light—it was as if the whole Hollywood press corps had set off their flash lamps—startled our troupe of actors. The wings dipped left, dipped right, and the plane dropped like a stone.

Someone screamed. The lights in the cabin went out. I kept my eyes—popping, as was their trademark—on the window glass. The world outside, the whole of the Bavarian Alps, had turned dark as night. Up ahead Serge, Von Beckmann's valet, started to sob. Sampson Frank, one of the actors, called out, "What has happened? Have we been struck by lightning?" Then a voice—how to describe it? Husky? Throaty? It was known the world over for its vibrato, like the string of a violin or violoncello—floated through the blackened compartment:

"Don't worry, little lamb. All will be well."

Naturally, a shiver ran the length of my spine. I knew that the words of Magdalena Mezaray had been meant only for me.

Then another voice came from the rear. "Please, ladies and gentlemen. There is no cause for alarm. The aircraft has been designed for such conditions."

I turned, glancing over the back of my seat toward the gyrating tail. A man—rather, a youth, no more than twenty—was half-standing there. This was the chancellor's adjutant, blond-haired, fine-featured, in the uniform of an Austrian lieutenant. "You see?" added our escort as the American-made craft leveled off and the lights blinked back on over our heads. "The shock of electricity has already been dissipated."

"What do you know? You are a stupid man. A stupid soldier." These words came from the front. Serge, the valet, was leaning into the aisle. He was trembling. He was whimpering. His face, sharp-chinned, with the skin taut upon it, was like a fawn's. The curls of his hair tumbled to his cheeks. On the seat beside him, I knew, was the tank of oxygen that he kept close to Von Beckmann, whether his companion was asleep or awake.

Now the impresario himself rose from his seat and made his way toward his shaking servant. His upper body, the massive torso, completely filled the aisle, though it rested upon a pair of long and spindly legs. The face was full, puffy, sallow; the dark eyes were drooping and heavy-lidded, as if pulled down by the pockets of flesh underneath. On the thick lip, a thin line of moustache. A cape, a carnation, a monocle on a ribbon. When Von Beckmann turned toward the lad, I could make out the celebrated profile: a jaw that jutted prognathically forward, while the hair—jet black, save for a frostbitten shaft of white—sprang to the rear. What a large head! I'd already made a bet with my old friend Basserman that there wasn't a store in Berlin, Paris, or Vienna that could supply him with a ready-made hat.

"What is this? Tears, *mein Honigkuchen*? Is the little bird weeping?"

Von Beckmann, crouching, took the valet's face, with its high cheekbones, its pinched Tartar's eyes, into both hands.

"We're going to crash! I know it! Into the ice!"

Von B shook his great head. "Dear boy, you must be making a joke. You wish to amuse me. You know that cannot be the fate of Von Beckmann—to be crushed at random, without meaning, against the side of a rock. Like an insect. Ha-ha! What a silly child!"

Serge laughed, liltingly, as if he had never had a care. In the flickering lights I saw how, when the impresario rose again, the boy licked the palm of his hand, the way a deer might, for the taste of the salt.

From across the aisle, opposite my seat, came another laugh. There sat Albert Basserman himself, hatless, the white fluff of his hair parted on one side so as to cover the pink dome of his scalp. The wattles of his chin were pressed against the silk stripes of his four-in-hand. How unruffled, unflappable my old friend was—or seemed. Again he gave his lighthearted chuckle. Was it the exchange he'd just heard that he found amusing? Or something in the copy of *Figaro* he'd picked up in Paris? Although I knew he'd been a featured player in films going all the way back to *Das Gelobtes Land* of 1909, I still thought of him as the great interpreter of Ibsen and as a stage performer for Reinhardt and Von Beckmann. The strange thing was, he hadn't performed for the impresario in over ten years; yet he had willingly abandoned his new country and his family, so recently settled, at nothing more than the great man's call.

Was that it? The reason we were risking, with these aeronautical acrobatics, our lives? Basserman wasn't the only one who had come at Von Beckmann's summons. Sampson Frank, who was to be our Tiresias, was sitting one row back. That six-footer, with his patchy beard, his wire spectacles, had been with Von B from the beginning of his career. It would have been a surprise if he *hadn't* been on board. And Reynaldo Flatow, the playwright? He had adapted all of the director's classical productions, from the early *Orestea* cycle to last December's *Medea*. It was only natural that he should join us at Salzburg.

But what of Magdalena? At the thought of her, the mental murmuring of her name, I pushed myself upward and twisted about in order to peer into the rearmost rows. Fitting that I should see first the crossed legs in their patented fishnet stockings. Then I looked up to what at that moment was the most famous face in the world: the arched eyebrows over the half-closed eyes; the strong cheekbones and sunken cheeks; and, beneath the pillbox hat, the streaming waves of what Louella would call honey-colored hair. I thought I could see, in the full lower lip and the hint of a knob at the chin, something of the girl—a shopgirl, was she? Modeling hats?—that Von Beckmann had discovered during the war. Her first role for the director had been that of Ophelia, in the scandalous *Hamlet* of Berlin. Throughout the twenties, in the public mind, and in reality too, the impresario and the actress had been inseparable. You'd have to search long and hard to find a publicity photo in which they were not physically linked: strolling, laughing, shoulder to shoulder; she bending to hug him round the neck while he sits lost in thought; or extending her arm either to light the tip of his cigarette or dangle, from the tines of a fork—this might be in Maxim's or a taverna, a trattoria—some morsel that her mentor grasps between those white, even, surprisingly little teeth.

Through the whole of that decade, during which the actress never appeared except as an extension of, practically an extrusion, a beautiful bulge, in that big man's ectoplasm, there had hung about them an air of titillation and scandal. He was, after all, old enough to be the fräulein's father. He had found her, shaped her, created her; could he not, like a Pygmalion, a Svengali, use her as well? Of course she drew men, the way the bright petals of a flower must draw the busy, bumbling bees. But this was the question that the gossip columns, hinting and smirking, inevitably asked: were they for the protégée or for the master?

All that ended—when was it? In 1930. The two of them had agreed to sign a long-term contract with MGM and, on the *Normandie*, had sailed for New York. The couple got no further. For some reason Magdalena boarded the Twentieth Century Limited by herself, and she was alone when she arrived at Union Station on the Super Chief. Nobody imagined that, by herself, with only her own wits and talent, she would be able to complete a single picture. Well, she'd made a score—the first for MGM and the rest with Granite Films. With Victor Granite as her producer, she'd become an even greater star, more beautiful in my opinion, more glamorous, even more mysterious, than she had been in Europe. As for the impresario, he returned on the *Normandie*'s next sailing. Who could say why? There were stories about threats, and a looming scandal, from other studios, especially from Granite. All anyone knew for sure was that by the time Magdalena headed west, he was already on his way back to the continent where every literate citizen knew his face, his name—Von Beckmann, the famed Von B—and would step into the gutter to allow him, his jaw jutting forward, his hair streamlined behind, to pass.

The storm outside our twin-engine airship grew steadily worse. It felt as if the wind, like some whimsical giant, was tossing us from hand to hand. A flash, a thunderclap, and once more the lights went out. A little glow came from up front on the left. A match flare. Rudi Von Beckmann was lighting a cigarette. He and Magda had been separated now for almost eight years. Yet all he needed to do was snap his fingers and—*poof!* There went her contract; *poof!* goodbye to Victor Granite, her producer, her lover—she had come.

But not before asking me to join her. That had been at the farewell párty she'd given last New Year's, in the final hours of 1937. "Come with me, lambie. Rudi wants you, only you. For the role of Haemon, yes? Antigone's cousin. Also her bridegroom." She took my hand and squeezed it. She stepped behind me and kissed my neck. "Don't you want to be my lover?" I could still feel, under my camel-hair collar, the nibbling lips; still smell, in our tossing cabin, the musk of perfume: Was Frauen Träumen. "What Women Dream." To be her lover! At the thought my palms grew damp. After all, perhaps it was what those lips said—*Rudi wants you, only you*—that held the clue to this mystery: was I, Peter Lorre, tossing in the stratosphere for the same reason as all the others? Was it simply because Rudolph Von Beckmann had called?

The lights came on, flashing like a movie marquee. I reached into my left-hand pocket. I took out the scrap of the *Examiner* I'd bought on the day I took off from Van Nuys. The "Merry Go Round," I saw, was still spinning:

> It was so warm in Palm Springs over the weekend that I had more than my share of the old-fashioneds that Nick whips up so expertly at the Desert Inn bar. I had planned to be *hors de combat* for a few days, but I couldn't help noting how Lady Castelross's Schiaparelli dress auto-graphed with the names of all the movie stars drew so much attention and how Tyrone Power sat like a lost soul bluer than blue at the Ellsworth Vines–Fred Perry matches be-cause Janet Gaynor had hied herself off to Washington. Ty's making no secret of the fact that he's never been in love like this before. "Louella," he told me, "this is the real thing." I hope that puts an end to the rumors that some of our prying journalists—some people can't resist getting a Hedda!—have spread about Ty doing the Big Apple with the vivacious young Lana Turner who continues to make a name for herself after Les Kahn, the publicity boss at Gran-

ite, put out the word that she was discovered over an ice cream soda at Schwabs.

Metro's rush act in bringing an unknown boy from Salem, Oregon, sight unseen to play the young Nelson Eddy resulted in bitter disappointment to both the child and his mother. By the time they arrived the studio had decided to put William Cody Jr. into the role. Leo the Lion tried to compensate the mother by offering her a job but she turned it down, saying she had no ambitions as an actress and that her place is with her husband, who is a prune grower.

From THE CHATTERBOX: Doc Mosk reports that Mrs. Stan Laurel is at the Wilshire Hospital with a nervous collapse. J. Carrol Naish and his wife now have separate addresses. Rudy Vallee removed his raincoat while having a picture taken on the Warner lot; seems like he didn't want Florida to get the wrong impression. The Binnie Barnes–Jean Negulesco romance threatens to get serious; they were cooing for hours at Ciro's last night. Chick Chandler, he of the dimpled chin, was seen lunching with Frances Langford, which can't make his new friend, the raven-haired Rochelle Hudson, jump for joy.

All those doubting Thomases who scoffed at my exclusive a few months back that Greta Garbo and Leopold Stokowski were romancing are going to have to eat their hats when they find out that the conductor has just left in secret for Europe and that the Swedish star is waiting for him in her native land. It certainly appears that Greta does not "vant to be alone" any longer and that the doting duo will be married soon. Speaking of long distance lovebirds, don't be surprised if Magdalena Mezaray, who recently threw over old flame Victor Granite in order to return to Europe, falls once more under the spell of Rudolph Von Beckmann, who will be her director at this year's Salzberg Festival. If you think Victor was upset, you should have heard his handsome brother, Manfred, when he discovered his top femme star had torn up her contract. Even if I wanted to, Mr. Hearst would not let me print that flying filmmaker's words. If Magda and Rudi step over the border to visit the old country, they'll find that nobody's sleeping in the gutters anymore and that the streets are spic and span. Maybe, as Mr. Hearst always says, we should try a little of Herr Hitler's elbow grease in the good old U.S. of A. One person who won't be raising a stein of beer is Peter Lorre, who is also on his way to join Von Beckmann's Salzburg premiere. He changed his name from Laszlo Loewenstein for a good reason, though his fans know him as Mr. I. A. Moto. I've heard that Granite is planning a whole new series of adventures for the slant-eyed sleuth and—

I crumpled the newsprint. Good news! Chick Chandler, it seemed, was seeing someone besides Miss Rochelle Hudson, with whom we both had worked in our last feature. Bad news, too. More Moto! Moto to the crack of doom! I had already made four of those pitiful pictures, and the fifth, *Mysterious Mr. Moto,* was scheduled for production in May. Here, then, was the real reason I found myself on this ill-fated flight. The eyes of the world would be on Salzburg. Was it foolish of me to think that with such an international success—and as the romantic lead! Opposite Magda!—I would have enough stature to break my Granite contract? Would Von Beckmann really free me? I glanced forward to where a coil of smoke, like a ragged wreath of laurel, rose above the impresario's head. A cold shudder ran through me. I must have been a lunatic, a *Dummkopf,* to put my faith in the man. There would be for me no happy ending. Rather, my end had been determined at my beginning—from my very first picture. The brand had been chalked forever upon my back: *M.* For Murder. Malice. Madness. For Macabre. For Melodrama. Above all, for Moto.

At that moment the stewardess—a brunette, with her eyes set a little too close to her longish nose—stepped through the door that separated the passenger compartment from the cockpit. "*Mesdames et messieurs,*" she announced, "*le pilote désire . . .*"

What the captain desired was to inform us that we could not continue circling much longer and that unless there was a break in the weather soon, he would have to divert our flight to another destination.

"How soon?" Basserman inquired.

"*Dix minutes,*" the stewardess replied.

With my index finger I performed what everyone recognized to be the international gesture of apprehension: I crooked it under my collar. "Excuse me. Where, please, will we land? In Linz?"

"I regret to say," said the stewardess, "the storm is moving to the east. The visibility there is worse than here."

"Innsbruck, then?"

"The aerodrome in Innsbruck is not equipped for electronic operations. There too it is as dark as night."

The passengers, each one of us, turned to the glass of the nearest window. But there was nothing to see but the charcoal-dust of the clouds.

Basserman, with his practiced sangfroid, folded his newspaper into a square. "Very well: we return to Paris. You know, I believe that might be best, after all. I now remember I left a pair of shoes at the hotel."

At this little joke the stewardess managed a lipstick-stained smile. "I, too, monsieur, would prefer to spend this night in Paris. Alas, we haven't the petroleum for the flight. Our reserves are too low to reach even Vienna."

Flatow wiped, with a handkerchief, the top of his shining bald head. His eyes were swimming like goldfish in the lenses of his glasses. "No Paris," he muttered. "No Linz. No Vienna. Where on this earth can we land?"

The attendant, in responding, shifted to the German word: "München."

"Munich!" a half-dozen voices cried.

"*Oui.* The distance is one hundred twenty kilometers, and the sky is clear. Even if the storm should outrace us, they have the instruments for such a landing."

Basserman chuckled. "*Landing?* The difficulty is not with the landing. How will we take off, my dear? There are no instruments for that."

I reached into my pocket, this time the right-hand one, and took a pinch of powder between my fingers. "You can joke. But what about me? I am known in Germany. My name is on a list. Yes! Yes! It is Loewenstein! Laszlo Loewenstein!" Quickly I inhaled the magic potion. "Fine for you to laugh: Albert the Aryan. But what about us Jews?"

"Yes, yes," cried Flatow. "What about us?"

Magda leaned forward. Once again her words were meant only for me. "Do not be alarmed, my lamb. I have met Herr Hitler. Just before I left for America—and even before he became Reichskanzler. He was pleasant. Yes, even gay, even flirtatious. He smiled with his little cheeks, his little moustache. How he stared with those eyes! He'll listen to me, I feel certain. I won't let him touch a hair of lambie's head."

"No, no," came a voice from the rear. "I, too, have met Herr Hitler. Eight days ago, Fräulein Mezaray, not eight years."

The speaker was the man in uniform. Now he stood upright, so that his handsome blond head brushed the compartment ceiling.

"You?" Serge exclaimed. "Why would he meet with a little lieutenant?"

"I accompanied Chancellor Von Schuschnigg to the conference at Berchtesgaden, above which we are circling now. I can assure you that the Führer was not gay. There were no smiles. It was our Austrian chancellor who was forced to bow, to make pleasantries, to play the diplomat. We stood on that mountaintop, from where we could look from peak to peak down to Salzburg itself. The chancellor said that he hoped that in their coming talks they would be able to see as clearly. Do you know what Herr Hitler replied? *We are not here to discuss the view.* It was terrible! The man got everything he wanted. His troops will infiltrate our armies. His supporters are to run our Federal Police. We couldn't get in a word. It was like talking to a Martian!" The poor patriot, in his agony, had begun to twist his cloth cap in his hands. "We came down the mountain in a half track. When we reached the bottom, Von Schuschnigg said to me, *He will break his word on everything, Anton. You cannot make a gentleman's agreement when there is only one gentleman.*"

Sampson Frank stood at his seat. In the flickering lights his spectacles blinked like semaphore signals. "Why are you telling us this? Is it to frighten us? Young man, you are succeeding."

"I merely wanted to say that it is impossible to land at Munich. A planeload of exiles bound for the festival at Salzburg, accompanied by the personal adjutant of the Austrian chancellor—this would be just the pretext the Reichskanzler is seeking. No, no, mademoiselle. We must not land in Germany. It will create an international incident. It is not just a matter of risking our lives. It would be risking war."

From all of us a moan went up that mimicked the sound of the laboring engines. The stewardess, to whom these last words had been directed, stood petrified.

"Intolerable! It is an intolerable situation! I shall speak to the pilot." That was Von Beckmann. He, too, had risen from his seat.

"Monsieur Von Beckmann, *je vous en prie*—"

The stewardess begged him to sit down and to extinguish his cigarette. The director did neither. Instead, he stepped into the aisle and moved toward the front of the plane. At the same time the aircraft nosed downward, as if the sheer bulk of the man had unbalanced the DC-3, the way a standing passenger will tip a canoe. Trailing the exhaust of his cigarette behind him, Von Beckmann pushed through the door that the stewardess attempted to bar and disappeared inside the cockpit.

Almost at once another flash of lightning engulfed our craft. It seemed as if, just beneath us, the pagan god of Bavaria was hurling these bolts in his fury at our intrusion into his space. Or else he was enraged that we dared to challenge the Lord and Master at the one spot on earth, Salzburg, he most despised. Like a leaf, slipping and sliding, we tumbled downward through the blackening clouds. Of course I knew that it wasn't Salzburg that Hitler loathed but what Salzburg had become. The decadent plays of Von Hofmannsthal, the conducting of Walter and Klemperer, the staging of Reinhardt; worst of all, the audience, sophisticates, cosmopolites: it was as if this jewel of the Alps, for a thousand years an archbishopric in which no non-Christians had been allowed, had suddenly become a Jewish ghetto. And all within eyesight of Berchtesgaden! Not just eyesight. Do you suppose, if the wind were right, he could actually smell us, and hear the screech from our violins?

The little plane, our aluminum coffin, was still plummeting downward, faster than any elevator. The cabin lights sizzled, like the spark at the end of a fuse. Once more I reached into my pocket for the potent powder. Then I saw the stewardess trying to make her way down the aisle. Were those tears in her eyes? Dark eyes, I noted, small and brown, like coffee beans. Each of her hands, with their long red nails, was wringing the other. Without speaking I patted the cushion of the seat beside me.

"*Merci*, Monsieur Lorre," she said, and sank upon it.

"You know my name?" I inquired.

"*Oh, mais oui!*"

"From pictures?"

"*Certainement.*"

"Raskolnikov, eh? Hitchcock, ha-ha-ha! Don't be frightened: from *M*?"

"*Non! Non!*" She put her thumbs to her eyelids and pulled upward. She gave a toothy grin. "*Voilà!*"

Downward, upward, round and round we circled. The engines were coughing like a man on his deathbed. I looked through the double panes of the window. Nothing to see save my own worried reflection, as round and pale as a Limburger moon. Next to me, the Parisienne panted, heaving sigh after sigh. I looked at the frills and frous of her Air France blouse. Did I dare to take her hand? To brush the tears from her cheek? At the thought a thousand fountains opened at my hairline and beneath my arms. Pipes burst between my shoulders, upon my chest. What bitter irony! Here sat I, a personal student of Freud, of Adler, liberators of the erotic emotions, pioneers of sexual freedom; yet the nearness of this coquette had made me awash in perplexity and perspiration. Were we about to die? To be squashed—what had Von Beckmann said? Like an insect against the Alps? And would I not act? I breathed deeply. I turned toward her. *Mr. Moto Takes a Chance.*

"*Chérie,*" I said in my smoothest voice, "do not be afraid. I have something for you. A little treat. Want to see it? Want to feel it?"

Impossible to ignore the spark of interest that lit the irises of those cocoa-colored eyes. I seized her hand. I guided it, without resistance, toward my lap. I opened the flap of my camel coat. Suddenly she raised her head, so as to sniff the air. "*Qu'est-ce que c'est, cette odeur?*" she exclaimed. "*Une odeur des amandes amères!* Is it nuts?"

That was the moment that the door at the front swung open and Von Beckmann squeezed through into the passenger compartment. All eyes turned toward him. "We shall not land in München," he declared. "We shall not land at any city of the Reich."

Delighted, Serge clapped his hands together. "Bravo!" he cried.

"*Pardon, monsieur,*" said the stewardess, jumping to her feet. "But how is this possible? We do not have the fuel to reach any other destination."

Basserman: "And we can't keep circling. We had ten minutes. Ten minutes have passed."

"Then," said Von Beckmann, "we must land in Salzburg."

Sampson Frank lost his nerve completely. "But the clouds! The storm! It's madness! We shall crash into the peaks!"

Here the impresario pulled himself up to his full height, so that the top of his head pressed against the cabin roof. It might have been a practiced pose, chin high, defiant, like Rodin's Balzac—except that the director had drawn the folds of his cape about him, instead of the immortal's dressing gown. "The clouds," he declared, "will part."

I hardly heard him. Did I really smell like almonds? That's what I was thinking. It was because of my glands. The excitement. Suddenly my bitterness spilled out in words: "*The clouds will part.* Is it Thor who speaks to us? The word of God?"

The director only smiled. He brought his cigarette to his mouth. "You have instead the word of Von Beckmann."

"Wait! Wait! There! The clouds *have* parted! I can see it! Look! The bridges! The river! It's a city!"

No sooner did Magdalena utter those words than everybody jumped to his feet. There was a rush to the port side of the plane. Even the stewardess hurried to one of the windows. "Where?" she exclaimed. "I see nothing. *Rien du tout.*"

Neither could the former Laszlo Loewenstein. All I could make out was the blinking beacon at the tip of our wing. That and the frightening flames that came from the engine cowling.

Then Serge cried out. "Look! There! It's true! Don't you see? Streets! And streetcars! The buildings! The people! It's the city of Salzburg!"

"Yes, yes!" That was Flatow, the Austrian native. "There is the Mönchsberg! There is the square of the Residenzplatz!"

The pilot had seen the sight, too. With a roar our plane banked, turned, and dove through the break in the clouds.

Basserman: "We're saved! It's a miracle!"

"Why are you surprised?" asked Magda. "The clouds have parted, just as Rudi predicted."

My nose was now pressed to the porthole. Inches away, the mists and vapors streamed by. I clutched my collar about my throat, as if the winds were inside the cabin and not whipping along the metal surface of the plane. Still I could see nothing of the scene below. "Miracle? Miracle?" I muttered. Then, more loudly, I spoke in the voice of the agent of the International Police. "Miracle of radio. No doubt honorable pilot has given our friend weather report."

At that instant the airliner broke through the layers of overcast and pulled up, shuddering, not above the old town of Salzburg but over a blaze of light. All of us gasped. For there, on the northern slope of a hilltop, winking and blinking, was a great bonfire in the shape of a swastika.

Anton, the adjutant, said, "Berchtesgaden."

Basserman gave a wry smile. "It's German intelligence. The Gestapo. They've discovered the hour of our flight. It's a warning."

"A greeting," said Sampson Frank, "just for us."

The plane flew on, sinking toward the aerodrome across the Austrian border. Basserman and Frank were incorrect, or such was my opinion. Like all actors, they were in the habit of putting themselves center stage. No wonder they thought that the cartwheel of light, its arms pinwheeling beneath us, had been ignited as a welcome especially for ourselves. But I had no doubt that, strolling on their boulevards or moving up the river in their barges or looking out the windows of their gingerbread houses, the citizens of Salzburg had also felt about their hearts that chill that is the sole purpose of the swastika, as well as its deepest meaning.

Amazing how, ten minutes after we landed, the last wisps of the stormclouds had blown away. The afternoon sun beat down upon us. Through the windows of our limousine I saw the waiters on the Gran Europa pavilion throwing white tablecloths over the tables and setting the placeware for cakes and tea. We didn't stop at the hotel, however, but went straight on to the Domplatz in front of the cathedral. Here crowds were waiting. They gave a cheer when our two black Mercedes came to a halt on the edge of the square. They pushed against the rope barricades. On the steps of the cathedral, which had been modeled on the Roman St. Peter's, the red-white-red flags of the Austrian Republic were flapping in the breeze. A platform and a podium had been set up in front of the triple-arched facade. Dignitaries, in dove-gray coats, in top hats and fedoras, were standing there, behind a bank of microphones.

I got out one door, with Flatow; Basserman and Frank got out the other. Instantly we were confronted by members of the press. They milled about us as if this were a premiere. Albert displayed what in America is called a Pepsodent smile. The glare from the flash lamps struck my face like a pair of white gloves. A shout went up. The crowd—fifty, sixty, perhaps a hundred people—had broken through the restraints. They dashed over the cobblestones and surrounded the first limousine. They pushed against the fenders and clambered onto the running boards. Anton, the lieutenant, forced his way out the front passenger door. He barked a command. But these were citizens, not soldiers. They brushed him aside and opened the door at the rear. Magdalena emerged. A veil from her hat covered her eyes. The crowd fell back. "Magda!" they chanted. "Magda! Magda!" Then the star began to sign autographs.

None in that throng had noticed how Von Beckmann had stepped from the other side of the Mercedes and was staring up at the cathedral's two great steeples. Stonily he stood. Nothing about him moved—not his arm, which he held out stiffly to the side, or his cape, or even the smoke from the cigarette in his rigid fingers; nothing, that is, but his shadow.

Those of us in his troupe approached him. Basserman asked, "Rudi, what are you doing? What are you staring at?"

"The cathedral. The steeples. The Mönchsberg. Here we shall perform our *Antigone*. On April tenth. At seventy-seven minutes before sundown. We must end precisely one minute before the hour of seven."

"But why," asked Frank, "such precision? That hour? That date?"

"Because on that date the sun will set only minutes before the moon will rise."

"I don't understand you," said Flatow. "How do you know these things? Have you consulted an almanac? And why are you standing there like a statue?"

"So sorry: not a statue," I interrupted, using the language of Agent 673,

International Police; for I had seen how the shadow from the impresario's arm continued to creep over the cobblestones. "A sundial!"

Von B's thick lips compressed in a smile. He lowered his limb. "Correct. A sundial. At the climax of the play, when Antigone is condemned to the underground, this same sun will descend with her. The earth, our stage, our audience, the square and the cathedral, all will be covered in darkness. Just then we hear a voice. Is it Haemon, calling the name of his bride? No. Not just Haemon. We hear many voices. It is the chorus, the stricken conscience of the community—the Greek community, the city of Salzburg, yes, even of Austria; perhaps it is the conscience of the wider world that has let this innocent be sacrificed."

Frank murmured, "Wonderful. Miraculous."

"At first the call comes faintly, from a great distance—the heights of the Mönchsberg. What is that sound? Is it the wind? The very wind, like the sun, must perform for us too. *An-ti-go-ne-e-e-e-e!*"

"My God," said Basserman. "The hair on my head is standing."

"There! The voice is a little louder, a little nearer: at the steeple of the Kollegienkirche; then closer, at St. Sebastian's; now it is at St. Margaret's. All those in our drama can hear it. Naturally, Tiresias is first; then Ismene, Antigone's sister, and her mother, Eurydice; next the soldier, the messenger; then each member of the chorus of Thebans. Still the voices sound, nearer, always nearer, from steeple to steeple. Only Creon, as deaf as he has been blind, hears nothing—that is, he hears nothing until the call reaches our own cathedral towers, from which, suddenly, the birds come swooping down. Yes, even animals will feel the affront to their conscience. The swallows of Salzburg shall be in our cast."

Anton alone seemed exempt from the director's spell. "Our swallows," he stated, "have long since flown south. They will not return by April."

Von Beckmann paid no heed. "Now all through the city there echoes the unmistakable cry: *Antigone! Antigone!* And all the while the sun is sinking, sinking. The shroud of dusk has fallen over the crowd."

There was a pause. Incredibly, a chill, a cold shudder, ran through us, as if the sun had fallen indeed.

"Suddenly, everything is reversed. Bells begin to peal, joyous bells. First from our cathedral towers, then farther off, from St. Margaret's, until the last tolling, the final chime, echoes from the Mönchsberg, where the call began. Now into the darkened sky climbs the moon. Not just a moon. The new moon. A sliver of moon. Like the slip of that girl. How pale it is! How delicate! Our hearts are full to have glimpsed—what is it, after all? According to your calculations, your *almanac,* it is one minute to seven and this is a cold, lifeless satellite. But could this slice of light, this thin splinter, a fingernail, a transparent peel, not also be the soul of the maiden, our Antigone—the wisp of her spirit, upon its flight?"

Everything, everyone, in the square was hushed. Even the flags had fallen still about their poles. On the far side of the car, what was left of the crowd stood motionless. Magdalena stepped forward, to our side of the automobile. She came up to Von Beckmann. "My darling," she said. "My master." And with an off-white handkerchief she wiped the tears that worked their way down the cheeks of the genius.

Ladies and gentlemen. Ministers of our beloved republic. Honored guests of Austria.

A voice, amplified by loudspeakers, filled the square. On the platform, a tall man, hatless, leaned into the microphones. His hair, long on top, was cropped close at the sides. Wire glasses sat upon the bridge of an aquiline nose. In our midst the lieutenant had come to attention. "Quiet, quiet," he admonished us. "This is Schuschnigg."

Behind his wooden podium, the chancellor started his speech. "I wish to speak plainly. My country has reached a moment of crisis. The master of the Third Reich has massed his forces across our common border. At any moment, on any pretext, he will pour across it. For some time now his plan has been to create the very anarchy that he will then claim it is his duty to suppress. *Germans,* he will declare to the world, *must not shed German blood.* I must tell you that against such an onslaught, the elements of the army that have remained loyal to the fatherland shall not be able to hold out for more than two days. We shall experience an instant *Anschluss.*"

He halted, gazing through his round lenses across the Domplatz to our little band of actors. Albert Basserman and Magdalena Mezaray had gone pale enough; my own face was undoubtedly an eggshell white. "You must be wondering what all this has to do with why I have summoned you, and why you stand now in this hallowed square. Surely you understand how Salzburg occupies a crucial position, not just geographically, at the border between eastern and western Europe and between the two German nations, but ideologically as well. Its values are those of the true spirit of Austria. They are opposed to everything represented by National Socialism."

By a conditioned reflex I began to grope in my pocket for my fairy dust. I leaned toward Basserman and, *sotto voce,* said, "*Geographically.* Do you know what that means? It means that this bone of Salzburg, stuck in the Führer's throat, will be swallowed in the first gulp. I knew it! We have been brought here as hostages. Hostages!"

Von Schuschnigg continued. "From one viewpoint, we have no allies—neither England nor France, not Hungary, and least of all our former protector, Mussolini. From another viewpoint, we have more than any other nation. These are the citizens of the world who venerate the music of Mozart and Beethoven—yes, and I dare say the symphonies and songs of Mendelssohn. It is this international community that provides our best hope of survival in the difficult months to come. You will perform the *Antigone* and the world will recognize that Austria is as weak, and as strong, as that Grecian girl."

In the square there rose, from the diplomats, and from a portion of the crowd, an echo of applause. All I could think was, if eight days before Von Schuschnigg and Hitler had stared from the heights of Berchtesgaden to the city of Salzburg below, what was preventing the Führer from observing the Domplatz and the meeting within it at this very moment? A sensation like frozen fingers crawled up my spine.

The chancellor held up his hands, so as to continue. "England is secure behind her channel, as America is across the sea. France is safe behind her wall of concrete. Our culture must form one part of our Maginot Line. The other part of our defense must be the will of our people. That is why I am now announcing a national plebiscite. It will be held one month from today, on March thirteenth. If the Austrian people vote yes, they shall declare themselves free and Christian and united. If no, they shall express their desire to form a union with Germany. People of Austria! Hear me! Give me your answer. Do you wish your independence? *Ja oder Nein?*"

Now there was an uproar. Half the people in the square began to shout *Ja!*, the other half *Nein!* There was a surge from behind the barricades. A score of men, two score perhaps, ran toward the parked limousines. They wore, I saw, red feathers in their Alpine caps and white stockings pulled over their calves. Autograph seekers, or so it seemed—except on this occasion they did not cry *Magda! Magda!* but, at the top of their lungs, *Lorre! Where is Lorre?*

"Here I am!" I responded, not without a tingle of appreciation. "Over here! Perhaps you admired my portrait of Abbott? Ha-ha! You know, the anarchist? In *The Man Who Knew Too Much?*"

"Fool!" That was the adjutant. "Quick! Get into the car!"

Too late. The crowd of whitestockings drew up before me. One of their number swiped off his hat—he had a clean-shaven head underneath it—and, as if deliberately offering an insult, used it to strike me across the cheek. The man next to him, red-faced and stout, spit upon the lapel of my camel-hair coat. A third man shouted, "Loewenstein! *Ein stinkender Jude!*" Then the whole mob, cursing and shouting, closed in upon me.

Think Fast Mr. Moto! If only I now possessed, as I had in that picture, a bulletproof vest, or if I had performed my own stunts instead of leaving the task to others—then might I have picked up the first of these gentlemen and, employing the principles of jujitsu, in which the force of a person's own leverage is turned against him, used his body to knock over his fellows like tenpins. As it was, the hatless man lowered his head and thrust it into my solar plexus. I doubled over. This permitted another to bring his fist down upon the back of my head.

"So! The Yid wants to be Antigone's lover!"

"Her bridegroom!"

"We have laws against that!"

Those were the words I heard as I collapsed to the ground. As one they fell upon me, kicking with studded boots, beating with fists, with sticks, with bottles still filled with beer. Someone screamed. It was Magda. A shot went off. I saw Anton struggling to reach me, aiming his pistol into the air. Then there was a cracking sound: one of my own ribs. Another crack, from another bone. My head flew back, striking the stones. Blood, thick and salty, rather like Granite Films ketchup, spilled from my mouth. A curtain, also red, dropped before my eyes. *Mr. Moto's Gamble.* Clearly I had lost it. There was nothing save for the sound of heavy breathing, of snorting, and the thud of the boots upon my flesh.

Then of a sudden the blows came to a stop. I struggled toward con-sciousness, as if it were a rope that had been thrown me, or a plot of dry land, an isle, an islet, in that sea of pain. When I opened my eyes I saw Von Beckmann. His head was aglow with flashing light. Was it, in his hair, the streak of silver? No! The monocle! He had turned it upon the mob, the whitestockings, as if he meant to incinerate them, the way a glass will start a blaze by concentrating the rays of the sun. Then the director turned, facing the cathedral. He raised his arms as if calling on the gods to intervene, to shake the earth or send their angels or bolts of lightning. Instead, from far away, from as high, it seemed, as the heavens, there came a faint, high-pitched cry.

Magda was the first to hear it. "What's that? Listen!"

The cry came again, louder than before. Even the whitestockings heard it. They lifted their hatted or their unhatted heads. The long drawn-out wail floated down from the sky.

An-ti-i-i-go-ne-e-e-e!

Basserman's voice rang out from nearby. "Did you hear? Did you hear that cry?"

Reynaldo Flatow said, "I don't understand it. Where does this come from? What can it mean?"

"Is it a trick?" asked Anton. "Is it ventriloquism?"

The attackers, some standing, some on their knees, shaded their eyes and looked skyward. For the third and last time the word echoed through the square.

An-ti-i-i-go-ne-e-e-e!

As if that call had been meant for them, the beaters, the kickers, pulled back from where, completely unconscious, I. A. Moto lay curled into a ball. Then, without a signal, without a word spoken, they sauntered off across the Domplatz and disappeared.

Immediately the rest of the troupe ran forward. The weeping Magda was in the lead. She bent over the shape of ex-Loewenstein. "Peter! My lamb! My lambkin! Can you hear me? Are you awake?"

No: he was, as they say, dead to the world. Thus he could not see how the head of Von Beckmann still tilted upward, nor the animation in the great man's face: the lips that moved; the tic that twisted the flesh of his cheek; and, on his forehead, just off-center, the blue vein that seemed to snap like a spark. Slowly he took off his cloak and waved it once, above his head. The whole world knew the mysterious way in which the director was able to relate to his actors. Now everyone saw how he was able to communicate with animals as well. It was a kind of telegraphy without wires. How else to explain how in the next instant the air of the Domplatz was filled with swallows? Scores of swallows. Hundreds of them. Thousands. They tumbled down from the steeples. They swooped and dove. They were like a second cape, no less black, swirling and billowing over the human heads.

"This is impossible!" Anton exclaimed. "I know that those birds migrated long ago."

From outside the square came the heehaw sound of a European siren. Flatow shouted, "Here is the ambulance."

"Thank heavens," Magda replied.

But Anton continued to follow the flock as it darted back and forth like arrows over the square. "They should be in Italy. In Morocco. In the deserts of Arabia."

The birds spiraled upward, caw-cawing like crows, and swirled back into the steeple top; they were like some dark liquid, ink or oil, that was being sucked into an invisible drain. In that belfry, high over Salzburg, they settled upon the wooden beams and the stone shoulders of the saints. Through the louvered windows the wind came whistling. It crossed the mouth of the brass bell, making a moaning sound—like the mournful note struck by a boy when he blows over the lip of a bottle. And here came a boy, the servant Serge. He crossed to the ledge of the steeple and leaned out. His sharp chin was on his hands as, grinning like a gargoyle, he stared down at the people of flesh and blood so far below.

LUCIFER CAFÉ

One month after the catastrophe in the Domplatz—more precisely, just a few hours before the dawn of Saturday, March the twelfth—all of Von Beckmann's troupe were seated in a nightspot called the Lucifer Café. It was located not in Salzburg proper but in the Nonnthal suburb, off to the south. There was no quaintness, no gingerbread here. The old Uhlan barracks were occupied by the salt miners and railway workers who made up most of the population of the district. The café itself might have been consciously modeled on that for which the Von Sternberg film *Der Blaue Engel* had been named—or so it seemed to me, peeking through my bandages at the dim, gas-fed lamps whose light glittered on each of the hundreds of glasses and gleamed on the brass of the twisting staircase. Lucifer, of course, was an angel, the one that fell from heaven. That meant he presided over crossed borders— not just the one between heaven and earth, but those between rich and poor, right and wrong, and whatever it was that my old teacher Freud had discovered between the part of the brain that was rational and the part that governed our instinctual life. Hence in that café, beer-swilling policemen could sit at the same narrow bench as socialist miners; and the table of self-conscious decadents, the bohemians and homosexuals, was set cheek by jowl with that occupied by the children of Salzburg bankers. Perhaps that explained why I was permitted to sit there myself, a Jew in the roomful of gentiles.

A simpler explanation was that, wrapped head to toe in bandages, I had not been recognized. Hard for me, still, to get over the feeling of amazement that I was even alive. No one, after my beating, thought I would be able to resume my career. More important, at least to the beaters, the wave of cancellations that had come in from America and other countries made it seem certain that the production of *Antigone,* and indeed the festival itself, would have to be called off. It was Von B who saved the day. The part of Haemon, he announced, would be played by an ordinary Austrian, a citizen of Salzburg whom he himself would choose at an open trial. Overnight the whole of the town became an audition stage. Everyone, from the shoeshine man at the Gran Europa to the florist who sold the director his boutonniere, was constantly winking, posing, gesturing, or greeting the impresario with one or another of the doomed lover's lines. Indeed, the excitement soon spread far beyond Salzburg itself. The choice took on the same aura of mystery and near supernatural speculation that accompanied the selection of Jesus by the town of Oberammergau.

The trouble was, with only a month to go before our premiere, no Haemon had been found. Hundreds of aspirants, amateur and professional, had paraded before the impresario at the Lucifer Café. Even with the youngest, the handsomest of the would-be heroes, there was always a fatal flaw: the voice, the carriage, the lack of magnetism, the lack of élan. The auditions had continued through this evening and into the wee hours of the morn. At that very moment I could see one such boy rise from the bankers' table and step onto the dance floor. The little orchestra—an accordion, a fiddle, a piano, clarinet, and drum—immediately stopped playing, and the dancers, as if they were engaged in a parlor game, stood motionless in place. The lad, dark-haired, with striking gray eyes, moved between them until he arrived at the table in front of Von B. The director broke off his conversation and nodded. The hopeful Haemon, like all those who had tried out before him, removed his jacket and shirt—revealing, in this instance, pale, pimply shoulders and a hollow at the center of his chest.

> *What have you done, my foolish father? A brave man will not fight against a helpless girl.*

Von Beckmann gave his cue, a crushed cigarette, and at once the band struck up an out-of-date American tune. The auditioner retired as the dancers glided this way and that across the polished floor.

As best I could, I rolled my eyes, in search of a cocktail waitress. Impossible, within my linen cocoon, to sniff my drug of choice. Instead I held in my hand a glass of whiskey, which I sucked into my mouth through a straw. Another straw, inserted into what I can only call my penis, drained what hadn't been metabolized into a rubber pouch. *Mr. Moto and the Mummy.* A waitress, with wiry red hair-ends and breasts bared almost to the nipple, passed by. With pneumatic gestures I tilted my head and lifted a bandaged arm. The frizzy fräulein waved back and went off to fetch a drink.

Outside, on the twisting street, a bonfire was burning. I could see the leaping flames through the blue mist that filled the room. I knew that ever since Schuschnigg had declared the plebiscite, the *Jas* and the *Neins* had been burning their wagons, their porches, even the bedboards from their beds, to see which side could set the more impressive blaze. At first, or such had been my impression, those who wanted their country to remain free had had the upper hand. *Ja* placards sprang up on every lamppost in the city, and the chancellor's name was scrawled on the sidewalks and the cobblestones. All day long airplanes crisscrossed the sky. They dropped leaflets that said, *We Vote Yes!* Soundtrucks moved through the streets playing "Oh, Du Mein Österreich." That word, *Austria,* had become the daily greeting between friends and strangers alike.

But it did not take long for those wanting to become part of the Reich to take action. In Salzburg, even before the chancellor had finished his announcement, crowds began to tear down the loudspeakers that carried his words. All too soon the chant of *Red-White-Red* was drowned out by shouts of *Sieg Heil.* In Vienna, in the Leopoldstadt section, Jews were chased out of their homes and thrown into the canal. In Graz, Hitler's supporters stormed the Berghof and replaced the Austrian banner with the German swastika. There, as elsewhere, the police refused to intervene. The situation drifted steadily toward civil war. Everything that had been forbidden was now allowed. "Heil Hitler," the Horst Wessel song, and the stiff-armed salute preceded every public meeting. Whole segments of the population, huge swaths of the country, were behaving as if they were already part of the Third Reich.

In the last few days, as the time for the vote drew near, the situation had reached a crisis. Ominously, the Wehrmacht began to mobilize along the border. Hitler addressed the Reichstag in a speech that all of us heard on the radio. Already he seemed to be assuming sovereignty over seven million of Austria's citizens: *All those who are suffering because of their sympathy for the German race will henceforth be under the protection of the Reich.* On and on he went, half dry statistics, half foaming diatribe. "My God," Basserman exclaimed, while frowning at the Blaupunkt speaker. "He's gone on for three hours!"

"Only three hours?" came the hollow voice from within my carapace. "I'd swear I've aged ten years."

By the morning of the eleventh, with the vote only forty-eight hours away, the entire nation seemed to have come to a realization: the more likely it became that the plebiscite, which Von Schuschnigg had called "a last S.O.S. to the world," would actually pass, the less likely it was that Herr Hitler would permit such a signal to be sent. But how would he stop it? With an ultimatum? With invasion? As the hours went quickly by, those who had most vigorously supported a vote of yes fell suddenly silent. In the lull, Germany's allies held sway. I knew only too well that the fire on the street outside had been set by the *Neins*. Indeed, I could see them—as usual they wore their white stockings pulled over their calves—scattered about the room. I even thought I could recognize the beefy faces of those who had beaten me outside the cathedral. Yet the spirit of Lucifer allowed even those lions to lie down for the night with what Magda had always called her lamb.

The music stopped. Time for another audition. Now the candidate was a strapping youth. He made his way to our table and executed a bow. Off came his woolen sweater. This was no puny socialite. The muscles of the boy's chest bulged like those of a weightlifter. Another muscle twitched at the side of his jaw. A laugh went up from the benches across the room. The worker's friends guffawed as he began to stammer:

What have you done, my foolish father? A-a-a—

Basserman put in a helpful word: "*A brave man—*"

For a moment the boy only stood there, red-faced and grinning. The band leader waited for the signal to strike up a tune. Von B was smoking. Above his fingers, which clung to his face like a surgical mask, his eyes turned toward Magda. She stared back, the tip of her tongue darting between her parted lips, her parted teeth. It could have been a sense organ, attuned to the director's wishes. Then—it was only the slightest of movements—a sign, a shake of the head, passed between them. Von Beckmann lowered his American cigarette from his mouth and crushed it in the tray. The boy flinched, as if the stub had been ground against his own naked flesh. At once a waiter appeared with an armful of dishes; the woodwinds and the percussion started to play.

Magda laughed. Her earrings, crystal ones, shaped like Chinese pagodas, made a tinkling sound. "What have they brought us to eat?"

Because Flatow's nose curved all the way to his moustache, his voice had a reedy sound, like an oboe. "Salted eels," he said.

Anton, our lieutenant, added, "From the Salzach. A local specialty."

Serge already had one of the delicacies upon his fork. "Delicious!" he exclaimed, flashing his teeth and shaking his head of hair, which fell about his cheeks like a cluster of purplish grapes.

"Not for me," Basserman said. "I have not touched an eel since that scene with Rudi. You remember, Sampson. In the Red Sea."

Frank laughed. "Only too well! The summer of 1908. Rudi, we were shooting at Swinemünde, on the Pomeranian Bay. Have you forgotten?"

The director had already lit another cigarette and was smoking it in his usual fashion, that is, his hand was clapped to the lower half of his face, so that the cylinder seemed to grow out of it, like a sixth finger. "I remember better than you. It wasn't nineteen eight. It was nineteen nine. Also, we were not at Swinemünde but to the east, at a Polish village off Stettin Bay."

Basserman: "I'll never forget it. How could I? My first motion picture! Frank was the featured artist. The Moses. A skinny boy with a pasted-on beard."

Von B: "That boy and I had already completed a dozen pictures. This is the one that brought him fame."

"Wait, wait!" said Flatow. "I know this film. *Das Gelobtes Land.* It made a sensation in Vienna. Moses puts his hands out and the Red Sea parts. Yes, yes, it was *The Promised Land!*"

"Nineteen nine," said Basserman. "I was—let me see: aged thirty-eight. I can't imagine why, with my work in the theater, I agreed to play a film pharaoh. Think of it, an Egyptian chasing the Israelites across the Red Sea. Oh, it comes back to me. Rudi was filming from a bluff. What I recall is this youth with a large head and long legs, like stilts, inside of his windy trousers. First Sampson Frank, our Moses, stretched his hand out over the water, and then, hours later, the men and women and children of Israel walked across the muddy straits."

Behind his half-inch lenses Flatow's eyeballs expanded in recollection. "In Vienna we could talk of nothing else. The waters rolled like a rug out of sight. We all knew it was a trick. But no one could imagine how it was done."

Von B exhaled a cloud of Virginia. "It was not," he said, "a difficult effect. I knew that the lower reaches of the bay emptied out every twelve hours. I calculated that if I put the camera on a tripod and opened the shutter each sixty seconds to the count of two, the result, on film, would make it seem that the sea withdrew in under four minutes."

Flatow said, "To us, in the theaters, it was a miracle. Those were the days when people would scream at the sight of a train coming at them from the screen. No wonder grown men thought that here was the proof of what they had read in their Bibles. It wasn't just Sampson Frank who became a star. From that time on we began to hear the name of Von Beckmann. To the man in the street he had the same powers as Moses."

Basserman, elegant in his cream-colored suit, gave a rueful laugh. "It wasn't so wonderful for those of us on the ground! We Egyptians had to wait until the tide began to turn back at midafternoon. The heat was terrible. Rudi moved down from the bluffs and set up his camera on wooden planks in the middle of Stettin Bay. When he gave the signal we charged straight at him. All around me and my chariot, people were shouting. I shouted, too. We waved our swords. We cracked our whips. *Death to the Jews! Death to the Jews!* And then our wheels ground to a halt in the mud. But why were the horses rearing? Why were my men, the Pharaoh's legions, starting to scream? I looked down. Not mud! Eels! Black eels! The floor of the bay was alive with them. They were already coiling around the horses' hooves. They were wrapped around the spokes of my wheels. Our army slashed at the beasts with their swords. Alas! The serpents coiled around the tin blades, too. What a terrible moment! Like a plague not written down in the Bible! And what was the worst? That we had to remain there for another ninety minutes, so that at intervals of sixty seconds the waters that had parted for the Israelites could return and sink us."

Frank: "As it is written in Exodus, like lead, like a stone."

Basserman was still lost in his reverie. "Why, you wonder, didn't we turn? Why didn't we run back the way we had come? The waters steadily rose—to our knees, our waists, and soon over the chariot tops to our chests. All the while the eels were writhing and coiling and clenching, more frightening now that they were covered by the waves. Still we remained. People were thrashing. They were weighed down by their armor. They were not acting when they called out for help, for mercy, from the great god Ra. Were we paralyzed? Had we become slaves ourselves? The answer, I believe, is *Berufsausübung.* Professionalism. Do you understand? We identified with the men whose lives we were portraying. The soldiers of Pharaoh's army, like Pharaoh himself, thought they were pursuing the Jews of their own free will. Little did they know that it was the Lord of the Hebrews who had hardened their hearts and that each of them was playing a part. That camera, which floated before us on its raft of planks—it was like the unblinking eye of some god. And Rudi beside it: he transfixed us. Better the serpents than risk the lash of that frown, the thunder in that voice."

Flatow removed his eyeglasses, which caused his eyeballs to dart back to the safety of their sockets. He gave a nervous laugh. "So Rudi can command a performance from—what are they, these eels? Fish? Reptiles? The same as he did with the swallows."

Basserman wiped his brow with his handkerchief, as if he still felt the heat of the Egyptian sun. "Those hours! Hours of misery! Yet in the finished picture the scene of the flood took only three minutes. And me? I had only seconds upon the screen! Just a glimpse of a fool in armor. But that was enough, that hint of immortality. Of course, I continued in theater, but from that moment on I knew that films would become my career."

Von Beckmann quietly said, "And I, from that moment, knew I would abandon filmmaking for the theater."

Little Serge leaned toward his master. "How can that be? Everyone knows the picture was a success."

What Von Beckmann said next shocked them all. "Because I understood even then what is now obvious to all—that this new medium, and the industry that was bound to spring up around it, would inevitably be dominated by Jews."

A gasp went up from the table. I gasped myself—not so much at the sound of that forbidden word as from a sudden thirst. My throat felt as if I had eaten a plateful of the salt-encrusted animals. Luckily the waitress, with dimples in her cheeks and hair like fire, now appeared, carrying my soda-whiskey. With a playful hop she settled upon my lap. Then she pried my stiffened fingers from the empty glass and curled them around the full one. "Thank you," I intoned from inside my unyielding corset. Her own corset, I saw, could barely contain her lively bosom. A lather formed upon my brow. The small of my back turned clammy. Prettily smiling, the waitress lifted my arm and directed the straw—it might just as well have been a feeding tube—into the gash in my linen. *"Trinken,"* she said. *"Trinken."*

Basserman was also holding a glass in his hand. He half rose from his chair. "A toast, friends!" he exclaimed. "How good it is to have Magda and Rudi united again!"

Everyone clapped. *"Prosit!"* they responded.

Flatow said, "A pity they were ever parted."

Frank: "How could such a thing be allowed to happen? It is almost a natural calamity. As if a continent had split in two."

Albert leaned toward the impresario. "Tell us the secret, Rudi. Why didn't you go on to Hollywood?"

Von Beckmann: "Secret? There is no secret. Didn't I just explain it to you? My presentiment had come true. In Hollywood, from the top to the bottom, you would find only Jews."

Serge put down his tumbler. "No, Rudi! Don't say that. Why are you so cruel to me tonight?"

"Cruel? I am not cruel. Please do not misunderstand my words. You must not think I hold any animus toward the Hebrew race. It has survived the rise and fall of one civilization after another, and will no doubt continue to survive until the end of time—or until the hour of salvation comes for us all. What tenacity! How they cling to the world, these people! They affirm it with all five senses. But the world beyond those senses—*that* they have no regard for, no belief in, no way of knowing. It leaves them mystified. It leaves them cold. And this indifference, of course, affects their art. If one does not believe—as Antigone believes, to take one instance—in the reality of the other world, the afterlife, the land of the gods, then one's art turns toward the subjective. The mark of the Jew is that confronted by the existence of a world beyond his five senses, he adds a sixth: the psyche, which turns the unknowable world into an illusion. Does our poor heroine hear the commands of the gods? Then she must be having a dream—or, worse, she, and we in the audience, with our belief, our age-old folk wisdom, are suffering from a hallucination. *That* is what is meant by the worldliness, no, the *earthiness* of the Jew: that everything has an explanation."

A moment of silence fell on the table. The actors stared at each other. The blond adjutant said, "This is a deep analysis, deeper than I have heard."

"Then you haven't heard Goebbels or Rosenberg," muttered the mummy from deep inside his windings. I winced: little snails' trails of perspiration were stinging my eyes.

"All of this is interesting, it's an interesting philosophy," Basserman said at last. "But what has any of it to do with why the Jews—and it's true, I don't deny it: whether in Hollywood or Paris, Moscow, or, in the old days, Berlin, why they always seem to dominate our industry?"

"Is that a serious question? Surely you understand what the motion picture is—or what it has become? *The psyche of the human race.* Think back to when the Red Sea parted. I did not invent a new technique at Stettin Bay. Nor did, before me, Edison or Muybridge or Lumière. The lapse of time, the fact that hours of effort exist onscreen for only an instant, is intrinsic to the medium. Why these puzzled looks? These frowns? Consider, my dears, a single foot of the old-style film I used to shoot *Das Gelobtes Land.* That foot—it might very well be of our friend Basserman up to his neck in eels and water—diverts us for precisely one second while we sit warm and dry inside the theater. Upon this foot of film there are sixteen frames, each with its own separate snapshot of the drowning Egyptian. And since at Stettin it was a bright summer day, each of these little pictures was exposed to the light for no more, and probably less, than one five-hundredth of a second. The logic that flows from that fact is inescapable. The eye of the camera is open to the world before it for sixteen five-hundredths of the second it takes Basserman to gasp for breath and sixteen five-hundredths of the second it takes the twelve inches of film to travel through the projection machine. To reverse our proposition, the eye of the camera is shut and thus the film is blank for all but .032 of any unit of actual time. Ninety-seven percent of reality goes unrecorded. Yet Herr Flatow in Vienna was convinced he saw Moses raise his hands and the sea roll back, the safe passage of the Israelites, and the inundation of Pharaoh, even though what he witnessed was only three percent of what actually took place. The rest he only thought he saw. That is why the cinema is quintessentially the art of imagination. The truth is, it is almost exclusively made up of fantasies. *Das Gelobtes Land* was a five-reel film. It lasted an hour and a quarter. But the reality in it, the three percent that was verifiably recorded on the quicksilver salts of the negative, as opposed to the sluggish cells of the human brain, comes to two minutes and twenty-five seconds. Everything else was a figment of the audience's imagination."

On my lap the waitress shifted her weight from one full buttock to another. Unfortunately for the mummy, there was no way my hidden pouch could deal with the sweat that was gushing through the pores of my body. For an anguished instant I feared I might drown in it, like a deep-sea diver who feels the water rising in his rubber suit. I looked toward Rudi, who sat wreathed in smoke. The fumes poured from his mouth and his nostrils. He was like one of those oracles who speak from clouds of steam.

"Perhaps now you can grasp the idea I formed thirty years ago at Stettin Bay. This phenomenon, the way the retina of the eye retains an image long after it has ceased to exist—it is called, I believe, persistence of vision. It is a kind of hallucination. It is a dream. The Jews themselves, who long ago should have ceased to exist, are a kind of afterimage, a persistent vision, in the eye of mankind. Who knows what actually happened in Egypt millennia in the past? Perhaps the tide shifted and the children of Israel imagined the rest. A bush flares up, a whirlwind roars: and from that instant the Jews create the I Am That I Am. What they actually experienced took place in the blink of an eye, for sixteen five-hundredths of a second; but the reverberation, these centuries of dreaming, are what we call history."

The café orchestra was playing a hit tune of the twenties. The hip-hopping dancers were singing the words in accented English:

> *Now the folks in Georgia they done gone wild*
> *Over that brand-new dancin' style—*

My waitress, the darling, squirmed this way, that way, as if the platform of my loins were part of the dance floor. "So, fräulein, you do not think I am such an ogre? You don't wish to run away, like so many others, to the opposite side of the street?" In response the full-busted female threw back her head, exposing the white meat of her throat. *"Called shake that thing!"* she sang along with the others:

> *Shake that thing!*
> *Shake that thing!*

Alas, all too soon the orchestra, and with it my wriggling waitress, came to a halt. That was because yet another auditioner was making his way across the room. Here was, no doubt about it, the barrel's bottom. This aspiring actor was a man in his forties, thickly built, with the stubble of a beard upon his chin. Unlike the others, he removed neither his jacket nor his sweater when he came up to our table. Instead, with a bow, he swiped off his hat. His hair, I saw, was cropped, in the military manner. More surprising still, the auditioner wore a pair of white stockings pulled halfway over his calves. It was the enemy! The very man who had knocked me to the ground!

"I would like," said the intruder, "to ask Fräulein Mezaray for a dance."

All of us pulled back in dismay. But the whitestocking only smiled. He held toward Magdalena a tobacco-stained hand. It might have had a dead animal in it, judging from the look it drew from the actress. She turned toward Von Beckmann. To our amazement, he gave her a small but quite perceptible nod.

Immediately, as if an invisible makeup woman had set to work, the movie star's features were rearranged: the curled lip stretched in a smile, the line of vexation between her brows was smoothed away, and her narrowed eyes widened and actually seemed to shine, as if the instrument of the cosmetician had placed into each of them a single drop of pleasure.

"I would," she told her suitor as she rose from her chair, "be delighted."

The overhead lights shone onto the whitestocking's scalp through his closely cut hair. With one hand he tossed his hat onto a nearby table; with the other he reached for his partner's waist. Magda wore a black sleeveless gown, cut low in the front and with a slit on the leg, *im chinesischen Stil.* She allowed herself to be guided onto the dance floor. At once the little orchestra broke into a South American tango. The dancer, all eyes upon him, led the actress six steps forward and six fast steps on the return. At the end of each line he thrust his leg between hers and bent her back.

How the band played! The clarinetist's cheeks were puffed like a chipmunk's. The drummer, in the American style, was juggling the sticks to his drums. The whitestocking, with his powerful arms, drew Magda after him, crushing her against his chest. Scissoring his legs, he maneuvered her toward our table. He bent her backward, so that her hair touched the tablecloth. Her chest, slick and heaving, was revealed. Her partner looked into the eyeholes of my mummy's mask.

What could I do? My own partner's heavy haunches were warming my thighs. Far beneath my armor, as impenetrable as that of the Egyptians, my circumcised flesh had begun to crawl achingly up the length of hollow straw.

"*Gott im Himmel!*" That was the waitress. "What is that smell? Are you eating nuts?"

"Tell me something, my sweetheart," I moaned from the recesses of my sepulcher. "You do not find me unattractive, isn't that true? You see, in this beast, the beauty? That is because I am an actor. I can portray what is human inside the monster. A ghoul on the outside, yes? Pop-eyed. A five-footer. A head like a balloon. But inside, sensitive, feeling, and delicate. Like a poet! Do you feel that? Can you imagine it? Do you know what it is like to be me?"

At that the waitress gave a laugh and, for an inexplicable reason, began to clack her teeth together. "*Ja! Ja!*" she exclaimed, chop-chopping her molars. "*Banzai! Jujitsu! Hara-kiri!* Ha-ha! Ha-ha-ha!"

I sat thunderstruck as the redhead leaped upright and ran to the other side of the room. Helpless, abandoned, I began to tip sideways, like a melting snowman. The laughter of my Lorelei rang in my ears. Then, just before toppling, I righted myself. Was it Moto she mocked? If only she knew of that detective's magical powers. Even then I could see how, on the dance floor, the whitestocking was moving not only his hips but his lips. Naturally, Agent 673 was trained how to read them.

"Listen carefully, Fräulein Mezaray"—that's what the tangoist was saying. He leaned over her rag-doll form so that his coattails divided over his buttocks. "You must return to your homeland and to your own language, the language of our folk. There you will be a star. It won't be like Hollywood: jazz bands and eastern decadence. We are disciplined. Our art expresses a vision for the future. You can see it in the faces of the people when they sit in our theaters. The pride on their lips. The unity in their eyes. Not like America, where it is every man for himself. Do you understand me? Do you know who has sent me? A great man. The most famous man in the world. He has asked for you personally. It is his wish that I bring you over the border. Are you listening? Do you hear me? Will you come?" For a moment the whitestocking buried his face in his partner's neck. But the great star remained silent. She hung slack, unresisting, in the man's grasp. Impossible, viewing this scene, not to think of a motion picture from the land of jazz bands and decadence. *King Kong*: the dark gorilla, pale Fay Wray limp in its arms.

"Listen to what I am saying, fräulein. The situation here is critical. You are in danger. Do you hear me? *Something is going to happen.* No one will be able to defend you. The Austrian government? In twenty-four hours there will not even be an Austria. What is it you want? Do you want money? You can name any sum. Don't think the great man is used to being disobeyed. That will not be tolerated! You must understand that he is trying to save you. To protect you. Come with me. Come now. The tanks are at the border. The planes are on the ramp. Look. Look out the window. Soon it will be dawn."

Was it true? I wondered. Was there to be an invasion? Would Austria cease to exist? Be that as it may, it was an Austrian, our own handsome lieutenant, who now came to Magdalena's rescue. He rose from his chair and in three quick strides took the German by the collar of his coat. There wasn't a scene. The whitestocking took out a handkerchief and with that flag of surrender mopped his brow. Magda dropped half fainting into her blond bodyguard's arms. He led her back to our table. She leaned on him, her arm around his neck. She didn't let go when, still limp, legs sprawled wide, she dropped down into the seat beside him. She lowered her head against his shoulder. I saw how the cheeks of the fair-skinned man broke into a becoming flush.

Serge leaned over. "May I help you?" he inquired. He dipped his napkin in a glass of water and touched it to the actress's brow.

Magda pushed his hand aside. A recovery was already under way. The sweat on her skin made her glitter, as if she were being photographed through a special lens. Diamonds of light winked on her body. Energy bubbled through her like champagne in a glass. It was as if she were drawing strength from her escort, against whom she continued to lean.

The lieutenant sat at a kind of attention in his chair. It was clear from the expression on his face, perplexed and doubting, that he was having difficulty reconciling the flesh-and-blood woman beside him with the fuzzy figure, thirty feet high, made from shade and shadow, that he had so often seen upon the screen.

"Oh, dear," said Magda. "I've lost my earring."

The adjutant looked more confused than ever. He pulled back, so that they were staring face to face. "*Nein,*" he said, pointing to where both of the brilliant crystals swung at her ears.

"You are mistaken," said Magda. She removed one of the little Chinese pagodas. She tipped her chair backward and tossed the jewel under the table.

The lieutenant hesitated. He looked all around. "Allow me to find it for you," he said.

He dropped to his hands and knees and disappeared beneath the edges of the starched white cloth. In their places, the actors, Basserman and Frank, pretended not to notice. Flatow finished his drink and called for another. My own drink was nearly empty; I sucked on the straw until the air at the bottom of the glass rattled like the breath of an expiring patient. Only the jealous Serge seemed unable to take this event in stride. "No, no," he cried. He was shaking. His face was twisted in anguish. "Rudi! Don't do this to me! Your *Honigkuchen.* I am suffering! Rudi, I beg you!"

The great Von B blew two columns of smoke from his nostrils. Serge looked up at him, his chin trembling like a child's. He said, "Won't you have pity?"

In the director's eyes two large tears formed. They slid onto the puffy skin of his cheeks. He reached out to stroke the dark curls that fell from the boy's head. *"Mein armes kleines Vogelchen,"* he said. *My poor little bird. "Mein unglücklicher, kleiner Spatz."*

"Thus life follows art," I murmured to myself; for it seemed to me that we were still on the set of *Der Blaue Engel* and the spectacle of the vanishing lieutenant resembled nothing so much as the celebrated scene in which Von Sternberg's camera had followed the puffing professor as he moved on all fours beneath Lola-Lola's dressing table. Who could forget the closeup of Jannings's face only inches from Dietrich's ankles, her calves, her stockinged thighs?

In this way a good five minutes went by. The orchestra ran all the way through "The Dipsy Doodle," last year's hit American tune, and began it once more from the top. "Stay. Don't follow." That was Rudi, addressing his servant. He rose from his seat and, without a glance back at the desolate Serge, lost himself among the crowd. Still the adjutant remained somewhere beneath the table. *When you reach your destination*—that is what Dietrich said to Jannings—*send me a postcard.*

Then the lieutenant emerged. The look on his face was no longer one of bafflement. On the contrary, one could see from his swollen eyes and the way his lower lip stuck out red and glistening that many mysteries had been solved. With those eyes he stared for a moment at Magda. She was much as before, tipped back in her chair with her legs, beneath the stuff of her slit evening gown, spread wide. He reached across the tablecloth and opened his fist. The crystal was inside. The actress ignored it. Instead she reached up to her other ear and removed the second pagoda. She let it drop onto the edge of her empty plate.

As one, the leading lady and the lieutenant got up from the table. They edged through the crowded room toward the staircase, which rose with a twist to the second floor. At first they moved slowly, hindered by the crush; but by the time they arrived at the first step, they were nearly at a trot. Magda went first, racing up the stairs. Just behind her, Anton took them two at a time.

With difficulty I rose from my chair. Where, I wondered, had that white-stocking come from? Was he really an officer of the Third Reich? Sent by none other than Hitler? So it would seem. *Take care, please, to observe beneath surface*: this was a Moto Motto. Was it not just as likely, therefore, that Von Beckmann had arranged for this little adventure? Could it not be the director, the impresario, who had written both the tango and the tango dancer into his script?

I headed, all too slowly, haltingly, toward the staircase. It did not take an Oriental oracle to know what was happening on the floor upstairs. At that very moment Magda rushed headlong into an unlit room and the lieutenant slammed the door behind them. In the pitch darkness they tore off their clothes. From below nothing could be heard save the dim thumping of the jazz band and a faint hum of voices. That was not enough to mask the sound of his ripping tunic, the fall of a button, the thud of a shoe. Then the lieutenant's eyes must have become accustomed to the dark. He halted. He pointed to the glow of a small, red, pulsing light. "What's that?" he said.

Another light, a forty watter, came on inside a paper shade. That was more than enough to reveal Magda, who still wore every stitch of her clothing. She stood stock-still for an instant and then made a dash for the door. The adjutant, caught bent-kneed, his trousers and shorts about his ankles, could not stop her. In a flash she was gone. Then he put his hands over his crotch and turned to face Von Beckmann, who sat in an overstuffed chair, the cylinder of his cigarette aglow.

"Who has Magda brought us this time? Ah! Our handsome lieutenant. Look how he stands there. A naked Pan! Like Nijinsky in *L'Après-midi d'un faune*. But this goat, he's more modest. No scandal here, as at the opening of the Ballets Russes. Such inhibitions! What did Diaghilev say to his dancer? *Astonish me!* But this one, he might be posing for a piece of kitsch, the misty maiden of *September Morn*."

The older man leaned forward; with a movement of his hands he seemed to part the curtains of his cigarette smoke. "Well, perhaps not so handsome after all. A disappointment. The eyes: a commonplace blue. What could be more trite than a cleft in the chin? Magda! Magda! This won't do. What could she have been thinking? Blond hair. The banality of the straight nose. Is this a person, ha-ha-ha, or a placard? It does not move. It does not speak. Yes, yes—it's a billboard for Aryan Youth."

Here the impresario struggled to rise from his cushioned chair. The effort left him breathless, a weakness he covered by screwing his monocle into his eye. "Does it, I wonder, even breathe?" So saying, he darted forward and pinched the officer's ear. "Ouch! Oh, ouch! What a brave soldier!"

Perhaps it was bravery that prevented the lieutenant from flinching—though even if he had wanted to flee, his movements would have been hobbled by the cast-down trousers and drawers. Von B stepped back, so as to inspect the young man through his glass.

"A soldier! That is undoubtedly why Magda's female heart went pitty-pat, patty-pit. *Frauen!* Show them a cheap uniform. A pair of broad shoulders with shiny epaulets. Brass buttons like a doorman. How their heads spin at a tunic that nips down to a tiny waist. Ecstasy at a pair of tight pants, at the red stripe down the side. Ah, if you only had a sword! When women see a soldier's hand on the hilt, it's more than they can bear. They faint if you draw it an inch from the scabbard."

Once more, nimbly, the heavy man skipped forward and pinched the soldier's ear. "Ouch, ouch! No, no—he's a poster. He doesn't feel a thing. He won't blink an eye. He refuses to remove those hands."

Was the lieutenant under a spell? In a kind of coma? He continued to stand immobile in his awkward pose, half sylph, half satyr.

Suddenly Von B broke into a loud laugh. "Ha-ha-ha! He won't speak. He does not feel pain. A feather on his lips would not stir. But he is alive! Real flesh and blood! I perceive it with this! My most sensitive instrument. Able to detect, in four liters of water, a drop of Chanel. But this is not perfume to my nose! Nor is it sweat, or the aroma of fear."

Von B lifted his enormous head to sniff, like a mastiff, the air. Then he lowered his voice. "Poor boy. It's your trousers. You've shat them. No reason to blush. Don't be ashamed. You have to learn how to eat and how to digest. I'll teach you. I'll be like a father. The momma bird who dangles the worm. Only the food I bring you—the fruits and the vegetables and the sweet little oysters—will be so refined you will never require a tissue. Do you understand me?"

Now the frozen figure—he could have been the toy soldier in yet another famous ballet—came to life. The shy hands moved aside. A grin spread across the poster-boy face. Then the adjutant, an amateur, began to recite:

What have you done, my foolish father?

Von Beckmann seemed beside himself with delight. "Oh, alive! As human as our baker, our banker, our railway worker! He wants to be an actor!"

The lieutenant, arms wide, concluded his wooden speech:

A brave man will not fight against a helpless girl.

"Marvelous!" cried Von Beckmann. "The taste! The phrasing! The feeling of it! What a treasure!" He took two, three, four cautious steps toward the naked man. "You shall be the talk of the city! What am I saying? Foolish Von B! The actor I shall create will possess the world!"

The nude lieutenant didn't respond. He had cocked his head, as if listening. But what was there to hear? The band below had stopped playing. Even the constant thrum of the voices had stilled. Then from the hallway came the thud and thump of a limping man. At the same time, from even farther away, a humming began, a distant drone. Suddenly the door burst open. I. A. Moto, wrapped like a babe in its swaddling clothes, stood in the doorway.

"Rudi!" I cried. "Look out the window!"

The impresario turned white with astonishment, with rage. "Lorre! How dare you? This is a private audition. I have found our hero, our Haemon."

What did I, at such a moment, care about that? I crossed the room to the shuttered window. "Don't you understand? There won't be a Haemon. There won't be an *Antigone.* It's over, Rudi. Everything's over. Kaput!"

With all of my strength I heaved my arms against the shutters. They flew wide. The light of dawn entered the room. Against the mother-of-pearl sky, black shapes were moving. Here was another migration of swallows, in numbers too great to count. The pulse of their engines caused a saucer on the table to rattle and, on the wall, a cheap landscape painting to shake. It was as if even inanimate objects were stricken with panic. The three of us leaned out the open window. Arrow after arrow flew overhead, from the north to the south, as if launched by a god's inexhaustible bow.

COMMAND PERFORMANCE

One month later, the Von Beckmann troupe set out for the Domplatz in two limousines. Who would have dreamed that after the new rulers had occupied the land, the premiere of *Antigone* would take place precisely as planned? Not I, and not I. A. Moto. Yet even before his troops had reached Vienna, the Führer had informed Dr. Goebbels that the festival he had attempted for so long to disrupt must go on. Not only that, the leader insisted on the same site, the same date, even the very moment of commencement that had been determined before. The cast would be identical, too—naturally, with one exception. Antigone's lover could not be played by Loewenstein-Lorre. Was this because of my injuries? Or was it because the Nuremberg laws forbade such amorousness between a pure Aryan Greek and a Jew? In any case, my new part was that of a one-man chorus.

I had fewer questions about why Rudolph Von Beckmann had agreed to perform for the new masters. Either the production took place in this city or it would never exist. The entire conception of his *Antigone* sprang from the topography, or as Von B himself had put it, the *cosmology,* of the singular site. A sundial can tell the time in any garden, but the sun that drew the shadows over the cathedral's marble facade and the moon that rose above the Mönchsberg belonged to Salzburg alone.

Our Auto-Union sedans pulled up at the back of the square by midafternoon. Even before the doors had opened, we were met by a squad of black-uniformed SS. Magda and Anton stepped from the first car, along with Von B. From our limousine came Basserman and Sampson Frank and the writer, Flatow. It took me, with my lame foot, my encumbered arm, a moment or two longer to stand upright on my own.

The Domplatz in April looked much as it had on that terrible day in February, and as it had for centuries past. The cathedral itself, with its twin towers, its great clock, and the hemisphere of the dome, rose as majestically as ever. Whatever changes had occurred were temporary—the two huge red-and-black banners of the Third Reich, for instance, which hung from the spires; the platform stage that had been erected in front of the facade; and the row upon row of empty seats that had been set up in the square. Another difference: all those slogans from the March plebiscite, those innumerable *Neins* and *Jas*, had disappeared. April showers? Only in part. Indeed, at that moment—I glanced up toward the medieval clock: ten minutes past three—a small crowd, dressed mostly in black, was crouched on the cobblestones, scrubbing away at the remaining flakes of old paint. One boy used his own toothbrush, one man the tip of his long black beard. These were, all too clearly, members of the community of Salzburg's Jews. The Salzburgers themselves stood about grinning. More Jews were at work, with slop pails and rags and brushes, on the cathedral walls.

That there were so few remaining signs of the old plebiscite could not hide from us the fact that on this very day, at that very moment, a new one was taking place. No doubt about the outcome this time—especially in Salzburg. These same citizens who at the moment of invasion had wept by their radios to hear Von Schuschnigg's last words to his country—*God save Austria!*—soon shed tears of joy at the sight of those who had come to destroy it. With my own eyes I saw the hundreds of thousands who had squeezed into the Domplatz to bury the Panzer units in flowers. On that March 12 there had been no feigning of frenzy. The crowd tore off the soldiers' buttons for souvenirs. In the days that followed, it was this gem, this center of art, of all the cities in Austria, that was the most enthusiastic. No other town in the entire nation had staged a public burning of books. And what were the first volumes consumed in this *auto-da-fé*? The works of those who had loved Salzburg best: Zweig, Zuckerman, every last book in the library of Reinhardt. That's why it was a foregone conclusion that when they were now asked, *Do you acknowledge Adolf Hitler as your Führer and the reunion of Austria with the German Reich?*, the people of Salzburg, along with the general population of Austria, would answer *Ja*.

Our uniformed escort formed a wall around us. They led us between the rows of seats and toward the cathedral steps. Through a gap in their ranks I managed to glimpse, among those scraping away at the red letters in the word *Schuschnigg*, the birdlike figure of Serge. His uncut hair still tumbled like grapes, all the way to his neck and over his high, chiseled cheekbones. Oddly, his plush jacket was worn front to back with the buttons done up his spine. It must have been a joke played by the whitestockings—rather, by the Salzburgers, since everyone in Austria was a whitestocking now. In his bucket, judging by the yellow burns on his sleeves and trousers, there was a solution of acid. The fumes had reddened his sunken, Slavic eyes.

At that moment Serge looked up and saw the SS officer who was well to the fore of our entourage. At once the boy threw down his bristly brush and ran toward him. In his broken German he said, "My name is Serge Maximovich Polyakov. I am a foreign national. A Soviet national. Therefore a citizen of a land that has a pact with the thousand-year Reich. Look, Herr Obersturmführer. Here is my passport—" Alas, in his front-to-back jacket, the servant was unable to reach the breast pocket, in which his papers were stored. The crowd laughed at the comedy. Serge appealed to the grinning onlookers. "Tell him. Tell him, friends. I am not one of your common Jews."

The officer merely pointed to a clean cobblestone at his feet. He wanted Serge to polish it all over again. The boy resisted. "I was born in the town of Odessa. On the Black Sea. I am an ally!"

An older man, in lederhosen, with Emperor Joseph moustaches, strode forward. "How dare this person not obey a lawful order to work?"

Now the rest of the Salzburgers crowded around the boy. Someone pushed him to his knees. Someone else brought up his pail, sloshing the contents over his cuffs and shoes. Serge dipped his brush into the acid, but when he looked up he must have seen, towering above our escort, the head, with its black hair, its white streak like silver piping, of Rudolph Von Beckmann.

"Rudi! It's torture! Why have you abandoned me?"

All of us heard that pitiful cry. The director drew himself upward, so that he was yet a head taller, and screwed in his monocle. His lip curled, his brow darkened, his glassed-over eye flashed fire. It was the Balzac pose, with folded arms and the cape swirling round his shoulders. He turned to the detachment of guards. "Who dares," he demanded, "treat my servant in such a manner?"

The black-suited soldiers only shrugged. The Obergruppenführer pointed off toward the cathedral, where a group of men were scrubbing the steps. "Don't worry," he said. "Those are just the local Jews."

"No, no. I am sure I heard him."

Said the German, "But where?"

Again Rudi stared out over the square. The very hairs on his head, like the quills of a porcupine, quivered with a kind of perception. Yet nothing met his eye. Around Serge the Salzburgers stood three or four deep. The Jews, the clean-up battalion, did not dare glance up from their work.

Von B's voice boomed out over the Domplatz. "I warn you. Not one of my company is to be harmed. It is a breach of our agreement to force my valet into labor. To hide him from me is intolerable. I won't allow it! He has my supply of oxygen. What if I should have an attack? Think of the scandal!"

Before the Obergruppenführer could reply, there was a movement, a quaver in the line of stalwart Salzburgers. For just a moment the crowd parted. A thin arm, a thinner wrist and hand, waved for an instant in the air.

"Rudi! Help me! Your *Honigkuchen*!"

Magda rushed to Von Beckmann's side. "It *is* Serge! Rudi, we must do something!"

Just then the lieutenant, in mufti now, and with his blond hair slicked tight to his head, also moved next to Von B. He put his arms on the taller man's shoulders. He stood on tiptoe, so that his lips brushed the impresario's ear. "Don't listen. This is nothing. It's only a jealous Jew." Then he added, with a dazzling smile, "Aren't I your *Honigkuchen* now?"

Von Beckmann peered down at his protégé. No one called him the lieutenant any longer. Everyone thought of him as Anton Döring, a local hero, the sensational actor who would soon step onto the stage in the role of Haemon.

Flatow spoke up. "It is now half past the hour of three. We must begin in two hours."

Von Beckmann slapped at his forehead. "Hurry. Hurry, dear friends. We cannot be late. Our makeup must be ready. And what of our costumes? Hurry. Everything depends upon our being on time."

Now we rushed forward, surrounded by our bodyguards. In a phalanx we moved around the broad stage, where at exactly 5:36 P.M. the drama was scheduled to begin. One after the other the actors climbed the steps of the cathedral, walked through the cast metal doors, and gathered beneath the great vaulting arch within. Puffing, limping, I lagged behind; a full five minutes later I reached the top of the weathered stones, where—is there a Jew who would not experience a chill, a shudder?—I too passed into the dim, spangled, and incense-filled air.

By five o'clock the falling April sun had already cast long shadows over the Domplatz. At that hour the seats in the square had all been filled. Only two places in front remained vacant: those reserved for Herr Hitler and Fräulein Braun. At the back, on beer-hall-style benches, was the contingent of whitestockings. Ahead of them sat the Wehrmacht officers and the uniformed SS. The front section was filled by officials of the new government, both local figures and others, like Herr Woltat, the new Salzburg *gauleiter*. Agent 673 was not surprised to see that this was the same bald-headed bully who had knocked him to the cobblestones and who had later danced with Magda at the Lucifer Café. The man still wore his Alpine hat, with its red feather; but the swastika now was openly displayed in his lapel.

The very first rows were occupied by plainclothed security personnel and many of the highest figures in the Reich, including Herr Heydrich and, in his schoolmasterish spectacles, Herr Himmler. On either side of the aisle sat the Bormanns, Martin and Albert, and ranged next to them were the latter's wife, Gerda; the bucktoothed, square-jawed, shaggy-browed Hess; and Linge, Hitler's valet, with Gunsche, his clean-cut adjutant. Near the center, flanking the two empty seats, sat on the left Dr. Goebbels, looking, with his full-sized head and shrunken body, and with his shiny silk waistcoat, a bit like a jockey; and on the right the plump Reichsmarschall Goering. All these dignitaries were twisting round in their seats, staring up and out of the square toward the distant Obersalzberg. Did they imagine they could see the Führer, or at any rate his command car, as it wound its way down the twilit slopes?

As the minutes went by, the Reichskanzler's continued absence created a number of problems. The security forces became more and more nervous. The tank squadron, which had deployed on either side of the Domplatz, repeatedly started and killed their engines, sending thick plumes of exhaust over the crowd. It was no trouble for those of us in the cast to pick out the plainclothes detail, since they kept rising from their seats to stare at those in the adjoining rows. More guards patrolled the length of the central aisle. In trenchcoats and slouch hats they walked up and down in front of the platform and even poked about—was it a bomb they were after? A hidden saboteur?— in the machinery below. There was a soldier at each portal of the cathedral and another high up on the gallery atop the facade. Binoculars flashing, this fellow peered off in the general direction of Berchtesgaden, as if he too thought he might catch a glimpse of the tardy suburbanite hurrying off to his night at the theater.

More smoke rose from behind the platform, so much that one might have supposed an additional Panzer detachment had been stationed in back of the stage. It was, however, only Rudolph Von Beckmann, lighting the tip of one Virginia from the butt of another. I stood beside him, pretending that the grains I took from the pouch inside my toga were only English snuff. Rudi wore, for this command performance, striped pants, a pearl-button vest with white gardenia, and tails. From time to time he would take off his top hat and peek round the wooden planks to see if the guest of honor had arrived.

For the impresario and the members of his cast, the Führer's absence amounted to a full-scale crisis. The sun would sink behind the monastery wall at 6:40 and below the horizon at 6:53. The vital thing was that the moon's miniscus, hanging in the blue like a sword sewn onto an Arabian flag, would rise over the Mönchsberg at precisely one minute to seven. One minute after that our play had to end.

Von B threw down his cigarette. He ground it out beneath the heel of his surprisingly small leather shoe. "The nerve of this man!" he muttered. "A Von Beckmann production cannot be stretched like an elastic waistband. It can't, like India rubber, be compressed." There was no need to explain that to me. I knew only too well how every speech of his actors, each of our gestures, our very pauses, had been timed with a stopwatch. All of my lines, from my opening address to the crowd—

> *I come to this stage with a tale of woe*
> *Of suffering, and faith, and insolent pride.*
> *You must hear every word before you can go.*
> *Don't try to escape it. Don't try to hide—*

to the admonition, which I intended to deliver directly to Der Führer, about how prideful men will always be chastened: indeed, each syllable of my speech had been rehearsed to the steady tock-tock-tock of a metronome.

Our curtain, an imaginary one, was scheduled for precisely 5:36. It was now—I glanced once more toward the hands of the cathedral's enormous clock—5:31. Five minutes to go! Von B shot his cuff and checked the watch on his fleshy wrist. Off went the top hat. He leaned round the stage. Of the Reichskanzler there wasn't a sign. He turned back to where I was waiting. "This is impossible! It's intolerable! Our moon will pause for no man, not even Herr Hitler. Does he think we'll wait? That I'll delay our drama? He would do better to ask me to make the earth stand still."

"Rudi! What can we do?" That was Magdalena, already in the robes of Oedipus's daughter. She darted, stooping, from under the platform, next to the machinery for the underworld. Her face beneath her powdery makeup was all foreboding. "*Die Zeit!* The time!"

To our surprise Von B stepped out from behind the platform. "Woltat!" he bellowed. "I want the *gauleiter!*" He strode up the first four rows of the central aisle. No less astonished, the SS ran forward to head him off. The *gauleiter,* hearing his name, rose to meet the director.

Von B: "We must begin at once. I insist upon it."

"But you see for yourself, our Führer has not yet arrived."

"You are responsible for everything that happens in Salzburg. You control the festival. We have to begin."

"You have made a mistake. I only carry out the wishes of others. And for those others, we must wait."

Von Beckmann looked once more at his watch. He groaned. "Five thirty-five! We have only one minute! A single moment! It is *my* wishes that the cast will obey! I have only to give the command."

That we might well obey his command was true, but how could he give it? He was closed round on every side by uniformed soldiers. They had even pinned back his arms.

It was at this moment—indeed, the very moment our play had to begin—that the Minister for Propaganda and Public Enlightenment came to the rescue. Without rising, merely by lifting his bony chin, he signaled the guards to step back. "On reflection," he said, "I cannot believe the Führer would object if we keep to the announced schedule. What is it our enemies say of us?" Goebbels's thin lips spread in a white-toothed smile. "That we make the trains run on time?"

For a moment Von Beckmann stood dazed, as if he had not fully grasped the favor that had been granted him.

The minister, still smiling, nodded his pomaded head. "Herr Régisseur, you are free to begin the drama."

"*Los!*" Von B cried, almost shrieking in his excitement. He thrust, both in triumph and as a cue, his fist into the air. "Commence!"

With no thought of my laggard leg, I sprang at once onto the platform. One arm was taped to my body. With the other I pretended to draw aside a nonexistent curtain. Then I poked my head, on which the hair was combed into Roman-style bangs, through the invisible folds. For a moment I simply stood there, not saying a word. I was intoxicated less by my fairy dust than by the tale that, somewhat in the manner of a nightclub entertainer, with a light, wry, ironical patter, I was about to tell:

The sons of Oedipus ascended to his throne,
But when Eteocles continued to rule too long

It stuck in Polynices' throat like a bone.
He warred with his brother to right that wrong.

Even as I chanted I could not help but note how the audience at the front leaned back in revulsion. They were actually cringing, as if they feared contamination from my shadow or sputum.

What rage, what fury, the tears in a flood
When brother seeks to shed brother's blood.

The distaste of these dignitaries filled me pleasure. Now I knew the real reason Der Führer had delayed his appearance. How could a man like that, the leader of the master race, agree to dignify by his presence an actor like the ex–Lazlo Loewenstein, the present Peter Lorre: *ein Juder aus Hollywood?*

With a kind of glee I continued the words of Flatow's prologue. I told the discomfited crowd how Polynices had hurled his armies against Eteocles, sending seven generals against the seven gates of Thebes. But when the fighting, with all its terrible bloodshed, was done, the issue remained unresolved. Finally the brothers agreed to settle their dispute by single combat. In the ensuing struggle, each killed the other. Creon, uncle to the slain warriors, then took over the throne. Immediately he decreed that all those who had attacked his city, but especially Polynices, must remain unburied, to be devoured by bird and beast and hungry dogs.

When those who disobey that rule shall be found,
They shall pay for their sin by a life underground.

Suddenly Antigone, the slain youths' sister, appeared behind me on the stage. She declared that she was determined to obey the gods by giving her brother full burial rites. I turned toward her, bowing slightly, as if introducing an act, an entertainer. Then I contrived to disappear through the same trapdoor from which Magdalena had arisen. A few seconds later I emerged where Von Beckmann was waiting behind the stage. We each had the same thought. Perhaps now, after the Israelite's exit, Herr Hitler and Fräulein Braun would consent to appear. We both peered round at the audience. Alas, there was still no sign of our honored guests.

The tragedy continued. Ismene refused to help her sister with the burial ceremony. A guard announced that someone had *sprinkled thirsty dust* on the unburied corpse of Polynices. Basserman, as Creon, demanded that the culprit be found. Through it all Von Beckmann and I kept staring at the two empty seats in the front. How to account for this absence? Could it be the new plebiscite? Perhaps the returns had not been as favorable as everyone supposed. Or did the Führer object to Sampson Frank, old Tiresias, for the same reason he did to me? That would mean he would miss the entire play!

Half of that drama had gone by already. The guard returned to announce that the guilty party had been caught in the act. It was Antigone! Now Basserman and Magdalena, the man of might, the voice of the martyr, engaged in the great dialogue that is the heart of the play. As each asserted his claim to the right—on the one hand, the needs of the state; on the other, the claims of the gods—the sun sank steadily lower. Blue shadows, gray shadows, enveloped the square. The crowd disappeared in the darkness. Then, as if the gloomy arms of the night had reached out and seized her, Antigone was led away to her doom.

In my opinion, what happened next was one of the great moments of the modern theater. If only scholars knew of it, they would still be writing of the daring of the conception and the unique interplay of setting and action. I looked toward Von Beckmann. His head was back, straining to hear the expected cry. I caught my breath, listening too. Was that it? Or was I imagining the sound? Yes! There! Yes! *An-n-n-n—* That first syllable, no louder than a robin's chirp, came floating down from the Mönchsberg. The hairs stood on my nape as the rest of the word echoed from the heights:

An-n-n-t-i-i-i-go-n-n-n-e-e-e-e!

Next, from the Kollegienkirche, a little less faintly, came the identical call:

An-n-n-t-i-i-i-go-n-n-n-e-e-e-e!

The whole of my body shivered, though whether that chill was caused by the note of the boy soprano or by the breeze that, at day's end, swept through the square, I could not say. Now the cries came one upon the other, calibrated, syncopated, an elaborate round; that is, just as the call died away from St. Sebastian's, and the even closer St. Margaret's, and then from the cathedral itself, it began all over again from the heights of the Mönchsberg:

An-n-n-t-i-i-i-go-n-n-n-e-e-e! An-n-n-t-i-i-i-go-n-n-n-e-e-e!

Near and far, the city of Salzburg rang with that name.

The audience sat rapt. Von B was beaming. That was because Anton, having heard of the fate of his betrothed, was about to make his appearance. Impossible not to see how proud the impresario was of his protégé, so young, vibrant, and striking in carriage. Von B grinned and put a finger to his lips: a kiss of encouragement. Then the smile faded from the director's face. I saw what he did. The crowd of dignitaries, the soldiers and whitestockings, were not looking toward where Haemon had entered. Their gaze was directed elsewhere—toward the clear space at the left of the Domplatz. There an open Daimler, its twin headlights blazing, was making its way toward the front of the square. Hitler had arrived! He was standing at the passenger seat, his left hand clutching the top of the windscreen, his right arm bent upward and back in a salute. A roar of greeting rose from the crowd. It grew and grew, so loud, so all-enveloping, that I had to clamp my mouth shut to prevent myself from cheering, too.

The Führer's face was set, serious and solid. But it was clear to all of us that he was not succeeding in his efforts to repress a gay, a joyous smile. Throughout the day, until that very hour, he had been waiting for the results of the plebiscite. Now the results were being passed quickly from person to person in the crowd: 99.73. That was the percentage of Austrians who, in free and honest voting, had approved the union with the Reich. What astounded the audience, making them buzz with delight, was that the vote in Germany itself had been only 99.02. Best of all was Salzburg. *Ja*: 158,058. *Nein*: 463. No wonder Herr Hitler's lips kept escaping the clamp of his teeth and breaking into a triumphant grin. But I knew there was a deeper reason for the Reichskanzler's pleasure. From every church, every steeple, a cry rang out. Could anyone doubt that the Führer had timed his entrance in response to a heavenly call?

The limousine halted. Herr Hitler assisted his mistress from the back seat. Together—no, she trailed a half-step behind, like an Oriental bride—the two figures made their way to the empty seats in the front row. In the respectful hush, the chanted round began yet again, the sweet trill from the mountain, followed by the echoing sound from the steeples, which in turn were lapped, like a canon of Beethoven, of Bach, by the original notes.

Suddenly I felt my arm gripped—and tightly!—by Von B. His large head, still hatless, was thrown back. Like an animal, he seemed to sniff the air. "What's that?" he demanded. "Did you hear it?"

I listened as the voices, sweet to any ear, continued their cascade. "What do you mean? I didn't hear—"

"Quiet! Quiet! It's a false note. A false note. There! There!" The director was pointing upward, to the cathedral's left tower. "That's no altar boy. I've heard that timbre. But when? Where?"

It was time for the final repetition of the roundelay. Some hidden child high on the Mönchsberg poured out his refrain; the nightingale's song descended toward the darkened Domplatz. Von Beckmann remained motionless, staring up through the glass of his monocle as if it were a telescope. Still the sequence of calls tumbled down, drawing nearer and nearer. Now I, too, heard the discord. It came from the belfry! *An-t-i-go-n-n-e-e-e!* The correct word, the correct notes, but not in the voice of the boy soprano who had been placed at the top of that tower. I stared. I squinted. But there was nothing to see. No movement. No shadow or silhouette. Only the half-shut louvers, verdigris-colored, like copper exposed to the salt of the sea. What could the presence of this new singer mean? Who could it be?

Beside me, the impresario uttered a half moan, half sigh. "Ah. I know it. That voice. And so, dear Lorre, do you. You heard it yourself. Remember? Three hours ago. On this very square."

An icy hand, that's what it felt like, gripped the back of my neck. Serge! It had to be Serge! Now the blood in my veins ran cold as well. What was that servant doing so high in the steeple? Suddenly I recalled with a skip of my heart the words of the handsome soldier: *It is only a jealous Jew.*

On the platform there was a whoosh, a sizzle, a sigh. The torches, meant to guide Haemon to the underground tomb, had been ignited. Now Creon approached his son. Man and boy engaged in the play's second great dialogue.

HAEMON: *What have you done, my foolish father? A brave man will not fight against a helpless girl.*

CREON: *And an obedient son does not question his father. I would rather give up my power than be ruled by a woman.*

HAEMON: *The woman did not cause the calamities that afflict us. It is you, and your stubbornness, who have brought war and drought.*

I turned toward Von Beckmann. His skin had turned a ghastly white. His mouth hung open. He was petrified, frozen, like one of those mastodons that have been dug up from a glacier. "Anton! Anton!" The word forced its way out from deep within the director's chest. He raised an arm, pointing to the stage. "How beautiful he is. How vulnerable."

I saw in a flash what our director meant. The head of the Austrian lieutenant seemed to shine on the stage, bright, blond, and brilliant, like the tip of one of the torches. Von B grasped my toga in both his hands. "Peter, I beg of you. Do something. It's Anton. You have to save him."

But what was it Von Beckmann wanted me to do? Should I dash to the stage and pull the actor from view? Call to the sentries? Or at least shout a warning: *Get back! Get down! It's Serge! He wants revenge!* But what if, after all, Rudi had been mistaken? In the medley of calls, could he be certain that the voice he had heard was that of his servant? Perhaps the thick walls of the tower had distorted the sound, lowering the register, the way speed and distance alter the whistle of a passing train. I glanced up toward the belfry again. Above the louvers a vertical slot was cut into the stone. It was too high off the ground for an archer, too narrow for the traditional vat of boiling oil. But a man with a rifle—no end to the mischief he might do.

A gasp came from the crowd. Creon, in his rage, had just hurled his son aside.

You woman's toy! It is I who made the laws that are the only hope for our town.

Von Beckmann gasped too, not so much from pity as from terror. Anton, flung helpless to the ground, was now a perfect target.

I returned my gaze to the belfry. What was that? At the window loop— a glint of metal? The barrel of a gun? Von B had seen it, too. He dropped to his knees; he implored me. "Lorre. Dear Lorre. My pretty Peter. You have to do it. It's the only way. I am too old. My heart—it's failing. It's choking me. Look, I can't even breathe. You can run to the cathedral. You can climb to the top of the steeple. How young you are! How strong! Run! Run! Run! Go now!"

I didn't move. Even if the spiteful Russian was there—and who knew if the two of us had not been the victims of our fantasies and fears—what could I, alone and unarmed, accomplish? "But Rudi," I said, "you know I never perform my own stunts."

He didn't reply. He must have realized what I already knew: that there simply wasn't time for such an ascent. Anton would remain onstage for only another two minutes. He would be plunged into the underworld at precisely seven, one minute after the soul of his bride had climbed into the sky. That was when the great bells would strike the hour, not just at the cathedral's twin towers but throughout the city. I peered up at the giant dial. Six fifty-eight. Yet even as I looked a movement, at once microscopic and magnified, caught my eye: the enormous hand of the clock had hauled itself almost straight up toward the XII. Now I had it! Moto had discovered the M.O.! It was the same as with Hitchcock! The cymbals in the symphony! Yes! It was during that clanging and clangor that the shot would be fired. Heaven help me! I was the Man Who Knew Too Much. And the man who could do too little. No one, in such a din, the deafening tintinnabulation, would hear the report. Suddenly Von Beckmann struck his forehead with a resounding smack. Then he broke into a laugh. *"Dummkopf!"* he exclaimed. "Ha-ha-ha! Such a *Dummkopf!* I have been the victim of my own egoism! My narcissism! Always the center of attention! Fool! I am a fool! Lorre, don't you see?"

"You mean," I asked, "that it's not Serge in the tower?"

"Of *course* it is Serge. But Anton is not his target. No, no! That was only my own sense of grandeur. As if the boy would risk everything to revenge himself on *me!* It is *Hitler* that he's after. Adolf Hitler. Don't you see? It's an assassination. Serge is going to kill the master of the German Reich!"

Could such a thing be? Was the target really the man in the brown uniform, the man with the moustache? Was the whole course of history to be changed in exactly one minute? Why then did I, possessed of such terrible knowledge, simply stand there—not in horror but oddly calm, detached, pleasantly lightheaded, like the pale bubble of the moon that, I noted, was just then wobbling upward through a sky of aquamarine? From whence came this feeling of well-being? The sensation of the serene?

Sometime best to do nothing: another Maxim of Moto. Either Serge was in the tower or he was not. The bullet would find its mark or it would miss. In any case, as the Buddha has taught us, life would take its preordained course. I felt like the Buddha, or some other godlike, all-powerful creature, myself. I could do nothing. Or I might after all decide to lift my finger—or my foot, and step into the swiftly flowing current of time: *A half minute! A quarter, ten seconds, nine.* No need to be hasty. Take care not to panic. After all, had I not, in *Mr. Moto on the Spot,* defused the bomb that would have destroyed the city of San Francisco with only one second left? *Eight. Seven. Six.* In this case, however, it could justly be said that Herr Hitler was the bomb and Serge the defuser. Hmmm. That required some thought. The practice of the art of deduction. *Softly, softly,* in the words of Agent 673, *catchee monkey.*

On the stage, Anton had got to his feet. He delivered his exit line:

You cannot punish me. You will never, in this world, see my
face again.

At that instant the hand of the clock gave a last convulsive spasm and jerked to an upright position. I covered my ears. I squeezed shut my eyes. What was the use? No power on earth, not any amount of cotton wadding, could muffle the boom, the pealing and tolling, of the cast-iron bells.

Dong! Dong! Dong!

Hands waving, screaming like a banshee, the impresario ran pell-mell over the cobblestones of the square. His path took him straight toward the spot, midway between the front of the platform and the first row of chairs, where the Führer was sitting. Again and again he cried the same words, words filled with fury and indignation. "An outrage! An outrage!" He had almost reached what must be the field of fire. Still he kept going, shouting louder than ever, "To disrupt a Von Beckmann production!"

The audience, because they thought this was part of the entertainment, only tittered. But the SS knew better. They came sprinting toward the director from every side. In the front row everyone started to duck. Heydrich and Himmler threw themselves to the right; Goebbels and Hess went left, leaving Herr Hitler, his eyes wide, his black mouth open, completely exposed. Overhead a swarm of birds, Salzburg swallows, banked and wheeled. Had there been a shot? Impossible, in the tumult, the boom of the bells, to hear it. A scream rose from the midst of the crowd. Fräulein Braun. A second scream came from the opposite direction.

"Rudi! Oh, Rudi!" That was Magda, still in her Grecian gown. She stood frozen as the SS, both soldiers and men in ordinary clothes, fell on her mentor. With their fists they beat him to the ground.

And what, in this furor, of Der Führer? Was his reign done? I saw that he was still sprawled backward in his chair. His mouth, with its ever-present shadow of moustache, hung open, in either the agony of death or, at such effrontery, sheer amazement. I turned to the left-hand tower. There, above the slit in the stone, a white puff of smoke hung suspended. I knew full well that this must have come from the barrel of a gun. Had a shot indeed been fired? And who, if anyone, had been struck? Or had we all, such was my fancy, been transported to St. Peter's, the original one, at Rome; and had the College of Cardinals, with this sign of smoke, just decided upon the man who would be the pope?

BRIDAL SUITE

A lovely spring day in Vienna! Tiny white clouds, like the caps tossed by sailors, filled the sky. Flowers hung from flower boxes, and, under orange and green umbrellas, vendors sold ices *mit schlag.* All was in harmony: taxis beep-beeped, birds chirped, and human beings whistled and hummed. Those human beings! Their plump, ruddy faces bounded along the Ringstrasse, each one beaming and nodding, like so many balloons on a string. And we? Magda in the middle, Rudi with her arm in his, and I to the left—we moved along with the others, inhaling and exhaling the fresh breeze with the scent of pine needles in it.

On such a day even the flag attached to the facade of the Hotel Metropol seemed, if not exactly gay, then less menacing than before. You could almost say that the black-legged swastika was performing a cartwheel in the wind. Directly beneath it stood Konrad, the aged doorman, wearing his legendary high hat, the one with the powder-blue sash. Who could resist, with all its creases, its wrinkles, that sunny smile? Our tipsy trio grinned back at him. He put two fingers to his hat, as if to salute these heroes of the greater Reich: the saviors of Adolf Hitler! On we swept, through the double doors and into the shining arcade.

Everyone in Vienna knew this gleaming space. There was no other like it. The ground floor was lined on either side with fancy shop windows filled with furs and jewelry and, behind the plate glass of Konditorei Cilli, pedestals piled high with *Spanische Windtorten* and other treats. In the window of the toy store, Das Känguruh, a locomotive went round and around, in and out of its tunnel, the same way it had when I had come here for cakes as a boy.

The lobby proper was one floor up. That was where you'd normally find the desk and the pigeonholes for keys and letters, as well as the bellboys with blue-ribboned caps and shiny pointed shoes. They'd carry your bags up the grand marble staircase, sixty-five polished steps, with a banister of what looked like gold-plated brass. But there were no bellboys that day. We paused at the foot of the stairs. Rudi looked up the daunting ascent and, undoubtedly from force of habit, glanced round for the valet with the oxygen tank. Of course he wasn't there, either. Magda squeezed the director's arm in her own.

"Are you all right, *Liebchen?*" she asked.

Von B nodded, though his face, from which the smile had faded, did not look well. There was a bruise under one eye, the result of the pummeling he'd undergone six days before, and an unhealed split on his lower lip. A twitch hammered away at his cheek. Still, in a sally at jauntiness, he wore a new cape, his hair had just been cut, and he sported a fresh gardenia in his lapel.

The smile had faded from my lips, too. "Something is wrong," I stated. "It's not like what I remember. There's no one here. No porters. Look, no guests. Magda, Rudi, I don't like it."

Von B had lit a new Virginia. His hand was plastered to his mouth like a starfish to a clam. When he exhaled he said, "Why do you always find something to worry about? You know perfectly well the reason there are no guests. The Gestapo has taken over the top three floors."

"No, no. Nothing makes sense. Tell me why they have left old Konrad out front like a prop. And these shops, with no one to buy their goods— whom do they expect to fool? Not me! Rudi, I think we should go back."

"Go back? How can we go back? When Herr Goebbels summons, we have no choice but to appear."

"*We?* Why *we*? I wasn't summoned. Why am I here?"

Von Beckmann laughed. "Because when you are with me, you aren't under arrest."

Magda was wearing a gray dress with white pearls, together with a dotted veil that she lifted now from her face. The electric lights, reflected from the glass panes, flashed across her cheekbones, her red lips, the knob of her chin. "If you want to run, lambie, run."

Run, I thought. Run where? The borders were closed. I hadn't an exit permit. My passport had been seized. The surprise was that I hadn't been seized myself. Von Beckmann was right: I was like some pale mushroom that had been allowed to flourish only under the great man's shadow. "I can't run," I responded. "They will shoot me and say I was trying to escape."

Von B swirled his cape through the air, gathering it at his throat. "And why should you wish to escape? Wait. Be patient. When I come down these stairs, I shall bring with me permission to stage our *Antigone.*"

That thought gave me no pleasure. Was this to be my fate? Performing in that Greek drama in festival after endless festival? That was no better than a millennium of Moto. "No, no, Rudi," I protested. "You don't know them. You have no idea what they can do."

"You talk as if *I* were the one in danger. Do you really suppose they would threaten me? Imagine the scandal. The repercussions throughout the world."

"What are you saying? Have you forgotten their treatment of Mann? What about Einstein? Now it's the turn of Sigmund Freud. My own teacher! They ransacked his house. They've taken his passport. Freud! A prisoner! That's what they think of world opinion."

"It's deplorable, but the fact is, everyone knows these men are enemies of the regime. Two of them are Jews. My case is different. I think it likely Herr Goebbels has asked me here to thank me. No one in Austria has demonstrated his loyalty more forcefully than I. Herr Hitler owes me his life! What if I had not run out into the line of fire? Does anyone doubt that Serge would have shot the Führer instead of putting the barrel of the gun into his own mouth? *Der Retter,* that's what the masses call me—the savior. You've heard the rumors. I am to be made a National Dramatic Artist. There is even talk of appointing me Senator of Culture."

Von B's own words seemed to fill him with vigor. They were like the oxygen from his missing tank. With a clasp of my hand and an embrace for Magda, he bade us farewell. Then, alone, he began to climb up what looked like a Grossglockner of snowy white stairs.

The Reichsführer for Popular Enlightenment and Propaganda had his offices in, of all places, the bridal suite. It was there that, panting and puffing, Rudolph Von Beckmann arrived. Even before he knocked, the door, by totalitarian telepathy, swung wide. An officer, a huge SS Scharführer, stood in the frame.

"*Keine Zigaretten!*"

The impresario paused, then crushed his Virginia on the rim of an urn that stood in the foyer. The SS man moved aside, allowing the guest to step over the threshold into the parlor.

This room, with its facing sofas, overstuffed chairs, and mahogany coffee table, was quite elegant. There were books in locked bookcases, and on the rose-painted walls, watercolors of old Vienna: the Prater, the Hof Garten, the Danube, the Wienerwald. A door in the middle of the left-hand wall was open just wide enough to reveal a corner of the bridal bed and the edge of a glass-topped table. Through the parlor windows the late sunshine streamed, soaking into the burgundy carpet and darting dazzlingly across the surface of a large rectangular desk. Von B shaded his eyes to see the man seated behind it. It was Goebbels. He was leaning back in a creamy suit and dark tie, his black hair slick and shiny. He balanced himself on the triangle made by the two back legs of his chair and the kneecap he pressed against the desktop. The slot of his mouth widened as if to accept a coin.

"So here is our hero! Herr Von Beckmann! A pleasure to see you once more."

With that the chair tipped forward and Goebbels jumped from behind his desk and, hands extended, moved quickly forward. His special shoes, in gleaming black leather, disguised his limp. Indeed, his scrawny frame glided gracefully across the sun-spangled room. Through narrowed eyes Von B noted the hollow face, the shiny, receding hairline, the jacket's fancy tails. Who did this little jockey remind him of? He had it! The American! *Astaire!*

"Herr Minister, I have done nothing more than my duty," responded Von Beckmann, extending his hand. But Goebbels ignored it. He seemed to be glancing behind his guest, toward the still open door.

"And Fräulein Mezaray? Is she not with you?"

"No. I mean yes, she is here, but in the arcade. I left her with Herr Lorre."

"Ah! A pity! I had so looked forward to seeing her once again. The Führer, too, will be disappointed. I cannot tell you how many times since their first meeting he has spoken of the impression she made upon him. His eyes would light up whenever he heard she had made a new film—even from decadent Hollywood. He would watch these privately, in his own residence. It is his opinion that beauty like hers comes only from within, from deep pools of belief."

Von Beckmann gave a start as the SS man closed the door behind him. "Herr Doktor Goebbels," he began, "there is a matter between us that must be resolved. It has been almost a week since the *Antigone* was disrupted. I have come to Vienna to learn when the production will be permitted to resume."

"And I have asked you here to discuss precisely that question. Come, it is time we got down to work." So saying, Goebbels took the director's arm and led him toward the gleaming windows. At his desk, the minister slid into his chair, which he tipped back, as before. He motioned to another chair, opposite. "Please, Herr Von Beckmann. Won't you have a seat?"

The director sank down on the reed-covered piece of furniture. There was a brief silence, which the minister broke.

"Yes, what you have said is true. We have seen that you are a man devoted to duty—even at the risk of your life. That is why you flew through a storm, a most dangerous storm, at the request of Schuschnigg. Ha-ha! That fool! With his wire glasses! His Maginot Line!"

Without thinking, Von B flipped open his cigarette case and reached for a cigarette. Then he paused. Was there an ashtray on the desk? The sunbeams sprang off the polished wood like effervescence from a glass of salts. Through the glare he saw that the surface had been swept clean: no books, no papers, no phone. Only three green pencils lined up in a row. The minister jiggled a fourth between his fingers. Von B snapped his case shut. "Herr Minister, if you please. My time is limited. We are here to discuss the *Antigone.*" There was another pause. The director squinted. Impossible to see, behind that slab of reflected light, anything more of the little man than his hands. They were in constant motion: clasping his upraised knee, smoothing his hair, cupping his chin, twisting, almost choking, the colored pencil.

After yet another calculated silence, Goebbels started to speak. "Yes. The *Antigone.* I am pleased to tell you that a decision has been made. The production of the play will continue."

"And I am pleased to hear it. If you will tell me the date of the opening performance, my colleagues and I will throw ourselves into the work."

Goebbels leaned further back. In his lapel the party badge gleamed as if incandescent. "You will appreciate that not everything can remain precisely the same. The Salzburg Festival, for instance: it must be postponed until the traditional summer season—of nineteen thirty-nine."

"Nineteen thirty-nine!"

"Don't be dismayed. The Führer has promised to attend. Did you think he could be discouraged by the kind of incident that occurred at the Domplatz? A man who survived the trenches for years? Every day, in the streets, in the crowds, he risks the worst. Really, one must conclude that he is under the protection of a higher power."

"Are you proposing that I hold my company in readiness for more than a year? It's ridiculous!"

"Why so touchy? So quick to jump to conclusions? The festival will be postponed, but work on *Antigone* will begin at once."

"What does this mean? A separate production? But everything depends on Salzburg. You saw for yourself—the city is one of the chief characters in the drama."

Goebbels smiled, showing an even line of clamped teeth. "And so it shall remain. There will be no change in location."

"I want to be certain I understand. You wish to continue *Antigone* at once, in Salzburg, but not as part of the festival?"

"Precisely. The festival is performed for at most a few thousand people, and the greater part of these are tourists, the wives of Fifth Avenue furriers. The Führer wishes the production to reach the widest possible audience: the whole of the German people. Herr Von Beckmann, you are an intelligent man. Surely you realize that the only way to accomplish this is to make the *Antigone*, from the death of Oedipus and the pact between the brothers to the rising of your moon, into a film."

"What? A film? Impossible!"

"Why impossible? Would you deny this drama, with its feeling for the community, the folk, to the entire German people?"

Here Von Beckmann closed his eyes, which had, on the instant, started to ache. How he yearned for a cigarette! His voice, when he spoke, sounded rough and dry. "It is impossible because I am no longer working in cinema and have not made a single film in many years. That is a medium *run* by your furriers! No, I have devoted myself to mythic drama, works that express the deepest instincts of a culture. It was that, not Von Schuschnigg, which at-tracted me to *Antigone*. And that is why, throughout my career, I have con-centrated on the vision of the Greeks."

"And what better place than on film to capture that vision? It is an art made for the acts of the gods. Those transformations—now a man or a woman and now a deer, a stag, a bull. A lover descends to Hades. A stallion flies though the air. How else to represent the epic scale? A Trojan horse, a raging storm, the massing of the Aegean fleet? Faced with mere tricks, colored lights and rattled tin, the theater crowd is struck by nonbelief."

Von B: "There is, in my opinion, nothing wrong with nonbelief. The highest artistic emotion is a combination of, a collaboration between, skep-ticism and imagination. Three cheers, Herr Doktor Goebbels, for cellophane and tin! Not to mention an even greater problem—the Greek drama requires an audience, living spectators, from whom the chorus is drawn and whom, as ordinary citizens, it represents."

Goebbels: "Ah, about the need for living spectators we are in entire agreement. And what other audience is as willing to give itself to the illusion before it as the one of flesh and blood that sits before a film? Even I, who must see every motion picture made in the Reich, am not immune. In my screening room I sit with folded arms, aloof; but in the cinema, surrounded by representatives of the great German folk, I feel myself drawn in, captivated—no longer a separate man, a minister, but a part of the whole community."

Von Beckmann leaned forward. "There is no secret to this magic spell. It springs from far more primitive instincts than the wish to lose oneself in the masses. How could this not be? One sits in a warm, darkened, cushioned room. All about, the unseen presence, the breath, of others. The food we are fed—the candies, the ices—is that eaten by children. Before our eyes, shadows play. Not to mention the crouched, fetal posture—have you seen how the young people place their feet up on the seat before them, with the backs of their heads growing numb? All of that suggests a regression to the uterine environment—to, if not the womb itself, then the crib, the tub, where we are bathed in a stream of infantile fantasies and delights. The Greek theater, *my* theater, is where we are freed from those dreams, where we become citizens and adults. In the cinema palace we surrender our minds to the common cortex, spread out before us in the shape of a screen. It is a stage for psychologists and tricksters and hypnotists."

"And for the Minister for Enlightenment and Propaganda. We cannot dismiss so easily these primitive instincts. The Third Reich depends upon them, just as it depends upon the public in the cinema audience who sit openmouthed, with hearts beating like that of a woman about to be seduced."

"Von Beckmann has no need for such an audience. It is why I left the cinema. It is why I refused to accept the offer of the Jews from MGM."

"That is commendable," Goebbels countered. "But surely you realize that there is no such decadent heritage remaining at UFA. Obviously you have other reasons for refusing our offer."

"Now it is you who jump to conclusions. Have I said that I refuse?"

The minister brought all four legs of his chair to the carpet. He placed his lean face within the palms of his hands. "This has been, Herr Von Beckmann, a fascinating discussion. It stimulates me greatly. If only time could stand still and we could go on—like two old philosophers, eh? Like your Greeks! But time does not stop. I must ask you, do you or do you not accept the idea of the *Antigone* on film?"

Once more the director shut his eyes against the glare. Why couldn't he have a cigarette? He could no more think without filling his lungs than the Aeolian harp could play without the wind. Even the ancient prophets, the oracles at Delphi, drew their inspiration from a cloud of steam and smoke.

"I am waiting, Herr Von Beckmann."

"Before I can answer," said Von B, "there is something I need to know. Everything will be just the same? You insist on no other changes?"

The minister uncupped his jaw and, turning over his hands, cradled it instead. "Not exactly the same."

"By that you mean—?"

"To begin with, Flatow, and that Sampson Frank. I need not tell you the obvious reason."

Von B heaved a sigh. "Very well. Accepted."

"Now, as to the man who fled his country—"

"Do you mean Basserman?" Von Beckmann demanded. "It's true he left Germany, but that was because of his wife. Why punish the man?"

"Let us simply say that we have contacted Jannings for the role of Creon. His work is admired throughout the world. Nor has he been so foolish as to marry a Jewess."

"Obviously, Jannings would make a splendid Creon. I do not object. Is that all?"

"Not quite. We have some doubts about another member of your cast."

"Oh! You mean Lorre. He's not with the company any longer. Dismissed. I dismissed him. Don't be misled by appearances. He is an old friend of Magdalena's. He follows her everywhere. It is almost a sexual pleasure for him. You know the type. Why not give him an exit visa? Eh? He'd be gone in a wink of the eye."

"I was not, Herr Von Beckmann, thinking of Loewenstein."

There was a pause. Von B glanced toward the door of the bridal chamber, where it was just possible to make out the gauze tumbling from the canopy of the bed. It was like the spent smoke, blue-gray, shiny as taffeta, from a cigarette. If only he could disappear behind that familiar curtain, or draw it around him, like netting for mosquitoes. His mouth felt even drier, as if stuffed with biscuits.

"Not Lorre? Not Loewenstein? Then who?"

"Why," said Goebbels, "it's you."

"I? Rudolph Von Beckmann?"

Goebbels did not reply. He had his green pencil between his fingers. He drummed alternate ends on the tabletop.

Von B attempted to swallow the nonexistent saliva in his throat. "Herr Doktor Goebbels, you leave me at a loss. I don't know if I am expected to laugh. Is it a joke? I confess I came here this afternoon expecting to be thanked, to be praised—not only for the production at Salzburg, one that will become a landmark in the history of the stage, but also because of the role I played in saving the life of the Reichsführer. Do not misunderstand me. I do not claim to be a hero. I do not expect a medal on my chest. But to be accused of disloyalty, to have the minister entertain doubts about me, when only days ago I risked my life for Herr Hitler! Look here—my eye! You see my lip? These are the decorations I wear instead of becoming Senator of Culture!"

The director had, during this speech, worked himself up. By its end he was straining forward, clutching the edge of the desk. Goebbels, however, kept tap-tap-tapping. Von Beckmann had no choice but to lean back. The glare from the top of the desk was like that from an interrogation lamp.

Now the minister said, "As a matter of fact, that was another thing I asked you here to discuss. Perhaps you would be so good as to satisfy my curiosity about the first moment you realized something was amiss. Do you remember when that was?"

"I do. It was during the calls for Antigone."

"And what occurred? What was it that made you think the Führer might be in danger?"

"I had rehearsed each of the callers myself. I knew their voices. The call from the cathedral was to be made by a boy of thirteen. The voice of an angel. But the one I heard belonged to an adult."

"Did you recognize that voice?"

"Not at once."

"Did you notice anything else that might have constituted a threat?"

"I thought I saw—in the belfry, above the belfry—a glint of metal. I thought it might be a gun."

"You said you did not recognize the voice at once?"

"Not at the first call. I only knew it did not belong to the child I had rehearsed."

"When *did* you recognize it?"

"During the round. I believe at the second call."

"And whose voice was it?"

"That, Herr Reichsminister, you know as well as I. To Serge. Serge Polyakov. My former valet."

"And then?"

"Then I ran forward."

"To warn the Führer—?"

"That is correct."

Here Dr. Goebbels threw down his pencil and leaned back as before, with his hands around his upraised knee. "Forgive me if I repeat myself. I wish everything to be clear. You did not shout a warning, did not run forward, when you realized that the caller in the tower was not the person you expected?"

"No. I—"

"And you did not act when you thought you saw the barrel of a gun?"

"Not immediately. I was not certain. I was stunned."

"But you ceased to be stunned when you realized that the man in the tower, the man with the weapon, was your valet?"

"No. Not exactly. It was the bells. The church bells. I suddenly realized that it was under their cover that the assassination, if there was to be one, would take place."

Goebbels seemed not to hear the last words at all. He was staring at the plaster in the ceiling. "Let us say," he resumed, "that the voice you heard had belonged to an utter stranger. That would be, would it not, most suspicious, most disturbing? Allow me to continue. You only became thoroughly alarmed when you recognized the voice to be that of Polyakov. Did you know something about the valet that particularly alarmed you?"

Von B: "Ah. I understand your meaning. Yes. He had been seized by the Gestapo. He had been humiliated by them. Forced to wash cobblestones in the Domplatz. And he had been beaten. I feared he sought revenge."

"Astounding! You see what you take to be a weapon. You hear the voice of a man with a motive, a man seeking vengeance—and you do not act. You wait until the bells sound the hour—" Here, in mid-sentence, the minister brought down the front legs of his chair with such force that anyone in the suite below must have thought they were hearing the thud of a Goliath, not the weight of this jockey, weighing sixty kilos at most. *"When the life of the Führer is at stake!"*

"No, no," Von B protested. He waved his plump hands. "I did not think the Führer was threatened—at least, not at once. I thought he meant to shoot Anton!"

Goebbels leaned forward and, rather like a pianist, pressed all ten fingers against the wood. "Anton?"

There was a snap, a glitter of gold. The director had flipped open his cigarette case and was offering—*American? Pure Virginia?*—Dr. Goebbels a cigarette.

Impatiently the minister waved the case aside. He asked again, "Do you mean Anton Döring?"

"Yes," Von B responded. "He was onstage at the time."

What could the impresario do? Impossible to light up if the minister would not smoke. He let out a sigh, as if that were a substitute for exhaling.

"What reason would Polyakov have to take revenge against him?"

"Just because he *was* onstage, perhaps. Before his arrest, Serge was to have had a role. A small one. He might have felt that Anton pushed him aside."

"From the role of Haemon? Herr Von Beckmann, you will not talk absurdities to me. There must be another reason you thought he would attack the actor. What was it?"

"Another reason?"

"Allow me to help. Was this Döring not an officer in the former Austrian army? Assigned to the protection of Magdalena Mezaray?"

"Yes, yes. He was."

"And does he not serve at present as your valet?"

"I would say he is now an actor. My protégé."

"What I am in plain language attempting to ask is whether or not he took—whether this Polyakov might have thought he had taken—the assassin's place in *that* role, not the one onstage."

"We shall never know what Serge was thinking."

"You stated that he was humiliated. That he was beaten. This took place on the Domplatz. On the tenth of this month. Correct?" Goebbels did not wait for an answer. "Oh, of course! You were there. Outside the cathedral. He actually called out to you, did he not? *Rudi!* Surely you heard him. You must have. It was Döring who prevented you from responding. He took your arm. Could it be that Polyakov saw this? That he saw his rival whisper into your ear?"

Von B's voice, when he responded, was shaky. "Who told you these things?"

Goebbels: "What matters is what I tell you. Three hours later Polyakov was in the tower. He had a rifle. He sought revenge. But it was not the Reichsführer he was aiming at. And not Döring, either. The reason, my dear Von Beckmann, that you do not wear a medal on your chest is that *you ran into the square to save not the Führer's life but your own.*"

For a moment the older man stared, thunderstruck. Goebbels waited. Then, almost wearily, he said, "Why this look of amazement? What I describe is commonplace. A lover's quarrel. A trite triangle. A sordid homosexual affair."

Next came a surprise: Von Beckmann burst out laughing. It wasn't put on. He wasn't acting. The great shoulders shook. The tears fairly jumped from his eyes. It was Goebbels's turn to look dumbfounded. "Herr Von Beckmann," he said, "control yourself."

The director struggled to comply. He took out a handkerchief. He wiped his neck, his brow, and dabbed at his streaming eyes. Then he managed to gasp, "So that is your doubt about Von Beckmann! The reason the *Antigone* is to be taken from me. Ha! Ha! Forgive me. I ask your pardon! But you intend to remove me from my own production. Because you have discovered I am homosexual! Ha! Ha! Ha!"

"I cannot imagine what you are laughing at. At this filth? Do you suppose the Reich—"

The bold impresario cut him off. "I'll tell you what's amusing. *You* are! All your efforts, the cleverness, the circumlocutions—how you labored to build your trap! All for nothing. Do you think my life is a secret? Oh, it's true, in the wide world, the public world, I maintain a certain—ambiguity. The mystery of Mezaray, for example. A love story for the masses. But in the world of the theater, the cinema, the arts, there is no pretense. I confess! Ha! Ha! Ha! You have caught me! You see before you a guilty man. My crime is that of Michelangelo, of da Vinci. Am I to be arrested? Marched with a placard through the streets? I think not. Not any more than you would pull down the Sistine ceiling or cover the Mona Lisa with cloth. We are speaking of the nature of the artistic temperament, of the artist's sensibility. You will not deny me *Antigone* for that."

"No," said Goebbels. "Not for that alone."

"For what then?"

"Perhaps you might be better able to inform me. What is the one group that clings to art with as much leechlike fervor as the homosexuals? That, in the name of your *artistic sensibility*, sucks its lifeblood dry? No answer? No laughter now? Come, Herr Von Beckmann, we both know it is the Jews."

"The Jews? You did not listen! I spoke of genius! The great line from Socrates to Shakespeare. The Jews haven't such powers. They don't create the symphonies or the dramas. They fiddle, and they scratch out their criticism, and they strut on the boards."

"Very well put. Just as they have always done, and continue to do, in the productions of Rudolph Von Beckmann."

"But all that has been settled. Didn't I tell you? Lorre has been dismissed. Dismissed even before you made your demand. Also my associate Flatow— haven't I agreed to release him? What about Frank, a man who has been with me since the start of my career? Let him go back to studying the Talmud! I ask you, man to man, have I not been as cooperative as any artist in the Reich? As Furtwängler, let us say? You are not removing him from his orchestra. Yet the *Antigone* company is as cleansed of Jews as the Berlin Philharmonic."

"Not quite. Not completely. One figure remains."

"Who? Simply tell me and I guarantee I shall put your doubts to rest."

"Oh, about this we have no doubts."

"Very well. What is his name?"

"Well, that—the exact name is part of the problem. It is possible that about this, too, you might help us. Will you be good enough to tell me, where does the *Von* in *Von Beckmann* come from?"

"What? The *Von*? It has always been in the family. As far back as anyone can remember."

The sun, in slipping across the windows, no longer glared so blindingly off the polished wood of the desk. Von B could see his questioner plain. Goebbels was not merely leaning back in his chair; he was gripping the armrests. "That is odd. What you say contradicts the evidence our experts on racial purity have collected. They have searched through generations. There is no evidence of a title in your family line."

The director shook his head from side to side. The soreness in his eyes had spread from temple to temple, as if someone had pushed through his skull with a needle. His thoughts seemed to be draining from his brain. "All families exaggerate their past," he said. "They like to think their origins are grander and more distant than they are. The likelihood is that the emperor Franz Joseph bestowed the honor on my father's father at the battle of Sadowá. That would be 1866. My grandfather was a medical officer. He saved the life of a member of the royal family. A nephew, I think. Or it may have been that he merely prevented the loss of a limb. The title was his reward."

Goebbels grinned, grinding his matched rows of teeth. "Really, I should let you continue. It's first-rate entertainment. Sadowá! Where no doubt the record of the honorific was lost on the field of battle. Oh, wonderful! These fertile brains!" The minister stretched forward across the desk. He beckoned to the director with a crook of his finger. His voice dropped so low that Von Beckmann, too, had to stretch forward to hear it. "Come. Come close. I will tell you where you got the *Von* in your name."

That was the moment the Reichsminister sprang: up out of his chair, over the desk, with his hands outstretched and his lips pulled back from his teeth in a terrible grimace. It seemed he meant to throttle his antagonist by the neck. Instead he seized Von B's jacket with one hand and thrust the other into the pocket at his breast. "Here! Here!" The two words burst forth in a shriek. "Out of your fountain pen!"

It was that instrument, of ebony, banded in gold, that Goebbels held in his hand. He snapped it in two, spilling its ink onto the desktop. Both men stared at the puddle, dark and narrow-waisted. It might have been the blood of the mouse upon which the cat had finally sprung.

"You are," said Goebbels, panting a little, *"ein schmutziger Jude."*

Von Beckmann, or perhaps it was only Beckmann, was on his feet. His cape swirled through the air. "I deny it! You have no proof! How dare you make such an accusation?"

"Perhaps you could tell me, in what town were you born?"

"What town? I can't be sure. My family made many moves. From Berlin. From Dresden. From Heidelberg."

"Berlin! Dresden! Heidelberg! These are sacred cities. Are you not familiar with another place? The town of Zaleszczyki?"

"Of course I have never heard such an absurd name," Von B responded.

"The Vienna Bakery? The Red Star Matchworks? Baron Hirsch Avenue?"

Von Beckmann shook his oversized head. "Herr Minister. I ask you to entertain the possibility that you are making a terrible mistake. I have nothing to do with Jews or Judaism. Do you see this flower in my lapel? Every day a fresh one. Every day fresh perfume. That is the incense of my religion. I live for art. I believe in it utterly. It alone has the power to save and to redeem. If necessary, I can be a martyr and die for it, too."

By way of reply, Goebbels snapped his fingers. The muscular soldier marched from the closed front door to the bank of windows, where he began to draw the heavy drapes across the glass.

What was this, thought Von B as the Scharführer shut out the last of the sunshine and proceeded to turn off the standing lamp and then the overhead light. Was it torture? That awful thought seemed to be immediately confirmed when the staff sergeant lifted from behind the far sofa some kind of dark, intricate instrument, black and boxy with two metal arms, and carried it to the top of the nearby desk. By then the pupils of Von Beckmann's eyes had fully dilated, so that he had a better view of the infernal machine: a motion picture projector!

No one—not Goebbels, not Von Beckmann, and certainly not the Scharführer—spoke a word as the latter threaded a thin strip of celluloid through the gears. In less than a moment the machine came humming and whirring and glowing to life. A beam of light shot across the room, splashing against the wall. A white rectangle, filled with dots and dashes, like tumbling marks of exclamation, shrank, enlarged, and came into focus. In two seconds the title was jerking about on the rose-red wall:

This was replaced at once by a card, also in Yiddish, reading PARIS: NOR EIN YOR ZWEIG, *Only One Year Ago.* Now the wall came alive with scenes from the year 1894: stock footage of the new Eiffel Tower, horses and carts circling L'Etoile, crowds of dandies on the Champs-Elysées, and, last of all, a barge floating along the Seine. The projector clacked and groaned as it chewed up the brittle film. Now a new title card was displayed, DI HEIM FUN DREYFUS, followed by an all-too-quick glimpse of a thatch-roofed house, with what looked like Russian, not French, peasants leaning from the windows. DER KAPITAN, read the next card, which led to a medium shot of a brisk military parade. The jittery cavalry passed by, led by a handsome officer, dashing in kepi and cape, with an elegant little moustache.

"Ha!" snorted the Minister of Enlightenment and Propaganda, from out of the dark. "If that is Dreyfus, I am the chief rabbi of Paris. The whole thing is a charade!"

The next card, DER KORBEN, *The Victim,* led into a long shot of anonymous men walking up the steps of what could have been a courthouse but might just as easily have been the Opera or the Stock Exchange. Similarly, the card after that—DER MISHPET, *The Trial*—depicted a jury in a jury box and the white-wigged figure of what looked suspiciously like a British judge.

"Ha! Ha! Ha!" Goebbels was holding his sides. He slapped his thigh. What he was laughing at was the section entitled DI BUSHE ZU DI FRAN-ZEUSEN: a tricolored flag was jerkily descending a flagpole. "Look! Ho-ho-ho! Beckmann, look! What a treat! That's supposed to be *The Shame of France!*"

But Von Beckmann did not look. Indeed, he hadn't once raised his eyes from the top of the desk, where the ink, in its figure-eight configuration, glistened in the castoff light of the projector. Rather, it could be said that he was watching a different picture, one that consisted entirely of flashbacks. If it had a title it would have to be the outlandish

ZALESZCZYKI.

Here was the kind of central European village that possessed as one of its chief features a puddle, thick and broad in springtime, narrow and shallow in the fall. In Zaleszczyki this landmark was located at the intersection of Baron Hirsch Avenue and Zosina Wolja Alley, the main crossroads in town. No matter how hot, how withering the summer sun, or how far the thermometer dropped in winter, the puddle never dried up or froze completely. This was the natural feature that Von Beckmann saw while he gazed at the spill from his pen.

And in his mind it must have been springtime—in fact, the spring of 1885—because now the puddle had swollen to the size of the Mississippi, or at any rate the Peltew, an affluent of the Bug. How will the town's fancy ladies manage to cross from the Vienna Bakery on one side of the street to the fruit store catercorner on the other? The answer? They will cross on the boys' wooden ferry. What a boat! Just planks nailed together. And what boys! With shaved heads, with ringlets, and legs so thin, like pencils, you would have thought an epidemic of rickets had befallen the village. First on board, Frau Dicker, the horsedealer's wife. With letters to mail at the post. She is joined by Madame Jungermann, spouse of the timber lord. The one holds aloft her envelopes; the other lifts the hem of her dress—the latest fashion from Minsk—well away from the mud. The ship's captain is the tallest of the boys, sad-eyed, spindly-legged. He raises an arm. He shouts the command: *Coolies! Northward! Commence!* At once a half-dozen of his Chinamen, with hemp ropes over their shoulders, run the length of Baron Hirsch Avenue. A scream from Frau Dicker. Madame Jungermann throws her arms round the captain. Slowly the ship and its cargo begin the perilous journey from curb to curb.

The fruit store, the Vienna Bakery, and the Royal and Imperial Post were located on three of the four corners of the main intersection. The fourth was taken up by the multistoried Red Star Matchworks. If the children were coolies on the street, in this factory they were slaves. All day long they toiled in the joinery, pushing raw wood into grinding machines and plucking out the finished sticks. The younger boys work in the drying chamber, and those younger still, age seven, or six, sweat in the packing room, where they remove the sticks from the frames and stuff them into the little wooden boxes with the red star. In every room the fumes of phosphorous, of sulfur, hang, palpable and all-pervasive. It is these vapors, not the lack of Vitamin D, that have affected the children's bones, turning their legs into little more than the matchsticks their labor has helped produce. That red star clearly has nothing to do with the Revolution, which is only a glimmer upon the horizon, some thirty-two years—they might as well be thirty-two centuries—away.

In winter the factory windows are shut and the clouds of sulfur thicker than ever. The little workers have to fumble at their labor in the gloom. On one such day Rudi—he was, of course, the ferryboat captain—is practically green himself from the fumes. Against the rules he pushes one of the panes open a crack, to get a breath of air. Suddenly he stiffens, peering into the street below.

There, a crowd of Zaleszczykians has gathered at the intersection. All of them are staring upward, with their mouths open like the pipes of drains. Rudi leans farther out and twists his head to look upward, too. What he sees makes him race down the steps two at a time, with a band of knock-kneed *kinderlekh* close behind.

THE GREAT GRANACH, *Der Greusser Granach*—that is the sign painted on the side of a canvas-covered wagon that stands off to one side of the avenue, attached to a chestnut mare. Granach himself is great, indeed—not in size, because his height is only average, but in his resplendence: brillian-tined hair, splendid hook nose, a fur-trimmed frock coat, and, most striking to the Zaleszczykians, real rubber heels on his shoes. With him is a lady, in green tights and spangles. In one arm she holds a baby, a wizened little brown-skinned chap, and in the other a small red drum.

Those Zaleszczyki natives—there must be a hundred of them around the puddle's frosty perimeter—stare and stare into the sunless January sky. The reason is the rope that has been strung across the intersection between the top of the post office on one corner and the roof of the match factory on the other. It is at a truly dizzying height. Fifteen meters! Suddenly the lady in spangles beats on her drum. From the heavens a trumpet answers. Jews and gentiles fall silent. The Great Granach cups his hands to his lips in order to speak.

"Friends, we have come all the way from Lemberg. And before that we were in Paris and London and Holland. In each of these places the kings gave us medals. Look." Here the speaker opens his frock coat to reveal the innumerable medallions pinned to the lining inside. Murmurs of awe rise from the crowd. "Why has our family of artists come to Zaleszczyki? Because you are good people, the salt of the earth, and when you see that we have staked the life of our son on the performance, we know that you will open your hearts to us. No, no, no. We ask for no money now." Again the artist breaks off, this time, clearly, because he is overcome. Tears well in his eyes. His voice, when he resumes, is choked with sobs. "No, we don't want a single kreuzer beforehand. If anything should happen to our son, we would have no use for money—no, not even any use for life. But if God should help this child on his journey, if he crosses from one building to the other above this hard, stony ground—Look, my friends! No safety net!—then my wife and I will allow ourselves, for the sake of both our sons, to pass the hat among you. You'll show the world that no one in Zaleszczyki is rotten enough to turn his back on artists who risked their child's life and who have medals from all the crowned heads of Europe."

By now more than two hundred people have gathered at the intersection. They're pale as parsnips. They're shaking with fear. Once more the lady with the babe, with spangles, beats on her drum. Once more the trumpet sounds from the rooftop. "Attention!" Granach calls out in Yiddish. Then he repeats the word in Russian and Polish and German and, though there are no Frenchmen to hear him, in French: *"Attention! Le spectacle commence!"*

So it does. To the gasps of the crowd a tow-haired boy appears on the Greek-style cornice of the Königliche und Kaiserliche Poste. He can't be more than eight or nine, yet his muscles bulge, they ripple beneath his shining clothes. Holding a pole at his waist and with a sky-blue scarf round his neck, he puts one foot on the rope and starts to cross.

The whole population, sly-eyed Jews, slack-jawed peasants, the poor father and mother and babe in arms—all stare upward without a word. Captain Rudi is spellbound with the rest. His heart swells in his chest like a waterlogged sponge. His short, sharp breaths wave like handkerchiefs in front of his mouth. He has never seen—that flaxen hair, the shiny silk shirt, the silver tights that cling to buttocks and crotch—a sight so beautiful, so exciting.

The other boy, the one in the sky, with his firm calves and thighs, has already moved a quarter of the way, a third of the way, across the chasm. Now he's over the half-frozen puddle. But what's the matter? He places one foot ahead and pulls it back. His long pole tips left, tips right. A low moan goes up from the Zaleszczykians. Suddenly, piercingly, a heartrending wail comes from on high:

"Foter! Der vint! The wind!"

All the people below give a shudder, as if they were themselves caught in the gale. The Christians cross themselves. The Jews start to rock. Rudi stretches upward, on tiptoe, and holds out his arms. "Help him, God," he shouts. "He's such a darling!"

Of all the prayers going up at that moment throughout the world, this is the one that is answered. The daredevil lifts his pole, straightens his back, and marches on—ten steps, eight steps, four steps to go. Then, to a tremendous cheer, he's on top of the Red Star factory, smiling and waving and tossing his handsome head at the sight of how the hundreds of people below, including Jungermann, the timber magnate, and also Herr Dicker, shower the artists with kreuzers and kroner and rubles and shillings.

Back in Vienna, more than a half-century later, Von Beckmann was still in his trance and Dr. Goebbels was practically in a fit of hysteria. He was pointing to the square of light on the wall, in which, first, a card read DI TREURIBE MAME; that was soon replaced by the image of an old, shawl-covered woman, who alternately threw her arms to the heavens and used them to beat her breast.

"Ho! Ho! Ha! Ha! Are you watching closely, Beckmann? That's supposed to be Dreyfus's mother! His mama! His *mamele!* This is better than the Jew Chaplin! Better than Hollywood!"

For Von Beckmann this is neither a time for working with his coolies at the factory nor playing with them by ferrying rich ladies from the bakery to the post. Instead they are studying the Talmud that, on broken-down tables in a broken-down building, is spread before them. Old Rabbi Blitzer, his chin propped on his palm, is snoozing at the front of the room. Again the spindly-legged boy tiptoes forward. In one hand he holds a candle, in the other a box of Red Star matches. When he reaches the rabbi he pauses, strikes the match, and puts the flame to the candle wick. Then, while the whole class watches, the grinning atheist drips the hot wax onto the old man's beard, affixing it to the top of the table.

And when the rabbi wakes up? The ten-year-old captain will not be there to see it. Already he has wound his way to the top of the matchworks. He is dressed in his usual rags, except that he has sewn pieces of metal—the tops from tin cans, the bit from a horse, and dozens of nails—to his clothes. In this gleaming armor he stands, one foot drawn up, like a stork or a flamingo, and the other upon a rope that is stretched on the rooftop tar. His arms are outstretched. Genuine tears of fright and self-pity drip from his eyes. *"Foter! Foter!"* he cries. *"Der vint!"*

"Ha-ha-ha!" There was a loud burst of laughter. For an awful instant Rudi thought that someone—the head of the Red Star factory, or even Rabbi Blitzer—had seen him. Then he realized that the man who was laughing was not a dead Jew.

"Ha-ha!" went Goebbels once more. His finger was pointing to the bridal suite wall. There the words, white letters on a black card, read, GESHIKT IN GOLES, *Sent into Exile.* This was followed by a distant view of ships, steamships and ironclads, which tossed on the waves. Black smoke billowed from funnels. The whole sea churned into froth. The minister could not contain his glee. "Beckmann! Beckmann!" he cackled. "This is nothing! It gets better, I promise! The best is yet to come!"

The director did not respond. He sat hunched in his chair, head down, staring at what was now only a sticky black blot on top of the desk.

"Is something the matter?" asked Goebbels. "You don't find this amusing? What you see is supposed to be the French fleet. They're taking Dreyfus to Guiana. To Devil's Island! Ha! Ha! Ha! Next we'll see dancing girls and palm—"

The minister broke off. Speechlessly he watched as the large man before him performed a reckless act. From one pocket he took out his gold cigarette case and from the other—he'd come a long way from Red Star matches—his gold cigarette lighter. The reckless part was how, without bothering to offer the minister a Virginia, Von B proceeded to light one of his own. He inhaled behind his hand. He held in the smoke for what seemed forever. Then he exhaled a rolling blue cloud.

The sergeant took one step toward Von Beckmann. *"Rauchen verboten!"* he commanded, and raised his hand to strike the forbidden pleasure away.

Goebbels, however, waved him off. The Scharführer retreated to the whirring gears of his machine. Goebbels leaned back, his eyes fixed on the director, who drew in another puff. What he saw was the portrait of a man in bliss: eyes closed, smoke pouring from his nostrils, a smile on his thick, half-parted lips. What had so pleased him? The narcotic of nicotine? Not entirely. Nor was it the French frigates or the windblown coconut palms—the purported representation of the dread Devil's Isle—that came on next. It was the more potent drug of recollection.

These exhaled smoke clouds were almost indistinguishable from the wisps of fog that had covered the frozen pleasure grounds at Lemberg some ten years later. That is to say, the scene Von Beckmann was witnessing took place in winter, at dusk, in the year 1895. The wagon he sees is the same, except the sign upon it no longer reads THE GREAT GRANACH but THOMAS A. EDISON, JR. In the interval, the chestnut mare has become a swaybacked nag; the tiny babe has grown into a dark-skinned gypsy boy. His brother, too big for the high wire now, wears his sky-blue scarf and thrusts paper fliers—announcements for *Di Tragedie fun Dreyfus*—into the hands of the eager crowd. Granach himself shouts through his hands, and his wife, still bespangled, beats and beats upon her wooden drum. No need for a trumpet this time. The Jews come running from every direction. There must be a hundred already pressed against the rope—the same rope? the tightrope?—that separates them from the white sheet that has been hung from the limbs of a nearby tree. The evening mist hovers close to the ground, wrapping their ankles in what look like puttees.

"We want Edison!" shout the Jews. *"Der zun fun Edison!"*

The son of Edison, that's the captain's cue. Up he stands in the cart.

Removing his top hat, he takes a bow. No doubt about it: it's Rudolph Von Beckmann. He's run away with the family of acrobats. Now, at the age of twenty, he's got the same top-heavy body, the pencil-thin moustache wisp, the bottom teeth that, even when he's smiling, acknowledging the cheers, protrude beyond those on top. His hair is brush-thick, and the bleached patch, perhaps the result of exposure to phosphorous, is clearly visible on the right. Perhaps those same factory fumes may be the reason he's already adopted the trademark flower in his lapel: better the perfume of a gardenia or rose than the stink of sulfur.

In Lemberg the Jews start to ask Thomas Junior some questions. There's no end to the things they want to know. Why the sea's salty, for instance; and if it's the case that there are some lands where the people have only one eye in the middle of their foreheads; and why is it Turks wear red fezzes? "Is it true," asks a man without teeth in the front, "about California? That the melons there are as big as a bathtub?" To this and every other question the son of the sage has an answer. And to each new reply the crowd gives a louder cheer. Until, that is, a bespectacled young man off to the side puts up his hand. "If this is Thomas A. Edison, Jr.," he asks, "how come he's speaking Yiddish?"

A pause. Consternation. Edison, as if all his light bulbs had gone out, says not a word. It is Granach who saves the day. Putting his hands to his lips, he shouts, "Night, friends, has fallen. It's dark enough for our show. You'll know this is the son of Edison when you see him run the Kinetoscope!"

A murmur sweeps through the crowd. Someone yells, "We don't care about Edison! We want Dreyfus!"

That is the call. The chant rises from a hundred throats: "Dreyfus! Dreyfus!"

It isn't an American Kinetoscope that young Rudi is laboring over but a brand-new Cinématographe from the brothers Lumière. With some difficulty he ignites the ether lamp. A sigh escapes the crowd. The bedsheet lights up like the shade of a lamp. Rudi settles onto a stool. He turns the crank. Now the Lembergians gasp in awe. Before their eyes is the Eighth Wonder of the World: the Eiffel Tower. Nor is that all. Scene follows scene: the cavalry procession, the courthouse, jury and judge. Then the lowered tricolor. Then the mother in tears. From the crowd, a profound silence—save for, at the portrait of the breast-beating woman, audible sniffles, unstifled sobs. What a spectacle! History parading in front of one's eyes! Even the broken-down nag, seeing the phenomena pass before it, the fabled ocean, the tropical palms, pricks up its ears and switches a ragged tail. At last the taut cloth holds but two simple words:

"Cease!" bellowed the director. "Cease at once!" At the same time he thrust himself to his feet, toppling his chair behind him. Then he staggered across the wine-colored carpet to where the splash of light on the wall provided the illusion of an open window. He lurched toward it as if he meant to jump through.

"No, no," Goebbels calmly replied. "We come now to the most delightful part."

At those words Von B spread his arms, and with them his cape, as wide as he could. Then he brought his fists together under his chin. It was as if with that defiant gesture, the pose of Balzac, he meant to gather up and swallow the immaterial motes of light. Instead, the flow of images swallowed him. The shades and shadows played over his torso, making him literally the subject, the body, of the film.

"Herr Minister," said Von Beckmann, "won't you please turn off the machine?"

To that request, so humbly, so meekly delivered, Goebbels seemed willing to comply. He turned to the SS Scharführer. "*Halt!*" was the command.

The sergeant put his hand on the turning reel. Immediately the play of images stopped. Goebbels rose from behind his desk and moved to where Von Beckmann stood against the wall, arms outstretched, like a knife thrower's target. Now the minister, staring at the director's shirtfront, threw the knife.

"What's this? What's this I see? Could such a thing be?"

There, in elaborate letters, a final inscription had appeared:

A PRODUKTSIE FUN RUDOLPH BECKMANN

"How interesting," said the minister. "No *Von*. No title. No honorific. Just plain *Beckmann*, after all."

The director remained motionless on the spot. The title continued to dance across the trunk of his body in fancy script that curled up like Arabian slippers.

"And what do we make of such a name, eh?" said Goebbels, who stood now just outside the shifting beams. He pointed at the letters, which, in the heat of the projecting bulb, had started to curl. "I have become something of an expert on this subject. Is it not true that Beckmann as a Jewish name is an acronym? Does it not stand for *benei*? The sons. And *kedoshim*? The saints, the martyrs. Ha-ha-ha! What? No reply? Can it be that I know more on this subject than you? Beckmann! Beckmann! Son of the martyr! Ha-ha-ha! What a joke! Who is this man? The great Rudolph Von Beckmann? He is only a filthy Jew."

Von Beckmann did not move a muscle. The beams of light bored into him, fixing him, the way a needle might fix a specimen upon a board. A thin line of liquid appeared at the corner of his mouth and rolled onto his chin. Anyone looking on would have thought that the impresario was having a fit. Then the letters upon his chest, already curling, bubbling, turned crisp and brown. The martyr was on fire!

Immediately the soldier turned off the projector. But it was as if the switch had been turned on inside of Von B. He bounded away from the wall. In his old manner, he gathered his cape at his throat. With a full voice, his old voice, he started to shout. "I have admitted nothing! Nothing! This is an outrage! To accuse a man of being a Jew is a crime! It is an unbearable insult! What degradation will you perform next? Why not demand I pull down my trousers?"

"Oh, that won't be necessary," Goebbels replied. "We already possess testimony about what is inside them."

Von Beckmann, though still in a rage, could not help his voice from shaking. "Testimony?" he said.

"From Hauptsturmführer Döring. Surely you would not deny he has intimate knowledge of the evidence."

"*Hauptsturmführer?*"

"Yes. Of the SS. We arranged for his place in the Austrian army."

Von B reached backward for his chair and staggered awkwardly on discovering it was no longer there. With mock solicitude Goebbels set it right. The director sank down. "Anton," he muttered. "*Mein Honigkuchen.*"

In his specially built shoes, Goebbels walked limplessly to the far side of the desk and took his seat behind it. The staff sergeant removed the projector and returned to his post by the door. The Reichsminister leaned back, clutching his knee, just as he had at the interview's start. "Now you see," he said, "why the *Antigone* must undergo a few changes."

For a brief spell Von Beckmann sat with his head in his hands. Then he looked up. "I resign from the production."

Goebbels: "Accepted."

"And from the Salzburg Festival."

"Also accepted."

Von B: "We shall leave the country at once. Within forty-eight hours."

"I am afraid," said Goebbels, "that will be impossible."

"But I must make arrangements. There is no way I could depart before this hour tomorrow."

"You have misunderstood me. We cannot allow you to leave at all."

Von Beckmann stiffened. "Are you saying I am under arrest?"

"There is no need to phrase it in such a manner."

"But I am not allowed to leave the Reich?"

"No."

"And Vienna?"

"No, not Vienna."

Von B, with growing horror: "And the building? The Hotel Metropol?"

Goebbels unclasped his fingers. He turned his palms upward, as if to say *Alas.*

Von Beckmann said, "I see."

Then, in little more than a whisper, the minister added, "Perhaps, in exchange for a certain favor, we might be able to provide you with an exit permit."

"You mean, two exit permits. We are a couple."

"Very well. Two exit permits. They will be handed to you at the airport."

"And what," asked the director, "is that favor?"

Goebbels leaned forward. Glancing apprehensively toward the Schar-führer, he beckoned Von Beckmann to stretch closer, over the desk. Then he whispered a sentence or two in his ear.

Von B jerked backward. "What are you saying? Do you know to whom you are speaking?"

Goebbels: "I know precisely."

"There is no bottom to your well of filth. The vulgarity is endless."

"Then you refuse—?"

The large, rumpled man did not reply.

"I see that you wish to think over our proposition." Goebbels rose. He seemed to wish to end the interview as he would any other. Affably he took the director's arm. He walked him across the carpet. "Unfortunately, there is not a great deal of time to decide. I can give you two hours. Until six o'clock this evening. The last scheduled flight for Paris leaves Aspern at a quarter past eight."

The staff sergeant pulled open the door. Von Beckmann stepped through. Alone, stoop-shouldered, he walked away from the bridal suite.

Magda saw the impresario first. She sucked in her breath in a gasp. I turned around to see what she did. Von B was at the top of the stairs. He was pale. He was anguished. "Magda!" he cried, as he caught sight of the actress. "They know everything! Everything! Zaleszczyki! The wagon! The acrobats! All my years with the Granachs!" Now, with his cape swirling behind him, he started down the smooth, milky steps.

"What's that? Lambie, who is it?" Magda had shifted her gaze to the middle of the staircase. There, crouched on the steps, was an old man on his hands and his knees. With bucket and rags he was polishing the Italian stone. I strained to see who it might be. Impossible at the distance to make him out. "Oh, lamb! I'm frightened," said Magda.

Trembling with palsy, the aged figure raised his head toward Von Beckmann, who had come to a halt just above him. The director reached for his monocle. He screwed it into his eye. The next instant the huge man was hurtling downward in full flight. Not Goebbels in his special shoes, not Astaire in his magical pumps, could have taken the stairs with such deftness and speed. "Magda! Magdalena!" the impresario cried as he reached the bottom. Then he speared the actress's arm and dragged her along the mirrored hall. "That was Schuschnigg! The chancellor!"

In panic now, the couple raced past the jewels and furs, the ceaseless locomotive in the shopping arcade. I trotted after, no less frightened by the apparition myself. We made straight for the gold-and-glass double doors, in which Konrad stood smiling. That gentleman spread his arms. "I am sorry, Herr Beckmann," he said, neglecting on this occasion to touch the brim of his hat. "We must ask you to remain our guests."

Terrible sight! Two SS Sturmmänner were standing at attention on the sidewalk outside. We whirled: another pair of the black-suited corporals had stationed themselves at the foot of the staircase. Seeing this, I felt the bones in my legs, the tibias, the fibulas, turn to soft rubber. The jaws of a trap were about to close. All these glass walls were collapsing about me, as in a story by the American, Poe. A vision rose before my bugging eyes: millions and millions of cobblestones, all the cobblestones in Vienna. With a toothbrush, a hairbrush, with a rag made from my camel-hair coat, I would be condemned to polish every last one.

Von B, however, remained a prince of insouciance. "Oh, we are not leaving," he told the doorman. "We'll stay for something to eat, perhaps some *Doboschtorten*, before our flight."

Then he turned on his heels and led Magdalena and me on a stroll through the arcade. We paused before the window of the Konditorei Cilli.

This was, or had been, along with Demel's, the leading confectioner of Vienna. For the season the trademark *Windtorten* in the window had been brightened with a display of marzipan bunnies, chocolate rabbits, and hares in meringue. There was a spun-sugar Easter egg of jumbo size. Rudi pointed it out. "Look, my love. That must have been laid by an ostrich. A *Dinosaurier.*"

The actress pulled him a few steps aside. I watched as she lifted her veil. She said, "Rudi, tell me. What did the man say?"

Von B raised his arms. He placed his hands on her shoulders. His cheeks, I saw, were twitching. He was powerless to prevent his eyelids from snapping open and closed in a series of spasmodic winks. What he said was "My darling. You must not ask me to speak. My tongue is black. My lips are poisoned. If you kissed me they would kill you."

She said, "I shall take the risk. Tell me. Don't make me beg you."

Rudi faced the gleaming window. He pressed his face to the surface, like a famished person about to break the glass. But he turned to Magda instead. He lifted a wing of her hair and, into her ear, with its shining Chinese pagoda, he whispered what favor it was that the minister had asked her to perform.

She did not recoil. She did not groan. There were no tears. On the contrary, she thrust against him. Raising herself, she drew him down. Then she kissed him. Her mouth opened as if she wanted to swallow him. His mouth opened to drink her in. Goebbels, who had thought Von B's taste exclusively homosexual, would have been amazed to see how long they remained attached to each other. This was not a movie kiss, what Rudi might call a fantasy for the masses. For that matter, no movie theater would have been allowed to show his red tongue and the way he bent over her, nor the way, beneath his cape, her two arms encircled his buttocks and her two muscular legs gripped the shank of his own. Imagine a zoologist from another planet, from Mars: he must think this coupling, with its exchange of fluids, a means of propagation.

When they parted she gasped for breath. "You see," she said, panting, "I possess the antidote."

Rudi smiled, compressing the thick flesh of his lips. "Why are you doing this? Is it for me?"

She shook her head so that the veil descended. Through it she said, "Don't you understand? Not for you. For your *Antigone.* From me they want two hours. I will give them two hours. What you create will outlast their thousand years."

She turned to walk back to the staircase. Von Beckmann did not move to stop her. I, too, slipped back, out of her way. She passed by me without a word. The two black-suited corporals saluted as she climbed the steps, one by one. As for the old man, the one who had been cleaning the stairs—he had simply disappeared. Had it really been Schuschnigg? The former chancellor? Or had all three of us seen a mirage?

Von Beckmann arrived at Aspern at a little after eight o'clock. He watched as the passenger ramp was rolled up to the side of the French DC-3. That plane, with its silvery fuselage, the winged horse on its nose, might very well have been the same craft that had brought him and his friends to Salzburg just two months before. How much had happened! In so little time! He continued to watch as the passengers—almost all of them rich Jews, or ex-rich Jews, since they had had to pay a king's ransom for their exit permits—filed on board. Their faces appeared in all of the windows but one. That was the place left for him and Magda. And where was she? And where the promised permits? The director walked back and forth on the tarmac. Behind the glass of the terminal no one was stirring. At the Air France counter the last lights were flickering out.

Suddenly there was a high-pitched whine and one of the great engines came to life. Smoke poured from the cowling, covering Von Beckmann and dwarfing the little cloud that came from his only remaining cigarette. Now the other engine started turning, sputtered, and spewed out its own oily exhaust. The ground crew ran forward and set about pulling the chocks from the wheels. Von B trotted to the bottom of the ramp and started to shout.

"You can't leave! I forbid it! I insist that you wait!"

Above him a stewardess—yes, it was the same Parisienne, with the long nose, the slightly smeared lipstick—appeared, but it was only to lean forward and grasp the handle of the door. He shouted again, but the noise of the engines drowned him out. This was, for him, like an agonizing dream: he knew what he must do and where he must go, but his legs stood still, as if paralyzed. He watched, powerless, as the crew came forward to push the ramp aside.

Then, with a wail of sirens, with flashing lights, a limousine came racing over the slick black asphalt. It was a Daimler, with swastika flags flapping over each front fender. It came to a halt under the aircraft's huge silver wing. Everyone paused to watch, as if they sensed that the famous actress was about to alight. Even the engines, idling, lowered their pitch in anticipation. But when the door opened, only an SS man stepped from the rear.

"Anton!" Von B exclaimed.

In his demeanor the blond young officer was perfectly correct. He strode forward and handed the director a sealed envelope. "Inside you will find your exit permits. We wish you a pleasant journey."

Von Beckmann tore open the seal. As promised, there were two documents inside. He glanced at one but stopped at the other. "What is this? It is made out for Laszlo Loewenstein."

Anton shrugged. "We assumed you would wish to take your colleague with you. I can assure you, he is most eager to depart."

"Is this a joke? Take Lorre! *Lorre!*"

The officer gestured toward the limousine. "As you see, we have made every effort to bring him here on time."

"This is an absurdity! You know there is only one person going with me. Where is she? What have you done with Magda?"

"Fräulein Mezaray? At this moment I believe she is occupied with other matters."

"What are you saying? Call Herr Goebbels! Call him at once! He will tell you we had an understanding."

A baffled look crossed the SS man's handsome face. "Herr Goebbels? But he is the one who sent me here."

"No, no! It was a definite agreement! I have kept my part! Herr Goebbels said he would provide Magda and myself with exit permits."

"There must be some mistake, Herr Beckmann. If you think back you may remember that you were told the Reich would provide you with two such documents. You have them in your hand."

"A trick!"

"Rather, an honest mistake. It is only natural to think that two Jews should wish to leave together."

"Never! He knew I meant Magda!"

For an instant the SS man let down his guard. In a low voice he said, "Don't be a fool. Do you think *now* we could allow her to go?"

"This is monstrous! It is inhuman! What will become of her?"

The Hauptsturmführer said something, but his words were lost in a new blast from the engines. At the top of the ramp the stewardess reached once more for the handle to the door. At the bottom the youthful officer shrugged and turned to go.

"Wait! Stop!" cried Von Beckmann. "Anton!"

But when Anton looked round, Von Beckmann said only, "You see? I am out of cigarettes."

The young man laughed, dug into his pocket, and threw the old one a pack.

Through the roiling exhaust, Von Beckmann hauled himself up the steep steps of the ramp. Halfway he paused. He swayed, as if he no longer possessed the strength to climb more. Then he glanced back toward the limousine, where someone else—not the glamorous movie star but a man born in the Carpathians, land of werewolves and vampires and ghouls—stepped from the rear.

"Greetings, Rudi," I somewhat sheepishly said.

For a moment he stared at me like a madman. "The bridal chamber," he muttered. "The bridal bed. The canopy. That vulgar gauze. I knew he was there. Not Goebbels. The lord and master. He was there all along. Listening. Oh, Magdalena! Can I do this? Can I leave her? Alone in a room with *him*?" The answer, it seemed, was in the affirmative, for the large man turned his back to me and continued the rest of the way up the ramp. Following behind, I was the last to board.

The engines roared. The plane rolled forward, making for the rows of lights at the end of the runway. The nighttime breeze was out of the east. We took off into it and made a wide banking turn to the north. By the time we straightened out on the route for Paris, we were already two thousand feet in the air. Everything was smooth. There weren't any clouds. Minute after minute we climbed. Then the wing dipped down and the plane banked to the right. Von Beckmann looked out the round window. Seated beside him, so did I. The lights of a city were blazing below. They gleamed and glided, like sequins on a songstress's gown. This might be Linz. This might be Salzburg. The director leaned back. I could smell the last of the perfume from his gardenia.

"Lorre," he said. "Imagine this. If from such a height a man cried out *Antigone! An-n-n-ti-go-n-n-e-e-e!* how much time must pass before his words could be heard?"

But I did not imagine it—nor did I calculate how long it would take before that cry of longing and despair might be heard by the busy millions on the planet below.

B UNIT

October–December 1940

VICTIMS OF NAZISM

It was a crisp fall night—or as crisp as October was likely to become in Southern California. After five years in those climes I still wasn't used to the way one blue day followed another, like the pages of a blank and endless book. Another thing I had not adapted to was the necessity, close to an absolute one in far-flung L.A., of driving an automobile. Which is why, on this crystalline evening, Rochelle—Miss Hudson, I should say, my leading lady in several of the pictures starring Agent 673, as well as the heroine of *Laugh and Get Rich, Curly Top, She Done Him Wrong,* and I don't know how many other Granite second features—yes, there was the Queen B at the rail of my terrace, awaiting the studio limousine. I shivered, less from the chill than from the glimpse of those plump wrists and plump fingers, the mound, like stacks of gold coins, of her pinned-up hair. She, too, gave a shudder and wrapped her furpiece—it ended, unnervingly, with the sharp little head, the brown beady eyes, of a fox—around her shoulders.

"Oh, Petey, just look!" She threw a bare arm out toward where, stretched out below us, the lights of the city were sparkling. Far off, on Wilshire Boulevard, two or three searchlights shone up at the sky, like straws in a cocktail. "It's so beautiful," the actress concluded.

I took a step closer. "Your hair, that is what's beautiful. What have you done to it?"

"Do you like it? Really like it? You can't see the roots?"

Now I drew up beside her, so that I could smell the Black Jack gum she was chewing. "Only in my memory. Do you remember, too? Our first picture? *Takes a Chance*? If I close my eyes I can see it. Your hair, black hair, Miss Hudson, against the white linen of my suit. Such a dramatic moment.

You wanted to comfort me because Bokar, the high priest, had just served me a dinner of my own carrier pigeon. Bested! Ha! Ha! Ha! Moto bested! *Fortunate not to send message by dog!*"

"Well, I've got to be a blonde for our next picture. Manfred insists. He says there's no two ways about it."

"Next picture?"

"Oh! Oh, golly! It's supposed to be a surprise!"

"Please don't be upset. I am calm. I am imperturbable. And the reason— you may congratulate me, Miss Hudson—is that this is the night I shall break my contract." That was true. I had worked everything out to what Americans call a T. Rochelle had offered to drive us to the Wilshire Ebell in her little two-door. There it was, on the driveway, a mint-green Plymouth. But I knew Manfred Granite would object. It wouldn't do for the studio's top money-maker to arrive in a chauffeurless coupe. Coupe? A coup! "Ha-ha-ha, Miss Hudson: Moto himself could not have devised a more cunning plan. Manfred will be trapped in his own automobile. With Victor. With my agent, too. He will have to hear me. He will have to grant my release."

The starlet's eyes, along with her lips, went wide with dismay. "But you can't! You mustn't! We're going to start next week. And guess what? Isn't it exciting? They've signed Chick Chandler."

"Chick Chandler! You know that name fills me with pain."

"Oh, everything's going to be different now. We're making a western! But, you know, high-class. The lovers, they're from families that are having a feud. It's like *Romeo and Juliet*."

"This Chandler. The hair part. The Adam's apple. The dimple in his chin. I could strangle him with these two hands."

"Don't be jealous, sweetie-pie. It makes your eyes pop out. I get, you know, frightened. It's like talking to a fiend. Be nice. Tell me again. The way you remember my hair."

The Queen B leaned closer. Through my silk trousers, and the silk of her plum-colored dress, I could feel the heat of her body. Close to one hundred Fahrenheit degrees. "Remember? I did more than remember. I have actually saved one of your—what would the columnist say? Miss Parsons? Your *raven-haired locks*."

"Don't be a silly! You did no such thing."

"Everyone laughs at me! No one believes me! But I too have a surprise. Shall we hunt for the treasure? You know the way." So saying, I turned my back upon her. I held my breath, while hers, heavy with sugar and licorice, played upon the stiff little hairs of my neck.

"No, no, Petey. It isn't appropriate. We don't have the time."

"Just as I thought. You don't remember. From *On the Spot*. When we escaped from the attic. Down the rope we made from your hair. That's when I cut it. With a little scissors. I kept a curl. A keepsake. A prize."

There was a pause. Below us, in the black bowl of the city, the lights were twinkling and swaying, like uncountable numbers of phosphorescent fish. "Oh, all right," said the actress, and thrust her hand into the pocket of my pants.

Instantly two fears overcame me: that the platinum-permed starlet might withdraw her fingers as suddenly as she had bestowed them; and that the stole she had playfully thrown over my head was either going to suffocate me or make me sneeze.

"There's nothing there," Rochelle announced. "I can't feel a thing."

"Just a little deeper. One inch. Two inches."

Behind me the Queen B labored to comply. In my ear the chewable gum made a snapping sound. Against the small of my back her abdomen—how large it was! My God! As big as her Plymouth!—thrust and ground. The nerves of my body began to grow warmer, like the wires of an electrical coil. *Further! Lean further!* That's what Coco, our director, had yelled at Miss Hudson at the very moment she'd thrown her hair from the attic; then he had trained the camera up toward a phenomenon that the Hays Office had not allowed in the finished film: her breasts, which, like pale babes fleeing a fire, were about to hurl themselves over the window ledge. I could sense them now, spreading like putty between my shoulder blades.

"What's going on?" asked Rochelle. "Are we going to be here all night?"

"One moment! Only one moment!"

Alas, a slick sheen of perspiration had begun to form on my cheeks, on the backs of my hands, on my wide upper lip. Tiny rivulets ran down my brow. I would have, if I could have, willed those ducts shut. But this was a curse. An affliction. My crown of thorns. Did the drops of blood sting the god of the Christians with any more fierceness than these clear beads of salt?

"I smell something," said the Granite Films star. "Is that the surprise? Marzipan!"

"Ah! Ah!" I responded, perhaps from the chill of the night, perhaps from the fluff of the fox fur. "*Choo!*"

I bent, in my spasm, double. My partner backed quickly away. "Tee-hee!" she giggled.

"Don't mock me, I beg you. These are involuntary glands."

"Sorry! Hee-hee-hee! You look so funny in that monkey suit."

Monkey suit! Where did Americans find such expressions? Did I look, in my tie and tails, like an ape? A gorilla? Perhaps the term came from the tight little jackets that organ grinders put on the primates who hold their tin cups. Fair enough. I was no less a beggar. Soon, in that limousine, I would be on my knees. "Then why not, Miss Hudson"—as I said these words I once more turned my back upon her—"finish our monkey business?"

With the third eye that I. A. Moto seemed to possess in the back of his head—was I not, in *Thank You, Mr. Moto,* able to see the villain's knife as it tore through the tent at my back?—I could well imagine the look of disgust that spread on the starlet's full features. That pretty pug nose was wrinkled, surely, at the acrid odor of the sweat that, like the residue of a sex act, now covered my body. "Oh, where are they?" she exclaimed, stamping the sharp heel of her shoe. "At this rate we won't even get dinner."

"Oh, no. No, no, no," I responded, turning about and swabbing my brow. "They won't start without the Granites. Think of how much they paid for their table."

"Speak of the devil," said Miss Hudson. Her ears, sharp as her Siberian fox's, had picked up the sound, like a man gargling, of pneumatic tires upon the gravel.

An instant later a Cadillac De Ville, its headlights ablaze, pulled up beneath us. Arthur, the colored chauffeur, stepped out of the driver's seat and opened the door to the rear. Music by Rachmaninoff floated up to my ears. *Click-clack-click* went the heels of the Queen B's shoes on my uncarpeted staircase. I watched as her pompadour flared like a match tip in the limousine's lamps, only to be snuffed out as she ducked into the compartment at its rear. Les Kahn, the Granite publicist, waved from the passenger side in the front. "Peter! Hurry up! We're already late!"

When I did hurry up—or should I say down?—to join those inside the custom-built car, I found that with the exception of Alexander, the studio founder, my fellow passengers were the most powerful figures at Granite Films. As for old man Granite, he wasn't a man at all. Rather, he had become the sort of legendary figure whom half of Hollywood thought living and the other half—mistakenly, as it happened—dead: an understandable error, since the nonagenarian had long since disappeared from the public eye.

But here were his sons, Manfred and Victor, the former in the cushioned corner, the latter in the opposite jump seat, practically knee to knee. Were ever two brothers less alike? Manfred, the elder, was solid and muscular. In the Sheldon system, of which I, as an agent of the International Police, had made a study, he was almost a pure mesomorph, with the numerical value

171. That is to say, his body was like a concrete slab, broad-shouldered, short-limbed, with, inside his barrel chest, a powerful heart that I had often seen beating through the veins in his neck and temples and arms. On that neck was a small, birdlike head, tiny-eared, flat-faced, out of which the narrow curved blade of a nose protruded like that of an owl, or the beak of that comic-book character—what was he called? Henry Hawk! Though he must have been well into his sixties, his hair had not turned white or even gray; it was, however, fair enough, and thin enough, to reveal the surge of his emotions, which regularly flushed the skin of his scalp primrose or vermilion.

"Hiya, Pete!" said Ernie Glickman, the agent. "Want a pick-me-up?"

Manfred said, "He can't hear you over the fiddles."

He meant Rachmaninoff, who was conducting himself on the Capehart, which was built into the bar that separated the two jump seats. I settled onto the one that was vacant and said, "Whiskey, please, and soda."

Arthur leaned into the compartment and poured the liquor into a glass. Then he laid a coverlet over my knees. An identical blanket, I noticed, had already been thrown over all three occupants of the rear seat: Ernie, across from me; Manfred, catercorner; and in the middle, hipless and thighless under the brown-and-gray wool, the Queen B.

"Say, Arthur, if you don't mind—" That was Les Kahn, who, from his spot in the passenger seat, thrust his empty glass over the rolled-down partition. The chauffeur took the tumbler from the pale-skinned publicist—perhaps because of the pink frames of his glasses, or the equally pink rims of his eyes, he reminded everyone of a rabbit—and made him a refresher. Then, in a sudden silence, we all watched as the spidery arms of the machine picked up the exhausted disk, turned it about in the air, and deposited it back on the spindle. Victor, spidery himself, said, "Second movement. *Allegro non troppo*"—the very words, as I glanced at Miss Hudson, at the bulge that moved down her swallowing throat, I whispered to my heart: *Fast. But not too fast.*

In the Sheldon system, the pure ectomorph is represented by someone whose body approaches, as far as humanly possible, a straight line. Like a Giacometti sculpture, for example, or one of those stick figures Kafka used to draw in ink. *Voilà:* Victor. In fact, he not only resembled those elongated blots, he favored Kafka himself, with the consumptive's bony face, alert, protruding ears, and low, near simian hairline. His lips, as at this moment, were often compressed around a cigarette, but when he smiled—an odd smile, with the lips turning down—his teeth, haphazardly strewn, showed through. His skin was sallow, like that of a Mexican, which of course he was not; it was as if the nicotine had suffused every part of his body, after steeping in the sacs of his lungs. There he sat, in a characteristic pose: legs crossed, arms crossed, as if he meant to X himself out. His clothes, in fact elegant, looked shabby because hot ashes were always dropping from his Chesterfields, scorching his jackets and pants. Sometimes, in violation of natural law, the sparks went upward, to smolder on the brim of the large felt hat he never removed from his head.

I knew all too well that with Victor, that wasn't the only natural law that was suspended: women, ordinarily attracted to somatotypes closer to 171, made an exception for this obvious 117. It might have been what they thought were his courtly Old World manners. Although nearly a decade younger than Manfred, he was the one who had kept his European accent, while his brother swore like a native. Or perhaps it was the way the mantle of genius had, since the death of Thalberg, been draped about this scarecrow's shoulders, attracting the birds instead of driving them away. Who knew the secret of such a success? It was a mystery to Moto. For all I could tell it was nothing more than his Adam's apple, which clogged his scrawny neck like a ship in a bottle or a piglet in the belly of a snake, and which—this was a myth, but stars and starlets believed it—indicated the size of its owner's penis.

In any case, Victor was proof that what my old teacher—his address used to be Berggasse 19, Vienna—said was true. The artist seeks three things: fame, riches, and the love of beautiful women. What women! Garbo! Dietrich! Clothed and unclothed, on her back, on her knees, Hedy Lamarr. Every great actress from Europe except—what irony here, since the whole world assumed they were lovers—Magdalena Mezaray. Fame? There was no end to the glamour, the awards: four Oscars already, his picture in every paper, his name on every tongue. Yet at Granite, riches lay elsewhere. Whereas the younger brother made, on average, two films a year, the older one turned out two, often three, and sometimes four a week. None of the Moto pictures, for example, had taken more than five days to shoot; yet each returned its costs tenfold and more. The plain fact was that while the A features brought the studio prestige, the B pictures kept it afloat. All glory to Victor; the money went to the mesomorph.

Arthur put on his driving cap and got behind the wheel. We coasted across the gravel to Fontenelle Way, then negotiated the hairpins to Stone Canyon. The ice cubes clicked like dice in my glass. Time to roll them.

"So, Manfred, isn't it pleasant to have these few moments together? It gives us a chance to discuss, I hope you won't take this the wrong way, my career."

The executive seemed to be taking a catnap, with his head stretched backward on the padded cushion. Drowsily, he replied, "There's nothing to discuss. We've got an unbreakable contract."

"Yes, yes, I don't dispute that. But the other day I was playing tennis with the Epsteins—"

"Those two?" Now he sat forward. The lids went up from his eyes. "I never should have borrowed them from Warners. Jesus Christ, Jack warned me. Tennis! I've yet to get a day's work out of either of them."

Victor said, "You mean they don't work on the lot, but—"

"Of course! Naturally! You defend them. You're the fourth for doubles. Peter, take my advice and keep your distance. Those guys are heading for trouble. Always for the underdog, like Communists. Dies is after them. I know for a fact they've been subpoenaed."

I had to raise my voice over the brass in a *fortissimo* section. "But this isn't about politics. They told me that Warners is planning another remake of *Maltese Falcon.* They thought, perhaps for the Joel Cairo part; yes, and I thought too—"

Was that a smile on Manfred's face? Or a grimace? All I could see was how, with his lips pulled back, his teeth flashed frighteningly, like bathroom tiles. "You thought what?"

"That that was a role for me."

"Are you crazy? Are you nuts? Do you think I'm going to let you tear up your contract? Just tear it up and flush it down the pot? Do you know what your grosses are? What did *Danger Island* do, Lester?"

"Two and a half million. That's net. *Mr. Moto's Last Warning* made almost that much just in Japan."

"Right! That's right!" Manfred yelled. "You're an idol over there, for Christ's sake. A god. Bigger than Gable over here."

Now Glickman spoke up from his corner. "Listen, Manny, you shouldn't let yourself get so upset. Peter doesn't want to break his contract. What we're suggesting is a loan-out. For a month maybe. A one-picture deal."

"*Mr. Moto Takes a Vacation,*" I interjected, citing the name of our latest feature, in which I had captured a gang of diamond smugglers in the Great Salinas Swamp. "Ha-ha-ha!"

Kahn said, "A million three, not counting foreign grosses."

Ernie sighed. He was a large, round man and, in my opinion, nearly a 700 on the Sheldon scale. It would be a mistake, however, to describe him as fat; that is, you could starve him and he'd still be an endomorph, only thinner. Indeed, he was close to his somatotype's ideal, a collection of near perfect spheres—an orange on top of a melon, with two gigantic grapes for an ass. According to Sheldon, if you peeled off that skin, you'd discover that everything inside, the heart, the liver, the kidneys, was also bulging and bulbous, like fruit. "As you know, Manfred, I also represent Julie and Phil. You owe Warners someone for their services, there's no way around that. Why not loan them Peter for a single picture? That way everybody is happy."

Manfred: "Not me, goddammit. I don't have to give Warners anyone for those jokers. I've paid enough in salary already. I'm going to pull them off the picture and send them back to Burbank."

"What picture?" I asked, not without foreboding.

"The same one you'll start at the end of this month."

"But I've heard nothing! Nothing! Are you going to take all my blood drop by drop? Yes, I am bleeding before your eyes. I am no longer an actor. You are turning me into a corpse."

"And," said Lester, "a very well paid cadaver."

"A well-paid slave. A slave in golden manacles. A prisoner in his palace. I don't even swim in my pool."

Just then our Cadillac turned onto Sunset and headed east toward Beverly Glen. The lights from the boulevard fell through the window glass onto Ernie's broad, freckled forehead and the backs of his freckled hands. His eyes, I saw, were brown, with segments in green. "This isn't fair, Manny. Peter has been asking for new parts for years. Each picture is supposed to be the last. You can't just spring a surprise."

"It's not a surprise." That was Rochelle, who had drawn the blanket all the way to her slightly double chin. "Petey's just pretending. I told him already. About the western. About the sweethearts and *Romeo and Juliet*."

"*Mr. Moto Wins His Spurs,*" said Kahn. "And we're very proud of the concept. In fact we're breaking ground here. A Far Eastern western, and I'm not making a joke. There are ranchers and there are miners. They're practically at war with each other because the hydraulic operation at the mine is consuming all the water that used to go for the cattle. Naturally, when the reservoir is dynamited and somebody cuts the pipelines, everyone in town suspects the Ranchers' Association. So Harwood, the mine owner, brings in Moto to find out who's behind the sabotage."

I felt carsick on the instant; I wanted to thrust my head out the window, the way a dog does, into the stream of air. Instead, I reached into my pocket for a pinch of powder. "Moto. Miners. Manure, undoubtedly, from cows. Manfred, should I beg you? Do you want me on my knees?"

"I am very disappointed, Manny." That was Ernie. "May I speak frankly? This is no breakthrough. It's nothing but the same old horseshit."

But Manfred, head lolling, seemed to have resumed his siesta. Miss Hudson answered instead. "You haven't told him about the ending, Lester. Don't you know what tragedy is? It's when the lovers die in each other's arms."

"I was definitely getting to that. Old Harwood has a daughter. MacDonald, the head of the Ranchers' Association, has a son. Annie and Raymond. In spite of all the obstacles, the bad feeling between the families, they fall in love. I know that's old hat, but what makes this different from the ordinary oater is just what Rochelle said, the ending. Raymond is captured by the miners and Moto helps him escape. Then, when Annie is trapped in a stampede, it's Ray and Moto who save her. The lovers run off together. Both sides, the posse from the cattlemen and the one from the town, chase them all day and all night. Even though Mr. Moto does everything he can to protect the couple, it's dark, no one can really see very well, and the two lines open fire on each other. The young people, they're caught in the crossfire—you know, in the hail of lead. Comes the dawn and the ranchers move forward and so do their bitter foes. They find the lovers in their last embrace. Moto has the last word: *Mankind must find way to peace.* Isn't that terrific? *Must understand there is plenty water for all.*"

As if on cue, the music of the Russian composer reached a climax and, with a last throb from the string section, the violas and violins, faded away. The Capehart clicked off.

In the quiet car, a bitter voice: "And who is this lover? The horse-opera he-man? Wait. Don't tell me. Allow most honorable servant to guess. Handsome Chick Chandler!"

At the mention of that name, with its cheap alliteration, Miss Hudson let out a half-suppressed squeal. What surprised me more was, from Manfred, a simultaneous sigh. I looked to where the two of them sat side by side. Suddenly that gap between us, so small that our feet nearly touched, became a gulf, a chasm, into which I felt myself falling. Where were Rochelle's hands? Invisible! And those of her employer? Not to be seen. Fool! Featherbrain! *To find best clue, just open eyes.* That blanket, the one that lay like a napkin under their chins: it was a pleasure tent. What was going on underneath it? One had only to look at Manfred's head, the color of a pomegranate, or listen to his breathing, which was like a blacksmith's bellows. Beneath that sheep's wool were the intricate embraces of Arabian nights.

"Stop!" I shouted to the blackamoor. The Cadillac, in response, swerved across two lanes of Wilshire and came to rest against the far curb.

"Hey!" cried the Queen B. "I mean *really*!" A little V of vexation appeared at the bridge of her nose.

"What the hell?" mumbled Manfred. He looked for all the world like a man who had been shaken from a dream-filled sleep. Had I, in my suppositions, been mistaken?

Arthur was staring at me over the back of the seat. Behind us, beside us, automobiles were honking their horns.

"Sorry," I said. "I forgot my ticket."

"You *what*?" yelled Manfred.

"That's all right," I said as I reached for the handle of the door. "I'll meet you. I'll take a taxi or something."

"But you don't need a ticket," said Kahn. "You're at the Granite table."

"Please, Arthur, go on." That was Victor, whose lips moved around the cylinder of his cigarette. "Peter, do sit. We need your help."

The chauffeur rolled down his window and stretched out his hand. Up ahead, five blocks, maybe six blocks, the lights from the Wilshire Ebell shone across the boulevard. On the sidewalks people were rushing in that direction. We inched back into the traffic's crawl.

Victor: "Did you see Louella's column this afternoon?"

"No, no. I was at Dick Carroll's. To fit this tuxedo."

From the pocket of his own dinner jacket the filmmaker drew a clipping from that day's *Examiner*. "Here. Wait. I am skipping the latest on Lana Turner. All right:

> "Rudolph Von Beckmann, who seemed to disappear from the face of the earth after the fall of France, was seen aboard the Swedish liner *Alvdalen* last week looking half his usual weight. What was his secret? It seems that he had spent the last three months at the internment camp at Gurs, which is not exactly a health spa. He complains that he had to live for weeks at a time on crusts of bread and the peels of potatoes, though Dick Mosk tells me that's where the vitamins are. Anyone who tried to escape was always caught and hung up by the heels. Sounds pretty horrid to me, but I just have to remember what Mr. Hearst always says: if you're building a new society, stern measures are called for. Mister Hitler has got to break a few eggs while he cooks up his omelettes."

"But Victor," I interrupted, "why are you reading this to me?" The fact was that in spite of Louella's words, Von B's adventure was no secret. The whole world knew that he'd been in Paris in June, when the French capital had been overrun; every newspaper outside the Reich reported that he'd been taken into custody while attempting to flee to the south.

"Patience," Victor replied, not taking his eyes from the scrap of newsprint.

> "My birdy in Berlin tells me that Rudi Von B was released at the personal request of Magdalena Mezaray, who has given such a headache to the folks at Granite by deciding to remain in her homeland. Looks like the fickle fraulein has saved the impresario from being strung up by his heels because she remains head over her own heels for him. Even in this coldhearted world it's impossible not to be touched by the power of love. A prison. Exile. A gal pleads for her beau. If Joe Green, that's Giuseppe Verdi, boys and girls, had heard about this, he'd have written an opera!"

Victor leaned toward me, across the surface of the bar. "Can this be? Peter, you were the last one to see them together. Is there any truth to his story?"

"What are you asking? If she's that close to Goebbels? To Hitler? How can I know such a thing? And if she had that kind of influence, would she use it? I don't know that, either. Rudi betrayed her, that's certain. But she already gave herself once so that he could go free. She might do it again." Even as I spoke a tide of bile, bitter and black, rose within me—not so much at the memory of the Hotel Metropol, with its parting scene, its poisoned kiss, as at the realization that the prison I found myself in was more secure than the one at Gurs, and that there was no one anywhere, least of all Ernie Glickman, who could get me out.

Victor rocked forward, so that the brim of his hat almost touched his knees. "I've flown to Berlin. I've flown to Munich. She wouldn't see me. She sent an aide with a card. Oh, I know her handwriting, that jagged script, like a line of barbed wire. She was happy in the new Germany—that's what she wrote me. My God! She was going to stay of her own free will."

Les Kahn shook his head. "Three projects canceled. Millions down the drain."

Now Manfred threw off the coverlet and, lurching forward, snatched the newsprint from his brother's hand.

"You're missing the point, goddammit! I could care less about the love story, Rudi's or yours. Here, Lester—you read it." He handed the column to the nearsighted publicist, who peered over the top of his glasses to make out the print.

> "Here's an exclusive that's a real Lolly-palooza. The *Alvda-len* was scheduled to dock in New York one week ago. Since then no one has seen hide nor hair of Rudolph Von Beckmann. Who can forget what happened the last time he set foot on American soil? He turned right around and sailed back on the *Normandie*. Don't say I didn't warn you if this time he shows up in Hollywood, the way he was supposed to a decade ago. In fact, the whisper in the wind is that he'll make an appearance at tonight's star-studded benefit for Jewish refugees"

"Jesus!" cried Manfred. He slammed his fist against the armrest. "Jesus Christ!"

> "and if Mr. Von B should wind up among us, will I be the only one wondering whether Magdalena can be far behind? That might save the day at Granite, which, except for that dapper detective Mr. I. A. Moto, hasn't had a hit in years. I can't wait to see the expression on the face of the super-tan Victor Granite, should his old flame walk through the Wilshire Ebell door. Of course, one can't help feeling for the long-suffering Giselle, née Fontenay—you remember her in King Vidor's *Proud Flesh* and *Wine of Youth*—who had to keep her upper lip stiff all the time that Berlin bombshell was being squired around town by our coffee-colored Casanova. The real fun will begin with brother Manfred. Of course he'll be glad to see the prodigal daughter back on the La Brea lot, but will the price be worth it? I'll bet dollars to donuts that when the great impresario makes his appearance, Manfred will wish he were high above the clouds in that studio plane I'd be so happy to take a spin in. Even now you still hear talk about how

Manfred, who's really a dear though he likes to play the part of Phineas T. Bluster, forced Von Beckmann to give up his contract at Metro."

"And I'll do it again! This is intolerable! Unbearable! I'll ruin the son-of-a-bitch!"

"Don't worry," said Kahn, folding the clipping into squares. "I've taken care of everything. We've called Louella. Just an hour ago. We gave her a hint—it was more than a hint—about who really got Von Beckmann out of Gurs. Old *Granach* was the name we used. We told her he bought him his steamer ticket, too."

"Was it the old man?" asked Victor. "Not Magda?"

Manfred's scalp, and his face too, and even the tips of his ears, had turned the color of one of the fire plugs along Wilshire. Who knew? Perhaps, beneath his cutaway and cummerbund, his whole body, which resembled one of those iron hydrants, had turned the same shade of crimson. "The idiot! A sentimentalist! He ought to be committed!"

What, I wondered, was the excitement about? What bee, to use one of Louella's own expressions, had the publicist put into her bonnet? And who was the foolish old man? But no sooner had I opened my mouth to ask these questions than Miss Hudson let out a high-pitched scream.

"Look! Over there! In the crowd! There he is!"

With that the Queen B threw the touring blanket from her lap and the fox fur around her neck. Then she began to climb over Ernie Glickman's lap toward the right rear door.

"Oof! Ouch! It tickles!" the agent exclaimed.

"Yoo-hoo! Yoo-hoo!" cried Rochelle. "Oh, Chickee!"

Once more I experienced the sensation of tumbling into the void. I glanced out the window on my left. A half-block away, in front of the theater, the crowd stood three and four deep. At the corner, the cluster of searchlights stretched into the sky like toppling Greek columns. And there, directly below the marquee, with a sharp chin and drooping moustache, stood the Romeo of the Ranchers' Association.

Even before Arthur could bring us to a stop, the Queen B had thrown open the door and stretched one leg toward the curb. There was a screech of brakes, from first our car, then those around it.

"Wait! Please wait, Miss Hudson!"

But she was gone, across the squares of the sidewalk and into the mass of commoners and stars who milled in front of the theater.

"Okay, Arthur," said the president of Granite Films. "We'll get out here, too."

The chauffeur engaged the emergency brake and stepped from his own door to stand by the open one at the back. By then Glickman had slid off the bench seat and touched down on the asphalt. Manfred did the same. Les Kahn exited from the front. Victor uncrossed his legs and his arms and followed the others. I was the last to depart.

Outside, the photographers from the *Examiner* and the *Times* were setting off what seemed like a hundred flash lamps. Ushers struggled with the felt-covered ropes. People shouted. They waved. I stood on tiptoe, attempting to catch a glimpse of my costar beneath the brightly lit marquee. There was no sign of her in the crush. I turned to look in the other direction. In so doing, I collided with the head of Columbia Pictures, who had just stepped out of his own limousine. In a fury he pointed up at the writing spelled out in blinking lights. "Relief for the Jews!" he bellowed into my ear. "What we need is a banquet for relief *from* the Jews!"

Inside the theater Wallenstein was conducting the L.A. Philharmonic. The horns were tootling, along with the bassoons and clarinets. The wooden baton waved in the air. To one side of the musicians, in the amphitheater, a crowd of over a thousand had settled into their seats. To the other side, up onstage, the bigwigs had already spread their napkins onto their laps. Each table had cost its studio ten thousand dollars—not to aid the Jews, exactly, but all "Victims of Nazism." Hence the white and red of the Polish flag on one side of the hall, the French tricolor on the other. The tables themselves, what with their white cloths and waiters scurrying between them, might have been in a restaurant, except for the row of blond young women who were dancing along the lip of the stage.

"Look at that," said Harry Cohn. "Dutch dames or something." He pushed by where I was standing and headed toward the Columbia table, where he sat next to Capra and Jimmy Stewart. He'd get his money back, at a thousand a head, from his contractees. Down in the pit, Wallenstein exhorted the violins. The percussionist stood up to strike his silver triangle. I recognized the music of Grieg. These maidens were not Dutch. These were the flying pigtails, the bouncing bosoms, of defeated Norwegians.

For a moment longer I stood undecided in the wings. Where was Miss Hudson? I stared out over the footlights toward the balcony, the orchestra, the mezzanine. All the faces looked the same, white, pasty, some with lipstick, the rest with the black line of a moustache. Impossible to pick out either the Queen B or—was her fox fur spread over their laps? Were they, beneath the plush of their chairs, playing footsie?—the handsome Chick Chandler. Was she onstage? I craned forward, in search of the Granite table. There, the brothers were just sitting down—Victor between Giselle and his daughter, Valentina; Georgia, Manfred's wife, at the latter's left, Burton, his son, to his right. Les Kahn was present, of course, along with Coco Goodheart, the asthmatic B-unit director. But the chair reserved for Rochelle Hudson was empty.

As I stumbled onstage toward my own vacant seat, Albert Basserman waved from the émigrés' table—not the one with the German directors, Zinneman, Lubitsch, Preminger, Wilder, together with my own ex-director, Lang; but the one that, given the nature of the occasion, the studios had had to subsidize for refugees without funds of their own. At that crowded table sat the Mann brothers, Thomas and Heinrich, and their children and wives, as well as the Schoenbergs, Feuchtwanger the novelist, and Reynaldo Flatow and Sampson Frank. Max Reinhardt sat surrounded by his full-grown sons. Grinning, Basserman held up a bottle of wine. To me he exclaimed, "*Vive la France!*"

"It's a little late," I replied, "for such sentiments."

Schoenberg, the composer, leaned toward us. "Is it too late for the rest of us? That is the question."

Little Lion Feuchtwanger was explaining how he had managed his escape. "I owe it to my wife. From the day Hitler took over, she wouldn't have sex unless I paid for it. Each time we performed the act I had to deposit one hundred marks in a Swiss account. That's what paid for my ticket and my Brentwood house."

Reinhardt, glancing toward where the author of *Jud Süss* and *Power* was fruitlessly fondling the buttocks of Erika Mann, asked, "And where is Frau Feuchtwanger now?"

"Oh," the writer responded, "that account is overdrawn."

The music came to an end. The nubile Norwegians made their bows. Onto the edge of the stage stepped Charles Laughton. From my nearby seat I could make out the way his eyelids fluttered and his teeth, in something like terror, ground together. His lips were twisted in a scowl. It was as if he were already performing: Captain Bligh set adrift, Henry the Eighth ordering the ax. Then someone in the audience yelled, *Finest hour,* and at once Laughton reached into his pocket and took out a cigar; out, too, thrust the bulldog jaw. The neck drew into the hunched-up shoulders. *Churchill.* Tumbling down from the reaches of the auditorium came the grateful applause. As well it might: these were the days of the blitz. We'd all read how, only nights before, the blocks around St. Paul's had gone up in flames. The children of Eton and Harrow counterattacked in their Spitfires. For the world, of course, the stakes could not be greater. Laughton's own response was to grow calm. The muscles of his face stopped twitching. I'd seen the phenomenon before—in the way, for instance, stuttering actors shed their affliction when delivering another man's lines. The British star put the cigar between his teeth and, with a growl, told us why so many owed so much to so few.

During the performance I continued to look from table to table in search of the absent Queen B. She wasn't with Zanuck, or Goldwyn, or Cohn. She wasn't with the crowd from Metro. Further off, at a double table, Selznick was presiding over the cast of *Gone With the Wind,* his hit from the previous year. Even Butterfly McQueen, a Negress, was there. With relief—what if she'd been sitting next to the charming Leslie Howard? Or worse! Gable!—I saw that Miss Hudson wasn't among them.

Where, then, could she be? I peered once more into the faces of the crowd. Unfortunately, the dimming houselights made it impossible to see. We were all being plunged into darkness. At the same time Wallenstein began to coax a soft, shimmering tone from his woodwinds, his strings. At the first bars Schoenberg jumped up from the émigrés' table. "This is a disgrace," he shouted. "Such music cannot be allowed."

Basserman—I couldn't see him, but I recognized his half-drunken voice. "Are they crazy? Why do they p-p-play such a thing?"

Now more voices came from the dark:

"It's shocking!"

"Make them stop! Stop the music!"

"We won't listen! Turn on the lights!"

I knew the notes the Philharmonic was playing. They were by Wagner. *Parsifal? Tristan?* No, *Lohengrin.* I could hardly believe my ears. How, on such an occasion, could they play the work of Hitler's favorite composer?

Suddenly there was a gasp throughout the hall. Out onto the edge of the stage a tramp came tripping over his cane. Charlie! Chaplin! There was a burst of laughter and applause. The tramp turned, just in time to catch a large rubber ball that someone tossed from the wings. Not a ball, but a giant globe, the same inflated world that all of us knew from the actor's new picture. Now, to the vibrating strings, he performed the *Great Dictator* ballet, embracing the earth, tossing it skyward, wooing it, then caressing it like some great breast he meant to suck dry. I stood in awe. Amazing how the vagabond's familiar moustache became that of the tyrant, how the stance of a man submissive to the world became the stride of one who was its conqueror.

Bang! Everyone had been waiting for the balloon to explode, and it did— right in Adenoid Hynkel's, *Der Phooey's,* face. There was a whoop of delight. The crowd stood up, clapping like crazy. Then the lights came on and I saw how, over at the Warners table, Ernie Glickman was trying to catch my eye. My heart leapt up. Had the agent made a deal? For *Maltese Falcon?* As I approached I heard a burst of laughter. The Epsteins were keeping Bogart and Cagney and everyone else in stitches. I heard Julie say, "This is really some event."

Phil, his twin brother, said, "I can't remember anything like it since Jack threw that banquet for Reinhardt—you know, at the premiere of *A Midsummer Night's Dream.*"

"All right, boys," said Warner, at whom the remarks were directed. "Knock it off."

"Who could forget," Julie persisted, "that magnificent brochure?"

"The creamy paper."

"The embossed medallions."

"I remember," said Cagney, who at that earlier banquet had been a guest of honor. "A profile of Shakespeare on one side, all in gold, and on the other a profile of Jack L. Warner."

"Neither one of whom," said Julie, "ever heard of the other."

Warner, with his salesman's moustache, sighed. "Will no one relieve me of this burden?"

As if in answer to this prayer Manfred Granite came storming up to where the writers were sitting. "You sons of bitches have some nerve turning up here. When you didn't show up at the studio this morning. Or yesterday, either. Don't try to talk your way out of it. I've checked. I've double-checked. You behaved the same way at Warners. Right, Jack? I should have listened."

One of the Epsteins—it was unlikely that Manfred himself knew which, since the bald writers were as much alike as two eggs in a carton or peas in a pod—replied, "Manfred, please. The waiter wants to clear our places."

"At least he's doing what he's paid for. You owe me eight hours a day. Read your contract. It says you have to be at the office by nine in the morning. Just like everybody else on the lot. What makes you two so goddamn special, you think you can sleep to twelve? Butchers have to be in the butcher shop on time. Clerks have to be at their desks. Even presidents of banks have to be in their offices."

"You're right, Manfred," Phil Epstein said. "Why don't you tell a bank president to finish the script?"

"He couldn't do any worse than you two, that's for sure."

Jack Warner grinned, so that his moustache stretched like a caterpillar on his lip. "You hit the nail on the head, Manny. You should see what they just finished for me. *No Time for Comedy*. I'll say! *No Comedy*, period. That should be the title."

Manfred: "Believe me, it doesn't compare with what these two clowns handed in last week. The scene where the mine owner dies. Jesus, no wonder we're losing a fortune. That was the worst piece of garbage I've seen in my life."

Julie turned toward his brother. "Do you remember the scene we did last week?"

Phil: "I certainly do."

"Something is terribly wrong here."

"There must be a misunderstanding."

"Manfred," said Julie, rather sweetly, "what you say isn't possible. That scene was written at nine."

The others at the Warners table, Muni and Garfield, Ed Robinson and the rest, made halfhearted attempts to muffle their laughter. Warner himself put a hand up to hide his twitching moustache. Manfred's face turned the color of raspberry sherbert. He wheeled upon me. "You! What the hell are you doing here? Working out a deal with Glickman? Forget it! Stay away from these guys, I'm warning you. They're Communists. They're going up before the committee. We've got to stay clean. I'm not going to let them do to Granite what they did to Jack and Harry."

"Now what is it?" asked Phil.

"Don't play dumb with me. You undermined studio authority. During the strike, when those picketers got shot. Everybody knows what the two of you said about the logo."

"You mean," said Julie, "*Combining Good Picture-Making with Good Citizenship?*"

"Why all the fuss?" asked Phil. "We just changed a word or two—*Combining Good Picture-Making with Good Marksmanship.*"

There was more laughter. Julie scratched at the smooth surface of his head. "Let's see. What's the Granite logo? *Rock Solid Entertainment?*"

"People who show films in crass houses," said Phil.

"Shouldn't throw stones—"

"That does it!" Manfred yelled, thrusting his fists into his pockets with such force that the stitches gave way. "Jack, we have to renegotiate our deal. I can't say you didn't warn me. As for you two, you're off the picture. Not only that, I want a refund. You're in violation of contract. I want back every penny I paid you."

Julie said, "I'm sorry you feel that way, Manfred. Especially since I know that Phil has already spent his share of the money putting in a new pool."

"But if you're in the Palisades," Phil added, "I hope you'll feel free to drop in for a swim."

There was a great guffawing. Bet Davis gave a shriek. Cagney and Bogart, it seemed, prevented each other from falling off their chairs.

A growl—it might have resembled the sound of the Messerschmitts over the city of London—came from Manfred's throat. Clutching my arm, he propelled me back to the Granite table. By then the spotlight had come up on a black man, dressed in black too, except for his white spats and white gloves and the white paint around his lips. He dropped on one knee and spread his arms.

I'd walk a million miles for one of your smiles, my Mammeee!

Valentina, Victor's daughter, tossed her head and pushed away her plate.

Manfred said, "My niece is making faces. She's going on a hunger strike."

Burton, in his cream tuxedo, with a green-and-gold foulard, was dressed better than anyone at the table—probably better than anyone in the room. "It's not the food, Dad. It's Jolson."

"Oh yeah? What's the problem?"

Giselle smiled at her daughter. "I think it's a protest."

Valentina was as dark as her father; impossible to tell from the skin of her cheeks whether or not she was blushing. "It's no longer appropriate for white people to mimic Negroes."

"I'm not in the mood for one of your lectures," Manfred said. "Jolson is a great artist."

Valentina, only a teenager, would not back off. "If it ever was."

"Maybe you'd prefer the real thing. Someone like Robeson? In my book a man like that is poison. Give me Jolie in blackface any day."

Giselle said, "Why are you prejudiced against Robeson? Because he really *is* an artist? Because his color isn't painted on?"

"Prejudice? It's not prejudice. It's politics. The only color I can't stand is red."

"Calm down, Manny," said Georgia. "You're turning pink yourself."

Valentina turned toward me. "He won't understand. Peter, you tell him. How demeaning this is."

"Yes, yes. I agree. The act is out of place." I said that much aloud; but what I was thinking was that with the whole of Europe overrun by people with death's heads on their helmets, the entertainer was not singing the most appropriate lyrics:

> It isn't raining rain, you know—
> It's raining violets.

The song concluded. The evening wore on. There was a speech by the former French consul, followed by a speech from a fighter in the Lincoln Brigade. Three actors, Conrad Veidt, Ann Sheridan, and Ronald Reagan, read a script-in-hand scene from a new Irwin Shaw play. Then Thomas Mann stood up at the table of refugees and walked toward the mike.

"Who's that?" Manfred inquired.

"It's Mann," said Coco Goodheart. "The writer."

"Yeah? No kidding. What's he get?"

The spotlight focused upon Germany's most famous novelist:

> For the duration of the present dark age in Europe, the center of Western culture will shift to these shores. To the open arms of America.

No one paid much attention. A steady buzz of conversation rose from the stage. Agents, like honeybees, were up and about, moving from blossom to blossom. Columnists, too. I watched as Louella made—the correct phrase would be a beeline, to our table. She smiled and nodded and cocked her little rouged head. To Manfred she said, "Is it true you're lending Peter to Warners? Don't try to fool me. I saw him tête-à-tête with Ernie and Jack."

"It is *not*."

"Or to Selznick? He was staring and staring at those folks from *Gone With the Wind*."

"Put this in the paper: Lorre's not going anywhere."

"Oh, but he is," said Louella, with a girlish giggle. She moved behind my chair and—her sting was in her pencil—pressed its point against my neck. In my ear she whispered, "Let's have a word."

It was not a summons to be denied. I followed her to the wings, where she turned, the rubber eraser propped under her chin. "I love it whenever

Jolson sings that song. You've heard the latest, haven't you? About how Al and Ruby may be on the rocks?"

"No, no. I know nothing about it."

"She thinks he's too old for her. Isn't that silly? Personally, I like a man who's mature. Look at Manfred, for instance. I wonder what he sees in Georgia? If anything, she's too young for *him*."

"Louella, we both know that's not what you want to talk about."

"Oh, there's no sense beating around the bush with you! The truth is, I thought you might be just the one to help me with my exclusive. I've never been so thrilled. The intrigue of it. The romance."

At that word I felt a sharp, stinging pain, as if the columnist had plunged her graphite stiletto into my breast. Before my eyes, as though the pages of the *Examiner* had been spread wide, appeared the headlines of the next day's "Merry Go Round":

GRANITE STAR RUNS OFF WITH LEADING MAN
Hudson-Chandler Elopement
Exclusive Details of
Steamy Love Match

"Romance?" I echoed weakly.

"Are you pretending you don't know? When it has such an impact on you and your studio?"

"Well," I ventured, though with a growing sensation of dread, "maybe I could guess. A romance. You mean with a man and a woman? Maybe a leading man? Eh? With a moustache? A hit in *Hotel for Women*? And the paramour—plumpish? Platinum?"

"Laszlo Loewenstein, what *are* you talking about? Do you think you can pull the wool over my eyes? Mr. Hearst has done you plenty of favors. He could destroy you like *that*. What if he started writing about Japs? The yellow peril? Where would you be then? Now put on your thinking cap, for heaven's sake, and tell me where she is."

"But Louella, that's the very thing I wanted to find out from you. I've been looking everywhere. In the audience. On the stage. She's disappeared! Tell me! Can't you see how I'm suffering?"

"He's lost his mind!" cried the newspaperwoman. "He's trying to get information from *me*!"

"Yes! Yes, I am! I am begging you! I saw her on the sidewalk! She's wearing a fox fur! She's wearing a plum-colored dress! Now she's gone. Gone with Chick Chandler! Oh, why did he have to be born? I could kill him! With my hands! With my teeth! It's his profile! That chin! That Adam's apple! The muscles in his calves! Oh, I can't blame her. How could she resist him? He could have anyone and he chose Miss Hudson."

So swiftly did Louella lift her head from her notepad that there was an audible crack in her neck. Her nose, like an animal's, was sniffing the air. "What did you say? Do you mean Rochelle Hudson? That bottle blonde? This sounds like a scoop!"

A sudden chill swept over me, as if someone had opened the door of a refrigerator. What had I done? "Not Hudson! Ha-ha-ha! You misunderstood me. Or else I made a slip of the tongue. *Hanson!*"

"I've had just about enough of this. I don't believe I've ever—"

"*Munson!*"

"What on earth has come over you?" The columnist was staring at me with wide-open cadet-blue eyes. "Is it possible you really don't know anything about it? The star I'm talking about is your friend Magdalena Mezaray. Didn't you read today's paper? I heard she freed Von Beckmann. I heard she might follow him to this country and might even come here tonight. Of course, if she did I knew she would contact you. You would know when, and where, she'd appear. Oh, let's hope it's true. What excitement! The story of the decade!"

There was, in the auditorium, a smattering of polite applause. Mann gave a stiff bow and returned to his place. At the dignitaries' table—I saw the mayor, a senator, and, next to Marion Davies, the aged Hearst himself—a man got to his feet. This was Magnin, of the Wilshire Boulevard Temple. Rabbi, as the saying went, to the stars. The clapping wasn't perfunctory now; it thundered down from the balcony and the mezzanine. Amidst this standing ovation, the rabbi, as tall and stout as a tree trunk, approached the microphone.

Back among the émigrés a man unsteadily rose. Basserman turned, sloshing wine over his waistband, and caught my eye. "Ten d-d-dollars!" he bellowed, waving a banknote in the air.

At once Louella lifted her nose, sharp as her pencil point. "What's that? What's Albert saying?"

"Oh, it's nothing. We have a bet."

"What? A bet? Tell me!"

"About the keynote speech. I say that Magnin will give the whole of it without mentioning the word."

"Word? What word?"

I bit my lip to hide a smile. This time *Mr. Moto's Gamble* would not be lost. I glanced toward the Warners table, at Robinson, Garfield, and Muni. Names at birth: Goldenberg, Garfinkle, Weisenfreund. "Why, Louella, the word *Jew*."

At the front of the stage Magnin's spectacles flashed in the spotlight beams. Everyone knew that the guiding principle of the rabbi's philosophy was that the more you talked about how the Jews were suffering, the more the gentiles thought there must be a good reason for it. One of the Epsteins' jokes had gone all over town. Magnin flies to Poland to rescue the Jews but is caught by the SS and put up in front of a firing squad with one of the coreligionists he had hoped to save. The thoughtful Obersturmführer asks his victims if they would like a blindfold. The Jew reaches for the cloth, but Magnin jabs him in the ribs. *Shah,* he hisses. *Don't make waves!*

After a moment or two the rabbi raised his hands. He motioned for this great congregation to resume their seats. Then, as the applause died away, he seized the microphone stalk in both hands. At his first two words Basserman sank crestfallen onto the seat of his chair. What Magnin said was, *Fellow Americans . . .*

As the speech droned on, Louella plucked my sleeve. "*Is* it true, Peter? About Magda? I'll tell you a little secret. As I was dressing for the banquet this afternoon, I got a call. You know, from a birdy. He said I'd made a mistake, that it wasn't Magdalena who had arranged Von Beckmann's release. Do you know anything about this? Do you? Tell!"

"Why does everyone keep asking me about Rudi and Magda? It's been over two years since I've seen either one of them. All I know about Gurs is what I, too, heard this afternoon: that the Germans had been bribed by—I don't know, really, just somebody called the old man."

"Yes, exactly! That has to be Alexander Granite."

"Maybe. That makes sense. I heard about him from the Granite publicist. He said that the old man bought Rudi's ticket, too."

"But it *doesn't* make sense. Why would the studio want to buy him his freedom, and bring him to this country, when the whole town knows that ten years ago they did everything they could to keep him *out*?"

"But you are the one who said the old man was Alexander."

"No. The birdy did. He said *Granach.* That's what the Granites used to be called. In Europe. In Poland. Before they came here and changed their name."

I stood, not daring to utter a word in response. Certainly the family of filmmakers had made no secret of their past. Indeed, everyone in the industry knew the story of how they had crisscrossed central Europe with what amounted to a nickelodeon on wheels. They showed their pictures on a tablecloth or a sheet. Over the years they managed to save enough money to purchase the American patents to the Cinématographe from the brothers Lumière. Alexander brought both sons from Europe in 1906 and soon increased their fortune many times over in a settlement with the Edison Company. The terms of the agreement forbade the family either to use the Lumière equipment or to open a theater east of the Mississippi—which accounted for the fact that the two boys and their father were able to snap up five large lots on a deserted stretch of La Brea and open Granite Films the same year America entered the First World War.

But Granach? *Granach?* Where had I heard the name before? Yes! I had it! The Hotel Metropol! On the staircase! When Von B, pale and in anguish, threw out his arms to Magda: *They know everything! Everything! Zeleszczyki! The wagon! The acrobats! All my years with the Granachs!* Involuntarily I sucked in my breath, inhaling the words, "Ah, so!"

"*Ah, so?*" echoed Louella. "So what?"

But I held my tongue. *Two and two,* said the Asian agent to himself, *makee four.* That wagon—it had belonged to the family of Granachs. Von B had worked with them. Traveled with them. He must have been like a third brother. No wonder he hadn't dared show his face in Hollywood. If he had, a certain blue-eyed columnist might have learned that the famed reviver of classical drama, the interpreter of Old and New Testaments, and the most respected theatrical artist in all of Europe was in fact part of a family of minstrels. *What a Lolly-palooza!*

As it was, the columnist's fingernails were digging into my wrists. "Don't hold out on me, Laszlo Loewenstein. Do you think I don't know what's in your pockets? Your habits and little pleasures?"

"Wait, Louella. Look. Listen." I nodded toward where Magnin was concluding his peroration. Even as I did so I saw something beyond him, in the shadows of the opposite wings: a slash of white, like a chalkstroke on a blackboard or a lantern held up against the dark. My heart doubled its beat. Could this be?

Magnin: "And now, dear friends, I'd like you to meet our guest of honor, one of the few who has escaped from the jaws of the lion. No one knows better than he what it means to be a Victim of Nazism. Ladies and gentlemen, Rudolph Von Beckmann!"

Beside me, Louella had started to tremble; even the strands of her pixie cut shook. "I see," she said. "You saw him first."

That wasn't quite true. Even now, save for the streak in his hair, I had trouble recognizing this thin, hunched figure. He walked past the microphone and stood center stage, blinking and looking about.

Louella—her face had turned as red as the hair of Rita Hayworth—could barely contain her emotion. "And Magda," she hissed. "Where is she?"

Just then Max Reinhardt got up from among the refugees and walked over to Von B. "Rudolph," he declared. "Not dead? Not a prisoner? I see it really is you."

Now Flatow jumped up from the same table, and so did Sampson Frank. "You escaped!" cried the writer. Tears the size of polliwogs welled behind his glass lenses. "It's a miracle!"

At this the other Europeans, the big shots this time, rose from their chairs. They, too, surrounded their former colleague. With Louella in tow, I came forward to join them.

"Welcome to California," said Lubitsch. "The Golden State."

Von Beckmann looked about as if bewildered. "Is that where I am?"

Lang: "Didn't you notice that the sun keeps shining?"

"Like the face of a mongoloid idiot," said Wilder. "It can't think of anything else."

Zinnemann, who had remained at the table, called through his hands. "Rudi! We never thought we'd see you again."

Lubitsch: "It's a hairbreadth escape."

Wilder: "A happy ending."

Lang said, "We heard you were interviewed by Herr Goebbels. I had the same experience, you know. He offered to put me in charge of the German cinema. Because his Führer liked *Metropolis.* Naturally—it's full of Nazi slogans, all spoken by criminals and madmen. These people cannot recognize themselves."

"Do you know what I'd say?" interrupted the star of that director's *M.* "I mean, if Goebbels made that proposal to me? *So sorry! Germany has room for only one mass murderer at a time.* Ha-ha-ha!"

With a smile, Lang resumed. "Well, I didn't say anything. As soon as I heard them praising me, I left for Paris. That night."

Von B leaned toward the shorter man. "I, too, left for Paris the same night. But their offer was not so attractive."

Lang sighed. With a hangdog look he said, "Sometimes I wonder whether I should have left. Now I am out in the desert, shooting westerns."

For the first time Von Beckmann raised his head high, though there was no cloak to sweep under his chin. "There's no shame in that," he responded.

"Is not the western the way the history of this country is recorded? Not only its history but its mythology. It is what the saga of the Nibelungen was for us in Europe. The Wild West, they call it, no? In such a place gods and furies are born."

You could have heard, in all of that vast auditorium, the drop of the proverbial pin. At the uppermost reaches of the balcony, people strained forward to hear. It was not difficult; even without a microphone, Von B had found his voice.

"It may be that the western is the only form left to us in which we can sense the working of fate, of predestination. Where else in this century do we find such a clear code of honor, the right against the wrong, the white hats, as they say, against the black? And the bloodiness! Greek tragedy was born on just such a frontier. Civilization has to be constantly rewon—it does not matter whether it is from Indians, or barbarians, or the landscape, all of which are nothing but the wilderness of our own nature."

"Hee-hee-hee!"

At the sound of this laughter, so mocking and gay, everyone whirled around. It was Valentina. She tried to suppress it with a napkin to her mouth. But her shoulders shook, and her dark face, from the effort, grew even darker. "Hee-hee-hee!" she giggled again. Now she pointed straight at Von Beckmann. "What's the matter with it?" she exclaimed.

At the table Georgia addressed her niece. "Valentina, it's rude to point."

Victor said, "And it's rude to keep secrets. What is it you are laughing at?"

"Ha-ha-ha! His hair!"

Everyone, those on their feet, those at the closest tables, turned back toward Von B. His hair, with its white badge, its thick bristles, was brushed back as usual. His dark eyes, enfolded in pouches, stared at the girl.

Abandoning herself, she allowed the words to gush out. "A bird made poo on his head!"

The child thrust herself back in her chair, collapsing with mirth. Von B stared for a moment longer. Then he moved with surprising quickness until he loomed over her. "Stop laughing," he told her.

For some reason—the deepness of the stranger's voice, perhaps, or its seriousness—she obeyed him.

In the same tones he said, "Now sit up."

She obeyed that command as well.

"Now lift your chin." The surprise, now, was not that she did as she was told but that the others remained mute, merely watching.

"I want you to turn your head to the left. Further left. A little more."

Solemn now, unquestioning, as if that white patch that she had dared make fun of had become a physician's headlamp or a hypnotist's unblinking light, she craned around as he demanded.

"Push those silly curls from your forehead."

Valentina did so. Now the impresario leaned back, folding his arms. "Look—do you see the ducks? Tell me. What do ducks say?"

With no hesitation, Valentina went *Quack! Quack! Quack!*

At that Burton raised his arm between Von Beckmann and his cousin, as if he meant to break the stream of light, the beaming rays, that seemed to flow between them. He grinned. "How marvelous! What a trick! How do you do it?"

"A trick? There is no trick. I am merely observing this child. Note her profile. It is classical, is it not? The pouting lips, the rounded chin, the way in which the nose and forehead are joined with hardly an indentation. I've seen the same on coins from Greece."

Burton: "Little Val! My little cousin! Ha-ha-ha! A Greek goddess!"

Von B leaned close to Manfred's son. "Do not be upset. I have not failed to notice you. Those strong muscles! On your arms. On your chest. Like an athlete from Olympia! I can see you high above us. On a wire. On a beam. Yes, in tights. So that we can appreciate the tendons in your legs. Shall we try it? Eh? Yes! Let's dare!"

So saying, the released prisoner snapped his fingers. At once a waiter, in all likelihood a drama student at UCLA or USC, darted forward. Von B made a small gesture. The waiter lifted an empty chair onto the tabletop. Then he balanced another chair on the seat of that. Rudi turned toward Burton Granite. "Now, my pretty boy. Up, up into the sky!"

Amazingly, Burton stood without a word. He placed his hands on the tablecloth and sprang lightly onto the table itself. Then he turned toward the tower of chairs.

But before the enchanted youth could actually climb them, Louella dashed forward. "Mr. Von Beckmann, it's a thrill for me to make your acquaintance. I wonder, could you tell me when Magdalena Mezaray will be arriving?"

A tall woman in a hat made from parrot feathers—this was Hopper, of the *Times*—elbowed her way to the Granite table. "Or is she already here? Won't you tell us?"

Louella: "Tell *me!*"

Von Beckmann, as if he were under a spell himself, looked from one of these women to the other. Now Ernie Glickman forced his way through the crowd. He stood rubbing his thumbs along his shirtfront, as if snapping an invisible pair of suspenders. He was smiling so broadly that his upper lip actually became everted, as sometimes happens in apes.

"Mr. Von Beckmann? Ernie Glickman. I don't expect you'll remember me. In fact we've never actually met. I've worked with Magdalena since 1930. I set up your contract, too. It's a pity it didn't work out. We were all great pals—I mean, me and Magda, and Victor and Peter. The four musketeers. Maybe you could tell us—is she okay? We've been worried sick."

Von Beckmann turned toward the agent. "I was released as a favor to Magda. Hitler's own adjutant brought the order to Gurs. He told me that she is in the best of health. And as beautiful as ever. As to the concerns of these ladies, she will join me in Hollywood when I ask her to come."

"So it's true!" cried Louella. "She's coming back!"

Hopper: "And she arranged your release. That's fascinating. Does she really have that kind of influence in the Third Reich? Could it be that she and Herr Hitler—? Are they really on such intimate terms?"

Here Les Kahn jumped up from the table. "Don't answer! I mean, there's no reason to discuss these matters in public. Louella, Hedda—you've got your story. *Mezaray and Von Beckmann to be reunited! Ten-year separation ends! Together in a production of Granite Films!"*

All this time Manfred had sat motionless, his face and throat filling with blood. On his scalp, at his temples, the blue veins twisted like the lines of rivers on a map. Now, in a low, ominous voice, he said, "Sit down, Lester. Mr. Von Beckmann will not be working at Granite. As for Miss Mezaray, she is in violation of her contract."

Immediately a chair scraped noisily against the floorboards nearby. It was Cohn, at the Columbia table. "Hell, they can both come to work for us."

Sam Goldwyn said, "I don't like this funny business with Hitler. Anyone can see he's a bad apple. Still, if Manny doesn't want to present the Mezaray–Von Beckmann reunion, we do. Ernie, I want you to put Goldwyn at the top of your list."

"Just one minute," said Zanuck. "Mezaray never made a nickel in those arty films for Granite. Let her come over to us. We won't mismanage a talent like that."

Now Selznick got to his feet. "Darryl, we both know that's a lot of crap. Magda would be wasted at Fox. Ernie, think about Selznick International. I've got a new star. Ingrid Bergman. We'll put her and Mezaray in the same picture. Von Beckmann can direct. We'll beat any bid. I guarantee it."

All of a sudden a half-dozen voices were shouting at once. Even L. B., over at the Metro table, chimed in. "It surprises me to hear this kind of talk. It's as if people were ignorant of the facts. The contract we have with Rudolph Von Beckmann remains in force. Isn't that so, Mr. Glickman? You told me it was ironclad."

Now Manfred leaped from his chair. His face was going alternately purple and pale, like a blinking stoplight. "This is insane! You people don't know what you're saying. Hedda! Louella! I'll give you a story. What the hell! Where's Winchell? Where's Whistler? I'll tell them, too. Why don't you write about who this man really is? He's a Granach! One of the Granachs! He showed pictures on a sheet. From the back of a wagon. The great Rudolph Von Beckmann? He's just a little kike like the rest of us."

From everywhere onstage, from throughout the auditorium too, came gasps of astonishment.

The two columnists simultaneously said, "What a scoop!"

Manfred turned to Von B. "I warned you," he said. "I warned you ten years ago."

The impresario smiled. "Ten years ago I was a different person. How can you harm me now? By not allowing me to direct at your studio? By disgracing me in public? I am already ruined. I am the scum of the earth. You see before you a penniless refugee."

The only one at the table who had not gotten to his feet was Victor Granite. He continued to sit, his legs customarily crossed, while the smoke from his Chesterfield ballooned around the brim of his hat. "I do not agree that you will not direct at Granite. Yes, it is true that Rudi was one of the Granachs. He did show films from the back of our wagon. But he also understood that the very same Cinématographe that projected the old images we spliced together with glue could also be used to create new ones. It was he who had the inspiration to make *The Story of Jesus Christ.*"

From every part of the stage people leaned forward to listen. In the vast reaches of the auditorium the spectators were on the edges of their seats. Victor's was the only voice in the Wilshire Ebell Theater.

"We arrived with our Lumière at a little Jewish town. When the Jews gathered round, Rudi simply ordered them to perform."

"I remember! *Gott,* I remember it all!" That was the actor Sampson Frank.

Victor's mouth twisted down in what was in fact a smile. "Yes, Mr. Frank was there. A yeshiva student. There was always a yeshiva student. *By whose authority?* That's how he challenged us."

Frank: "Yes, yes. *By whose authority.* Those were my words."

"The Jews echoed them. They refused to perform. Rudi was wearing Granach's old frock coat. Then he opened it to reveal the velvet interior and the dozens of gleaming medals—there was one from the queen of Sicily and a shiny one, in nickel, from the Belgian king—that glittered in the sunlight."

Now the grown-up Rudi pulled himself upright and repeated what he had said forty years before: "By the authority of Franz Joseph, the *Königliche and Kaiserliche* emperor!"

"And the crowd," Victor resumed, "kneeled on the ground. *He's a count!* somebody shouted. Then all the others shouted, too: *Von! Von! It's a Von!*"

There was a pause. Victor brushed the sparks from his lapels. "Thus two things of great moment occurred. Sampson Frank launched his career in the role of Jesus, and Rudolph Beckmann put the Von in his name."

Manfred turned on his brother. "He made his name, all right. The film was a big success. And what did he do? He left us! With our camera! A thief! A betrayer! That's how he paid back our father. And that's how he drove our mother mad. That drum! She never stopped beating it. *Rudi! Rudi!* That's who she was drumming for. But he never came back. Drahomira! She's still in Lemberg. Still in the nuthouse. My God! Is she still beating that drum? Still calling his name?"

Von B! Von B! In Los Angeles the audience certainly was. They had begun rhythmically to clap their hands.

Magnin, at the microphone, gestured toward the disgraced refugee. "Come, they are calling for you. They want you to speak. Don't you see? In these times every victim is a hero."

I have never been able to get over how the city of Los Angeles, for all its cosmopolitanism, has remained in essence a provincial town. One sign of this is the ease with which it gives standing ovations. Each year at the Shriners Auditorium, the show always stops for the elephants in *Aïda*. Now everyone got to his feet as Rudolph Von Beckmann came to the front of the stage. As the applause mounted around him, he stood unmoving, the stalk of the microphone like the third of his spindly legs. He did not have to hold up his hands to quiet the crowd. At his very first words the audience fell hushed.

"I come to you from the dead."

The silence was so sudden, so pronounced, that in the whole of that vast theater the only audible sound was the gurgling noise—it was like a man smoking a hookah—made by Coco Goodheart struggling for breath.

"What you see before you is not a man but a ghost. A ghost who has escaped from hell. I speak of the concentration camp of Gurs. It is true that they beat us and starved us; it is true that we suffered torture, shocks of electricity, the bitter lash of mockery and scorn; it is also true that they murdered those of us who tried to fight back or escape. Nonetheless, this was only a little hell, the first circle, the smallest fraction of the greater hell that is to come."

"Of course that's an exaggeration," said the endomorphic agent. "We have to be optimistic."

In the spotlight, the speaker whipped round. Then, with a smile, he said, "Mr. Glickman, in spite of the size of your body, its bulk, its solidity, you are a ghost as well."

In the auditorium someone, and then someone else, started to titter. The refugee whirled round again. "Who laughed? You? Or you? You are specters yourselves! You are shadows! At this very moment, as I speak to you, the Jews of Paris are being hunted down. Tomorrow it will be the Jews of Budapest and London and Rome. Do you think the Jews of New York will be spared, or those that live here, in the City of Angels? And not just Jews! Half Jews! Quarter Jews! Non-Jews with Jewish faces or Jewish husbands or Jewish wives. There will be no end to it. The Poles! They are next. And then who? Slavs. Yellow Mongolians. Negroes in Africa. Arctic Eskimos. The population of the earth will be turned into Jews!"

The silence that filled the hall was now complete. Even Goodheart was holding his breath.

"And where will they be taken? To another Gurs? A far worse Gurs, I promise. Do you think you can sit back, in the sunshine, in Hollywood, and not be affected? Here is a fact you must face: you have had a role in creating this camp. It was built because of your failure. Oh, I am not talking about politics. Speeches and fund-raising and banquets like this. I mean a failure of imagination. For centuries men believed that they would be punished for their sins in a place much like Gurs. They imagined it fully. Fire, yes? And sulfur and torturing demons and eternal labor before the flaming ovens, at the edge of the pit. Are human beings different now? Has mankind improved? Are we so innocent that there is no longer a need to pay for our sins? I think not. Our guilt, the psychic need for retribution, is as powerful as ever. What has shriveled is our ability to believe. We can no longer grasp with conviction, or depict, or imagine such places. I warn you: when the imagination is destroyed, the unimaginable will happen. Thus what was once buried deep in the unconscious—so deep that it was always, everywhere, thought of as existing far under ground—is now being transformed into reality on the surface. Now we shall have hell on earth."

There was no laughter now, no tittering. Here and there, on the stage and in the audience, a number of people had started weeping. Even some of Wallenstein's musicians wiped away their tears.

"Do not weep. Do not despair. Are you not the people who invented conscience and imagination? Do you not make your living through the art of film? Therefore you have a weapon to fight back with. Before it is too late you must turn to your craft. Through it you must create a motion picture powerful enough to confront your foe. This must be a new kind of film, one not based on tricks or games or illusion. It must show life as it is, not the sliver of reality that you allow to pass through the shutters of your cameras. Not a fraction of experience, the five-hundredth, but the full glare of the sun. So return to your work. To your sets, your soundstages, your cameras. Prepare yourselves to make a picture so great, so truthful, so unavoidable, that it, and not Herr Hitler, will capture the world's attention."

"Not us," someone cried from the crowd. "You do it."

"That's right," came another voice. "You'll show us how."

Immediately similar cries came from every direction:

"Help us!"

"We'll work!"

"We're ready!"

Von Beckmann shook his massive head. "Not I. I am sixty-five years old. I am tired. I have not made a film in many years. I can only point out the path that others must follow."

"No! No! We can't do it without you!"

Von B: "Think. Reflect. Our enemy has great resources. All of Europe is under his sway. With its treasure he is determined to build an empire that will last a thousand years. To expose him, we shall need great resources, too—not only energy and will and determination but financial commitment."

At his table, Goldwyn jumped to his feet. "We'll budget a million dollars."

Cohn: "That's small potatoes. At Columbia we'll make it a million and a half."

"All right. All right," shouted Selznick. "Two million. That's more than we spent on *Gone With the Wind!*"

Now L. B. got to his feet. He did not have to shout; when he spoke, everyone listened. "Why are we competing with ourselves? It's unseemly. For a project like this, if it stars Magdalena Mezaray, if it's directed by Rudolph Von Beckmann, there should be cooperation. It's in all our interests to expose this Hitler, so we all should contribute."

At this remark, so sensible and fair, a tremendous cheer rose toward the high, cream-colored ceiling. There was, however, one discordant note. At the table for refugees, someone was standing. He was shouting louder than everyone else.

"W-w-wait a minute! Just a minute here! There's a little bit of a p-p-problem."

Consternation throughout the hall. Everybody strained forward to see who was speaking. But I knew just by the sound of the voice. This was the man who had just completed *Moon Over Burma.*

"Sit down, Basserman," someone cried from across the stage. "You're drunk."

That much was obvious to all. The actor's face was bright pink, and he was swaying. His necktie, normally so elegant, was as twisted as his tongue. "*You* sit down! No, no. I mean *he* should sit down. What he's saying, it's a lot of b-b-b-bull!"

Little Feuchtwanger, the author, leaned across the table to take Basserman's arm. "Albert," he said, "you'll make a fool óf yourself."

"I'm n-n-not the fool! Don't tell me I d-don't know what I'm talking a-a-a-abooot. I was there. Present, sir! I saw it all!"

By then a lot of people were hissing. There were catcalls. Two waiters, big as bouncers, hurried toward the drunkard's chair. Von Beckmann remained at the microphone. His jaw stuck out in anger; his lower teeth protruded. Then a strong, familiar voice, Manfred's voice, rang out over the others.

"Where were you? What did you see?"

The hubbub subsided. The waiters paused, uncertain. Basserman said, "I was at S-S-Salzburg. I was Creon in the play! I performed for, ha-ha-ha, Adenoid Hynkel!"

Now Victor stood up next to his older brother. "Our colleague is not sober. We can understand that. He, too, is a refugee. I am sure Mr. Basserman will sit down. He'll let us continue our program."

"L-L-Like hell!" Basserman shouted. "You havta listen. I was right there. I saw everything. Serge had a gun. Serge had him in his sights. All he hadda do-o-o was pull the trigger. Bang! Like Hynkel's ba-a-a-a-lloon!"

There was an indistinct murmuring, the kind of mumble-mumble-

mumble that stage directors ask for when they want to show the reaction of a crowd. Manfred said, "All right. Go on. What happened? Who did Serge— was that Von Beckmann's servant?"

"Servant! Right!"

"Who did he have in his sights?"

"I *told* you. Her-r-r-r Hitler!"

"And what happened?"

"He saved him! Rudi did! I d-don't know why! If I were a god I could tell you. Maybe he's a spy or a G-G-German agent or something. I saw him do it. He r-r-r-ran up. He waved his arms! He saved Hitler's life!"

The noise in the hall abated as everybody strained forward, staring at Von Beckmann. He stood stock-still, his face the kind of green that statues take on when they have been exposed to the elements. Suddenly he clutched his throat. "Water!" he shouted. "Water! An oxygen tank!"

A gasp of sympathy went up from the crowd. Von Beckmann staggered backward and dropped to one knee. Instantly Burton Granite leaped up from his table, a glass in his hand. He took the spilling water to Von B. In the auditorium the crowd rose to get a better view. Meanwhile Rabbi Magnin moved to the lip of the stage and leaned over the orchestra pit.

"Dr. Wallenstein," he intoned, "couldn't we have a little music? 'La Cucaracha'? That's a lively tune."

But Von Beckmann, gulping water, had already revived. His obvious distress seemed to turn the tide of opinion. People began to shout for Basserman to sit down. They wanted him to be thrown out of the theater. Victor held up his hands.

"It's all right. There's no need for that. I think it's clear that there's been a mistake. After all, if what Basserman has said were true, if Rudi Von Beckmann had saved Hitler's life, he would be a hero of the Third Reich. Instead he was driven into exile, hunted through the streets of Paris, and starved in a concentration camp."

"Of course!"

"That's right!"

"He should apologize!"

Now a new speaker put up his hand and began to shout through the din. "Another drunkard," he said, "wishes to speak." This wasn't, strictly speaking, an alcoholic. No. He was intoxicated by a different drug. "I was at Salzburg, too. I can confirm everything. If Rudi had not interfered, Hitler would be a dead man. It's not Albert who should apologize. It's Von Beckmann. How dare he come here and say that he wants to expose the tyrant before the world? It's utter hypocrisy. He was the one who saved his life!"

"You are a fool!" cried Von Beckmann.

No doubt you have guessed the object of Rudi's wrath. Loewenstein, Laszlo: lunatic. What he—or rather I—said was, "With that, I am in complete agreement."

In response Von B turned to the crowd. "Part of what you have heard is true. My servant had a gun at the top of the Salzburg cathedral. He used it to kill himself by his own hand. Did he wish to assassinate the head of the Third Reich? No one will ever know that for certain. But let us grant everything that has been said. What if by some terrible accident I saved Hitler's life? Would I not be eaten by remorse? Would I not wish to make amends? Do you not think I would insist on dedicating the rest of my life to making up for that error? Yes, now I see. You were right to make these demands upon me. We shall make our new film. A great one. At one and the same time a great Greek classic and a revolution in the cinema. And who would be better suited to direct it than I?"

It was Basserman who replied. "M-M-Maybe no one. Maybe anyone. But this picture won't be made."

Victor: "How can you say that?"

"You will say so yourself when you realize there is no way that M-M-Magdalena can be in it."

The thin Granite brother, darker than any Latin star, went visibly pale at the remark. "What are you saying?" he demanded.

"What the hell is going on?" cried Harry Cohn. "We only committed ourselves when we heard Mezaray would be part of the picture. If she's out, so are we."

L. B. said, "We are not in business to lose money. With Mezaray and Von Beckmann we have a hit, even if we put them in *Andy Hardy*. Without them—"

Von Beckmann had hold of the microphone. His words echoed through the theater. "Magda sacrificed herself for me. She knew it was better for one of us to leave Vienna than for both to stay behind. She wanted it to be me. I swear that she insisted. It was so that I could complete my life's work. Do not be deceived. If I call to her now, she will come."

Basserman: "And what if she can't?"

Von B: "You mean, if Goebbels won't let her out?"

"It's not G-G-Goebbels I'm thinking of. Do you know what happened to the women in Hitler's life? A-a-a-all of them? They committed suicide—or so it was made to seem."

At these words there was an outcry throughout the hall. Victor staggered backward, as if struck by an invisible opponent. "What are you suggesting? That he had her killed?"

Von Beckmann, in a sudden gesture of rage, cracked the metal pole of the microphone into two pieces, as if it were no stronger than Louella's pencil. "No! It's not true! It can't be! She was the one who got me out!"

Then Louella herself started to speak. "No. That isn't true. I know who it was. A birdy told me. You can read about it tomorrow!"

Von Beckmann seemed to go into a swoon. For a terrible moment it looked as if he were about to topple off the edge of the stage. People ran forward to catch him. I was among the first on the scene. But I did not put my hands out. Instead I stood paralyzed by the sight that met my eyes. For there in the orchestra pit, between the bassoons and the clarinets, sat Chick Chandler and the Queen B. Side by side! Shoulder to shoulder! Cheek to cheek! Inch by horrible inch I felt my heart climb up my throat and into my mouth. I chewed on that bitter fruit.

At that moment of dismay and chaos an old man, thin-faced and wrinkled, started to make his way down the central aisle. He moved haltingly, hunched over, with the aid of a cane. Those in the hall who recognized him nudged those who did not: here was the former Alexander Granach, the grand old man of American film, known affectionately to the industry as Alexander the Great.

"Poppi! Poppi!"

That was Valentina. She ran to the front of the stage and hopped like a schoolgirl at the sight of her grandfather. The old man stopped, squinting up at the child, who was in fact taller than he. Then he continued to totter down the length of the aisle. As he neared the orchestra, the nonagenarian halted, lifting his cane. At the sight of that stick, so threateningly raised, the whole room grew silent. They wanted to hear the words of the patriarch.

"Where is Von Beckmann?"

Rudi leaned over the lip of the stage. He stared down at the aged figure, who looked as old as Methuselah. He said, "*Vater,* I am here."

Alexander Granite raised his head, entirely bald save for an uncut fringe whose snowy locks fell almost to his shoulders. His skin looked, in color and texture, like a walnut's shell. "I paid Hitler a fortune to get you out of that camp. Every Granite theater in Munich and Berlin. The least you can do is come down here where I can see you."

Von Beckmann obeyed. He moved down the four short steps and strode into the aisle. Old Granite did not wait, however. He turned his back upon him and started to address the near breathless crowd.

"The whole world knows the product put out by Granite Films. *You're never more than a day's walk from a Granite picture,* that's our motto. One day! No matter where you are in the world. I could read you letters I get from places like Borneo and the Arabian desert. Also from Africa, where we have wide distribution, and from South America, too. Only in Germany, and the nations conquered by Germany, is this no longer the case. This makes me sad. It breaks open my heart. Think of it! The little towns I worked in—I never forgot them. I gave them lots of money. There's a Granachstrasse in every one of them—or a Granach Fountain, a Granach Library, the Granach Baths. And they, of all the people on earth, cannot see a Granite picture!"

Impossible for all the film folk at the Wilshire Ebell not to feel the pathos in his words. They knew it was this aged man who had helped create the audience for their medium. It was he who had first hung a sheet from a tree limb or a clothesline or a window and, with the beams from his ether-filled lantern, covered it with seeming quicksilver. Was just such a sheet, or something like it, hanging at this very moment beneath desert stars or jungle moon? Is that what the Wild Man of Borneo walked a whole day to see?

Alexander Granite had more to say to his colleagues. "Now every Granachstrasse is a Hitlerstrasse or a Goeringstrasse or a Goebbelsstrasse. Even in Lemberg, my beloved Lemberg, the Granach Polytechnic Institute is now the Himmler Museum. What a desecration! What a disgrace! I could not save my name. I could not rescue my buildings. But I could free Rudolph Von Beckmann. That's why I brought him to America. Where is he?"

Directly behind the old man's back, Rudi said, "Here, Father."

The Great Granach looked up at the tall, gaunt man before him. "No, no. I want the director of *Antigone.* The man who made *The Story of Jesus Christ.*"

"But I am Rudi. Don't you recognize me? I was a member of the family."

Frowning, fumbling, the aged man reached into his pocket for a pair of spectacles and placed them on his nose. Then he stared with his blue eyes into the sagging brown ones of the person who stood before him. "What is this? A trick? A prank? Who is this old man? Get him out of my sight!" With that, the tottering nonagenarian began to brandish his cane. Valentina screamed. Rudi leaned backward, so that the stick came down, without much force, on his shoulder. Immediately Granite raised it again.

"Impostor!" he screamed.

His target, bent over, his shoulders hunched with humiliation, was already lurching up the aisle toward the rear doors.

Now all hell broke out. People were running this way and that, shouting and waving their arms. Manfred marched to the edge of the stage. He shook his fist at the back of the departing figure. "Out! Out! You're not part of the family! You'll never direct at Granite! Never!"

Now Rabbi Magnin attempted to edge Manfred aside. He leaned out toward the tumultuous crowd. "Wait! Wait, everybody!" he cried. "I have a telegram from Mrs. Roosevelt!"

All this while the former Laszlo Loewenstein stood in a daze above the orchestra pit. Below me I saw how the Queen B's plump calves were entwined around those of Mr. Chandler. And worse! Far worse! Her hand was inside his pocket!

At that sight a wave of hot fury broke within me. The saliva boiled in my mouth. I reached out and snatched the baton from Alfred Wallenstein's hand. But the instant I raised it into the air, intent upon bringing it down upon the head of Chick and his chickadee, the one hundred members of the Philharmonic reached under their seats for their Mexican sombreros. The next moment they started to play "La Cucaracha."

There was no saving the evening now. Men and women were rushing for the exits. More people were pushing into the wings. Waiters ran about, scooping up silverware and dishes, and the stagehands started to lower the asbestos curtain. It was like a scene from a comedy by Mack Sennett—who, of course, had been present all along, and who now, alone upon the stage, calmly finished the piece of rum cake he was having for dessert.

Outside, in the chilly night, limousines were gunning their engines and honking their horns. I pushed through the doors of the theater and looked about. How, I wondered, was I to get home? I thought I saw, inside the black Cadillac, Arthur, the Granites' chauffeur; but when I waved, using my handkerchief, he drove off. Suddenly I felt something that choked me and simultaneously tickled my nose. I looked down into the beady black eyes of a fox. Rochelle! I whirled around. The Queen B was standing there in her plum-colored gown.

"Miss Hudson!" I exclaimed. "What are you doing here?"

"Trying to figure out how I'm going to get home," the starlet responded.

"Why," I began, not attempting to disguise the irony that filled my voice, "don't you have a ride with—what's his name? Like something that came out of a shell. Big hit in *Honeymoon Deferred.* Muscles. Moustache. Ah, I have it! Mr. Chick Chandler!"

What the platinum-haired actress said next brought so much joy to her costar that all the difficulty and pain of this long evening fled from my busy brain and heated heart: "Who? That jerk?"

It was a long walk to Fontenelle Way. I offered Miss Hudson my arm. She took it. We started off down the boulevard. For a time we moved in the glare of the searchlights and the streetlights' glow. But soon we found that the dark of the night closed in upon us and swallowed us up.

CHAPTER

T W O

OCEAN DEPTHS

It was, or had *recently been, the season to be jolly. Christmas decorations hung the entire length of Santa Monica Pier. Ivy, maybe mistletoe, twined up the lampposts, at the top of which acorn-shaped globes threw their rays into the damp, dark air. Stars with light bulbs inside them were stretched over the boardwalk. The glow they made, together with the illumination from the surrounding city, obscured the real stars in the heavens above. Not only that, clouds were moving in, with a chill fog, creating an overcast.*

Who was that, shivering upon the wooden planks? It was the former Laszlo Loewenstein, Moto manqué. He glanced over his shoulder; at Jack's-at-the-Beach the windows were lit up and steamy. The music and laughter from inside the restaurant assaulted his ears. Overhead, a sleigh and reindeer, respectively candy-apple red and chocolate brown, were suspended on invisible wires. Not even the pasteboard Santa, or the three-dimensional presents spilling from the two-dimensional carriage, could lift his gloom. Oh, those packages! With bows! They gave him a particular pang.

Laszlo moved on, down the length of the dock. He passed couples, sailors in sailor suits with women in blouses, women in dresses. They strolled with their arms about each other, or they leaned against the rail, kissing and kissing. Some of the girls wore open shoes or leather sandals, so that he could not help but see how they had painted their toes in seasonal red. Covering his eyes, he fled onward, beyond the last rays of light. Here it was darker, quieter, more peaceful—no noises, no decorations, no groping between the sexes. At the rail were the bundled-up shapes of solitary men, six of them, eight of them, watching the lines on their fishing poles. This was a sight that fit Laszlo's mood: the patience, the resignation, fate and its fickleness.

"Good evening, fellows," he called out, with as much cheeriness as he could. "Are you having good luck?"

Only one of the men, a grizzled old-timer, bothered to respond. He turned and—was this a charm to secure good fortune? To ward off ill?—spat all the way to the intruder's shoes.

Some thirty yards remained between Loewenstein and the lap-lap-lap of the open sea. He crossed them. The sodden boards gave like canvas beneath the fall of his feet. A smell like old dollar bills rose through the cracks in the wood. He came to the thick, salt-splashed pilings at the end of the dock. Here civilization seemed to come to an end. The whirligig of the metropolis, and the whole pulsing continent, had at last come to a stop. The actor looked down. It wasn't a blue sea or a green one. The water was black as oil. The waves, little wavelets, broke against the piles, turning suddenly white like buds of cauliflower. Overhead, an invisible bird, a gull or a pelican, or not impossibly a lone, lost albatross, uttered a cry: carrow-ow-ow, untranslatable into human terms.

Between two of the giant, slippery timbers, an iron ladder hung almost to the surface of the sea. Loewenstein-Lorre sat beside it, with his feet dangling down; he might have been a fisherman himself. In his left hand he held a dough-covered sausage, the kind that comes warm from a vending machine. He placed it beside him. With his right hand he took from his pocket a package, a small one, no larger than a saltcellar or a bottle of ink. He put that down on his right. Then he raised first one leg and then the other to the bulge of his belly and, grunting, removed both his shoes. Still seated, he took off his camel coat, damp at the armpits, and folded it behind him. He sat for another moment, in thought. Then he took off his Gruen watch with the luminescent hands and placed it with care inside one of his shoes. His wallet? He took that out as well. Without further ado he stood, placed one stockinged foot on a rung of the ladder, and descended to the Pacific Ocean.

One moment later and the waters had closed over his head. Down, down, down he tumbled, thrashing with all four limbs. Both Granite brothers had a pool. So did Basserman. Ernie Glickman's was shaped like a harp. Phil Epstein had put one in at his house in the Palisades. Even Schoenberg, the avant-gardist, splashed around up to his hairy shoulders. Alone of all his friends, alone perhaps of the entire population of Southern California, Laszlo Loewenstein-Lorre had not learned to swim. Those scenes in Last Warning? The underwater struggle between Mr. Moto and George Sanders to save the French fleet? Done with a stunt man. Al Fox. Also five feet, four inches. A mere bathtub, with its lion claws, its sinister steaming, caused Lorre unease. Even at that moment, sinking *in coldness, in blackness, he shuddered at the memory of the chlorine odor that hung over his section of Bel Air.*

What a tub he found himself in now! Like a mudbath, thick, viscous, murky. It was as if some octopus or squid had squirted him with its ink. He could feel the icy tentacles wrap around his chest, his neck. He struggled against those myriad arms. Impossible, in their unyielding grip, to breathe!

Up he shot in a foaming cascade. He-e-e-l-l-p-p! he started to shout, until he reminded himself that help was the last thing he wanted. He shut his mouth and, for two or three seconds, floated on his back like a child's toy—a duck, a duckee, a duckling. Then he rolled over and, as effortlessly as Johnny Weiss-muller, plunged headfirst into the world's greatest sea.

Contrary to legend I did not see my life pass before me—only the last two months. That was bad enough; for, as I had feared, just days after the debacle at the banquet for Victims of Nazism, work began on *Mr. Moto Wins His Spurs.* From the start, everything seemed to go wrong. Horses stepped into gopher holes and spilled their riders. Clouds billowed up out of nowhere, dropping inches of rain exclusively, it seemed, on the block bounded by Olympic and La Brea. If automobiles didn't blow their horns at just the wrong moment, then airplanes droned slowly overhead. Once a transformer over-heated, and before Maynes, the gaffer, could do anything about it, a whole row of klieg lights exploded, one after the other, like a string of Chinese firecrackers. Those little delays stretched what had been meant to be a five-day production all the way to the end of October, and still we weren't done.

In those days, of course, it was nothing for the major studios to turn out a picture a week, fifty pictures a year, the way Ford turned out automobiles. But that kind of schedule was difficult for places like the Granite B unit, which had only one soundstage and where on occasion the very film in the cameras had to be pieced together from the short ends left over from Victor's high-budget productions. On La Brea Boulevard, instead of an assembly line, they used what had come to be known as the leapfrog system. While the *Spurs* cameras were grinding away on scene 25, *Annie pleads with her father to divert water to the suffering cattle,* the assistant director did the setup and rehearsal—*Sheriff Clayton passes out rifles to his deputies*—for scene 26. When things were going smoothly, the director could move from one set to another without having to do much more than say *Action* and *Cut.* In the meantime, the frog, as the second director was called, was already at work on the next setup, *Tipped off, the Ranchers' Association passes out rifles as well.*

Hank Sumner, a gray-faced man with an equally gray moustache and a curved clay pipe like Sherlock Holmes's, made all the oaters at Regal-Titanic—the same way Coco Goodheart, who was actually the frog on the *Moto* production, shot the grass-skirters. Sumner claimed he could direct a western in his sleep—which in a way he did, since twice a day he would retire to the cutting room and lie down with his red, ether-soaked scarf over his face. When he emerged, glassy-eyed, he'd light up his pipe and work six hours without stopping once for a break. Tinkles, the crew called him, because of the sound of the glass vials of anesthetic that knocked together inside his pockets.

When did the real trouble begin? I think it was at scene 41. This was when Raymond, the son of the big rancher, and Annie meet secretly behind an enormous pile of discarded quartz—only to be discovered by a gang of miners. It was late in the day. Perhaps an hour of sunlight left. I was preparing for scene 42, in which Moto lassos the rogue he has caught in the act of diverting the town's water supply. For the moment all was confusion. Tinkles was shouting through his megaphone and grips were hammering last-minute nails; Maynes was on all fours, splicing electrical cords; and Lizzie, the redheaded script girl, was looking through her glasses at the pages that were balanced on her bony knees. Ellie, from wardrobe, was putting pins into the back of Miss Hudson's rawhide blouse. Extras milled left and right. Over at the water pipe, where Coco was setting up scene 42, Fox was practicing tricks with his lariat. He waved for me to come over. Yet I lingered. Miss Umin, who always prepared the Moto makeup, was slicking my hair with Wildroot Cream Oil. Her own hair, like that of a palomino, hung down in bangs over her forehead. She blew on my spectacles and shined them with a piece of lace she drew from her flat bosom. "There," she said. "Now we're ready to go."

But I didn't go, even though Coco had started waving, too.

"Action!" cried Tinkles, from near the pile of stones.

Immediately, inside my chest, my heart started to flutter. It hopped like a canary from rib to rib. That was because Rochelle Hudson had stepped from behind the boulders of quartz. Her breasts reared like horses out of her buckskin halter. Anxiously she twisted her hands. Then a smile spread like jam on her plump, pouty lips. Chick Chandler, also known as Ray MacDonald, ran into the frame of the picture. He dashed to his lady love. I just had time to see his dimpled chin, his hangdog moustache, the oddly pale eyes in the tanned skin of his face, before each of those features disappeared behind the Queen B's pompadour. They kissed with wide-open mouths.

Instantly, like water streaming from a showerhead, a hundred rivulets ran from my pomaded hairline over my pancaked skin. "Oh, Mr. Moto," exclaimed Miss Umin, "look what you've done to your makeup."

I blinked the sting of salt from my eyes. The hated kiss continued. It was as if the saliva that bound their lips together were made out of glue.

"This is too much," I muttered. "I can't bear to look."

Miss Umin, also like a palomino, tossed her head. "But they're only kissing," she said. "It's all in the script."

I groaned aloud. My skin, I noticed, was shining more brightly than the radium dial of my watch. "Not kissing—look, he's biting her ear. He's biting her neck. Is that in the photoplay? Certainly not!"

With horror I saw that Annie had gone limp with passion in the rancher's arms. She had fainted!

Miss Umin sniffed the air. "What's that smell, I wonder? Almonds? *Amaretto?*" She placed a hand on my bicep. "That reminds me of *amore. Amour.*"

I paid no heed. Deep within, below the solar plexus, a word was taking shape. I fought to keep the single syllable down; yet it rose, past the diaphragm, the windpipe, the larynx, the throat. "Cut!" I cried.

All those within earshot—the actors, the director, the script girl and stunt man, and even Kleinbard, who ran the sound—stared at me as if I had dropped to earth from another planet. "Ha-ha!" I laughed, displaying my artificial incisors. "So solly!"

"Hey!" yelled Miss Hudson. If she had fainted, she was wide awake now. "What's the big idea? We were making sparks!"

"To hell with it," said Tinkles. "Let's break for the day."

"Okay! That's it, people!" Meltsner, the production assistant, shouted this through his two cupped hands. "We'll start here, with 41 and 42, tomorrow morning."

Miss Hudson stamped the heel of her western boot. "I've had it up to here with your funny business," she declared—no need to say to whom. "Sometimes you just make me sick." Then she strode off in the direction of her trailer. The others moved away, too. With no less alacrity, Coco's crew abandoned their set. All the grips and gaffers disappeared. Only a crowd of black-eyed miners remained. They trudged off across the deserted lot. One of those extras, taller than the rest, halted; then he turned back toward where I was standing alone.

"One moment," he called.

I looked more closely. This man's face was covered with coal dust. His clothes were grimy and torn. But I knew who it was: Rudolph Von Beckmann. It was the first time I had seen him since he had been driven in disgrace from the Wilshire Ebell Theater. We all knew that Manfred had hired him for the B unit—not out of softheartedness, just the opposite. He gloated at being able to lord it over this broken man, who, with his matted hair and ragged clothing, the dark, charcoal-rimmed eyes, had been reduced to little more than a husky hobo. The extra, low man on the totem pole, leaned close to me.

"What would you do to get out of this picture?" he asked.

"Anything!" I responded.

"We can do it, you and I. And we might, my dear Lorre, be able to rid you of Mr. Chick Chandler, too."

Rolling over and over, *like a log in a logjam, the drowning man rose a second time to the surface. Here the currents spun him onto his back, where he floated a moment, spewing saltwater upward as high as the spout of a whale. He just had time to think, with a certain grim satisfaction, that the third time down was the last time when, indeed for the third time, he went down.*

Now the whole weight of the sea, the pressure of countless fathoms, sat like a hippopotamus upon Loewenstein-Lorre's chest. His eyes, already exophthalmic, bulged from their sockets; they were as big as Jerry Collona's. A stream of bubbles, like a cartoonist's indication for thoughts, came from his mouth.

What were those thoughts that ran through my mind? How, in the dark of that night, while Blowen the gate man was dozing, Von Beckmann and I took down the boulders of plaster and replaced them with stones weighing fifty, eighty, one hundred pounds. Hideous! Horrible! The devil's work. The impresario, at least, acted from artistic motives. Nothing fake, no illusions: this was to be a new cinema of the real. I had no such ideals. All I wanted was an avalanche, a rock slide, under which my adversary would be buried up to the chin. For an hour and more I staggered under the burden of stone. I paused. I panted. I wiped my brow. But Von B did not stop to rest. He heaved one of the last rocks to the top of the pile. Then, grunting, he stooped for another—a huge piece of flint, bigger than I was. When he stood, raising it over his head, he looked like Atlas, bearing the weight of the world.

Came, as the poet puts it, the dawn. And with it the grips, the gaffers, and the rest of the crew. The actors stationed themselves as before. In due course Hank Sumner cried, "Action!" There was Miss Hudson. There the doomed Chandler. They met. They embraced. They kissed. All within the shadow of the quartz.

"It's so real!" said Miss Umin.

I did not reply. *Real?* What was real? Above me, at the back of the Granite lot, rose the great cyclorama, covered with ponytail clouds. Impossible, at the glimpse of that peacock blue and those wisps of white, delicate as eyelashes, to tell which was the actual sky and which the work of art. Once more the Queen B went limp in her lover's arms. Did I interfere? Did I object? I did not. I merely watched, half hypnotized, as the morning sun lit up her locks—the way a miser might be transfixed by a pile of gold coins. But all the while my ears were alert for the approaching vigilantes. And of a sudden, here they were. The ragged crowd of miners fell upon the lovers. They surrounded them with revolvers and pistols. From among their midst a man with a tin star on his chest stepped forward to put Raymond under arrest. But Chick Chandler was not going to be taken without a fight. With a blow of his fist he knocked Sheriff Clayton back into the arms of the miners. Now those men leaped forward to right that wrong. The brawl that followed was tremendous, with some deputies flying left, some right, and others going head over heels.

I tried, at this fateful moment, to look away, but could not. My eyes would not close. They would not blink. A miner aimed a blow at Chick Chandler's chin. The rancher, as choreographed, ducked, and another of the extras flew by him, straight into the keystone that held up the pile of rocks. There was a pause. Then the whole mountain of stone started to shudder. Beside me, Miss Umin uttered a scream. "It's moving! Watch out!"

One, two, three: one could have counted, it seemed, to an infinite number before that great rock pile, like a sawed-in-half redwood, decided to fall. Another scream, this time from Rochelle Hudson, and the entire mountain tumbled with a roar to the ground. Then, in silence, a huge cloud of dust rose into the air. From every direction people came running. I ran with the rest. We dashed round to the back of the pile, where, from beneath a heap of flint and quartz and granite, a pair of boots protruded.

"Who is it?" cried Kleinbard, the sound man.

"Help him!" the script girl howled.

"Yes! Yes!" shouted Chick Chandler. "Get a doctor!"

Chick Chandler? I whirled about. There stood the actor, his lantern jaw quivering with emotion. The Queen B, all atremble, clung to his arm.

"What is the matter with you?" called out one of the extras. His face was covered with charcoal dust and so was his hair, so that it was impossible to see its white stripe, like that on the back of a skunk. Von B! "Are you just going to stand there?" he shouted. "Like nigger zombies?"

With that he bent down and began to pluck away the rocks that had crushed the legs of the victim. He threw the stones aside with as much ease as he had earlier put them in place. Now the others dashed forward to help. Slowly the body of the poor wretch emerged. A cry went up. "It's Bernow!" And so it was, Steve Bernow, the assistant prop man. His legs had been smashed to smithereens. His pelvis, like a broken dish, stuck jaggedly through his clothes. But his chest rose and fell and rose once again. Breathing! Alive!

Now Manfred Granite—surely he had heard the roar and seen the dust cloud—strode over from the executive building. "Jesus Christ! What's going on here? Where's Sumner? Who the hell is in charge?"

Miss Hudson ran to him. "Oh, Mr. Granite! There's been a terrible accident!"

"The whole rock pile!" cried Bill Maynes, the gaffer. "It's fallen."

Hoffman, the key grip, approached the studio boss. "It's Bernow. My assistant. What an idiot! Who told him to use real rocks?"

Manfred: "I don't believe this! Another day lost! Call Glickman! I want another prop man. I want him now."

Here Rudi, still holding a giant boulder, approached the head of Granite Films. "That won't be necessary. There's no need for an agent. As you see, I am able to carry the load."

Gasping, gagging, thrashing *his arms like a boiling lobster, Loewenstein-Lorre clawed his way once again toward the surface of the Pacific. "Oh!" he started to say, as in Oh, what a fool I have been!; but the minute he opened his mouth, ten thousand gallons of seawater, that's what it felt like, poured into the gaping O. It might have been that heavy ballast that weighed him down, or the burden of guilt, like an anchor, a cross. In any case, he sank so suddenly that anyone would have thought that boulders of quartz had been tied to each of his limbs.*

Scene 50. *Jailbreak.* The town at night. For once the setup, which Coco Goodheart was conducting, seemed to go smoothly. Maynes had arranged the klieg lights to enhance the glow of the rising moon. George Hoffman was checking the chain that would be looped around the bars of the prison window. Clayton, the sheriff, was pinning his badge to the fringe of his breast. The cameraman, Nakhimovsky, measured the distance between his lens and the jailhouse wall. And inside that prison? Behind the wall of brick? The crouching Chick Chandler. Irony of ironies, the man who would free him was none other than Agent 673. Bucktoothed and buckskinned, I sat upon a reddish stallion. On my head, a white sombrero, from whose stiff brim hung small cotton balls. On my lips, a smile of grim satisfaction. Mr. Ray Mac-Donald might think he was about to escape from imprisonment into the arms of his Annie. But I knew the Queen B was far away in her trailer; I also knew who the prop man had been and which way the bricks would fall. This time Chandler would not have a chance.

Hank Sumner, who would actually shoot the scene, was still asleep in the cutting room. Coco would take us through the single rehearsal the B-unit budget allowed. He clapped his hands for attention. This director was a tall, thin man with white, wispy hair and a nose as long as a collie's. He had worked in Hollywood for over a quarter of a century and was an object of everyone's pity—not so much for his asthma, which made him hawk constantly into his handkerchief, but because the innovations in the industry had long since passed him by. Poor Coco! He could not bring himself to embrace even sound, much less color. *Art is Art and Life is Life:* that was his motto, by which he meant that each so-called advance in filmmaking blurred the crucial distinction between the two. "In the talkies, a pistol goes off, does it not, with a terrific report"—this was how Coco often made his case. "In a silent picture the pistol is pointed and instantly a flock of pigeons wheels into the air. Answer me, which audience hears the bigger bang?"

Just then Mike Meltsner, the production assistant, shouted through an old-fashioned megaphone. "All right, everybody. We're going to run through the rehearsal. George, did you check the chain? Make sure the end is attached to the saddle. Peter, you'll ride up and attach it to the window. Okay, let's have the sheriff over there. When the bars pop out, Chick is going to come out shooting. Clayton, you fall right there, in the middle of the road. Kleinbard! Set for sound? Lizzie? No slate board this time. Okay, Coco, she's yours."

We all turned toward the leapfrog director. For a moment Goodheart stood, making a noise like a man drinking the last drops of a soda through a straw. Then even that sound ceased. The silence that fell upon the once bustling set was as complete as if someone had closed the lid on a bottle of buzzing flies. Coco raised his hand, then dropped it down.

I kicked my spurs into the side of the stallion. The well-trained animal trotted up Main Street toward the jailhouse. With both hands I clung to the saddle. All unbidden, Mr. Moto's mount came to a halt beneath the high, barred window. Standing in the stirrups, I stretched all sixty-four inches upward and wrapped the clanking chains around the stout metal bars. Then I delivered, through the same jailhouse window, the scene's only line:

> *Honorable sir! Have no fear. Moto will bring freedom before*
> *you can say Mr. Jack Robinson!*

Once more I dug my spurs into my horse's flanks. The animal wheeled, whinnied, and galloped away. The metal links of the chain, firmly bound to my saddle, grew taut. The next instant the entire window came flying out of its frame. That much had been planned. What was unplanned was how the bricks in the jailhouse also went flying and how, after a terrible moment of suspense, the wall itself collapsed to the ground. Also on the ground was Mr. Moto—that is to say, I had been catapulted over the head of my horse the instant the chain had brought that steed to a halt. For a moment I lay dazed, while spots, or perhaps they were balls of cotton, danced before my eyes.

Now everything happened with amazing speed. The sheriff ran toward the jailhouse. A shot rang out. Coco Goodheart, in the throes of an asthma attack, brought both hands to his throat and stuck out his tongue. By then the cloud of dust had lifted from where the false front of the jailhouse had stood. As it did so, I gaped. So did the entire crew. For there, upright in the moonlit space that had once been the jail's interior, were Chick Chandler and Rochelle Hudson; rather, he was upright, with his denim pants about his ankles and a smoking gun in his hand, while she was kneeling, with her arms around the pale pillars of his thighs.

Once again I found myself thinking of a bottle of flies, though this time I imagined that I and my colleagues were inside it with the air running out. I wanted to speak but could not. I wanted to move, to rush forward, but felt impeded by an invisible wall of glass. The next instant, as if an unseen hand had removed the lid, everyone began screaming and running about. The sheriff got up from where he had dropped in the road. Inside the jailhouse Chick Chandler lifted his trousers and Miss Hudson ran off toward the trailer.

Everyone else, Moto included, rushed to where the leapfrog director had been standing.

"Oh, no! Oh, no! They've killed him!" shouted Lizzie, the script girl.

"Jesus!" cried Michael Meltsner. "That was a real bullet!"

"Stand back! Stand back! Give him air!"

The crowd drew away, revealing the pitiful sight of Coco Goodheart sprawled on the ground. His chest was heaving. His open eyes stared up toward the black and white of the sky and stars.

"Coco! Coco! What is it? What happened?" That was George Hoffman.

The director moved his lips to reply, but, as if he were a character in one of his own silent movies, no words came out. He had heard the bigger bang.

"Call an ambulance!"

"We did! We already did!"

"It's too late! He's dying!"

"Coco!"

Shaking, trembling, Liz lifted the director's head and undid the button that held his collar. Then everyone gasped. There was a hole in his throat. It gaped like a second mouth. Now the air and blood, mixing together, spilled like a tongue onto the ragged flesh. The sound he made, more horrible than his usual labored breathing, was like the last gallon of water draining out of a tub.

"Here, let me through," said Tinkles, awakened from his nap. He balled up the end of his scarf, which was red to start with, and thrust it into the wound.

"How could this happen?" somebody said.

Meltsner: "It's my fault. I did it. I loaded the gun. I got the box from the prop department. I'd swear they were blanks."

Kleinbard, the wiry little sound man, looked up from where he was kneeling. "It was an accident, Mike."

From the crowd an extra shouted, "Look! Listen! It's the ambulance!"

It took only a moment for the orange-and-white vehicle to drive through the main gate and make its way down the unpaved street of the western town. The attendants darted out with a stretcher and lifted the stricken man onto it. Then they climbed back into the rear of the ambulance and pulled the door shut behind them. Lights flashing, and with its siren full blast, the vehicle raced for the Olympic Boulevard gate, which the guards, Lydon and Kuttner, threw open. Those left behind stood shocked, neither speaking nor moving.

All this time I had remained quietly off to one side. The sequence of events had stunned me, the way two terrible blows of a hammer might stun a cow on the way to the abattoir. The first, of course, was the sight of Miss Hudson clasping the bared loins of Chick Chandler. Cuckolded! The second blow, even more staggering than the first, was the tragedy that had befallen poor Coco. It wasn't the sight of the director on his back, or even the gaping wound, with the slick spill of blood that had come lapping out of it, that had shocked me so much as the following thought: what if it were *not* an accident? What if that bullet had been yet another of Von B's attempts to create the *cinema of the real?* Alas for Coco: his philosophy had been just the opposite, *Art is Art and Life is Life,* and he had striven through the whole of his career to keep the one separate from the other. Now an actual bullet had taken the place of a blank. A fictional shooting had given way to a real one. It was that bitter irony that made me stagger like a beast on the slaughterhouse floor.

Yet in spite of my state of shock, I felt—oh, terrible confession!—a surge of joy. Surely now, after so many delays and with the twin tragedies to Bernow and Goodheart, the production of *Mr. Moto Wins His Spurs* would have to shut down. Not only that, without a second director to run the leapfrog system, the entire B unit, together with every new Moto feature, might be disbanded. "What a pity," I remarked to Manfred Granite, who had once again arrived belatedly at the scene. Then—clap, clap!—I chopped my en-larged teeth together. *"Sometime smart man know when to quit."*

Manfred responded more like a grizzly than a Granite. Deep within his throat he growled.

Then from behind me I heard a familiar voice. "Oooh," it said, as a hand began to fumble at the pocket of my western breeches. "Isn't he a wonderful man?" The Queen B!

Coldly, without turning around, I said, "What are you doing here, Miss Hudson?"

"Can't you tell?"

"Those days are over. I can't wait to hear the story you'll tell me. About you and Mr. Chandler. Maybe you were just inspecting his scar, is that it? Ha! Ha! From an appendicitis operation?"

"You know I wasn't."

"Yes, I do! But I don't care! I don't care about anything. I'm the same as a dead man. It should have been me who was shot. Go on. Tell me your lies. Nothing you say could make me forgive you."

Rochelle, going up on tiptoe, plunged her hand a little deeper. She wig-gled her fingers as well. In spite of myself, I peeked over my shoulder. Her face, I discovered, was stained with tears. Her lipstick was smeared and wet. Out of her vocabulary of hundreds of words, she chose the only two that could melt the frozen water that had replaced the blood in my heart: "Forgive me?"

Melt I did. A wave of emotion rose within me, together with an effluvium of almond and ammonia. "*Wonderful man.* Why do you say that? I'm just—how do you say it in America? An ordinary Joe."

"Oh, Petey, I didn't mean you."

Black bile, and gall, flooded my internal organs, as if I were the one with the defective appendix. "I understand. You mean Chick Chandler. Because of his Adam's apple. That is only a myth. A myth! The same as the manly cleft in the chin."

"Silly! I don't mean that bum, either. Look at him, will you! I get the shivers, like there's a spell upon me. Do you see him? It's that Von Beckmann!"

I turned, following the Queen B's gaze. She was looking toward the cyclorama. Now, at night, nothing was visible in it but the brushstrokes of the clouds. Beneath these curlicues and commas, my pitiable stallion was circling in a frenzy, more like a dog chasing its tail than a horse. The links of the chain were hopelessly entangled about its fetlocks, threatening with each new turn to bring it down.

There was a man beside it. Von B. He drew near the animal, which, hobbled as it was, tried to rear. Failing that, with bared teeth and a crazed look in its eye, it lunged toward the prop man. Von Beckmann held his ground. From the far side of the lot the whole cast and crew watched, spellbound, as the former impresario moved in front of the startled steed. The white shock at the front of his hair might have been, from the stallion's point of view, a lump of sugar. Immediately it quieted; that is, it stood, every muscle trembling, as if it were warding off ten thousand invisible flies.

"*Still sein, mein noble Ross.*"

Now even the twitching stopped. Von Beckmann walked to the side of the roan. He passed his hands over the sweat-streaked body and then bent to uncinch the saddle, which slid in a heap to the ground. Daintily, the horse lifted each hoof from the loosened chains. Von Beckmann pointed back toward the prison. The obedient animal trotted to its place beside the crumpled wall.

The trainer of animals followed. "To work! Why are you standing there? Get a new saddle! Get a new chain! Here! You! Maynes! I want a floodlight here. Don't you see the shadow of the boom on the bricks? Not allowed! Carpenters, masons—get that wall up! Put the bars in the window! We shoot in an hour!"

Manfred, seeing all this, turned on his heel. "I'll get Sumner," he said. He might just as well have declared that we now had our new frog. My heart sank; but it soon rose again. Miss Hudson was reaching into the depths of my pocket.

"Oh, Petey," she said. "I've never been so excited!"

Up shot Loewenstein-Lorre, *as high as a porpoise, spewing seawater from his mouth, his ears, his nose. He hadn't the least doubt he would soon sink again. He might as well be one of those mortals or demigods of the ancients, condemned eternally to rise and eternally to fall, like a dumbwaiter at an endless feast. Why was it that when Fredric March wanted to forget his sorrows, all he had to do was walk into the waves at Malibu Beach? There, in a neat pile, were his bathrobe and his thongs. With a pang Lorre thought of his own effects, the jacket and shoes, the pretty little gift box, the watch and wallet and half-eaten sausage, scattered at the end of the dock. There would be no Janet Gaynor to bewail his fate as, without a struggle, he slid once more into the bottomless deep.*

There had been yet one more disaster for the *Spurs* production. It had occurred just ten days before, while Hank Sumner was preparing to shoot the scene of the great stampede. Even now, thrashing at the bottom of the sea, Lorre could not help but groan at the thought that by that date a whole month had gone by since Coco had been shot and over two months had elapsed since the start of what had been scheduled to be a five-day production. *"Sometime,"* he found himself moaning aloud, to the kelp and the fishes, *"hands of clock move slower than snail."*

Much of the last month's delay had been caused by the demands of Rudolph Von Beckmann. The way he set up a scene for Tinkles took longer— four times longer, five times longer, a whole day and then overtime at night— than shooting the action itself. With Von B the lighting was always wrong; the sound was never right; one had to wait, as in Salzburg, for the perfect angle of the sun. Worse than that, with the Epsteins dismissed, Rudi felt free to make changes in the script. Just lines at first, then whole scenes, would be altered or written in. He even had the nerve to drop characters, which wasn't as bad as adding them: a son for the sheriff, a sister for Annie Harwood. That meant further delays in order to audition the actors, hire them, and rehearse and then rerehearse all the new lines. No wonder Manfred had been heard to complain that as far as he could tell from the balance sheets, this B picture was turning into an A.

At long last, before dawn on a December morning, everyone gathered for the big stampede. This was to be one of the most elaborate shots ever attempted on the Granite lot. For reasons both aesthetic and mundane, the scene was scheduled to begin at 6:15—to catch the first light and, as the police had insisted, to clear the lot of cattle before the rush hour began. Just before the appointed hour we all heard the faint sound of glass striking glass—just what you would expect from the milkman so early in the morning. But it wasn't the milkman. It was Hank Sumner. We could see the glowing tobacco inside the bowl of his curved clay pipe. The bottles in his pockets continued to jingle as he went from one camera position to another.

"Good morning, folks! I see that George has got everything ready."

What Sumner meant was the piano wire that Hoffman and his crew had stretched the length of Main Street. Behind that invisible corral, the onrushing cattle couldn't get to the buildings—except for the church and the livery stable, which, with their supports sawed nearly through, were supposed to come down. Now the director called out to the script girl.

"Liz! Where are you, sweetheart? I want you in front of this camera. We'll roll here first when the steers charge."

The frizzy redhead moved into position. On her slate board, which she clutched to her chest, it was just possible to make out the chalk marks for scene 62. Take one and only, as Sumner went on to explain.

"This isn't a run-through. We aren't going to have more than one chance at the stampede. Those sets come down, they aren't going up again. Even if we had the time, folks, the animals don't. Take my word for it, once they've been riled up, there won't be any calming them down."

On cue, from the south there now came the mixed sound of truck engines, the squeal of brakes, and the lowing of cattle. Off to the east, over downtown Los Angeles, the sky was starting to turn the color of tinfoil. Nearer by, the streetlamps, on automatic timers, began to wink out. The early morning breeze broke up the trail of pipe smoke that Sumner lay behind him as he moved to the second camera, and the third. It brought with it, too, the unmistakable odor, sharp as persimmons, of the frightened steers.

"Wow!" exclaimed Ernie Glickman, who had made it his business to be present for this historic shot. "Pee-yew!"

Then Mike Meltsner clapped his hands for silence. "All right, people. Let's have quiet, please. The rodeo riders should get into position. Billy, time to turn on the lamps."

There was a brief flurry of activity as the horsemen got onto their mounts and cantered into position. With a series of soft thuds, like someone plumping pillows, Maynes turned on the lamps that, at Rudi's instructions, I had filled to the top with kerosene; this was to create the illusion of an inhabited town. Simultaneously the first red-hot wires of sunlight began to glow in the sky. By then Sumner had reached the boom that had been set up in the middle of the street. He climbed on board and was just swinging up over the packed dirt of the road when, unexpectedly, prematurely, the voice of the leapfrogger said, "Commence."

"No! No!" cried the director. "I've got no cameraman!" Too late. The stampede was under way.

No one who was there that morning will ever forget what happened next. Even now, at his last gasp, while tumbling helplessly in the depths of the ocean, Mr. Loewenstein-Lorre could not help but see those events projected before him—as if that school of smelt, darting by, had formed a silver screen in front of his bulging eyes.

"Run!" somebody had shouted.

"An earthquake!" cried Kleinbard, ripping off his headphones.

"No, it's the cattle!"

And so it was. The first steers, heads down, their muzzles drooling like the jaws of rabid dogs, appeared at the western end of the street. The sound they made, a single low-pitched note, was like foghorns. The drumming of their hooves was so much like thunder that half the crew members instinctively looked upward, into the pinkening sky.

"Action! Roll camera one! Roll camera two!" That was Mike Meltsner, shouting through his megaphone. Liz, loyal, thrust the slate board in front of the camera lens. But Nakhimovsky was already running pell-mell into the nearest building, a mockup of the town barbershop. In the blink of an eye the other cameramen followed suit. The human stampede was no less frantic than that of the beasts. Everywhere men and women were in full flight ahead of the herd, like daredevils in the streets of Pamplona. Others dashed to the upper stories of the flimsy facades—the saloon, the general store, the assayer's office—as if they were seeking higher ground in the midst of a flood. There was no stopping this tide. Even the expert rodeo riders were caught up, shouting and shooting their six-guns, like so much flotsam in the middle of a deluge.

This was the moment at which Mr. Moto, seated upon his roan stallion, was to win his spurs. My job was to gallop across the street, well ahead of the maddened herd, and catch Miss Hudson as she leaped from the top of the Fancy Free Hotel. But at my first glimpse of the cattle, I knew that something had gone terribly wrong. They rolled forward like a foam-flecked wave of mud, shaking the ground beneath them. The livery stable went down, as planned, in a storm of splinters. Then came a second crash. The top floor of the church, with its high steeple, was crumpling slowly onto the floor below. With horror I saw that these were not the only buildings in danger. As the crazed beasts careened by the covered walkways, every structure on both sides of the street started to sway. The piano wire, strong enough to yank marlins out of the ocean, might just as well have been spun from cobwebs. Here and there strands of it were snapping atonally, like notes in a Schoenberg concerto.

On swept the steers, toward the spot where Sumner, his smoking pipe clamped between his teeth, rode the boom. The herd, snorting their own smoke from their nostrils, swept underneath him, even as the director ground the camera in their wake. The trouble was that the herd, spreading wide, was now charging against the gallery posts on either side of the street. The awnings went down in their wake, like flyswatters too slow to catch the nimble flies. Now the buildings were not simply swaying; they were teetering, lurching, tipping, as if this Wild West town had been transformed into one of those drunken ghettos in the paintings of Chagall. It was from the largest of those sets, the three-story front of the Fancy Free Hotel, that there now issued a terrible scream.

Eeee! Eeeee! Eeeeeeee!

At that moment I saw, stretched out of the third-floor window of the reeling building, a pair of woman's arms. They were white, smooth-skinned, and plump.

Chickieeeeeeee!

Rochelle! I watched as first one leg, also plumpish, and then another came over the sill. She was going to jump!

"Miss Hudson!" I cried, bellowing louder than the most stentorian steer. "Wait! Moto is in motion!"

My stallion, however, would not budge. Instantly I threw down my sombrero and jumped from the saddle. I dashed from the roadside into the path of the galloping herd. Trouble, friends: for as fast as I ran, those horned heads were quickly closing the gap. Behind me, a blur of dust, matted hair, saliva; ahead, the desperate starlet, already half out of the window frame. The entire facade, mere plywood, with struts at the back, seesawed around her. Could this be happening? Was it real life? Or were we all characters in a movie, like one of the cliffhangers that the B unit was so expert at producing? The answer, more's the pity, was real life: the actress uttered a high-pitched scream and launched herself into the air.

"No! No! Oh, no!" Moto moaned. I stretched out my arms. I increased my speed. But there was no way I could catch her. Down came the Queen B, her nightdress ballooning around her. I saw her bare legs, like the pale stalk of a dandelion tuft, and—the shame of it!—the little roll of fat where her buttocks were pinched by her panties. This was no dandelion. She dropped like a bucket to the ground.

Unable to look, I closed my eyes. When I opened them, I saw that Rochelle had landed in the arms of—this was not in the script—Chick Chandler. Moreover, she had her own arms around that cowboy's neck.

"Miss Hudson! Honey!" I shouted. "Are you all right?"

"Oh, yes!" she replied.

Our reprieve, however, was a short one. The bellowing herd was almost upon us. I could make out the very lashes over the beasts' rheum-filled eyes and the horny sheaves of their hammering hooves. Our little love triangle was about to become what geometricians call a flat plane.

"Mr. Von Beckmann!" I heard the actress cry. "Help us! Oh, help us!"

Miraculously, that is just what Von B did. From out of nowhere he stepped into the path of the steers and held up both arms. Was it this gesture that spared us? Did the shock of white in his hair somehow remind the onrushing animals of the blaze upon their own foreheads? Or did the tide turn because at that very moment the sun, struggling up over the pits of La Brea, went off like a flare in everyone's eyes? Turn it did, for whatever reason. The blinded cattle in front slackened their pace. Those behind reared up over them, and those still further back simply came to a halt. There was a moment of thrashing and milling, and then the entire herd began to stampede back the way it had come.

Nothing, this time, stood in its path. On the south side of the street, half the buildings were already crushed. Now those to the north went down like dominoes.

"Hank! Hank! For God's sake, run!" somebody—it was the gargantuan Glickman—cried out.

Sumner was still on the boom, which, for a more dramatic shot, he had lowered to the level of the steers. No one can say whether, if he had taken his agent's advice, he might have escaped the sudden return of the rampaging beasts. What doomed the director was his six-foot scarf. The rising sun struck it head on, making each of its fibers burn magenta. Might as well wave a red flag before these maddened creatures. They made for him. The scaffold went down with no more resistance than a blade of grass. The director was hurled into the air, his pipe in his teeth and the scarf trailing like a banner from a biplane behind him.

For an instant, while Tinkles went flying, we all dared to hope that he might be thrown clear. Indeed, his trajectory took him out of the path of the trampling hooves. The director landed at the side of the road with the sound of a crushed cocktail glass. The vials of ether! In an instant his clothes were soaked through. And an instant after that, the sparks from his meerschaum set the poor man afire.

"Eeeeee!" Rochelle shrieked at the sight, but her cry was obliterated by the more terrible scream that came from the director's throat. Fully ablaze, he leaped to his feet and outran those who, from every side, were rushing to his aid. He made first for the Swallow, which was one of the few sets left standing. No sooner did he reach it than the kerosene I had placed in the lamps burst into flame. So did the lamps in the courthouse next door. Sumner didn't stop. He cut across the lot toward the soundstage. As soon as he entered the door, the huge building erupted. Like a human torch, the director ran on—to the executive building, the writers' huts, the dressing rooms. Everywhere he went he left a trail of fire behind him. At last he staggered to his own den in the cutting room, where the film stock, coated with silver nitrate, simply exploded. He was engulfed.

From all over the studio, and from the streets outside, people came running to fight the conflagration. The studio's own firetruck was first on the scene. This was a model built in the twenties that Manfred had bought from the old Mack Sennett studio. What followed might just as well have been filmed by the King of Comedy himself. The hoses were connected to the pumper and the four-man crew duly pumped. The stream that emerged was not much stronger than the spill of a man's urination, and described the same paltry arc. By then the sirens of the municipal equipment had drawn near. But the entrance on La Brea was blocked by the empty chutes and flatbed trucks that had set up to receive the stampeding cattle; when the gate man, old Blowen, sent the firemen to the Olympic entrance, they found it choked with the frantic cattle. None of the equipment, not the red trucks from Los Angeles or the off-red ones from Beverly Hills, could get through.

Thus the fire had to be fought with handheld extinguishers and a makeshift bucket brigade that stretched from the water tank to the burning buildings. In my Moto costume, with sparks like bugs in my hair, I hurled my bucket along with the rest. Futile effort. The leaping flames kept my puny spray well out of range. Since we had no way to fight it, the blaze continued through the day and well into the night. So great was the heat that the branches of the plastic palms on the South Seas set melted off the trunks of their trees. The soundstage and the western town, as well as the cutting room, had been consumed. The roofs of the commissary and the studio garage were destroyed. The losses, as Louella reported in her next day's column, were expected to amount to over six and a half million dollars, which, as everyone knew, was far more than the total profits of both units since the founding of Granite Films. Of the body of Hank Sumner, who had been undone by his neckwear as surely as the famed Isadora Duncan had been destroyed by hers, they had been able to find only a few charred bones.

''Poor Tinkles!'' Loewenstein sobbed, *though his tears added but a mite to the sea of sorrow in which he was about to drown. Now he had all the water anyone would need to douse a blaze, whether the real one at Granite or the re-creation, by Selznick, of the burning of Atlanta. More irony! Another splendid joke! Perhaps it was convulsions of laughter that sent Lorre, like a yo-yo on an invisible string, up through the pitch-black waters to the ocean surface. Like a buoy, or balsa, he bobbed. He opened one eye. Above him, through the night fog, several stars floated on a sea of their own. If only he could be as peaceful, as serene, as they. He accepted his fate. He desired it, with its darkness, its oblivion, its freedom from pain. In resignation, he spread his arms to make the final descent. Alas, pale and buoyant, he floated like a piece of lard atop a bowl of baked beans.*

"Oops! Pardon! Entschuldigung!" *gulped the nonswimmer, who, perhaps because he had consumed precisely those legumes for lunch, now emitted a jet of flatulence into the otherwise calm Pacific. That was enough to upset his equilibrium; like a stricken steamship, the* SS Loewenstein-Lorre *slipped once more beneath the waves.*

At long last my racing thoughts caught up to the present: the evening of December 23, 1940. Rudolph Von Beckmann was having a party at his house in Venice—not the one in Italy, the one in California. He had invited several of us from Granite Films for a late-night meal. Miss Hudson and I had driven to the beach together in her green Plymouth coupe. We parked on Ozone Avenue and walked by the sagging houses—they looked as if they were made of little more than tarpaper and wood—that lined both sides of Speedway. Von Beckmann's place was more substantial, three stories of brick with curtains at the windows. When we rang the bell, the host himself ushered us into the foyer. Rochelle said, "Are we late for dinner? I could eat a horse!"

"No, no," said Von Beckmann, kissing her hand. "We shall eat later on." Then the impresario turned to me. "But where are the Granites? I thought you would be driving together."

"The Granites? They're coming in the limousine. Miss Hudson and I, we wanted, you know, to be alone."

Just then a faint sound of coughing floated down from the floor above. Rudi put a finger to his lips. "I have a friend upstairs. He is suffering from a slight fever. Let's not disturb him. This way, through here—"

So saying, the director led us into another room, where several guests had already assembled. Von B began the introductions.

"Miss Rochelle Hudson, here is Reynaldo Flatow, from Vienna, and here is Sampson Frank, my oldest colleague—we have worked together since our first film, about Jesus. And our film about Moses."

Of course I had worked with both men myself. The actress, curtsying in the sheath of her sequined, silvery gown, said she was charmed. Now the Epstein twins rose from chairs in the corner. "Do you know why there are so many pictures about Moses?" asked Julie, as he shook hands.

"Sure," said Phil, also making his greetings. "*Because he looks so good in the rushes!*"

"Ha-ha-ha!" boomed Ernie Glickman, whose upper lip turned inside out. "That's a good one, boys!"

"I don't understand," said Miss Hudson. "Is it a joke?"

From the back of the room came a sound, like a wheezing radiator. "Coco!" I cried, and spun round to see the wounded director. He was sitting upright in a wheelchair, with a thick bandana, a kind of cloth napkin, around his neck. "Good evening, Peter," he said in a high, squeaking voice, like the note that comes from a bosun's pipe.

Miss Hudson, leaning over to embrace him, addressed the director by his given name. "Shhh. You don't have to talk. I'm so glad to see you, Eugene."

Behind the wheelchair, in the role of a nurse-companion, stood Lizzie, the script girl. Her red hair was calmer than usual, and her blue dress, long-sleeved, came up to her neck. She welcomed us with a smile.

Von B took a puff on the cigarette that lay in the web of his fingers. "You asked about the dinner arrangements, Miss Hudson. They are in the hands of our friends Herr Frank and Herr Flatow."

I took a better look at the two refugees. Each of the gentlemen wore an old suit and tie, in the case of Flatow a bow tie, with a handkerchief in the breast pocket and a stiff white collar around the neck. The dark material of these outfits was worn in some places to a shine and elsewhere had been eaten by moths. Threads stuck up from the seams. Hard not to smile upon seeing that the pant cuffs of the writer were rolled up over his calves and those of the actor were pinned to the same height.

The former, Flatow, removed his glasses, in which his eyeballs seemed to be trapped, and wiped the thick lenses with his handkerchief. "We'll do our best," he said.

Frank said, "If we don't starve first."

"They fooled us," said Flatow. "They said this was the land of plenty."

One of the Epsteins said, "Plenty of hunger."

The other added, "You aren't the only ones to find that out."

Coco, in his corner, gasped so hard with the giggles that Liz had to pat him gently on the back. Glickman haw-hawed, snapping his nonexistent suspenders. "I get it!" cried Rochelle. The twins looked at each other and simultaneously threw up their hands.

Sampson Frank sitting down was as tall as Flatow was standing. "Yes, we found that out," he declared. "How do I spend my time? Daytime and nighttime are occupied with thoughts of food. *Kalbshirn im Muscheln*, for instance. My dear Reynaldo, do you remember the way they served the calves' brains? In scallop shells?"

"*Ja, ja*," Flatow replied. "But what I can't get out of my mind, it's like an obsession, are *Leberknödel*—the livers, the milk, the butter and onions. Oh, these little balls!"

"Hey," said the actress. "What are they talking about? I'm in the dark."

Glickman said, "It's different things they eat."

Frank: "I have an obsession, as well. A good hearty *Tafelspitz*. My friends, you have not lived until you have had this dish at Meissl und Schadn's. This is an establishment in Vienna. Twenty-four different cuts. Mahler used to order the *Kruspelspits*, number sixteen, and Richard Strauss had only to walk in the door and they would start to boil a *Riedeckel*, which was number two."

"True! Absolutely true!" Flatow exclaimed. "The secret of that establishment was that they fed their herd on sugar beets and molasses. That's why the meat was so sweet."

"Once I ate upstairs," added Frank. "On the second floor, you see, the horseradish is mixed with whipped cream."

Von Beckmann, who was now squatting halfway up the staircase, sucked on the stub of his cigarette. "To think I have been associated for so many years with two such fools! You are like those freezing Arctic explorers—they believed they could warm their bodies with thoughts of food."

Flatow: "No one is freezing in California, Rudi. Here we are at the end of December, temperature Fahrenheit sixty degrees."

The impresario ground out his Virginia. "If only you *were* in California. But you have never left the continent of Europe. I know what's in your heads. Liver dumplings! Calves' brains! And Bayreuth and the Wienerwald and the waltzes of Strauss. Don't you understand that this is nostalgia for a land that no longer exists? It never existed! The books we wrote, the music we played, the productions we mounted, and our newspapers, publishing houses, the great emporiums—they were all a gigantic misunderstanding. We never had a childhood. Our boyhood friends are now our bitter foes. If we attempted to share memories, to express ourselves in a common language, they would rip our tongues from our mouths. Our kneepants and high socks have turned into a prisoner's striped pajamas. Do you doubt me? Take an airplane trip. Ride on a steamship. Return to the streets of your youth. By all means do not fail to visit Meissl und Schadn's. They have a new cut. *Judenfleisch.* Number twenty-five."

In the shocked silence that followed it was possible to hear, through the open window, from the nearby beach, the thump of the breaking waves and even the hiss of the foam as one after the other they expired upon the sand. The tide, it seemed, was rising.

Then the doorbell rang. Flatow, bending to pick up one of the buckets that was piled in the corner of the room, went to answer it. We could hear him introduce himself to the newcomers. Then he said, "I hope you will excuse me. I must see if our dinner has arrived." As he went out, the new guests came in. They crossed the foyer to join us.

Here were the Granite brothers. Manfred, by way of greeting, shot his wrist from his cuff and checked his watch. "Look at the time. Already ten o'clock! I told Arthur to stop at all of Burton's haunts. We must have been to every nightclub in town. I don't know where the boy is. Hey—!" Here the studio president whirled round, pointing his finger at the Epsteins. "What are *you* two doing here?"

"Well," said Phil, "I thought we were invited for dinner."

Julie: "But now we're not so sure."

"What do you think of liver dumplings? Or *Kruspelspits*?"

"*Kruspelspits*? I don't know. I think they're against my religion."

Manfred's entire head looked as if it had been splashed by red paint. "What is this? What's going on? You two are off the lot. I fired you two months ago."

"I know, I know. It's the *Leberknödel.* Who could resist?"

Manfred turned to Von Beckmann, pointing a finger up toward his face. "Listen to me. These boys are poison. I'm not talking about wisecracks. I'm talking about un-American behavior. I happen to know they're about to be called up before the Dies Committee. Then we'll see who gets the last laugh."

Julie: "Oh, we've already heard from the committee. We got their questionnaire."

"That's right," put in Phil. "There were just two questions."

Julie: *"Are you now or have you ever been a member of a subversive organization?"*

Phil: *"If so, name that organization."*

"Good," said Manfred. "It's about time. Let's see how you wriggle out of that one."

"What do you mean?" said Phil. "We certainly have no such intention."

"In fact, we've already filled out the questionnaire."

"To question number one, about belonging to a subversive organization, we answered *Yes*."

"All right," said Manfred. "At least you were honest."

Julie: "And to question number two we answered, *Granite Films*."

Von Beckmann put up his hand to stop the burst of laughter. "I invited these gentlemen here. I want them to work on our new script when we resume."

Manfred: "Resume? Resume what?"

"Why, our film about the American West."

"What? The Moto picture? *Mr. Moto Wins His Spurs*?"

Von B smiled. He lit a new cigarette. "We must find a new title, I think."

"You must be crazy," Manfred declared. "The B unit is completely destroyed. Every building is down. We're out of the B-picture business."

Music to Moto! I approached the director. "It's true, Rudi. All of us have started to look for other work. I've been talking to Warners. You know, about *Maltese Falcon*."

"But I am not thinking of a B picture," Von Beckmann replied. "I have prepared a budget of two million dollars."

"Two million?" Manfred shouted. "Why not three? Why not ten? Why not a billion?"

But Miss Hudson was delighted. She took a little hop like a schoolgirl and clapped her hands. "Oh, this is wonderful. It's the break I've been waiting for all my life!"

Coco signaled to Lizzie to wheel his chair forward. When he spoke, the words came out accompanied by a rush of air, the way music does from a flute. "Rudi, I think I will be able to serve as your frog, the way I did for poor Tinkles. I won't be in this chair much longer."

Von B smiled down from his perch on the stairs. "Good. I had hoped to make you both part of my production."

At this Manfred made a choking sound, as if he'd swallowed something down the wrong pipe. Victor, cupping an elbow in one hand, his chin in the other, finally spoke up. "You haven't grasped the situation, Rudi. Things are very grave. It's not just the B unit. We've lost the capacity to produce A films, as well. I don't think we'll be able to shoot on the lot for—well, for almost a year."

"Who said anything about the lot? I think you should know that a short time ago our colleague from Berlin, Herr Lang, drove me to the state of Nevada to see a true ghost town. Pandaemonium, it's called. It was built in the center of a meteor crater, right above the meteor itself. Everything there— the mine shaft, the buildings, even the furniture inside the hotel—has been dried by the desert air. Imagine, if you can, an entire town that has been made from petrified wood. I am going to take Miss Hudson and Mr. Good- heart and the entire crew to that spot. We do not need the soundstages of Granite Films. We do not require your buildings or your labs. The sets that have already been filmed we can re-create on location. So. Do we understand one another? I have a paper here. A contract. Mr. Glickman will be the witness. Manfred, will you be the first to sign?"

Manfred's face had turned so red it looked as if it were being photo- graphed through a number 9 gel. "Do you think I've lost my mind? That I'll let you take a production into the desert? Do you have any idea of the costs? You have to feed people. You have to send the rushes back to the studio every day. What happens if somebody gets sick? If it rains? When the actors throw tantrums? I'd rather put an army into the field than have those kinds of headaches."

"But Manfred, my dear," Von B said sweetly, "what choice have you? We all heard what Victor said. You will make this picture or there will be no picture at all."

"That's an exaggeration. We're going to have the A unit up sooner than anyone thinks. All we have to do is collect the insurance."

"Insurance? Am I in error? Are there not some problems with insur- ance?"

"There aren't any problems. I had Kahn check it out. Every premium was paid on time."

Here Von B took a scrap of newsprint from his pocket. Everyone in the room recognized that it was from the *Examiner*. "The difficulty is not with the premiums. Perhaps you missed yesterday's paper—?"

"I read the goddamned paper," Manfred growled.

But Von Beckmann, holding the sheet up to his monocle, read nonetheless.

> "It's all hush-hush-hush at Granite but it seems that the big blaze that destroyed so much Hollywood history might not have been an accident after all. Over at the insurance company everybody's as tight-lipped as that curly-headed Marx Brother, but I've learned in an exclusive that the investigators have turned up evidence of arson, including—"

"That bitch doesn't know her ass from a hole in the ground," shouted Manfred. "They didn't find anything!"

Von B did not miss a beat.

> "—including rags soaked with gasoline and holes in the hoses of the antiquated fire wagon. There is even suspicion that someone deliberately gave a signal that started the cattle on what turned out to be their deadly stampede."

At these words I broke into such a sweat that the back of my jacket and the seat of my pants were immediately soaked through, as if the unknown arsonist had doused me with kerosene. Kerosene! The lamps! The start of the fire! I looked around. For some reason all eyes were upon me.

"Maybe we should open a window," said Ernie Glickman. "It smells like nuts."

"It's already open," said Sampson Frank.

Manfred strode toward me, his hands balled into fists. "If someone set that fire, I'd like to get my hands on the son-of-a-bitch. He's guilty of murder!"

"Ha-ha! *Man who plays with fire sometimes gets burned*. Moto Motto."

Von Beckmann held up his hands. "Really, Manfred. I don't know why you are carrying on. It's not such a mystery. This will not be the first time a man burned down his own property for the sake of insurance."

"I don't have to listen to this! Come on, Victor. We're getting out of here."

But Victor did not budge. He stood in his familiar pose, the sole of his right shoe crossed over the shoe on the left. He still kept his chin cupped in his hand. "Rudi, I will be frank. I have seen every picture you made in Europe. Again and again my breath was taken from me. Indeed, the pity is, in my opinion, that you left films at all. Ah, if only we had such a record of your plays! I have also seen the rushes of *Spurs*. Oh, I know the work, the real work, was yours, not Sumner's. I am struck with admiration. Rochelle, Peter, Chandler—their performances have been beyond anything we could have hoped. But as head of production I have more than artistic responsibilities. Can even your vision—very well, allow me to say it: your genius—transform this script and this cast and crew into a production that justifies a budget of two million dollars—or half, or a quarter, of that sum?"

"It's a joke," muttered Manfred, who had already moved into the foyer. "We can't raise a dime."

Von B : "There have already been changes in the script. The Epsteins will make many more. As for the cast, there will be changes as well. I want Laughton, to start with. He will play the sheriff. I want Cooper—"

"*Gary* Cooper?" Miss Hudson exclaimed. "I'm going to play opposite Gary Cooper?"

Victor waved her to silence. "Even if we could get them," he responded, "and I don't think we can, we couldn't spend anything like what you're asking. It's twice as much as any picture has cost us before. I'm sorry to say— and I *am* sorry, believe me—that the answer must be no."

"Do not be sorry. You will change your mind."

"Yeah?" said Manfred. "What makes you think that?"

"The fact that I have finished the list of those I will add to the cast."

"Okay, who?"

"Fräulein Mezaray."

"Magda!" gasped Victor.

The Queen B stepped forward in her metallic dress. "Well, you can forget about your deal, then. We all heard what Basserman said at that banquet. She's dead as a doornail."

"Is that so?" asked Von Beckmann as he reached into his other pocket for a clipping. "Who then is performing in this UFA feature?"

Victor had gone pale—that is to say, his swarthy skin had turned the color of scraped toast. "Is it true? Is it Magda?"

"See for yourself. This is the *Deutsche Zeitung.* She is to star in a film with Jannings. *Liebe auf den ersten Blicke.* Allow me to translate for Miss Hudson: *Love at First Sight.* Apparently the Third Reich makes B pictures, too."

Victor snatched the newsprint from Rudi's hand. "I never thought she was dead! I swear it. There were times—because I thought I could hear her, her words, her thoughts: at those moments I thought I must be losing my mind. Sometimes, at night, I was sure I was dreaming her dreams!"

Rochelle: "So what? Huh? So what if she's alive? She won't leave. She wouldn't do it even when you went to wherever she was and begged her in person."

Von B: "Well, Victor, Mr. Glickman is holding the contract. Will you be the first to sign?"

"If Magda were to appear, of course I would. We could finance the picture on her name alone. On the reunion of the two of you. But I fear Rochelle is right. I did beg for her return. Twice. She refused both times. How can we know that they will allow her to leave—or, if they do, that she will agree to come?"

"Forgive me, but there is a difference between your request to her and mine. In any case, the choice may not be entirely Magda's. Granite Films still has more properties in Europe that our old friend Goebbels desires; and Goebbels, in Magdalena Mezaray, has a property that is sought by Granite Films. You'll see—we can do business. If old Alexander could negotiate my release, he can do the same for Magda's."

Victor wrung his hands in despair. "Our father—you saw how he is. He can't go to Europe. Neither could you. They would throw you back in the camp."

"That may be so. That is why Herr Lorre will go. Magda will listen to him. Especially if he has a message from me. In return you'll release him from his Granite contract."

Had I heard Rudi correctly? Joyfully I whirled about, so that a gown of moisture swirled around me like the spray from a garden hose. "Done! It's done! Goodbye, Mr. Moto! Sayonara to the sleuth!"

"Out of the question!" Manfred bellowed. "We need him more than ever. I've already bought the rights to a brand-new feature. *Mr. Moto Meets the Sphinx.* Eh? How about that?"

Von B turned to the younger Granite. "Victor, I warn you. Do not make difficulties where none exist. Do not hesitate. After all, if Herr Basserman was right, if Magdalena is truly in danger, our efforts might yet save her life."

"Boy," said Ernie Glickman. "And I thought I knew how to bargain."

"All right," said Victor, taking the contract from the agent. "I am signing with a condition. That Magda is released and that she play the lead in our new feature western."

"The lead? *Magda?* What about *me?* Petey! Tell them! I'm signed for Annie—Annie Harwood! It's my chance to be a star!" With that the Queen B fell upon me, throwing her arms about my neck. Our bellies touched. I felt her breasts, in their tin cups, press against my damp nipples. But my head was still reeling from Manfred's revelation. "*Sphinx?*" I echoed. "*Stinx.*"

"Oh, shut up, you idiot!"

Von B: "Miss Hudson, do not be upset. Remain with us, please. I can guarantee you another part."

But the Queen B was already headed for the door. "*Another part!* I like that—*another part!* If you don't think I've got rights, you've got another think coming. Ernie, you made that contract. You damn well better make it stick. As for you, you stinkpot"—and here, standing in the entrance to the foyer, Rochelle whirled about to address none other than her sweating swain—"I don't ever want to see you again!" Then, with a click and clack of her heels, the actress crossed the uncarpeted floor.

"Wait! Miss Hudson! Honey!" Slipping in a puddle of my own perspiration, I started after her. Too late. She slammed the door behind her with a bang.

"Now what?" I inquired.

With aplomb Von Beckmann replied. "Now? Well, Victor has signed. Mr. Glickman, will you bring the contract to Manfred? It's his turn."

"Over my dead body!" bellowed Manfred. He threw the paper down. "There won't be any picture! I don't want Magda even if you could get her. And I'll never give that miniature Moto his release!"

But no one was looking at Manfred Granite. Instead, we had all turned to gaze toward the top of the staircase, where a new guest had appeared. That person was wrapped in a sheet and a blanket. Or half wrapped: the bedclothes were over his shoulders, but the front of his body, with the black hair on his chest and his legs and his groin, was exposed. His sexual organ hung down like a sausage in a butcher shop window.

Lizzie, at that sight, let out a scream. The young man shivered. His teeth made an audible chatter. I recognized him. I knew him well. Burton! Manfred's son!

Manfred had recognized him as well. The top of his head looked like a glowing furnace. He thumped his breast once with his fist, as if his heart had stopped and he wished to restart it. Then, with a terrible cry, he flew through the air and fastened his hands around the throat of Rudolph Von Beckmann.

"Blackmailer! You want to blackmail me with my son!"

The two men fell to the floor. For a moment Lizzie and Victor, Glickman and Sampson Frank, stood appalled. Manfred, meanwhile, his arms locked straight, his fingers spread in a death grip on his antagonist's windpipe, choked the life from his victim.

Then the two Epsteins sprang forward. One took Manfred by the back of his jacket. The other seized his arms. Together they hauled the madman to his feet.

Said Julie, "You didn't know I was a professional boxer, eh? Three fights. Right after Penn State."

"Yeah?" said Phil, panting a little. "What was your record?"

"Two wins," said Julie, still with a hammerlock on his former employer. "One draw."

"Why'd you quit?"

"I wanted to retire undefeated."

Manfred wrenched himself free. He moved away. He turned to the wall. "I don't mind the sex part, the animal part. Two men in the dark, two animals in the dark—what is the difference? It is the human condition, for Christ's sake. Sad, okay. Okay, pathetic. What I can't bear is the idea of two men kissing mouth to mouth. That means there's *feeling*. It turns my stomach!" Here Manfred gestured toward Rudi. "The man has lips like a camel!"

Von Beckmann did not reply. He merely held out his pen to the eldest of the Granite brothers. Manfred took it.

Meanwhile, I had started from the room. When I reached the foyer I looked back over my shoulder. Manfred stood, head hanging. "Louella's going to find out about you two. She's uncanny, the way she finds out everything. *Guess who's gazing into each other's eyes?* That's what the bitch will write in her column. *You'll be surprised to hear who was at Ciro's. Holding hands!*"

Then, stepping through the doorway, all I could hear was the scratch-scratch-scratch of the gold-tipped pen.

The long agony of *the nonswimmer was coming to an end. Loewen-stein-Lorre had become so waterlogged, or had swallowed so many gallons of the Pacific, that he could no longer rise. For a brief spell he simply hung sus-*

pended, midway between the surface and the muddy bottom, where scavengers creeped and crawled. Ancient galleons, he'd heard, could float this way for eons after they had gone down with their treasure in the Sargasso Sea. Time now, in the last seconds remaining to him, for the truth. The fact was, the loss of his hopes for Maltese Falcon, *the suspicion of arson, of murder, the ruin of his reputation—none of these things, nor all of them taken together, had caused him to plunge into the briny deep. It was what had happened next, with Miss Hudson.*

At the thought of that anguished actress, the actor felt a terrible pang— worse than a pang: a searing pain struck him, not, as one would suppose, in his heart or even his lungs, but in the flesh of his buttocks. A shark! thought Peter Lorre. He was being eaten alive!

Immediately after leaving Rudi's house on Speedway, I'd trotted back toward Ozone Avenue. My hope was to intercept Rochelle Hudson before she could drive away. But to mixed feelings of relief and dismay, I found that the little green Plymouth was parked where we had left it, with no sign of the actress anywhere about. I retraced my steps along Speedway, past Navy and Kinney and Ashland, toward Ocean Park Pier. The bright lights of the concessions blinked up ahead. Crowds were pouring out of the late-night shows at the Rosemary Theater and the Dome. A bitter thought struck me: soon, along with *Partners of the Plains*—that was the Hopalong Cassidy feature displayed on the billboards—there would be six more Moto pictures to draw in the eager throngs. No end to it! Agent infinity!

Still no sign of the Queen B. I was beginning to worry. I knew she was distraught at losing the part of Annie. Was it possible that in her disappointment, her torment, she might do something rash? "Miss Hudson!" I called, standing on tiptoe. "Where are you?" I trotted along the boardwalk, with its honky-tonk attractions: the Skee-Ball machines, the rolling barrel, the House of Mirrors. I passed the merry-go-round, a whirl, in reflecting mirrors, of color and light. The music in the center came from real instruments, piccolos and trumpets and cymbals, played by unseen musicians, like a band in a picture by Disney. The triple thump of the drum echoed the boom-boom-boom of my own troubled heart. Next was the penny arcade, where a brown wooden gypsy in a glass cage promised over and over to tell my fortune. Did she know where Rochelle might be? I tarried a moment, watching a boy in short pants attempt to grasp, also over and over, a wristwatch in the fingers of a mechanical claw. A feeling of hopelessness clutched my throat, with a far firmer grip. Had the Queen B decided to escape this vale of illusion and vanity and pain?

Just then, when my thoughts had turned most dire, I spied the actress. With one hand she was dangling a french fry over her open mouth, the way an Englishman from the gentry will eat an asparagus spear; and with the other she was pulling the lever on a horseracing machine. The darling! So like a little girl! Playfully, I snuck up behind her and gave her a squeeze.

"Hey! What's the big idea?" She wheeled round to face me. "I was betting on Gallant Fox!"

I pulled her toward me, away from the flashing machine. "Never mind. Come with me. I have something for you."

She put her arm through mine. "We never got anything to eat at that party. What a gyp. Buy me some sugar corn?"

Of a sudden I realized that I was ravenous, too. I bought her the caramelized popcorn and, as we strolled down the boardwalk, watched with pleasure as she turned each little piece around in her hands, like a squirrel with a nut. Couldn't I, a small, pale man, and a little pudgy too, be thought of as just such a white, exploded kernel? How delicious to be pecked at, adjusted this way and that, and then popped into that warm pink mouth. My perspiration came bubbling out, like the colored streams from the fountain at Santa Monica and Wilshire.

"Miss Hudson, come this way. I'll give you a special treat."

"I'm still hungry. What about corn on the cob?"

I bought her that, too, and watched impatiently as she ate the buttery stick like a person from another planet, nipping vertically instead of on a line.

"This way. This way. It won't take more than a minute."

"Oh, Petey, for heaven's sake!"

I drew her away from the crowds, into the shadows. Dubiously, she followed. Then I turned and faced the wall of an abandoned building. I spread my arms against it, like a suspect in a crime. "Go on," I told her. "You know what to do."

"Petey, *honestly!* There are people."

"Everybody's having a good time. No one will notice."

"Oh, all right. But don't take all night."

She stepped up behind me and thrust her right hand into my trouser pocket. I could feel, against my torso, the weight of her bosoms, as heavy as a mountaineer's backpack. Her hand, with its sharpened nails, trod along my thigh.

"Gosh, Petey, you smell like an Almond Joy."

"It's not me. It's the hair oil. Ha-ha. Wildroot."

"There's nothing there. I can't feel a thing."

"A little more. There! Almost! A little deeper."

"Uh-oh. What's this?"

"Why don't you take it out and see?"

She did so, balancing the pretty little package on the palm of her hand. "A present!" she exclaimed. "Is this for Christmas?"

"No, not for Christmas. Open it, why don't you?"

She did that, too, snatching at the ribbon, the bow, the shiny blue paper. Then she opened the box and stared—I turned round, wanting to see her expression—at the glittering band upon the plush. "Oh, Petey! A diamond! A diamond ring!"

"Ha! Ha! The hardest substance known to man."

"Oh! Oh! Isn't it beautiful? And look how it fits!"

"So does that mean it's all right and everything?"

"It's perfect! It's like it was made for me!"

"So you will?"

"Will what?"

"You know. Marry me, Miss Hudson."

There was a pause. The Queen B stood like a statue, with her hand upraised, so that the sixteen carats sparkled in the stray beams of light. She was like the goddess at the start of a Columbia picture. Then she put both hands on her hips.

"*Marry* you? Marry *you*? Are you kidding? Ah, ha-ha-ha! Ah, ha-ha!"

Her laughter rang out over the boardwalk. It drowned out the sound of the sideshow barkers and even the screams from those coming over the top of the loop-the-loop.

I grinned too, wiping my dripping brow. Then I drew a quarter from my pocket and put it into a nearby machine. "Ha-ha. I feel like a Pronto Pup."

Out came the hot dog, encased in dough, like a full-scale version of a cocktail wiener. Miss Hudson's laughter did not stop. It rang in my ears, piercing and high, indistinguishable, finally, from that of the mechanical woman who screeched endlessly in front of the House of Mirrors.

"Here," said the actress. "Take it."

She pushed the box back into my pocket. My heart, which had ceased all activity, gave a tentative thump when I saw that the ring remained on her finger. Did that mean that all was not lost?

"I don't know about you, Peter, but I'm going to bed. Thanks for the sparkler."

She turned on her pointed heel, sharp as a nail, a needle, and walked off to the south. The agent of the International Police remained half in shadow, wiener in hand, so that it was understandable that several passersby thought they had witnessed a man who was exposing himself.

Then the Queen B stopped. She turned around. Tears were streaming down her face. Of self-reproach, perhaps. Or remorse. "*Marry me!*" she shouted, so that people could not help but glance in her direction. "*Marry me!* Ha! Ha! Ha!"

It had taken Peter *Lorre only half an hour to walk from the board-walk at Ocean Park to the tip of Santa Monica Pier. And how long had he been in the water? Another half-hour? The whole of the night? A lifetime? The pain in his buttocks was unbearable now. Why didn't the shark finish him off? If only, like the whale with Jonah, it would swallow him whole. He squirmed round. There was no shark. Nor even a mackerel. Yet the sharp, burning pain only increased with each move he made. He reached back, groping through the murky waters. What was this? A fishhook! And a fishing line! He was hooked!*

Bit by bit the taut line hauled its catch to the surface. Lorre thrashed there like a bluefish before it is hauled into the net. From above him, at the edge of the pier, a voice said, "Oh, fuck! Will you look at this?"

It was the old fisherman. The one who had spat at his feet. After all, he had had good luck. In spite of everything, a strong feeling—it was determination, it was hope, it was almost like joy—surged through the body of Loewenstein-Lorre. "Help! Help me, sir! I want to live!"

The old-timer spoke through his beard. "Then get off my line and get out of the water."

Lorre, desperate now, beat the sea about him to a foamy froth. "No, no! Don't you see? I can't swim!"

The fisherman spat again, this time from disgust. "What's the matter with you? Just stand up. The water here isn't three feet deep."

"What?" said Peter Lorre, but already he was feeling downward with his stockinged toes. They sank into the mud. Streaming water, he rose upright. The Pacific Ocean came only to his waist.

Within minutes I had put on my jacket and shoes, reclaimed my watch and my wallet, and was walking southward along the deserted streets. In a little while I came once more to the amusements at Ocean Park. The bright lights at the concessions were off, as were those at the Rosemary and Dome. Like Hopalong on the poster, I limped by the pier. No music now, no loop-the-loop. The laughing lady at the House of Mirrors had fallen mute. Gallant Fox had run his last race.

On I went, in my squelching shoes, until I had retraced my steps to Speedway. What I saw next made my breath catch in my throat. The Plymouth coupe! Still parked on Ozone Avenue! I lifted my head, listening. All I could hear was the slap of the onrushing waves. Could it be possible that my worst fears had come true? Had the poor girl, crazed with regret, decided to end her life? After all, if I had decided to kill myself for love, why couldn't she?

In terror now, I stumbled across the street and into the first narrow alley that led to the beach. I paused to remove my shoes and roll up my pant cuffs. Then, with my heart in my mouth, I gazed over the desolate strand. No corpse, not even a hunk of driftwood, had been thrown onto the shore. What could I do but keep looking? On I plodded, for an hour, and then an hour after that. Still a third hour went by. Not even Magellan, I thought, had gone on such a journey.

"Miss Hudson! *Hola!*"

The only answer was the *ow-ow-ow* of a passing gull and the mindless thump and crash of the waves. There was, however, one change: the last of the nighttime mist had now lifted. The whole sky, I noted, was filled with stars. The Big Dipper. The Little Dipper, too. A full moon tugged at the incoming tide. Seaward, a line of light, like a drawn line of chalk, marked the breaking waves. I could feel their concussion beneath the bare soles of my feet. I trudged on, the black strands of seaweed clinging to my ankles. Then, from the darkness ahead, I thought I heard voices. A cry. A laugh. A shout. What was that before my eyes? Dark shapes, silhouettes, were moving along the shore. Were they human beings? A strange metallic light seemed to come from under their feet. Through all my veins and arteries the blood raced round and round. I broke into a loping trot.

I saw soon enough that I had not been mistaken. Those were people ahead. They were dashing in and out of the swirling foam. Spellbound, I drew closer. What made my breath catch in my throat was the way their legs seemed to be lost in puddles of molten metal. It was as if some giant, a great philanthropist, had strewn the beach with silver dollars, or as if the ocean itself, like an enormous gaming machine, was disgorging a fortune in coins. The figures, the shadows of men, were bending, standing, bending again; greedily they stuffed their pockets, their shirtfronts, the very sleeves of their coats. Flakes of silver, like silver plating, rubbed off onto their clothes. The beings were beginning to glow in the night.

"Hey, this is terrific!"

I knew that voice. Ernie Glickman!

"I cannot believe my eyes. My senses. Such a thing is *wunderbar*!"

I knew that voice, too. Reynaldo Flatow, the Viennese playwright.

"We don't have this in Europe. This is a phenomenon only of the New World."

And that was Sampson Frank. Yes, I could see his flashlight stabbing up and down. There was a glint of light: the spokes of the wheels of Coco Goodheart's chair. And there was Lizzie beside him. They were all on the beach! Both of the Granite brothers. The Epsteins. Everyone! Then, a little further away, I made out the unmistakable shape of Rudolph Von Beckmann. And who was that with him? Holding on to his arm? An answer to a prayer: Rochelle Hudson!

With a gleeful smile, I continued toward them; upon reflection, however, I slackened my pace and in a moment or two came to a halt. There I remained, with my hair still damp with seawater and both hands inside my sodden pockets. Soon the waves advanced around me. In no time my own feet were surrounded by gasping fish. Flopping and squirming, they burrowed into the sand. I wasn't quite sure what, beneath the brine, the seaweed, I smelled; it might be the eggs, the sperm, of the spawning grunion. Then Rochelle turned. She waved her hand, the one with the ring that sparkled like fire.

"Oh, Petey, look," she said. She pointed—away from the beach, away from the heaving silvery lava, and up to the sky. There the moon had inched itself further into the heavens. How large it loomed. How bright. Upon its surface was an etching of a face. Suddenly I understood what Miss Hudson wished to say: here was the god or the goddess who had driven all those on earth into such frenzy.

GHOST TOWN

August–October 1941

SCREENING

Dust, a cloud of it, hung above the bone-white plain. It was moving slowly from right to left. Was it a tornado? A thunderhead? The next instant desert sand flew by, as if viewed from a magic carpet. Quickly the mystery was solved: the dust was caused by a wagon train—no, one wooden wagon pulled by a score of mules. On flew the carpet, closer and closer, until it came to a halt in the very midst of the cloud. Directly ahead were the mules, short, squat, straining, like the team in the ads for Borax. White alkali powder had settled on the animals in patches and streaks. It clung to their muzzles like foam on a mad dog's mouth. Up on the box the driver's beard had turned all snowy. The man beside him, riding shotgun, had a bandana over his face. His eyebrows looked like spun sugar.

Now the escort, four, six, eight men on horses, galloped by, kicking up a chalky exhaust of their own. They were racing toward a hump in the road ahead.

"Ho! You mules!" cried the driver, cracking his whip along the animals' flanks.

The poor beasts, striped like zebras, hurled themselves against their traces, trying to create enough momentum to carry them up the steep incline. The hacking cough of the mules, the thud of their hooves, and the squeal of the unoiled wheels were mingled together. At the top of the rise, the wagon came to a halt. A third passenger, a rifleman—he was played by Sampson Frank, the European actor—polished an old-fashioned telescope, like a sea captain's glass, on his shirt; he put the instrument to his eye.

Rifleman's point of view: to the rear, well in the distance, snow-covered mountaintops, which looked as if they too had been dipped in a pot of alkali.

To the north and south the desert stretched away like the surface of a glassy sea. Ahead, however, dipping down from the crest of the thrust-up ridge, lay an enormous basin, baking in the noonday sun. The white salts, not stationary at all, shifted about in the wind. In places the earth underneath was swept bare, momentarily revealing a maze of crevices and cracks that made the surface of the vast dish look, through the magnifying lens, like the glaze on an antique piece of ovenware.

Cut to a black bird, a buzzard or hawk, hovering overhead. If only these men, with their puny instrument, had been able to see with an eagle's eye, they would have realized that the line of the ridge which seemed to stretch off beneath them in a straight line was in fact curved and made a great circle miles across. The wagon was perched at the edge of a crater, the very spot where a comet had struck the earth, sending out this single ripple, like a seismic wave that had frozen in the once molten rock.

"Whatcher see there, Jackie?" the mule master called out to the man with the glass.

"Wouldn't you like a look?" the rifleman responded. "I seen this show before. In the city of Cincinnati. All you got to do is turn her around in front of the light."

The mule master said, "Give it here for a look-see." He seized the spyglass and squinted into the eyepiece. "Hoo-eee! There she be. Doing the hula dance."

Now the man riding shotgun pulled down his bandana and grinned. His teeth, an ordinary white, turned grayish against his powdered skin. "Henry, you hand her over. You mean that gal's got a skirt of grass?"

Henry, the mule master, handed the tube to his partner. The latter put down his weapon and lifted the telescope to his eye. "I don't see no Sandwich Island girl."

Jack laughed. "Sure you do. Just turn her around. That's what gives her the shakes."

Henry: "Faster. Give her a spin. Look how she jiggles them hips. Look— this is the way her arms go, see, like snakes, kinda swaying." The mule master dropped the reins and held his arms shoulder high, making them undulate in the air. The two men, Jack and Henry, roared as their companion rotated the spyglass without effect.

There was a whistle and a neigh. The crowded two-shot expanded to take in the mounted escort. They were waving the wagon ahead. Impossible not to wonder what was so valuable about this cargo. There was surely a hint in the shape of the container; that is, the wagon itself was nothing more than an enormous barrel laid on its side, so that the great metal hoops stretched up from below, like the ribs on the keel of an ark. The joints between the staves seemed to be slathered with pitch, and these planks formed not a circle but a half-crushed cylinder, like the tank of a modern truck—from Chevron, from Shell—for carrying gas.

But there was no petroleum here. Automobiles were a generation off, and the first oil well was yet to be drilled. Not liquid gold, then, but clearly worth its weight in the precious metal—hence the crack of the whip, the urgency and haste; and hence, too, the escort, which was calling out to those on the wagon. They were like ghosts, bandanas over their faces and white-washed head to toe. They waved their arms and started off, stringing out over the sun-baked earth. The wagon followed. Slowly the entire party began to grow smaller as it advanced toward the center of the dish. Soon the various sounds faded away. Heat rose palpably off the crazed surface, not so much in waves as in pulsing balls of light. Thus the wagon and its crew, fading from view, seemed to pass through the beads of an Oriental curtain. Vanished. Gone.

A voice, it was Victor Granite's, rose in the darkened room. "I hope everyone here will remember this moment. Why? Because after it the history of motion pictures will never be the same."

"I'll remember it, all right." The speaker was his brother, Manfred. He sat in the first row of the screening room, his arms on the rests of the brass-studded leather seat. "Because it's Granite Films that's about to become history. Have you any idea of the money that went into this scene? Kahn! Read him the figures. That wagon was handmade. You could buy a Stradi-varius for what it cost. At least a fiddle plays a tune."

In the dimmed light it looked like a swarm of fireflies were tumbling down Victor's shirtfront. He spoke around the Chesterfield in his mouth. "Don't think about music. Think about art. From that first moment, when we are flying over the ground, we are presented with a series of paintings. We are not in a theater, we are in a museum. There has never been anything like it."

"What are you talking about? Some big expert! Do you think that's the first shot taken from an airplane? I've flown the cameras myself."

"The beauty of the scene lies in the fact that it was *not* shot from the air. Rudi must have set up twenty cameras. No! That's my error. You don't have to shout about the expense, Manfred. There was only one camera. But he moved it to twenty different locations, so that with each shot we leap ahead, we stride magically forward in our seven-league boots."

"But our business is to make *motion* pictures." That was Lester Kahn, who sat two rows above the Granite president.

Manfred chimed in. "If we wanted paintings we could hire Picasso."

"We already have," Victor said with a laugh. "The point is, these positions were not in a line. They were set off from each other so that as we approach the wagon train we see the animals and the men and the turning wheels from a variety of jumbled angles. Doesn't that remind you of Braque? Of Picasso? I am attacked by pangs of envy. The man has created cubism with a camera."

"Quiet!" said Manfred. "Now what's going on?"

Up on the screen the same mules and men were reemerging from the folds of heat. On they came, sending up their funnel of dust. In the distance, more tornadoes appeared, twisting and whirling behind them like dervishes of salt and sand.

"My God," murmured Victor.

"Indians," said Kahn. "Apaches!"

Naturally, the men of the escort had seen them, too. They bent low over their horses, urging them on. Those on the wagon looked fearfully backward and began to level their guns. The mule master turned his team in a wide arc toward the camera. Hopeless: more warriors poured out of the lower edge of the screen, as if from the audience itself. They shouted and whooped over the sudden clatter of their horses' hooves. The dust devils that spurted behind them swirled over the lens.

For a good half-moment it was impossible to see, through that dust storm, what was occurring. Then, when the blowing sand settled, it became clear that the wagon had stopped and that the escorts had abandoned their horses and run behind it for protection. Atop their piebald ponies the Indians galloped on.

That's when the white men opened fire. Over the great distance the effect was almost comical: a rattling tattoo, like exploding kernels of corn; and then, boiling up over the flattened top of the cylindrical tank, like popcorn out of a popper or foam from a pint of beer, came thick white clouds of smoke. But the little fusillade had its effect. Two ponies stumbled. One of the Apaches hit the ground. In response the Indians split into two columns and streamed around the ends of the wagon. Immediately the defenders scrambled to the near side of the barrel. Some pressed against its bulging flank, some crouched beneath it on the ground; all kept up a stream of fire. By this time the pursuing natives began to appear out of the clouds of kicked-up alkali and join the throng of attackers. All the Indians circled the wagon, riding around and around, so that the white men behind it could no longer use the cylinder as a shield. It must have been as obvious to them as to those gathered in the screening room that they were doomed.

A voice, unmistakably Victor's, cut through the gloom. "Pay attention to what you are watching. Do you understand that the entire ambush has been photographed from a single location, in one unbroken take? Already it is longer, and finer, than the shot in *Citizen Kane* that everyone overly admires. And it is not yet done."

Far from it. Now four of the besieged escorts made a dash for their horses and, heads down, clinging to the flying manes of their mounts, began a desperate gallop through the ranks of their tormentors. For a moment the Indians looked on, bemused.

"Notice," said Victor, "how the reduction in scale tends to make the action almost comical—which is why, conversely, a closeup is always used when our feelings are meant to be magnified." It was true: on the screen the four fleeing steeds bobbed across the plain in a rocking-horse motion. Eventually the Indians, in a volley as disciplined as that from any white man's army, opened fire. All the riders went down. Above the thrashing limbs one of the animals raised its head and—another effect of Picasso?—let out a bloodcurdling shriek.

Now the Apaches turned their attention to the four horses that remained by the wagon. One after the other the sharpshooters brought them down. No: an error. Those shots were coming from beneath the wagon itself. The escorts were shooting their own mounts! Next they turned their fire on the mules. Odd how the beasts simply stood there, philosophically, while their fellows dropped to the ground or sagged against their traces. To this madness there was a method: the white men hauled the dead animals as best they could into a wall parallel to the tank, thus creating some degree of protection to their rear. From behind both barricades they kept up a steady stream of fire against their foes.

The redskins, undismayed, began to shift the bulk of their forces to the opposite side of the wagon. Still within the unbroken take, what had been a stationary camera moved with them. It tracked in a wide arc about the ambuscade. As it did so, the shooting continued—at least the white men went on blasting away at the Indians, who seemed content for the moment to hold their fire. On the far side of the wagon many of the tribe were deploying themselves like soldiers, almost like British dragoons, some kneeling, others standing behind them, while the late arrivals took aim from atop the backs of their ponies. No one dropped a sword; no one shouted the command. But at some hidden signal the whole tribe opened fire. The volley was aimed high, not at the men but at the wagon. Dozens of bullets raked the wooden tank, sending up a shower of splinters. Under the hail of lead the barrel rocked on its springs like a gigantic cocktail shaker. A second barrage followed and then a third, as if the inanimate cylinder were an enemy of the tribe, some hostile god or totem that could not be killed too many times.

The camera had come to rest among the Indian braves, revealing the feathers in their bonnets, the lightning marks on their cheeks. For the time being the shooting had stopped. The chatter among the natives—part guttural vowels, part clicking laughter—ceased as well. From offscreen came a hiss, a sizzle and splash. The camera, still without cutting, lengthened once more its focal plane. There was the wagon; it had sprung a hundred leaks. The cargo, plain water, shot from it under great pressure. Innumerable jets arced high and away, to be soaked up at once by the dusty ground.

Inside the private theater the viewers stirred with thirst. One or two groaned. No wonder. The sight of the wagon, like a gigantic lawn sprinkler or some machine that is towed through the streets to keep down the dust, would make the sides of any man's throat stick together. How clever, diabolical even, the photography; the outlines of each object had been blurred from the start, as if seen through the fumes that rise from an open tank of gasoline. The effect was to make everything seem as if it were melting in the rays of the sun. And if this little audience, with every kind of liquor at hand, should yearn for a few drops of water, how maddening it must be for the doomed men on the screen—consumed by thirst while crouching beneath a veritable fountain.

From the midst of the Indians a shot rang out. Ahead, in front of the wagon, a white man—it looked to be Henry, the mule master—slumped down below one of the gushing streams. Then a second man squirmed from beneath the wagon bed and cupped his hands under a jet of water. An Apache picked him off as well. A third man, shouting, waving his bandana in surrender, stumbled forward to drink. He was shot before he could take a single swallow. Then the rest of the escort came rushing out together. The Indians moved forward slowly, on foot and on horseback. Occasionally one or another of their number got off a shot, as casually as a hunter shooting at grouse. When the natives arrived at the wagon they dragged their victims aside and turned their own faces up into the shower.

No one could take his eyes from the scene of carnage. Little piebald ponies were guzzling from what, in black and white, looked like pools of blood and water. The Indians themselves were playing under the squirting jets. They laughed. They shouted. Their skin glistened. Their loincloths clung dripping to their loins. Everywhere a spray was flying, so that droplets clung to the lens of the camera.

Off to one side, under a spout of his own, stood a solitary redskin. Gradually the director began to focus on him. First he drank his fill. Then he stood motionless under the water. A gasp went up in the screening room. Somehow, under the force of the stream, like a figure in a fable by Ovid, the man was being transformed from one kind of creature into another: the blackness of his hair dripped onto his shoulders, leaving in its place long fair strands that were almost blond. The broad muscles of his back, a deep tan color, turned into a kind of mud, which ran to his waist, to his knees. This was no Apache! The skin underneath was as white as the quartz from the underground mine.

"What in heaven's name is this?"

Before anyone could answer Manfred's question, the bather turned. His eyes were light, pale, probably blue. The young man laughed, showing his teeth. Presumably that was the moment that Von Beckmann had said *Cut*; for the exposed film ran out, and black stock, covered with scratches, like vertical Japanese writing, filled the screen.

There was, in the projection room, utter silence. It lasted until someone— it was Ernie Glickman—said, "It's over. Ha-ha, let there be light!"

Upstairs, in the booth, someone turned on the overhead lights. There were a half-dozen occupants scattered throughout the room. Mr. Joel Cairo, that was my latest part, sat in the topmost row.

"Okay," said Manfred. "I'm spending the money. I think I'm entitled to an explanation. Who the hell was that?"

Kahn: "You didn't recognize him? That's John Payne."

"I know it's Payne, for Christ's sake! I want to know what he's doing there."

Burton, whom Manfred these days rarely let out of his sight, spoke up. "Don't you remember? He's the traitor to the town. He's joined the attackers. He's only an Indian in disguise."

"I don't want to hear from you right now, thank you. Do you know the nightmare you've gotten me into? With that bitch Louella?"

"*Hollywood's Hearst Lady*," said Lester. "Ha-ha-ha."

"It's no joke, goddammit. She wants me to take her up in the trimotor. Or she's going to write about Rudi's tastes."

Kahn, the publicist, said, "But she doesn't know anything, Manfred."

"Oh, yeah? She's threatening to write about Burton. She's going to use his initials, for crying out loud."

"That's just a stab in the dark."

"A stab at my heart! She knows more about this picture than I do! When we started out at the B unit, it was about ranchers and miners. Now it's cowboys and Indians."

Kahn: "But Mr. Granite, we've known for a long time that the ranchers were replaced by Apaches. The cowboys—they're still the miners."

"Besides," said Victor, "there's really not a fundamental change at all. The issue is the same: two forces struggle because there is not enough water for all."

Burton, it seemed, would not be silenced. "I should think you'd be happy, Papa, since the change isn't costing us money. Really, we're saving. I mean, we still use the Sumner footage from the stampede, only now we've cut in a few shots of the natives. They're real, you know, real Indians. Navahos, they tell me. All except John Payne at the end. We've been able to replace at least half of the extras, and boy, they're dirt cheap. I've gone over the figures, Papa. We're not paying for food or housing, not even tents. We pump their water, but they scrounge for food on their own. It's practically like buying Manhattan. For trinkets!"

"You dare talk to me about saving money? You've got figures? You pipsqueak, I've got figures, too!" Manfred swung forward in order to dig into the briefcase between his feet. "Here. Page after page. Fifteen thousand dollars for electrical cables. Nine thousand five hundred for dynamite! Sixty-nine hundred for birds. *Birds!* Do I have to read the rest out loud?"

"It's not necessary, Manny," said Kahn. "We all understand Von Beckmann has gone over budget."

"By four hundred and fifty-five thousand dollars!"

Even from my distant seat I could see the blood suffusing the top of Manfred's scalp. His whole head looked like a red rubber ball. Nor was he finished. "Not to mention he's—what? Forty, forty-one days behind schedule, and the picture isn't half done. Is he *trying* to bankrupt us? Is it some kind of secret plan?"

Victor: "My skin crawls when I hear this screaming over the budget. I am embarrassed for all of us. We have just seen one of the great sequences in the history of film. The only thing that matches it is the scene of burying old Harwood inside the mine. The genius of immuring him in a solid wall of quartz. The way the fuse ends lit the scene. The way they writhed like mourners."

"Well, my skin is crawling too. This scene you are so proud of because it was done in one shot. Did you happen to notice—or am I the only one in the studio who knows how to read a slate?—that it took thirty-eight takes? How many days did the production stand still so that one fucking stunt man could fall off his horse? Four? Five? Six? That's forty-five thousand dollars! Nothing. Spare change. Peanuts to you. All right, you don't want to speak about money, we won't speak about money. But what about the fact that time after time we come here to see the dailies—that's a joke, there are no dailies. It's a misnomer. *Weeklies*, we ought to call them. Well, we come here and we don't have any idea of what we're going to see. One day the mine owner, yeah, Harwood, has only one daughter. At the next screening he's also got two sons—this Payne and the guy played by Gorcey. I forgot to mention that Annie was already given a sister. Not only that, but all of a sudden she's not in love with the rancher's son anymore but—do I have this right?—with Chick Chandler, the son of the sheriff. And Apaches! Maybe you boys like the life of adventure. I've never in my life had a pleasant surprise. There is no supervision. There is no approval. There is no control. Every new line the Epsteins write—and you'd think at their prices they could do better than *Whatcher see there, Jackie?*—each new line changes what went before. Who knows what's going on? Does anybody know? I'm waiting to hear. Half the time I don't think Rudi himself understands what he's doing."

With both hands Victor pulled on his earlobes, a tick that explained why they were as long, nearly, as the Buddha's. "You speak so disparagingly of cowboys and Indians. What you have just seen is a critique of the banality of such scenes. To me, the lack of closeups, the stillness of the camera, were done on purpose; at arm's length, forced to watch at a distance, I felt as if I were looking up at a Greek frieze, like one of the battles on the Parthenon—civilization against the barbarians."

"One shot, goddammit, forty-five thousand dollars. We could *build* the Parthenon for less."

Then Glickman, like a student, raised his hand. "If you'll allow me, Manny. I thought the scene was breathtaking. You know, literally. I held my breath from the start until Payne washed off his greasepaint."

Victor: "That's what I mean by artistry. A cut in a film is like a comma. It tells you when you can breathe."

"Look, boys, what we have to cut is the crap. It's time to make some decisions. Victor, I know you don't believe it's responsible, and I mean *artistically* responsible, for us to proceed when we don't know what's going to be shot from one day to the next. Heaven forbid I should mention fiscally responsible, because no one wants to hear about the stockholders in this company, who are being asked to pay for a picture we can't describe to them except to say what we did at the start: it's a western and we're bringing Rudolph Von Beckmann, who half of them, believe me, have never heard of, and Magdalena Mezaray together. That's our selling point. Barbarians and civilization couldn't interest them less. Well, we've got Von Beckmann and all he's given us is a headache. And we *don't* have Magdalena, which is an even bigger pain in the neck. We can't keep shooting around her forever. For this kettle of fish I know who to thank." Here the studio boss half rose and pointed to the top of the screening room, where I was sitting.

"Me?" I responded.

"You know goddamned well *you*. We've put Mezaray off until you finish shooting at Warners. What's the matter with Huston? The other *Falcon*s were made in two weeks. He's already taken the goddamned summer. I always said never, never, never let a writer direct. Well, we aren't waiting any longer. We've booked a ticket for you. I want you on that boat in three weeks."

Three weeks! That was, for me, like setting the date of execution. "But Manny. Mr. Granite. You're asking the impossible. We're scheduled for looping. And I'm obliged by contract to attend the previews. The premiere's in October."

"I've checked with Warners. Your part is done. You can loop the Joel Cairo dialogue in two days, tops. And October—you'd better be back before then. You're going to work for us the first of that month."

"What? What are you saying? I thought that Ernie—"

Now the agent stood up to speak for himself. "Listen, Manfred. Be reasonable. This is a tremendous break for Peter. I've been negotiating with Harry and Jack. They've got new ideas for him. They're talking about a multiyear contract."

"And you're talking through your hat. I lent Lorre out for *one picture*. The *Falcon* remake. After that he comes back to me. Don't you read your own language?"

"Sure I do, Manny, but there *is* no work at Granite. You know that. Every penny is tied up in *Pandaemonium*. Besides, you've got no facilities. It's going to be another year before the B unit can start making pictures."

"That's what you think. I've worked out a deal with Fox. We're shooting there in the fall. *Mr. Moto Meets the Sphinx*. It's money in the bank. All kinds of people are dying in a terrible plague. Moto goes to Egypt to find the antidote. It's almost biblical. There's a scene inside a pyramid. There's a scene with the Sphinx. He's going to be a tremendous hero. He's going to save thousands of lives."

"I don't want to save lives. I want to take them. I want to rob! I want to kill! I want to plot and plunder! Ernie, get me out of this!"

Down below, Victor rose from his seat. He looked, with his slender body and wide-brimmed hat, like a capital letter T. "Wait. Wait. I've been thinking. Listen to me. These changes—what do they mean?"

"Who the hell knows?" answered Manfred. "We don't have the slightest idea what picture we're making from one day to another. Nobody's told me yet what John Payne is doing with that bunch of redskins."

Burton said, "He's fighting against his brother. You know, over the mine. Over the town."

"It goes back to when the old man died in the stampede," said Les Kahn. "The two of them, Ethan and Paul, argued about their inheritance."

"Yes, yes," said Victor. "The two sons quarrel at the reading of the will, when they discover they've been left the mine together. They have to find a way to share the riches, the power."

Glickman: "Sure, they decide that Ethan will run the town for a year, because he's the oldest. Then he's supposed to hand over the job to his brother, Paul. That's John Payne, who we just saw washing off his warpaint. He went over to the Indians when Ethan refused to resign. All these scenes we've been getting in the dailies—the Apaches attacking the town, burning the aqueduct, shooting the burning arrows into rooftops—those are Paul's ideas. The white man has become the Indian chief."

Victor was still on his feet. You weren't supposed to smoke in the screening room, but a cigarette dangled from his lips. Sparks rained down as he spoke. "Well, Manfred, I am happy to tell you that you won't be bothered by any more surprises. In fact, I'm going to inform you of what happens next. Peter, you could do the same, if you put on your thinking cap."

But there was only one thing I was thinking about: Moto. On the Nile. On a camel. In the lap of the Sphinx.

Victor: "The brothers are going to kill each other."

Burton: "Really? Is it true? How can you know that?"

"Well, since Mr. Moto will not, I had to deduce it myself. I knew one thing for certain. The scenes we have seen—not those today but all of them, every one of the rushes—were not made because of a whim. I also knew I had seen them before. I don't mean necessarily on the screen, in a picture. Where, then? When? I've had this feeling, a feeling of déjà vu, all along; but today, probably because of the talk about the Parthenon, about Greek art, I realized that the source had to be classical drama. There families turn constantly upon each other—wife against husband, father against daughter, son against father. Where was it, then, that brother turned his hand against brother?"

He paused. From under the broad brim of his hat his eyes lifted toward me. And by then I also knew. It wasn't all that long ago that I acted in the same drama at Salzburg. "The brothers," I said, "are not really Ethan and Paul but Eteocles and Polynices. The one goes over to the enemy when the other won't give up his rule over the town."

"Ah," Victor exclaimed. "I thought you'd guess. It's Sophocles! *Sophocles!* That turncoat, John Payne. He's going to be buried by his sister. The sheriff, that's Creon. And of course Annie—oh, what a perfect name: Annie! She's in love with his son. Rudi! Clever Rudi! He fooled us all! Manfred! Don't you see? He's making the picture he came here to do. The one he said would be like none ever attempted. This is no western. It's not about cowboys and Indians. The great Von Beckmann is making a film of *Antigone!*"

HOLLYWOOD MERRY GO ROUND

The birdies tell me that all is not sweetness and light on the Granite lot at Olympic and La Brea. That howling you might have heard lately is most likely studio exec Manfred Granite and not one of those saber-toothed tigers at the tar pits up the road. Ever since foreign-born director Rudolph Von Beckmann—they say he's an absolute genius—took over what was once a Mr. Moto vehicle last spring, there has been no end of trouble. Seems that this two-million-dollar epic is already way over budget and far behind schedule to boot. The whispering wind says that what was once a swell adventure has turned into a five-handkerchief drama. Who would have dreamed that the dynamic Manfred Granite, who always had his finger on the pulse of the public, would go arty on us? His pictures may not be Rembrandts but they certainly add up at the box office, and that's what counts in this business.

And if Manfred G. is on pins and needles, you should see his brother, Victor. Ever since *Pandaemonium*—that's what Mr. Von Beckmann is calling his picture, named for the ghost town in the wilds of the Nevada desert— that swarthy-skinned Granite, in his wide-brimmed hat he looks like a tanner, thinner Caesar Romero, has been as jittery as a Harry James addict. It's not that he's unhappy with the work of his old childhood chum—far from it. He told me himself in his courtly manner that the rushes he's seen so far have been mucho sensational and that everybody involved in this tragedy-as-a-western is going to win an Academy Award. Well, boys and girls, when a man like Victor Granite gets a burr under his saddle it doesn't take Bulldog Drummond to discover that it's the age-old question of *Cherchez la femme*— that's French, in this case, for *Find the Fraulein*! It's no secret that three years ago when the celebrated Von Beckmann turned tail from Austria he begged the woman of his dreams, the honey-haired Magdalena Mezaray, to go with him and the tantalizing Teuton turned him down flat. Seems she preferred the company of Der Fuhrer—they say he's got a twinkle in his eye where the ladies are concerned—to either the imperious Von B or pencil-thin Victor Granite, from whom she'd been inseparable during her eight-year rocket ride to stardom.

According to Granite publicist Les Kahn—those witty Epstein brothers once asked whether he was related to the fabulously wealthy Aga—the missing Magdalena is due to show up any day now at Granite's desert location. Well, it's Lester's job to be the cockeyed optimist, but the Granites have already been waiting long enough for poor Manfred to tear out whatever hairs were left on his handsome head. Only he knows how much it has cost to keep the production on location while the great director, the Great Dictator to most of his cast, has shot around the nonexistent leading lady. All of Hollywood knows that the only reason Manfred agreed to transform a B-unit western into a major motion picture was the tremendous public interest that would result from reuniting Rudi Von B and Magda M. I confess I can't wait to see the fireworks that will surely go off when Magdalena returns and has to choose between the two men who for so long have been carrying the torch.

Far be it from LOP to throw cold water on such a hot story, but it might just be that if and when the mysterious Mezaray shows up, she'll find that she's been replaced in Von Beckmann's affections by a certain someone quite a bit younger, a someone he was often seen arm-and-arm and eye-to-eye with at Rhumboogie and the Mocambo before he disappeared from sight in the desert sands. This is such a private affair that I don't dare give more than the initials, BG, and I don't mean the gorgeous-gammed Betty Grable but someone tall and dark and, if you get my drift, handsome. That doesn't mean that I believe the tall tales that some people who ought to know better have spread about the impresario being one of "the boys." Frankly, I think there are some writers in our profession—Jiminy Cricket sure was a *Hopper*!—who are old enough to have learned to let sleeping dogs lie. Some *intime* matters just aren't anyone's business.

What all Lollywoodians want to know is, will Magdalena Mezaray leave her native Germany or won't she? The best-informed man about foreign affairs, he's the dear friend of just about every world leader, is my own boss, Mr. Hearst. He believes that Herr Hitler has enough to do getting his nation's own house in order, and in W. R.'s opinion tremendous progress has been made in the land along the Rhine, without worrying about a domestic triangle of his own. In other words, in the view of this astute observer of international relations, the choice might not be Magdalena's at all. She might find herself a gal without a country once that henna-haired Hun, of course I mean the other woman in Der Fuhrer's life, the curvaceous Eva Braun, finally puts her foot down.

On the other hand, does it stand to reason that the powers that be at Granite Films, who are losing money faster than Hedy Lamarr changes husbands, can afford to stand around and wait for that day? To answer that question I called Alexander Granite, only to be told that the studio's legendary founder had secretly left town a month ago! Well, Lolly, I said to myself, there's more here than meets the eye—especially when one of my little birdies told me that pop-eyed Peter Lorre, who heroically saved the whole French fleet in *Mr. Moto's Last Warning*, had also disappeared at precisely the same time. You can imagine how my sharp little nose was up and sniffing. Lorre's no lover, but he might just be the man Magdalena Mezaray trusts most. And it seems that he and Alexander the Great snuck out of town together under cover of darkness, in the most mysterious getaway since Lana Turner motored to Las Vegas in the dead of night for her marriage to Artie Shaw. Speaking of Lana, I am glad to say that if the impulsive child who was discovered for the movies while drinking a milkshake at the corner drugstore ever marries Tony Martin, it won't be in a midnight elopement. Since her recent divorce she has grown up and has a new and most becoming dignity. "Louella," she told me at Guilaroff's, as we both were having our hair cut, "I am a very lucky girl. I almost passed up my movie career for marriage, and where would I be now if I had? I thank my lucky stars that I realized before I lost my chance that Artie and I were unsuited to each other." Incidentally, Lana, who had the most gorgeous titian locks when I last saw her, was a stunning blonde at Sid Guilaroff's studio. "Louella," she told me when I commented on the change, "I went blond for *Ziegfeld Girl* and I am afraid it is going to affect my kismet if I ever go back to being a redhead. I am so fortunate the way that picture just dropped right out of heaven into my lap and now I have *Dr. Jekyll and Mr. Hyde* with Spencer Tracy. I am really grateful to the people at MGM for giving me that chance." That attitude is really refreshing. Too often I hear actors complain about their studios and about the producers who make multimillion-dollar investments in them and build them into world-famous personalities.

I am sorry to say that Peter Lorre, who we were chatting about before I happened to think of Lana, is turning out to be just one of those ungrateful types. He has been getting such raves in the previews of *The Maltese Falcon,* but instead of thanking Manfred Granite for lending him to Warners, he immediately began to protest his new assignment in *Mr. Moto Meets the Sphinx,* which is scheduled for shooting at the start of October. It seems to me that before complaining an actor should consider the wishes of his fans. It is they who have made the oily-haired Oriental such a favorite that Peter is likely to continue in that role for many years to come. Anyway, it wouldn't surprise me one bit if the elderly Alexander Granite and the natty Nipponese have for some time been traveling together through the hills and dales and little cobblestone villages of the Third Reich, seeking like knights of old for their damsel in distress. The future of *Pandaemonium* and perhaps even of Granite Films may depend upon their success.

From THE CHATTERBOX: Jean Gabin and Michele Morgan are rekindling an old flame that started in France. Alice Faye told me by long-distance telephone she definitely intends to return to her career after her baby is born. "Louella, you know I am the restless type and won't want to be idle long. But what is money and fame compared with having a baby of my own?" I couldn't be more thrilled for her, especially because she used to be so moody—I was her next-door neighbor for months and I know—and is now completely happy and doesn't care who knows it. The real story of why Sterling Hayden walked out of filmdom at the height of his fame can now be revealed. Sterling was terribly in love with Madeleine Carroll, but Madeleine felt the difference in their ages might result in an unhappy marriage and harm both of their careers. She was very fond of Sterling and begged him to forget his love for her. Besides, Madeleine was already engaged to a French aviator. Speaking of aviators, Mr. Manfred Granite has been much more attentive to yours truly of late and has promised to take me up for a spin some time soon into the wild blue yonder. Wait until you see *Dumbo,* the little elephant with the big ears and blue eyes and his sidekick the mouse. This is a sophisticated comedy, full of pathos and delightful lyrics, to say nothing of Technicolor that is out of this world. There is so much of human nature in the mean, gossipy elephants and the fierce mother love that Mrs. Dumbo has for her long-eared son. Here's a combo at the Mocambo: Bruce Cabot and Carole Landis, dancing cheek to cheek. Mrs. Billy Gilbert parted with her tonsils at Cedars of Lebanon and is resting comfortably. That's all for today. See you tomorrow!

SPHINX

In June of 1941, one year after the fall of France, Germany invaded the Soviet Union. Ten weeks after that, just as Louella had written, the former Alexander Granach and his companion, the former Laszlo Loewenstein, sailed from New York and, after a smooth crossing, entered the North Sea on September eighth. The next day we steamed up the Elbe and docked at the port of Hamburg. Granite Films had requested an audience with Herr Hitler, a request that had only been granted after Hearst had persuaded Charles Lindbergh, the famed aviator, to intervene. At the time we arrived, however, the Führer was directing the operations of his armies in Russia and could not leave his battlefield headquarters, the Wolf's Lair. However, as an extraordinary act of courtesy, he dispatched his personal adjutant, SS Major Otto Günsche, the same dashing young man who had traveled to Gurs to secure the release of Rudolph Von Beckmann. It was he who drove us two naturalized Americans out of the hills and dales of Germany into the towns of the occupied east, thus permitting Alexander Granite, who had long since changed his own name, to see whether or not others had done the same thing to his monuments.

Above all it was the ancient city of Lemberg—it had gone through more than a few renamings itself: Lemberg in the empire, Lvov under the Poles, surely Lemberg again under German occupation—that the retired head of Granite Films was most eager to visit. So it was that six days after our arrival, the old man and I, still in my youthful thirties, found ourselves in an open sidecar, bouncing across the broad plain that led to the River Peltew. The engine of the motorcycle roared in my ears. The dust of the unpaved road had settled across the front of my goggles. It clogged my nostrils and, thick as the alkali of the Nevada desert, reached deep into my dry and cracking throat. The sight of the river, as flat and yellow as a lionskin rug, only increased the sensation of thirst.

"Stop! Stop!" I croaked, as our powerful machine approached the weed-strewn banks.

Günsche, also in goggles, applied the brakes. Even before the vehicle had ceased rolling, I had jumped over the edge of the sidecar. Scrambling to the edge of the water, I dropped to my hands and knees.

"*Achtung!*" shouted the blond-headed driver. "*Die Cholera!*"

I lifted my head from the silt-filled stream. There was a bubbling scum upon it and, further out, amidst the detritus, floated a human corpse—no, corpses, two of them, three of them, as if this were the Ganges and not a tributary of the Bug. In spite of my thirst, still unquenched, I could not repress the twitch of a smile. These bodies meant fighting somewhere to the north. Was the Russian counterattack at last under way?

Old Alexander, still in the sidecar, had no interest in tarrying for refreshment. He gave orders to Günsche as if the latter had been a Granite Films employee and not the personal adjutant of the Führer: "To Lemberg! The inner city! To the public gardens!"

The SS officer gunned the hot engine. As we sped along, Granite, his white locks flying about his shoulders, shouted to make himself heard. His high voice creaked like hinges. "Forty-six years ago. Eighteen ninety-five. The last performance of the Great Granach in Lemberg. This was the fourth city of the empire—after Vienna, Prague, Trieste. Here were living sixty thousand Jews. Look, there is the tileworks, just as in the past. And that is the factory for naptha. And there—you see? You see?"

The adjutant brought the cycle and sidecar to a halt at the spot where the old stone walls gave way to the open field that had once contained the public gardens. The nonagenarian struggled to his feet and pointed with his cane. "The tree! That one! That is where we hung the sheet. Look at it droop—it's even older than I am. It was night. There was fog. But we put on our show. Ta-tra-tra-tra—Victor beat the drum. He was skinnier than a drumstick himself. *Di Tragedie fun Dreyfus.* It was crap! It was dreck! But those dumb Jews didn't know any better! Ha-ha! Lemberg! With its university, its museum! And all they wanted to know about was California! About melons! When the ether lamp came on, those Yids were hypnotized. The same as in our theaters now. Those poor souls! Those pale faces! There wasn't a man who could take his eyes off our screen. Except for myself, the Great Granach. I looked that way. You see, gentlemen, over there—"

The old man pointed the tip of his cane off to one side. "That's where my dear one was standing. I can hardly bring myself to say her name. Drahomira! My heart! If you could have seen her in her youthfulness. With rhinestones and sequins and lozenges from glass. What breasts she had! White like cream, boys! Whiter than the sheet with Dreyfus on it, and Dreyfus's prancing horse."

"Maybe," I ventured, "we could discuss these old memories over a glass of beer?"

"You!" cried Granite, swinging around to the young man with the lightning bolts on his collar. "Now we shall see if Herr Hitler has kept his word." He aimed his cane into the distance, where the tower of the town hall soared over the central square. "Take us there!"

The roads were unpaved no longer. My teeth clacked together as the sidecar careened over the cobblestones. The main square, when we got there, did not look like a place that had recently been invaded and reinvaded. Its statues and fountains, the glass and stone and ironwork of its buildings—all were weatherworn and aged; yet all were scrubbed clean, perhaps by the same bent-over women who were at that very moment sweeping the steps and staircases with their brooms. The only sign of war was the absence of any cars in the street save for those, all of them black and shiny, of German manufacture—and, of course, the German soldiers themselves, their helmets no less shining and no less polished than the barrels of their guns. In groups of three and four they stood on every corner. Otherwise, or so it seemed, we might have been looking at a busy square in any European town. The sidewalks and streets were full of people. Horses trotted by, pulling their loads of straw. The bells in the Armenian cathedral rang out the hour and were answered by those of the Dominican church across the way. One thing, however, struck me as being out of place. The conquerors were dour, their mouths pulled down in grim frowns; the conquered, however, were smiling. Everywhere I looked the people streamed by with twinkling eyes and happy, cheery faces. Was it, I wondered, some kind of celebration?

"Loewenstein," said Granite, addressing me as always by my Austro-Hungarian name. "Even with glasses my eyes aren't good like they used to be. You go. That's the building. You look for me. Here's the Kodak. Take a picture for proof."

The oldest of the Granites held out a camera with a collapsing bellows between the film and the lens. I took it and climbed from the sidecar. I made my way through the pushing crowds to a large building with a facade of dark stone, like rough-cut marble, and a large arch at the top of—I counted them—eight steep steps. Curved above the arch was a sign in silvery letters:

INSTYTUT POLITECHNICZNY IM ALEKSANDRA GRANACHA

"You see?" said the adjutant, relaxing upon the leather seat of his BMW. "All this talk—persecution, and changing names, beatings and so forth: it is all lies, all propaganda."

But I saw more than I was supposed to, with the result that I had to put my hand over my mouth to keep from laughing out loud. The old fool! Was he totally blind? Didn't he notice that the fresh paint—yes, I could make out the old paint underneath it—was actually dripping? But those were not tears of merriment that welled in my eyes. Moto was the moron, not Alexander Granite. Why had I agreed to return to Europe? Why—and for the second time!—had I put my head into the lion's mouth? Did I really think Manfred would give me my outright release? What a laugh! What a joke! Even if I did manage to bring Magda to Hollywood, I knew that Joel Cairo—oh, I would kill and be killed for another such part!—would be transformed into the copper-toned cop as quickly as the Alexander Granach Polytechnic Institute was going to be converted back to the Heinrich Himmler Museum.

Perhaps it was, so to speak, to fix that paint forever that I snapped the picture of the facade. Seeing my Kodak, a group of Poles paused, smiling, on the steps for their portrait. I took it. After that a group of muscular laborers asked for a snapshot. I took that, too. They were followed by three blond-haired mothers and their flock of dumpling-cheeked kids.

"*Halt!*" Günsche gave the command from his cycle. "Taking pictures of the civilian population—this is *verboten!* Herr Lorre, *kommen Sie her!*"

With my heart in my mouth, a mouth so dry that I could have bitten that organ to taste the flow of blood, I approached the angry adjutant. The SS major did not confiscate my Kodak. Instead, with an oath he ordered me into the sidecar and started the engine. The aged Granite did not want to see any more monuments, no matter for whom they were named. He had, as it happened, a more urgent mission.

Off we roared, not stopping once until we arrived at our destination in the Lemberg suburbs. Günsche pulled up in front of a broken-down three-story building. Everything about it was in disrepair. Its portico had sunken in; its awnings sagged. The windows beneath them looked out at different levels, like eyes in a modernist painting. As soon as we drew to a halt, old Granach thrust out one spindly leg and struggled to climb out of the sidecar, the way a wrinkled chick will fight to emerge from the pieces of its shell. The sign over the door, in Yiddish this time, had not been repainted:

YIDDISHE HEIM FAR DI GUEISTIK KRANKE

Amazing how rapidly, thumping away with his cane, Granach-Granite loped over the porch and into the building. I followed. The ground floor was deserted. On both sides of the long corridor, doors hung aslant on their hinges. Bare bulbs were suspended at the end of wires, while the light-green shards of what had once been their shades glittered upon the floor. The adjutant thrust his handsome head into the entrance. "Come. You can see that this hospital has been abandoned."

Granite ignored him. He was trotting the entire length of the hallway, rapping with his stick upon every door. I looked into one of the rooms myself. In one corner was a bed with its coiled springs exposed. In another a cream-colored table with only three legs leaned against the wall. Nearby was a basin of chipped ceramic; over it a pipe glistened. I looked closer. A drop of water! The sight was as alluring as a diamond earring beneath a woman's ear. I lunged for it, twisting the handle of the faucet. Nothing happened. But when I licked the brilliant bead a fresh one, as cold and crystalline as the dewy droplet at an icicle's end, appeared to take its place. I bent to drink my fill.

Drahomira!

A chill went through me, as if this had been an actual icicle, to which my tongue had frozen.

Drahomira!

Again the cry, so piercing, so anguished, sent shivers up my spinal column. Of course it was Granite, calling to his wife. I could hear the old man toddling with his cane, two steps and a thump, two steps and a thump, back up the corridor. I remained where I was, lapping at the pipe.

"You! Günsche! What have you done to her? Answer me! Where is my sweetheart?"

"Why, Herr Granite, is it not obvious?" The SS man's voice came from just outside my room. "These patients have had to be moved for their own safety. All of them have been relocated to the east."

At the sound of those words the droplets of water turned bitter upon my tongue. They might just as well have been drops of developing fluid, for the photographs I had taken with the Kodak now swam before me. *Sixty thousand Jews,* Granite had said. That was before the turn of the century. There must be a hundred thousand now. With the lens of my mind's eye, I examined the images of those who had posed before me—those square-headed men and blond-haired women, the barrel-chested crowds—with as much intensity as, with the aid of my magnifying glass, I had examined the picture postcards in *Mr. Moto Takes a Vacation.* Ah, so! I had it! The terrible truth! Those photos: they were all of gentiles. Smiling gentiles. But what of the Jews? *Sometime must look no further than end of nose.* The hundred thousand that had disappeared from the population of Lvov—or Lemberg, or for that matter every town into which the armies of the Third Reich had marched: all of them, I knew now, were going to eliminated. And, unlike the erased names of the buildings, they could not be restored. I had proof! I had pictures! There was going to be a massacre!

Three days later, on the eighteenth of September, old man Granite and I found ourselves driving in a Daimler limousine through the nighttime streets of Munich. I leaned against the window glass. No blackout here. The reflections of streetlamps, of electric bulbs from storefronts, of flashing neon slithered over the waxed surface of our automobile. The plump Reichsmarschall in the front seat—I estimated him at a 484 in the Sheldon system—seemed to be reading my mind. "You see our gay lights? When the RAF bombs by day and by night? Might I be forgiven for thinking they are a personal tribute? A necklace, perhaps, or a decoration to be worn alongside my *Verdienstkreuz*? Please report back to the important men in America that our people are fearless. They know my Luftwaffe will protect them."

Neither Granite nor I said a word. Goering, from deep in his throat, gave a chuckle. "If your Roosevelt after all succeeds in drawing us into war, do you think New York City will be as brave? Eh? Do not believe it! Even with the ocean on one side and a continent on the other, the Broadway lights, the lights in the windows of the skyscrapers and on the speeding taxis—all will be extinguished. Well, that would be at least one happy result of the war: all those cosmopolitans, eh, the sophisticates, will get to bed at a decent hour."

Now Alexander Granite leaned forward to look at the bright lights through his rolled-up window. "What's that? That theater? Der Volkspalast? The People's Theater. Is that a joke? This was the Montezuma. It had a what-do-you-call-it—an Aztec design." The old man struck his cane, to little effect, upon the plush carpet of the floor. "You. Driver. Take us to Briennerstrasse. *Schnellstens, zum Excelsior Kino!*"

The driver of the limousine, a youth, an air cadet, did not react. Then Goering, in the passenger seat, made a nearly imperceptible movement of the head. The Daimler leapt forward, raced past two blocks, and swung left at the next intersection. Granite peered eagerly through every window. His voice, high and rasping, sounded like an off-key violin. "I see it! What does it say? Kino Horst Wessel! That was the Excelsior. A great Granite house. Fifteen hundred seats. An imported Wurlitzer organ. How dare you change the names of these theaters?"

"But Herr Granite," said Goering, "you sold them to us yourself. All the theaters in Berlin. All the theaters in Munich. Have you forgotten? In exchange for using our influence with the authorities in France."

It was true. These were the theaters given up for Von Beckmann's release. And now the studio was going to relinquish the remainder of the Granite properties—the theater chains in the rest of Germany and Belgium and France, a soundstage in Antwerp, and offices throughout occupied Europe: all of this in exchange for Magdalena Mezaray and a symbolic three thousand marks. No wonder Hitler had been so eager to please us, two sons of Israel, not only allowing us into the Reich but providing his own adjutant to aid in the search for old Granite's wife. On the other hand, so Moto mused, why had he refused to meet with us? Was it really because he couldn't leave Wolfsschanze at a crucial stage in the war? Then why, on this very night, had he suddenly agreed to come to Munich? Was he to abandon one hundred and twenty divisions to settle the fate of a middle-aged actress?

"Look!" cried Granite. "Look, Loewenstein. Am I seeing things? Is it a mirage?"

I leaned over so as to peer through Granite's side window. The good people of Munich were lined up under the dazzling Horst Wessel marquee. The blinking lights spelled out the title *Liebe auf den ersten Blicke.* I followed the sequence of bulbs that led me, as surely as parallel landing lights would guide the Reichsmarschall on a foggy night, to the names of the stars.

"No, Mr. Granite," I responded. "This is not a mirage."

EMIL JANNINGS flashed on and off. Beside it, the name of his costar: MAGDALENA MEZARAY. Ten minutes later the limousine moved slowly down the Prinzregentenstrasse, with its mall of dark poplars and lindens, and came to a stop in front of number 16. Party headquarters. On the top floor, *Der Führer Residenz.* A squad of SS, all in black, stood guard at the curbstone and on either side of the double doors. A corporal, a Rottenführer, opened the limousine for Goering. No one opened the door in the rear. I got out on my own and, moving around the automobile, pulled Granite—how thin his arms, his bones!—from the frame. Our little party of Jews and gentiles started toward the entrance. Suddenly I heard a far-off voice. It seemed to be drifting down from above. It wasn't speaking so much as—could this be possible?—sobbing. The others, including the blackshirted SS, heard it too. Everyone froze. Then someone—it was the cadet, hardly more than a boy—heaved a sigh. "*Ach,*" he said. "The poor Führer."

Goering waved us toward the double doors. "Come," he said. "Why such sad faces? Today we have had a great victory. Yes, at Kiev!"

Granite hesitated. "But what was that noise? That wailing? The boy said it was the Führer."

Goering: "You are mistaken. Do you see the cornice of the building? There the wind whistles by. It makes this mournful sound."

Ahead, both doors sprang open, tripped by an electrical circuit. The Germans started forward. It occurred to me that with their slow gait, their grim expressions, they could have been pallbearers in a funeral procession. And that weeping, that unearthly moan: it might have been the sobbing of the mourners. One thing was certain, it was not the wind. There was no disguising this pitiful wail that floated down from the eaves; rising and falling, now full-voiced, now fading, it was the echo of the rant and roar that the whole world had heard on the shortwave bands of their radios.

Inside the building a marble lobby, high-ceilinged and austere, took up much of the ground floor. I realized at once that this is where we were to conclude our business. Two tables had been set up opposite each other beneath red-and-black banners. On one were the agreements to be signed. The other was laden with food. The skull-like Goebbels already stood at the latter. Goering walked over. A small group of SS officers—I saw the handsome Günsche among them—moved to join them. That left Granite and me by ourselves, not far from the smooth soapstone of the staircase. The atmosphere about us remained hushed and funereal. The only sound was the click of the boots of the SS men as they moved across the polished stone floor.

Then everyone stiffened. There was a new sound, a whirring, followed by a soft thud and a clank. Someone shouted *Heil Hitler,* and the Germans raised their right arms. Hitler himself stepped out of the tiny box of an elevator. He took the salute in his usual fashion, his palm bent womanishly backward, as if submitting to the invisible shock waves hurled toward him by the upright limbs. Even from across the room I was struck by the contrast between the Führer's face, which was animated, the muscles twitching, the mouth chewing on the lips, and the eyes, never once blinking, the whites reddened as if caught in a flash lamp's glare.

Goering stepped from the crowd at the table. "*Mein Führer,* may I be the first to congratulate you on our victory. No one can doubt that it represents the turning point of the war."

"What?" said Hitler, looking from his air chief to the Minister of Propaganda. "Have we released the news from Kiev to the public?"

"No need to worry about our American guests," Goebbels responded. "Tomorrow our triumph will be the headline in the *New York Times.*"

Hitler: "And the day after tomorrow, I promise you, those headlines will be even bigger. We have swept past Kiev to surround an army of four hundred and fifty thousand men. As we speak they are in the process of surrender. The battle for the Crimea has been won."

Goering: "Not just the Crimea. On this day we have saved the civilization of the West."

Hitler turned. He looked directly past us, or through us, as if we did not exist. Yet it was plain that we were the subject of his next words. "We have present here two American Jews. I hope they appreciate how extraordinary this is. It has been allowed only at the request of Mr. Hearst and of Herr Lindbergh. Those are farsighted men. They understand that our victory today has been won not only for Germany but also for the United States."

Goering beamed. His chest puffed out. "I have today spoken by telephone to Lindbergh. In the opinion of my colleague of the air, it has now been demonstrated that the armies of the Reich, supported by the Luftwaffe, cannot be overcome—I will put his words into exact English: *by any conceivable combination of forces.* Of course he means by that that the chance of war between our great nations has grown inconceivably remote."

"For such a figure," added Hitler, "I will meet with these two Jews. I do not hide the fact that I admire Herr Lindbergh as much as any man in the world. Any man! His was the single most courageous act of our times. I declare here, before all my old fellow fighters, it was from him I learned the lesson of boldness. Yes, and of acting, when conditions call for it, entirely alone. There is much he and I have in common. Who else in all the world has known such terrible loneliness at a moment of crisis?"

Goering: "But our dear Führer knows he will never be alone. His oldest comrades will always stand with him."

I was amazed at the transformation that now came over the German leader. His face grew as white as the creamy staircase, and his voice, when he spoke, emerged in a strangled whisper. "Not alone? Herr Goering, have you gone mad? Do you know what day this is? A day on which, whatever the difficulties, I have always returned to München."

Goebbels spoke soothingly. "We feel ourselves, *mein Führer,* what you have lost. None of us have forgotten this anniversary, and—"

But the Führer was not done with the hapless Goering. "There is much, too, that *I* have not forgotten. Didn't the Reichsmarschall des Grossdeutschen Reiches promise me that the Messerschmitt 109 would make short work of the RAF defenses? Let us pray that we do not look back on that failure of the Luftwaffe as the *true* turning point of the war."

"Might I say to the Führer, the victory we are celebrating today would not have been possible without the air cover of the Messerschmitt and the tactical support of our Stuka dive-bombers."

"*Celebrating!* We are not here to have a celebration! Don't you understand? You say you are my oldest friend. You claim to have fought by my side. And still you know nothing of my inner life. I have just come from upstairs. From that sacred room. I have been weeping. Look! My tunic! Soaked with my tears. Oh, Goebbels! Has it been ten years? Ten years!"

Goebbels, glancing at his watch: "Almost to the hour."

Goering took the risk of saying, "A beautiful young woman. A noble spirit."

Hitler put his hand to his chest. "On that night, at that moment, my heart stopped beating. Tell me, why is it beating now? It is a traitor! Look at you, all of you—you obey me. All of Germany obeys me. Only my own heart ignores my commands."

Goebbels: "On such a night, at this anniversary, naturally you have such feelings."

"Yes, I am made of flesh. I do have feelings. They are deep, deep within. But do you think I am swept away by my emotions? I assure you I am not some woman who weeps at the cinema. I am not a boy who is overcome at the death of his dog. Painful memories do not prevent me from making rational decisions. Every creative spirit has at his center a store of ice. It is from this unmeltable core, with perfect calm, that I tell you I am aware of how much in these last ten years has been accomplished. Already we have achieved many of our goals in Europe. But I would give all of it up, yes, in an instant, without regrets, if I could have returned to me that dear girl."

Günsche, no dust upon him, no goggles, but smartly beribboned, spoke feelingly. "You must not say such things, *mein Führer.* What happened in that room was God's will. Nothing could prevent it. Such things are not in our power."

"*Kameraden!* None of you can know how much I suffer. Before my eyes I see that gay smile. I hear the mountain brook of that laughter. Geli! Geli!

Not once did I have to beg her. Never did I have to grovel. She did for me from the goodness of her heart what others did because of promises, because of fear."

The SS adjutant looked as if he might break into tears. "And so, too, all that we have attained has been according to God's will. You have no choice but to continue. You have been chosen by destiny. Nothing can be undone. Our only direction is forward!"

"Well said, Günsche," Goering declared. "The greater part of the task still awaits us. Not just in Europe. We shall be victorious on every continent."

"Ah! Ah!" Hitler exclaimed, peering upward either at the gilded ceiling or through it, beyond it, to the evening sky. "With my revolver! In my apartment!"

At these words a coldness came over my heart, as if some cruel person had plunged it, like an unwanted tabby, into a pail of frozen water. How could the leaders of the Reich allow me and Granite to overhear such remarks? Even worse, how could they allow us to leave the Reich once they had done so? They would have to shoot both of us, the way criminals must eliminate whoever has blundered across their crime. And even if we somehow managed to escape, how could Magda go with us? Hadn't she, like Geli, been Hitler's mistress? That meant that like his niece and every other woman who had shared his secrets, she must take, or seem to take, her own life.

Now I, like Herr Hitler, stared up toward the ceiling, where a great chandelier blazed above us. Would that, like the even grander fixture in *Mysterious Mr. Moto,* it might crash down upon us while I stood, in my cool white linen, calmly chatting nearby. *Auf Wiedersehen* to the leaders of the Reich! Alas, the chandelier hung as immutable as the candelabra of the heavens. The only thing that changed was the Führer's expression. He looked toward his visitors with—was that a wink? Beneath the brush of the moustache, was that a hint of a smile? Goebbels led him to where Granite and I were standing. None of us shook hands. But when the minister mentioned the name of the founder of Granite Films, Hitler looked him directly in the eye.

"I understand from Goebbels that you wish to see me about your properties in the Greater Reich."

"We have come, Herr Reichsführer, to make an arrangement concerning our assets. The minister has informed us that this must be done with you in person."

"I want to make it absolutely clear that you have been allowed into this room solely as a favor to Herr Lindbergh."

"We are grateful for his assistance."

Here Goebbels turned the old man toward the table and its documents. "There is no reason for delay. If you will sit, we can sign the contracts."

But Granach-Granite would not be budged. He kept his gaze upon the Führer. "Just one minute. I'm sure you can wait that long, since you are going to get our holdings at such a reasonable price."

"Do you think that is of the least concern to our nation? A reasonable price? The Third Reich does not haggle in the bazaar."

"The total sum," Goebbels interjected, "has been set at three thousand marks."

From ten feet away, Goering laughed. "Tonight the Kino Horst Wessel will take in three times that amount!"

"The board of Granite Films is aware that we are offering the Third Reich a gift."

"And what choice have you?" Herr Hitler asked. "We have seized all the theaters. It was our moral duty to do so. We cannot allow the good German people to be subjected to filth and lying propaganda. An entire generation has grown up with sirens and seductresses. With Chicago gangsters. With Negro music. We do not permit sexual relations between the races in the Third Reich. How then could we turn our eyes away from a more insidious kind of miscegenation? Through these images and sounds Africa and the Orient penetrate the mind of the folk. We can deal with degeneracy when we see it in our streets. But the soul, when it is polluted with foreign ideas, is harder to cleanse."

Goebbels: "The German film industry now corresponds to the same ideals one sees in all German art. The screen images spring from the soil and from the deepest yearnings of the folk."

To my own horror, I heard myself saying, "I saw that tonight with my own eyes. *Liebe auf den ersten Blicke,* with Mezaray and Jannings."

"If I am not mistaken, you intend a certain mockery," Goebbels responded. "Our people are at war. You are now aware they have just won a victory that will turn back the Asiatic tide. If each day they willingly shoulder such heroic burdens, we cannot deny their wish for relaxation and diversion at night."

Goering: "Herr Loewenstein does not mention that we also drove by der Volkspalast. Did he not see what is playing there? If not, I can tell him that it is a film that has brought enlightenment to the people in every city of the Reich. It is a useful corrective to the false notions spread by the Hollywood product. It is our version of *Jud Süss.*"

"The lines," said Lorre, "were longer at *Liebe auf den ersten Blicke.*"

Hitler turned to his Minister of Propaganda. "Goebbels, tell me, der Volkspalast—wasn't that the old Montezuma? Yes, I remember. That is precisely my point. Even before the film could be shown, the motifs of these theaters—primitive Aztecs, Egyptian pyramids, Chinese temples: by suggestion they were undermining the racial purity of our thousand-year Reich."

"Those pyramids," I, or the devil who had seized my tongue, replied, "have lasted longer than one thousand years."

Granite leaned forward on his cane, as if without it he might topple over. What surprised me was the way his voice, though still high and rasping, had nonetheless assumed the confident tone of a diplomat's. "Herr Reichsführer, you mentioned that because our assets have already been expropriated, the board of Granite Films has no choice but to offer them to you on the most generous terms."

"It is the only possible course."

"That is not the case. Not exactly. My government has the means to retaliate. Secretary Morgenthau has told me that you have the right to confiscate our property but that German assets worth tens of millions of dollars might be seized unless we are offered fair compensation. I mention this not to make threats or in order to bargain, but only to point out that we enter these negotiations as equals."

Here Goebbels stamped his weighted shoe on the stone. "Morgenthau! Bringing his name into the discussion can only be considered a provocation."

"I am worried," Granite continued, his little eyes still focused on those of the Führer, "that the agreements upon this table do not reflect such a reality. They are clearly one-sided. The contracts that I will sign as an officer of Granite Films have the force of law. They will be enforced by American courts. I am to give up my theaters and offices and a functioning studio. How can I know that what we ask for in return will in fact be forthcoming?"

Goering responded with what sounded like genuine shock. "Are you questioning the word of the leader of the Reich? You shall have your three thousand pieces of silver."

Granite: "The first signs have not been encouraging. I was promised the opportunity to speak with my wife. But when I went to Lemberg, she was not there."

Hitler: "Lemberg? Of course she's not in Lemberg. That was a mistake. She's in the east. The east! You wait—we'll take you to her."

Granite: "And what of Magdalena Mezaray? Herr Goebbels gave me his guarantee that she will be permitted to accompany us to the United States."

"What has that to do with me? The choice is entirely hers. We do not hold people against their will."

I could not stop myself from blurting out, "Then she agrees? She will come? We have her ticket."

Goebbels put his hand over his hair, which seemed to leave it even slicker than before. "We, too, must take into account discouraging signs. No one knows better than I the role of the motion picture in forming public opinion. This is no less true in America than in the Third Reich. Can you deny that a conscious decision has been taken by the owners of your studios, a decision to create a climate that will force America into the war on the side of Britain? This is not merely my own conclusion. It is an opinion expressed to me by Mr. Hearst and your former ambassador, Mr. Kennedy. Lindbergh says the same himself. Why do you bother to deny it? It is an understandable thing. Such a decision in an industry dominated by Jews is almost reasonable. They see that we have reduced their influence in our nation. They do not wish to lose it in their own. But it is no less reasonable on our part not to wish to assist them. That is the question regarding Fräulein Mezaray. We know a good deal about Hollywood. For instance, about Beckmann's new production. Will she not run to her old friend? Will she not do his bidding and slander her own nation? That is what that production is. A slander on the Reich! And there is nothing we can do, once she leaves our boundaries, to prevent this. So you see, Granach, that after all we are equals. We both must face certain risks."

Through this speech Hitler had stood, rocking on his heels, with one hand grasping his wrist. At last he blinked, slowly. When his eyes opened, they bulged wider than before. "Why are you here? What is it you and Morgenthau are after? And why on this day of all days? Do you expect to find me drunk on my own emotion? On my memories of poor Geli? Or do you have some idea of rescuing Fräulein Mezaray from some similar fate? You want a melodrama, is that it? To snatch her from the jaws of death! Perhaps instead of the news of the victory at Kiev, you would prefer to see those headlines in your gutter press."

Once more I felt the ice crystals stabbing at my chest. It was as if the master of the Reich had the ability to read my very thoughts. "Mr. Granite," I said, turning to my traveling companion, "why don't you tell him? We have no such ideas. We came here on business. We are nothing but businessmen."

Now the Führer's cheek began to twitch, like the flanks of a horse. His lower lip was slick with spittle. "Do you dare to imagine," he continued, as though he had not heard a word I'd said, "that I have forgotten what our enemies said? Ten years have passed and I have not forgotten! The stories on the radio. The stories in the press. That Herr Hitler killed his own niece, his own darling Geli! Yes, that he broke her nose! Covered her with bruises! And broke a few ribs for her, too! Worse! The stories were worse! That she killed herself because some Jew, an art teacher from Linz, had made her pregnant or—this was fantastic, sheer delusion and depravity: *Herr Hitler, we have heard, was the father of her unborn child.*"

Goering: "To speak that way about a love that was pure! Pure and spotless! About an angel!"

Goebbels: "We shut their mouths for them. We smashed their presses."

Goering: "We haven't finished yet. There is more smashing to do."

Here was a medical miracle: though my internal temperature had dropped to zero, I had broken into a sweat. "I don't understand such talk. Why are you making these threats? We came here in good faith. We want to do business."

Here Hitler pointed his finger at Granite and let out a terrible shriek. *"Then why doesn't he agree to sign?"*

Now the adjutant, Günsche, stepped forward and clicked his heels together. "Good faith, did you say? Strictly business? I am not so certain. *Mein Führer*, it is my duty to report that I witnessed this Jew as he was taking photographs in a restricted area of Lemberg."

For the first time Hitler seemed to become aware of my existence. His eyes, heretofore wide and white, now narrowed to glittering slits. "Can this be true?"

"I took photographs. I admit it. Of the Instytut Politechniczny im Aleksandra Granacha. Of the sign over the door."

Günsche: "There were also photographs of the liberated population. We have discovered the prints hidden in his luggage. In them you can see certain Wehrmacht installations and personnel. Also strategic streets and monuments. I am forced to conclude we may be dealing here with an adventurer, or more likely a spy."

"You searched my luggage? But that is outrageous! By what right was that done? Besides, I took no pictures of the German army. Those people were Poles. This is a mistake. A misunderstanding." So speaking, I backed away from the others, toward the staircase. There was in the back of my brain a whirring sound, a kind of whine—no, not in my brain, from somewhere in the building.

Goebbels: "Seize the Jew. He might have a weapon."

"What Jew? Ha-ha. I am a practitioner of judo, not Judaism. Here is Moto. Ally from Japan!"

Hitler went pale. "A weapon? We can't take chances. What if they want to harm Fräulein Mezaray? And put the blame on me? I know these tricks! Anything to create a scandal. Search him!"

Günsche made a motion with his hand. Three of the SS men stepped forward.

"Stop!" The order, amazingly enough, came from Alexander Granite. "You forget that I know a show when I see it. This has all been an act—the shouting, the tantrums, the misery of Herr Hitler. You've staged it all because you want my business. All right. You can have it. Every Granite property left in Europe. Give me the pen. The paper. I will sign."

With that the old man limped to the table and pulled out a chair. Goebbels, his own limp disguised by his built-up shoe, moved quickly to sit down beside him. He took an ebony pen from its holder and signed in three places. Then, as the small crowd gathered around, he handed the instrument to the founder of Granite Films.

While the Germans were busy watching the nonagenarian put his name down in triplicate, I managed to dart unnoticed up the stone staircase. Not surprisingly, perhaps, I could not escape the sensation that I had played this part before. Not once, a hundred times. Jewel thieves, kidnappers, gamblers, assassins: Mr. Moto knew how to foil them all. The trick, of course, was to remain both calmer and cleverer than any such villain. Mental jujitsu, that's what I needed—the ability to remain detached, floating in nonchalance above the foe. Alas, it was just that Asian aplomb that deserted me now. At any second I felt that my chilled heart would burst, the way a bottle of milk will explode in the freezer compartment of a refrigerator. My breath, vibrating in my chest, sounded like the seeds in a gourd shaken by Xavier Cugat. As I stumbled on, past the first story, up to the second, the whirring sound, the whining, continued to echo in my ears. Suddenly I recognized it. The machinery of Hitler's elevator!

With a groan I pulled myself down the hallway, past one shut door after another, until I came to the metal portal set into the grillwork of the shaft. There was a buzzer next to the handle. On impulse I pressed it. There was no answering bell. Through the mesh of the screen I could see the steel cables tremble with exertion. There, well below me, the cage itself, swishing and sighing, was on the rise. I went back to the door and peered through the round metal porthole, which, it turned out, matched an identical window on the lift itself. Thus, for a half-second I could look into the dimly lit interior as it glided unhesitatingly by. That was enough time for me to see that the metal box was occupied. I thought I had seen a woman. I thought she had been wearing a veil.

Up, up, up went the elevator, until even the dangling ropes underneath it disappeared from view. At the same time the whir of the engine high above also ceased, not because the elevator had stopped—on the contrary, I soon saw that it was once more descending—but because the tramp-tramp-tramp of the jackboots upon the soft stone of the stairs drowned it out. A search party! The SS! Panting now, I staggered back to the buzzer and jammed my finger against it. I pressed my bug-eyed face to the window. But the cage, with its mysterious occupant—not so mysterious; it must be Magda—flickered for an instant, porthole to porthole, and then sank out of sight.

What could I do? The ring of the boots on the stairway was louder. They were on the first landing; they were marching to the second. With my finger, it was numb now and tingling, I signaled the lift yet again. In due time the taut cable shuddered, stopped, and hauled itself upward. How long had Magda been locked within this cage, rising, descending, rising once more? For an instant I thought of something I'd read somewhere, or seen in a movie: a bird, not a hummingbird but more flamboyant—bird of paradise?—that died when it came to rest. Poor Magda! She was no less frightened than I of the SS.

Once more I pressed my man-in-the-moon face against the circle of the window. All hope was draining away. Two tiny blades, that's what it felt like, were sawing at my wrists. The pins and needles had reached as far as my toes. My eyelids, made from asbestos, fell over my eyes. Was this the end of Loewenstein-Lorre? No contract with Warners?

There was a clack, a click, then something was pushing on my chest— not from the inside but from without. It was the door! The elevator had stopped! With the last of my strength I stumbled inside. Both doors closed behind me.

"Magda! Darling! I am dying from a heart attack!"

The little room was warm and airless. A light bulb produced very few watts in the lampshade overhead. For a moment the two of us, actor and actress, hung motionless in space. She stared blankly, invisible behind her dotted veil. I leaned against the wall, panting, my tongue lolling from my open mouth. Finally, with an effort, I raised both hands and began to grope at my breast, ripping the buttons off my camel-hair jacket, tearing open the silk shirt with the monogram PL on the pocket, and digging into the stuff of my undershirt, as if I meant to claw through the flesh itself to get at my thudding heart. But it wasn't my heart I was after. From next to my skin I peeled away a photo of the Lemberg town square. I held the sticky print toward my fellow passenger. "Please, Magda. Take it. Hide it. You will save my life."

But Magda, if indeed it were she, turned her back. She reached for the slick brass handle of the controls and pulled it toward her. We rose.

The photograph dropped from my fingers. My head drooped on my neck, as if weighed down by the force of acceleration. We climbed to the top floor, the Führer floor, and halted. For a moment neither one of us moved. I remained slumped against the wall, panting for breath. She stood, swaying, her grip on the protruding lever. Then, with a gasp, she lurched against the handle, and we began to slide down the shaft.

My eyes were fixed on the floor of the cage, where the photo of Lemberg and its inhabitants lay face up. "Magda," I began, "we have to get out of here. Let's stop at the first floor, all right? We'll walk right by them. I'm only asking one thing. A little favor. Take the picture. Put it in your purse. They won't search you. That would be an insult to Hitler. He trusts you. Maybe he fears you. You are the one who knows his secrets. Or put it in your dress. They found the other photos. This is the only one left."

One by one, like the snap of a shutter, the floors slipped by the porthole lens. Above us, in the rafters, or on the rooftop, the cable unrolled with a humming sound from its spool. Magdalena made no response. She stood, shadowy in the feeble light, pressing against the controls.

"Have they told you why we are here? It's to take you back to America. Everything has been arranged. We have a kind of a contract. We'll sail on a steamer from Vichy France. Won't you turn around? Won't you look at me? Everyone said you wouldn't come back if I didn't ask you. Am I so irresistible? Ha-ha-ha. You know I missed you, Magda. I sent letters, but the letters came back. Such dark thoughts I had! Old Granite is with me. He wants you in Rudi's new picture. I told him you wouldn't act for Rudi of all people on earth. He abandoned you, didn't he? He left you in their clutches. It's the same with Goebbels—he's afraid you'll go back to Rudi, too. That you'll make propaganda against them. There are a lot of pictures these days about spies and adventurers and refugees. I made one myself. Right after I came back from Salzburg. *Mr. Moto's Last Warning.* It's set in Egypt. There's a spy for Germany there, it's George Sanders, and he wants to launch a sneak attack on the French fleet and blame it on England. An antique dealer discovers the plot; only it isn't an antique dealer, it's Mr. Moto. At the last minute, five fathoms down, he foils the Germans by setting off the charges prematurely. Only we couldn't say Germany. Not the actual word. We said *your employer* and *the foreign power* and things like that. I don't suppose you saw it? No, no—they wouldn't allow it in Berlin.

"You won't speak? Not to your old friend? Your lamb? Listen, love, I was angry with Rudi, too. Not just because he left you, but because of what happened in Salzburg. He cares too much about perfection. Art is more important to him than living people. Why couldn't he have just sat still? Why couldn't he have kept his mouth shut? Then Hitler would have been shot. Magda, listen to me. In the whole city of Lemberg, in the little villages, too. In Poland. In Russia. Where are the Jews?"

We had reached the ground floor. Magda sighed. I stood upright and pulled on the inner door. It did not open. I looked around at my companion. Her back was still turned. She seemed to be shuddering. "Aren't we going to go out?" I asked her. Apparently not. With a groan she threw herself upon the lever, and once again, inexplicably, we started to rise.

"Magda, I don't understand this. Are we going to go up and down all night? There's no air here. We'll suffocate. After the last Moto film I thought I wouldn't have to do another. Manfred actually lent me out to Warners. Oh, what joy! I was a man out of prison! Light! Air! The songs of the birds! But now I've got to go back to Granite. I've been on my knees praying there would be a war with Japan. That will be the end of my bondage. Goodbye to the gumshoe. Under water! With my hands tied! Inside a sack! Can you imagine it? Like a Japanese Houdini. And meanwhile the French fleet with all those French sailors on board was nearing the harbor. I was the only person in the world who could save them. *Moto! Moto! Do something! A miracle, Mr. Moto!*"

Still no answer. No response of any kind. Was she deaf? A horrible thought: she'd been tortured! She'd lost her mind! "Magda, if you want me to, if it's your wish, I will also fall on my knees. I'll pray to you. Who else besides me knows what is happening in the east? Granite—he's too old, he doesn't grasp it. He still thinks he can find his wife. Look at those people! The Poles. Why are they smiling? Why happy? *Only dumb man ask dumb question!* They have the Jews' apartments. They have the Jews' jobs. Don't you see? They've got the whole city to themselves! It's a Polish holiday!"

I broke off, but only to gulp, from the stagnant interior, a breath of air. I felt now that I dare not stop, as if the string of my words was, together with the strands in the cable, the only thing that kept us aloft.

"That photograph. Do you know what it is? It's the evidence of a crime!

Help me! You have to help me! Oh, in case you are wondering how I escaped, I had a steel file in my hand. The audience saw it in closeup. I cut through the ropes. I slashed through the sack. Then I swam to George Sanders, who was waiting for the signal to blow up the fleet. I attacked him with jujitsu, with judo. Right on the chin! I confess that in my heart of hearts I am not angry with Rudi. I am angry with myself. *I* was also at Salzburg. I was only ten feet from the Führer. I could have leaped from the stage and torn out his throat. Alas, I am only fearless on film. This is real life, Magda! Do you know what real life is full of? Doubts! And fears! Why did the Germans let me take those pictures? Why was I allowed into Lemberg at all? Did they *want* to let me in on their secret? What do you think? Is it an excuse to kill me? The way they killed that girl? That Geli? We used a water tank. The whole picture was shot on the lot. The camels and fezzes and the streets of Port Said. That was a double in the water. Al Fox. With buckteeth like a beaver. With my Wildroot hair."

The next time up we didn't go to the top but stopped at the fifth floor, one beneath the Führer's. Moreover, when we descended we didn't reach the bottom but halted at the second. And when we rose again we only went as far as the fourth. It had finally begun to dawn on me what was occurring—with Magda, with the polished handle—less than a yard from where I stood. I turned away my eyes. I put out my arms, so as to brace myself against the walls of the lift, which, from Magdalena's exertions, had started to rock. Now I didn't allow myself the least of pauses; if I did so, there was no way to avoid hearing the way she gasped with pleasure as she drew in her breath.

"Maybe I'm lying about my motives. Maybe I'm not so high-minded. I might be fooling myself, I admit it. Listen, Magda. If I have to do another Moto it will kill me. If it doesn't kill me I'll commit hara-kiri. This summer I finished my work in Huston's new picture. The remake of *Maltese Falcon.* We open next month in New York. I'm going to get raves. I'm going to be offered a Warners contract. It's the way out of the sack! Out of the elevator! You've simply got to help me! You've got to come back! I've seen the script they'll give me if you don't. *Mr. Moto Meets the Sphinx.* Oh, my God. My God. Back to Egypt! People are dying from a new kind of plague, of poison, only it's an old kind, and—can you believe this?—the antidote is buried inside the Pyramid of Cheops! They want me to take a time machine so that I can learn the secret formula from the pharaoh himself. Meanwhile here we are in the twentieth century in the middle of a tragedy. What's going to happen in the city of Kiev? It's surrounded. It's overrun. That isn't a shtetl. It's not even Lemberg. They will slaughter tens of thousands of Jews. If they're going to have a time machine, why do I have go back to the Fourth Dynasty, for pity's sake? Let Moto travel to the eighteen-eighties, as a peddler or a gardener or a household servant. He's good at that. A master of disguises! *Time for your tea, honorable Mister Schicklgruber.* Or, *How does the honorable lady wish me to prepare her pork sausage, her pork dumplings, her pig's feet, her bacon?* Mr. Moto knows herbs. He knows poisons. Just a pinch. Merely a drop. He won't have to kill his victims. He'll make these Austrians sterile. *Mr. Moto and the Miscarriage.* The whole course of history will be changed. Instead, I'm supposed to fly back thousands of years and answer the riddle of the Sphinx. You'll see. You'll see, Magda. I'll put a sword into my stomach. *Banzai!*"

The little cage that enclosed us was no longer traveling between the floors. At most we went up a few inches and, an instant later, a few inches down. A gentleman, an Old Worlder, this Herr Laszlo Loewenstein: I turned round completely and, as is the worldwide custom of those in elevators, faced the interlocked door. I was too shocked to say another word. Behind me Magda panted. She groaned. The smell of her sex filled the little room. Suddenly the lift stopped rocking. The machinery above us fell silent. Ashamed, abashed, I looked down at my hands. The light from the light bulb fell upon them like a dusting of makeup, turning the skin as yellow as that of the agent of the International Police.

"All right, Peter," said Magda in the husky voice familiar to millions. "It's over. You can turn around."

I did as requested. She was crouched on the floor. She had lifted her pillbox hat, and with it the veil, from her flowing hair, which was longer and darker than I had ever seen it before. Her face, I thought, was the same, with the thin, arched, penciled brows, the high cheekbones, and the full lower lip, after everything still like that of a pouting child. The cheeks were even deeper, hollower than ever, an effect, perhaps, of the overhead illumination. Her eyes, so deep set, also seemed darker, blacker, but that might have been caused by the dilation of her pupils in the inadequate light. Faintly she smiled, probably because she had caught me in the act of doing what everyone did at first impulse: glancing toward her legs. But they were folded beneath her, out of sight.

"Don't be upset, little lamb. It's over. I'm calm. I'm not troubled. Except for one thing. It is not true what you said about Rudi. He didn't abandon me. You mustn't think it. He told me what was waiting. I knew what was upstairs at the Hotel Metropol. I went willingly. I knew I wouldn't come down."

"Magda. Darling Magda. I wish I were not here. It would be better if I hadn't seen this. If I didn't exist."

The actress gave a laugh, surprisingly light, almost carefree. "This? It's nothing, lambie. I want you to understand about Rudi. I went because otherwise he would be a prisoner, too. All we could hope for was that one of us would be allowed to escape. Isn't it for the best that it was he? No, no. It's not just the obvious, that he can work without me and that—it's no secret, I've always known it—I cannot act without him. You're thinking of Victor? Of Hollywood? But I feel about that the way you do about the Moto series. What does Ernie call it? Slick shit? Horseshit? *Nur Scheiss*. No, I knew there was a great idea, a new venture, a production—I thought then it would be a film, a great new film—that he must complete. I sensed it every day, in every hour that we worked at Salzburg. That is why I climbed the stairs. I think the room they took me to was the bridal suite. *He* was in the bedroom."

I threw my hands over my ears. "I don't want to hear it! You have to forget about it. Don't you know about Geli? What they did to her? With Hitler's own pistol!"

"Then don't listen, lamb. Or don't remember what you hear. Are you afraid they will torture you for information? Or torture me? If they pierce me with burning wires I'll tell them that Magda does not know anything about the Jews. She also doesn't know why she did what she did in Vienna, or after Vienna, or whether she would do it again if she had the chance. The question I ask myself is, was all of it at bottom a kind of flattery? I knew he was the most powerful man in the world. But with me he was powerless. He was a beggar. I wish I could tell you it was torture. Or a humiliation. Or that it wasn't me. Do you understand? That I had abstracted myself, made myself into a machine without a soul, a body without a mind, or had turned myself into another person, the way I do before the camera. But it is pointless to pretend that I was anyone else but Magdalena Mezaray, the name I was born with, and that when he lay under me, like a baby, really, naked and helpless, wailing, covered with slime, I felt anything other than what he does when, with the might of his armies, he straddles the world."

"Magda, I—"

"Shhh. Lambkins, hush. I know what you are too dear a lamb to ask: why didn't I feel, instead of that glory, simple human revulsion? I did. But not until later, months later, when he started to use a piece of glass. It was a coffee table. I squatted on top. He was beneath with his bulging eyes. That was when I felt the disgust. Waves of it. And nausea. Because now that he was to be clean and pure, I felt covered with dirt. The only part of him I could bear to look at was his moustache, because it was a reminder, like a smudge of filth. Oh, these English words: *the pain of glass!* It shattered me, lambie. I'd lost him. That's what happened to that little girl, Geli; she'd lost him, too. *Liebe auf den ersten Blicke?* I made that to get back my power. I wanted to be a giant, a giantess, sixty feet high on the screen, with an audience of pygmies writhing beneath me. A colossus! A star! That's what I'd had before. The knowledge that at any one moment, in all the capital cities of the world, men were gazing at me. Devouring me with their eyes. I used to think of them: crowds of men, armies of men, *my* armies, with their pale white faces. There they are, turned like sunflowers—or moonflowers, if such a thing is possible—to the light of the illuminated screen. I would feel the heat of their breathing. I would hear their soft moans. Ah! To imagine the pleasure I gave them, those uncountable millions, as they touched themselves in the dark."

I did nothing. I do not think, through the whole of that speech, I took a single breath.

"But it was too late. My moment has passed. Does he care? He is indifferent. He is gone. So now, my lamb, you know why I came to this little room. No? Can't you guess? Of course you can guess! Because only a half-hour ago his hand"—and here she indicated the cool metal lever of the controls—"was on this piece of brass."

Mission to Munich: who would have thought it would end in success? When Magda fell silent I wanted both to embrace her and to flee in horror. The two impulses canceled each other out: I merely stood frozen. Nor did I move to assist the actress as she got to her feet and smoothed her gray skirt and adjusted the hat on her head. I did not even react when she picked up the photograph of Lemberg and slipped it inside her blouse. I could not imagine that either one of us was going to be allowed to live. Nor did I change my opinion when we both were permitted to walk unmolested across the polished stone lobby of 16 Prinzregentenstrasse and make our way—just the two of us, without old man Granach—to the steamer that waited in Marseille.

That port was like the closed gate of Hell, upon which half the world seemed to be beating. Those who escaped—robbed by the French and the Germans; humiliated, sad to say, by the American Department of State— huddled upon the decks of our craft. And were we then, as we steamed from the harbor, safe at last? All calm, Mr. Loewenstein-Lorre? All tranquil? *Pas du tout.* This must be a trick. A hideous tease. How could the hungry lion let us out of its mouth? All day long I scoured the horizon for the periscope of the *U-Boot* that was undoubtedly following in our wake. And through the night, during the hours of fitful sleep, my arms were crossed over my body, reassuringly, like the hug of a life preserver. After this long, fear-filled week, we arrived at last at the spot where the gray waters of the sea mixed with those of—Had we slipped the net? Were we free?—the mighty and sweet-smelling Hudson.

HOLLYWOOD MERRY GO ROUND

The big news from the Nevada desert, where Magdalena Mezaray has recently started work on Granite's *Pandaemonium,* is that there is no news at all. I can't remember such a top-secret operation since the time, exactly two years ago, that Darryl Zanuck confiscated the scripts after each day's shooting on what he pretended was *Highway 66.* I don't have to remind you that the truth about that production was revealed by none other than LOP. I've got to admit that was a more satisfying scoop than the breakup of those great lovers Mary Pickford and Doug Fairbanks. After all, there was plenty of Parsons luck involved in getting what the whole world thinks of as the greatest exclusive in newspaper history. If I live to be a thousand—and wouldn't the publicity departments at Warners and Para and Columbia just love that!—I'll never forget the day that Mary, usually so bright and bubbly, turned to me sadly at luncheon and said, "Louella, you are an old friend. You may write the story. Douglas and I are separating." But the account of the shenanigans at Fox didn't just fall into my lap like that. When my nose starts to twitch it means I smell a rat. But Darryl F. Zanuck was as silent as the tomb. And it would have been easier to break into Fort Knox than to get by those guards who were patrolling the *Highway 66* location. Mathematics may not have been my best subject at Freeport High—I wore the laurels for literary composition, believe it or not!—but I can add my tips together, and when I did I was able to inform all five continents that the mystery-shrouded feature John Ford was shooting in the valley was the highly controversial screen version of *The Grapes of Wrath.*

Here are the facts about *Pandaemonium*: for weeks now no one on La Brea has heard a word from the company on location. It's as if these hundreds of people, among them the famed Charles Laughton, not to mention the fabulous fraulein, had fallen off the edge of the earth. No telephone. No telegraph. Unbelievable as it sounds, not even the United States Postal Service, which fears neither snow nor wind nor dark of night, can deliver or pick up a letter at that once deserted ghost town. No wonder the Granite Brothers are fit to be tied. It's bad enough to lose control over a production, but it's really going to raise havoc when you've lost contact as well. If I were a betting woman I'd say this was no accident. All those guys and gals have deliberately cut themselves off from the rest of the world. I've heard they drill for their own water and eat their own livestock—the same poor critters you will see on the screen! People I have known for years, like the hairdresser for the mysterious Magda, and her seamstress, who broke into the industry with my recommendation, people who have never failed me—they all seem to have taken a vow of silence. Why the mystery? You would almost think they were making a secret weapon.

Well, the shocker is, maybe they are! Everyone knows Rudolph Von Beckmann has really got it in for Germany's leader. That's understandable when you remember how Magda dropped the famous impresario in favor of the brown-shirted Fuhrer. No wonder he holds such a grudge. I wouldn't be surprised if his motion picture was intended to be a bombshell that will blow his old rival, A. Hitler, and the great nation of Germany to smithereens.

If so, it won't be the first time that our industry has been misused for politics. The reason Darryl Zanuck tried to complete *The Grapes of Wrath* on the sly was that he was afraid of the big farmers and the banks. They disliked John Steinbeck's book, which unfairly made them out to be villains, and they thought the picture would be all black and white and inflame the people against them. Lollywoodians in the know still claim that even though the ending was changed, it was just those high feelings that caused the Academy Award to go to *Rebecca*. Shocking as it sounds, Rudolph Von Beckman wants to turn public opinion against Germany the way Steinbeck did against our patriotic businessmen and the banks.

I know what you're thinking: why would Herr Von Beckmann want to keep his work a secret? Wouldn't he seek publicity if he is making an exposé? That really was a puzzler—at least it was until I put the same question to my good pal Mr. Hearst. People complain about me splitting infinitives and sometimes getting this or that detail a tiny bit wrong, so I wrote down word for word what the publisher and statesman told me. "Louella, what Von Beckmann fears most is the reaction of his employers. He knows that the type of men who run the Hollywood studios are drawn most by the allure of money, just as they are repelled most by the prospect of its loss. He wants to confront the Granite brothers with a *fait accompli*. Louella, please let your readers know that he is playing with fire. I am in contact with the highest circles in Berlin. If such a hate-filled picture is allowed to be made, the relations between the United States and the Third Reich could be seriously harmed. I believe the government of Germany would view such an action as a deliberate provocation."

Far be it from LOP to meddle in politics, but it does seem just a wee bit surprising that Mr. Adolf Hitler, whom I wouldn't know from Adam and who wouldn't know me from Eva, pardon the pun, should be so sensitive to the way he is portrayed in American films, especially after he has banned their distribution in his homeland. On the other hand, I think we all can agree that people who are guests in our country ought to mind their p's and q's. While I don't pretend to be an expert in foreign affairs, I do know enough to defer in these matters to Mr. Hearst, who is always spoken of so glowingly by leaders at home and abroad. The last thing W. R. wants is for this country to allow the flower of its youth to be sacrificed in yet another foreign war. This is one fight we'd best stay out of. If Rudi Von Beckmann thinks he should have been made the head of UFA or if he's doing the slow burn over his femme star, then he should find some other way to express his frustration than by turning an innocent western into vicious propaganda that might drag this nation into far-off bloody battles. The same goes for Senor Schicklgruber. Settle your grudges somewhere else, boys.

That's all LOP had on tap for that story, especially when the talk in town has been so brisk all week. But not ten minutes ago a birdy was on my line with such sensational news that I'm going to take the time to pass it along. But before I hop off the movie-go-round, let me at least take a peek into THE CHATTERBOX and report that the Fred Astaires are expecting a visit from everybody's favorite stork. Clarence Brown has taken off twenty pounds peddling away on his new electric bicycle. Was that Jinx Falkenburg, once Bob Taplinger's heart throb, dancing with him and sending out sparks at the Beverly Hills Hotel? Lollywood's latest divorcée, Lana Turner, now that her long-term split with Artie Shaw is at last official, has been seen dueting with Tony Martin at the Tail o' the Cock. Adrian and Janet Gaynor stopped at Ciro's after gin-rummying at Jack Benny's until the wee hours. Peter Lorre will be up to his Asiatic antics next week when he starts filming *Mr. Moto Meets the Sphinx,* the latest in that delightful series that all his fans hope goes on forever. Annabella looked so cute in the hat she wore at the Brown Derby Las Feliz drive-in, where she and hubby Tyrone Power went for hamburgers.

She seldom wears hats. Just one message in THE LETTER BOX: Mrs. Edith Turnell, the man you describe in your letter does not sound like an authentic motion picture talent scout to me, and I would advise you not to allow your daughter to accompany him back to Hollywood.

I'm not going to keep my loyal readers sitting on the edge of their seats, because what the birdy just told me might make for one heck of a Lolly-palooza. First, I've got to reveal that the thin-as-a-thread Victor Granite never stopped calling me over these years to ask if I had any news about the missing Magda. What could I tell my sallow-skinned friend? It was never easy to get information from the close-mouthed Magdalena, who once told me, "Louella, a woman who will tell her age will tell anything." Of course I'd like nothing better than to be able to report that she had kept the flame alive for him all these years, and I'd like nothing worse than to play the hard-hearted Hanna and disclose that in my opinion Magda the Mum has been kicking up her heels in the old country.

Well, I hope this birdy won't be eaten by the cat I am about to let out of the bag, but my caller was none other than that half-pint body beneath the ten-gallon hat, Victor Granite! He told me himself in that delightful continental accent of his that he'll soon be going to Nevada in order to accompany his teenage daughter, Valentina, whom Rudolph Von B has personally summoned to play a small juvenile role. If you ask me, it's not likely the head of production for Granite studios would make such a long drive just to be a chauffeur. This trip only makes sense if he is going to do some serious trouble-shooting for his studio, not to mention that he'll be able to seek out his old friend the fraulein and confront her and his other rival, Herr Von B. How the feathers are going to fly! It wouldn't surprise me if he found that not all was peaches and cream between the leading lady and her director. The dailies stopped arriving at the studio just when she was supposed to start her first scene. Could she be ill? Or has she displeased the regal Rudi? Or maybe she, who wears the mantle of La Swanson, is in one of her famous sulks. Not only that, Charles Laughton, who is making such an impression with his just released *It Started with Eve,* has not shown up in any of the rushes, either. Can he be ill, too? And if so, what is this mysterious malaise? You can be sure of one thing: Victor Granite won't be the only one searching for the answers to these questions. That's all for today. See you tomorrow!

BURMA SHAVE

How hot it was! As scorching inside our Packard, almost, as in the desert that surrounded us. The portable cooler we'd rented in Barstow had worked for about an hour; now it only sprayed warm drops across the side windows. Victor, I knew, had the accelerator to the floor; still the black macadam, slippery-looking in the sunlight, stretched as far as the eye could see. From the back seat I watched him punch the tabs on the radio: not even static. I looked out the windows to the left and the right. In all the landscape, no life, no color, no movement. Where was, as the song had it, the tumbling tumbleweed? Here and there someone had planted cactus cutouts. Look again: the man-sized vegetation was real enough. The arms stretched upward imploringly, as if praying—for relief from boredom? For rain?

"*In the desert—*" came the singsong chant from the front passenger seat.

It was Valentina. In the mirror: dark eyes, dark skin, the flash of white teeth in parted lips. Her long hair, filled with highlights, was pulled straight back, a style she had adopted since the night—it was at the Wilshire Ebell banquet—that Von Beckmann had asked her to remove the curls from her forehead. The curls themselves had disappeared.

"*In our car—*" Victor answered, from under the broad brim of his hat.

"*Hit a salmon—*" came the nonsensical response.

There was a pause. The engine labored. The hot wind whistled by. Victor—with his hooded eyes and leathery skin, he might have been a desert reptile himself—stared into the empty sands. "I don't know, dear heart," he said. "I stand on the brink of defeat."

The girl wrinkled her nose. She giggled.

"One moment," Victor said. "Please start again."

"*In the desert*—" she said.

"*In our car*—" he said.

"*Hit a salmon*—" she prompted.

"*Caviar!*"

They laughed. They intoned together, "*Burma Shave!*"

"Almost!" she said, gloating. "Almost, that time."

"I was misled by the salmon. I nearly said *lox for four*. I think I shall claim a foul. You meant to say sturgeon. That's where caviar comes from."

"It certainly does not!" the girl sniffed. "I've had salmon eggs. The red ones. They are very pretty. They are translucent."

With his downturned grin, Victor said, "Very well. Prepare yourself. *In the desert*—"

She said, "*In the shade*—"

"*Shade?*" he repeated. "Shade in the desert?"

"I meant, "*In the glade*—"

"*Hit a tree*—"

"Um. Wait. Um. I got it! *Marmalade!*"

Together: "*Burma Shave!*"

Victor said, "Excellent. Such an intelligent young lady. She thinks it's an orange tree. In the middle of the desert."

Valentina: "I suppose you never heard of an oasis?"

"Certainly I have. But the trees in them are, I believe, palms."

"Okay. Fine. Say 'palm tree.' Start again."

"You're not getting tired? I thought you were going to take a nap."

"No. I'm *not* tired."

"Then we're keeping Peter up. *He* wants a nap."

"Again!" she said, more like a child than the pretty teenager that, in fact, she was.

"*In the desert*—" Victor said.

"*Among the huts*—" she said.

"*Hit a palm tree*—"

"*Coconuts!*"

"*Burma Shave!*"

The girl twisted about, leaning her chin on the back of her seat. "Peter! Uncle Peter! Why don't you play? You aren't paying attention."

"But of course I am. The trouble is, the trees you have in mind, the ones in the oasis—they're date palms. We had them in the shots of Port Said. Coconuts, they're in the South Sea adventures. Tahiti, you know. Hawaii."

"Peter the Pill!" Val exclaimed. "Why did you have to come?"

Aha! The very question I had become accustomed to asking myself. Why agree to the kind of trip that any sane man would have refused? Was my own being so deeply entwined with that of I. A. Moto that I had to throw myself into every possible adventure? What would Dr. Freud say? Or Dr. Adler? Death wish, from the former? The latter: need for self-assertion? For power? I knew what I needed—something to drink. My throat was parched. My eyes, as I shifted them toward the window, creaked in their sockets. What was that in the distance? Shimmering? A mirage! The same azure oblong as the pool behind Victor's house. This was Sunday. Sunday afternoon. I should be sitting on that flagstone after a game of doubles. How nice to watch Giselle swim her steady laps. Or see Miss Hudson, at the end of the diving board, tucking her curls into her bathing cap. Here comes Arthur with his tray of gin and tonics. *Gott! Gott!* I could actually feel in my hands, on the tips of my fingers, the surface of the silver cartridges, icy, heavy, dew-covered, that we used to fizz up our drinks with CO_2. Splash! The Queen B was in the water. I could see her form, like some kind of insect deep in blue amber.

There was a thump beneath us—not loud, not jolting, in fact barely perceptible. We didn't change speed. Nor alter course. I glanced through the rear window. A snake was writhing in agony on the road behind. Had Valentina, the lover of animals, seen the blow? I looked toward her; two red dots, of chagrin perhaps, lingered on her cheeks. She stared, eyes wide, mouth open, into the landscape. Then she said, "Do you know what Tacitus said?"

"Not at the moment," Victor replied.

"Yes, you do. Everyone does. Even Peter. It's famous."

I took a stab: *"Burma Shave?"*

"Of course not. We studied it. The actual speaker was Galgacus. He was talking to the Britons about the Romans, just as they were going into the battle. Tacitus was only quoting."

"I get the picture," said Victor. "What did he say?"

"They made a desert and called it peace."

Her words, for all the stifling heat, gave me a chill. What frightened me, of course, was the knowledge that we were driving toward a wilderness more barren, even, than this. I remembered all too well the scenes from the rushes: the cracked plain, the alkali, the tornadoes of dust. Was Victor as mad, as reckless, as I? Of course Louella was right; he wasn't escorting Valentina so that she could perform some kid's part in the production. Among other things, she couldn't act. I'd seen her play a Wise Man—quite awkwardly, even Giselle said so—in the Crestview Christmas pageant. No, this trip was about Magdalena. If she were not being used in the lead, then—and Manfred had been firm about this—Victor was to shut down the picture. But would he do it? Would he, to use his own words, throw ink at a Rembrandt?

Not likely. Once again the answer was in the "Merry Go Round." Victor was traveling to see Magda, plain and simple. A few weeks ago, at the end of September, he'd been at Union Station, standing like a lovesick boy with his arms full of flowers. But, grinning and sweating, I got off the Super Chief alone. How to explain? Les Kahn had spirited her away at the Pasadena stop—supposedly to avoid the press, but in reality to drive her to Pandaemonium before the couple could meet. The look on Victor's face! How clever Louella, with her language of love: *Keep the flame alive. Carry the torch. Burning with passion. Sending out sparks.* Anyone who had seen Victor then, the waste of him, his blackened body, would know that sheer longing had burnt him to a cinder.

How much further to go? Miles and miles. How much longer? Hours! Could I open the window? No. The blast of air would be like that from a furnace. Get a drink from the canvas bag that hung from the bumper? But the water was sickening, warmer, greasier than that from a bath. I closed my eyes. Ah! Instantly, in my reverie, I saw Miss Hudson. She shot upward, breaking the surface. Her white cap sprayed water the way a hundred-watt bulb strews light.

"Do you think"—that was Valentina, following some train of thought of her own—"that England can win the war?" I opened my eyes. I licked my chapped lips. But before I could answer, her father spoke up.

"I don't know. I am not an expert. Grim, that is how things look to me."

"I read in the *Los Angeles Times* that the Germans are going to take Moscow."

"It looks that way, sweetheart. Unless it starts snowing. Winter can defeat them, if England can't."

"So Hitler is greater than Napoleon. Napoleon, you know, could not enter Moscow. Have you read *War and Peace?*"

"I don't know if *great* is the word I'd use. Formidable. How about that?"

"And Genghis Khan and Darius the Great. None of them could conquer the whole continent of Europe. Isn't Hitler the master everywhere? Didn't he defeat Vienna and Paris and even the city of Athens?"

Victor didn't answer. Neither did I. What answer could we give? I glanced forward just as Valentina looked round. I noted the crease in her forehead, the kind of vertical line one rarely saw on a child. "Athens," she said, "is the cradle of Western civilization."

Victor: "You should try not to be upset. It has been invaded many times before. Wasn't it Byron, the poet, who helped throw out the Turks? Did he not die in the attempt? The Parthenon still stands."

"The Germans are worse than the Turks."

"On that, dear heart, we agree."

"And they are winning. I think they have won. The paper said when they enter Moscow, the English will also have to surrender. There won't be anyone left to fight them. It's worse than Attila the Hun. Because this time Italy is on his side. Rome is also an important center of culture. Oh, everything is hopeless!"

"Don't say that, Valentina. Don't say hopeless. Because things look bad at the moment does not mean the war has been lost. At bottom, you know, this Hitler is stupid. He is going to do something colossally dumb."

"We are the ones who are stupid! Especially the people in America. They don't care. They don't see what is happening. I am very well informed. If Hitler is so stupid how did he get, you know, Austria and Czechoslovakia without a fight? How come he snaps his fingers and all these great countries, like Poland, like Holland and Norway and France—they just surrender. They're like children following the Pied Piper of Harlem."

"Hamlin," said her father.

Valentina ignored him. "And Greece is lost forever! That is the place where the things that are important, the things that matter, the idea of the citizen and the idea of democracy, were born. And it is obvious to anybody who doesn't want to be fooled what is happening to Jewish people. Uncle Peter, why do you just sit there? I saw your photograph. I know what it means. Do something! You have to do something!"

"Yes, yes. But what? I talk. I talk some more. But no one listens."

The girl's cheeks were redder than ever, as if rouge had been smeared upon them. Her skin, for all the heat, was oddly dry. "The Jews gave the whole world the idea of one God. And all of this is just allowed! It's like, I don't know, people *want* it to happen! It makes me angry—the dumbness of Americans. It is complacency! Everybody at school goes around singing 'The Woody Woodpecker Song.' Can you believe it? Or 'Deep in the Heart of Texas.' The boys throw baseballs back and forth as if everything were normal, as if life were just going on. Wait a minute. Just a minute. All right. Now listen.

The mountains look on Marathon,
And Marathon looks on the sea;

And musing there an hour alone,
I dreamed that Greece might still be free.

Beautiful, right? Noble. You don't have to tell me about Lord Byron."

Victor sighed—in part, I knew, because with the windows up he could not smoke a cigarette. "What do you wish me to say? That the words of the poet are superior to"—and here the filmmaker rapped his knuckles four times against the dash and in a cracked voice crooned, "*deep in the heart of Texas!*? But what are you asking of people? Are they supposed to stop singing, my dear?"

"Yes! I mean, no. Or what I really mean is that I don't expect you to say anything different—or Uncle Peter. The two of you have devoted your lives to pictures that mirror the popular culture. I shouldn't expect you to try to help the Jews."

The words stung, no question. Naturally, with my cliff-hanging adventures and Houdini escapes, I could only plead guilty. And Victor, for all his reputation as a genius, a Thalberg, our one great artist in film, had never been under any illusions. He knew that his very livelihood depended on the manipulation of emotion: the ending of *Boys' Town,* the throb of gypsy violins, a cat up a tree. He reached over and touched the arm of his demanding daughter. "What is it? Why are you speaking like this, my heart? Do you know that you're hot? Should I stop? Are you feeling ill?"

"No, Victor. I want to apologize. Oh, I can hear myself! So arrogant and brash and removed from the masses. I mean, I understand this really could be the end of the world and the beginning of the dark ages. What excuse do I have for pushing that knowledge to the back of my mind and playing Burma Shave jingles?"

The masses! Where did she get such language? She sounded like a member of the Screenwriters Guild. Not to mention *translucent* and *complacency* and the rest. I could not quite repress my smile. Over these last five years the little girl I knew had grown up. She *was* well-informed. She had an interesting mind.

"You know," said Victor, "you are hard on yourself as well as on us. We have, in the first place, already played ghost and alphabet tag and odds and evens on license plates until we were the only car on the road. Thus our jingles. In the second place, it is a bit early to consign us once more to the dark ages. Not everyone has surrendered. Half the world is preparing to fight. The battle of Marathon—that's where Greece was saved, you know: well, it has to be fought over and over again. I wish I could tell you what is going to happen in the next few years. I cannot. No one can. There is no way to judge the future, unless it is by what has occurred in the past. That is why I said Hitler is going to do something stupid. Perhaps he already has, by invading Russia. I read the papers too, Val. I read that in some places the early snow has started. Just like Napoleon, he may have to make a disastrous retreat. Or perhaps what happened in the last war will repeat itself in this one—we shall join the fight. In my opinion, that is more than likely."

"I wish you were right but you're wrong. You think you know how to judge the Americans and their opinions but you don't. All you know is what movies they go to, but that doesn't tell you what they are thinking. I'll tell you about this German boy in my class. Gerhardt. He looks just the way you would think he would: tall, you know, and straight blond hair and blue eyes and this nose like an eagle. Actually it is a nice face in spite of the stereotype, impressive sort of, except for his mouth, which is always smiling—not pleasantly but with his lips curling with, oh, what is the word? When you look down on someone?"

Victor: "Disdain?"

"With disdain. As if the rest of us don't really exist."

Again I felt my eyelids, as if weights had been sewn into them, inch down and down. Up ahead the road, rising and falling out of the gullies, had begun to undulate, like the waves on a rope that somebody shook.

"Nobody cares," Valentina went on. "People admire him. He has a following. He is a leader."

Victor said, "I am becoming worried about you, Valentina. What is the point of this story about the boy? Why are you telling me this?"

"But I just told you the point. People *admire* him. *We* are the ones who are alone. Listen, do you know what Gerhardt used to call me? *The Jewess!* Even though he knew it wasn't true. I told him. Only you, only my father, is a Jew, which means in the Jewish religion I am not; and of course my mother is a beautiful blonde and a definite Christian who takes me with her to church. Gerhardt said that in his country if only one of my grandparents was Jewish or even if a great-grandparent was Jewish, which is a percentage of one out of eight, I would have to wear a yellow star and my name would be changed to Sarah and we couldn't have servants or sit on a bench in the park. All that with his smile! Naturally I told him he was a guest in our country, I wasn't living in his, and can you guess what he said then? He said, *Yes, you are right. You are not a Jew. You are a gypsy. A dark-skinned gypsy!*"

I gave, at those words, a start. Involuntarily I glanced once more at the rearview mirror. There was no question the girl had inherited her father's coloring—tawny, that would be the generous word for it, swarthy more honest, perhaps: but the features, particularly the jutting chin, the full, pouting lips, the strong, straight nose that went directly into the convex brow, were like the profile on a coin or a medallion, the classical Athena, the American Liberty, or La Belle France. Those looks, the beauty, came from her mother.

Valentina had not stopped speaking. "I laughed. That's how ridiculous it was. But he would not stop. *Gypsy!* That's what he called me every day. And the others did, too. My classmates. My friends. Even my friends who were Jews. The teachers knew, but they didn't say anything. I think they enjoyed it. It was the joke of the school."

"Val," said Victor, "tell me, are you all right?"

I was no less worried about the girl. Her eyes were black and lusterless, like the sewn-on eyes of a doll; and the blush in her cheek was now as bright as the pimiento in an olive.

"No! I am not! I feel terrible! It's because of what I said to him. I said— oh, I was wearing Giselle's gold earring, I *stole* it, ha-ha, like a gypsy! And I had her scarf, the purple one, and I used her mascara. I waited for him after school. We were alone on the soccer field, and I said, *Yes, you are right. I am a gypsy. Give me your palm.* He did. He just gave it to me. I looked at it, at his hand, it was white like alabaster, and I saw the heart line and the life line and the love line, and suddenly I knew how to read them. I knew the story of his life. I saw it before my eyes—a terrible fate! Horrible! The longer I looked, the deeper I saw. There was the blood in his veins. There were the beautiful bones underneath. I think that was the worst moment in my life. I could not breathe. My head was pounding. Victor! I really had become a gypsy! I truly possessed x-ray eyes. Spread before me was all the pain of the future. What should I do? What should I say? There we were, alone in the sunshine. I wanted to rush forward and hug him. To embrace him and protect him. Poor Gerhardt! Poor German boy! I never knew until that moment how unhappy he was. *You are going to be rich and successful and marry a beautiful woman,* that's what I told him. But I knew it was a lie. I knew that in less than a year he would put a gun to his head. It's a fact! He is going to blow out his brains! I see it! I know it! It's true!"

It goes without saying that Victor's hat was pressed firmly to his head. Nonetheless, I thought I could see with my own x-ray eyes how the thin strands of his hair stood up from his scalp. My own hair felt as if it had been passed through an electrical current. Couldn't we hurry? I leaned forward. The needle of the speedometer was stuck at sixty-six.

"Oh, Val. Dear heart," said Victor. He was trying to make his voice sound light, jaunty. "Can you see far enough into the future to know if there is a place ahead where we can stop for a nice cool drink?"

But Valentina didn't hear. She was leaning, eyes closed, against the passenger door. Asleep? Swooning maybe. Or was it a kind of coma? Victor took the car out of gear, stepped on the brake, and pulled to the side of the road. He opened the front door and gasped at the blast of sand-filled air that swirled about him. Quick as he could he unhooked the canvas bag from the front bumper and carried it around to his daughter's door. She slumped against him when he opened it. He poured the lukewarm water into the palm of his hand and dabbed it against her cheek. He dribbled more of it over her hair. She opened her heavy-lidded eyes, but the stare she gave him was without recognition. She refused to drink from the spout. Her lips, I saw, were swollen. It was sickness. It was fever. And all in the middle of nowhere.

Victor returned to the front of the Packard, where he hung the canvas sack. Then he knocked on my window. I rolled it down, squinting against the blowing sand. "Is she ill?" I asked him. "I mean, really ill?"

"I don't know. It may be so. Her skin is burning."

"What should we do? Can we go back?"

"Not to the coast. That would take twice as long as to go on."

"What about that town we passed? Where we got gas?"

"Hiko? I doubt there are a hundred people in the place. I don't think we could find a thermometer, much less a doctor."

"Then let's go on. We'll go on, Victor. Dick Mosk is still on location."

"Yes, I thought of that. But—"

"But what? He'll take care of her if anyone can."

"The thing is, Peter, the possibility exists that we are lost."

Lost! I could barely take in the word. My head hung from the window, like that of a dead tortoise from its shell. The rays of the sun beat down upon it; they were like the flaming arrows of the Apaches. "But how can we be lost?"

"I did not say we were. Perhaps we are not. We were supposed to go left at the third dirt road after the intersection. We passed two for certain. But the third one—it wasn't really a road. It was like, I can't say: a wagon track, or an abandoned trail. So you see, do we double back and take it? Or go on and look for a better road?"

What could I, a nondriver, say? I only shrugged.

"Okay," Victor said. "We risk it. We double back."

First we moved poor Valentina into the back, where she lay against the hot upholstery. I got into the passenger seat. Victor swung the car around and raced back over the macadam. We came to the dirt track and turned right upon it. We bounced along the ruts, sending a funnel of dry spume into the air.

The better part of an hour went by. The sun, moving down the sky, seemed to be spinning, its rays like the teeth of a saw. Valentina lay out of the glare. She hovered between what looked like sleep and what looked like trance. Victor hunched forward, so that his hat brim touched the wheel he clutched in both hands. We both jumped at the sound of the voice behind us.

"Cold blood," it said.

"What is it, dear heart? Are you cold?"

"Killed in cold blood."

I turned round. Valentina was still stretched out on the seat. Was she having a dream?

"Who?" Victor asked. "Who is killed? What are you saying?"

"He'll freeze! At night he'll freeze! He's a cold-blooded animal!"

I fought back a feeling of panic. Was she becoming delirious? From a thousand motion pictures I had formed the idea that every fever ended in a crisis. Was this it? She sat upright now. Her face was twisted, as if she were about to cry.

Valentina: "The desert will be cold. Too cold. His temperature will change. We learned that in school. Mammals shiver. Dogs—what they do is pant. Superior humans perspire. If it gets too hot, if it gets too cold, he'll definitely die. That's what it means to be cold-blooded."

Victor risked a glance backward. "I do not understand, little dove. Who are you talking about? Is it that German boy? Gerhardt? Or the Germans? Are they the ones who kill in cold blood?"

Slowly at first, then rapidly, she began to whip her head back and forth against the cloth of the seat. "One drop. That's all they need. Then they kill everyone."

I looked ahead to where our car was hopelessly chasing its own elongated shadow. It seemed to me that her head, jerking left and right, was actually shaking the sedan. Now she leaned forward. With her fists she beat at the back of the seat. Before I could react she aimed the blows at her father's shoulders. She cuffed at the crown of his hat. "It's your fault," she shouted. "You are the one who did it. He wasn't hurting you. Why did you do it? You think I didn't see. But I did! I told you I see everything. Why didn't you stop? It was cruel!"

At last I understood: the snake. After all, she had seen us hit it. I felt for the poor reptile a surge of delayed pity. Victor, it seemed, understood as well:

"I am sorry, dear heart. I am sorry, Valentina. It was an accident."

At those words she relented. She sat back. Then her mouth dropped open and tears gushed as if from a broken pipe. "Oh, Daddy," she wailed, and her whole face crumpled. "Are you going to marry Magdalena Mezaray?"

Neither of us said a thing in reply. Valentina dropped back into her speechless stupor. In the brief silence that followed, the engine roared and the wind whipped over our streamlined hood. Then Victor caught my eye, motioning toward the dust-covered windscreen.

"What is it?" I asked. "There's nothing to see."

The filmmaker put his finger to his lips. "Shhh," he said. Then he resumed in a whisper. "That's just it. There's nothing. The road has ended. We are lost for sure."

It was true. The flat sand stretched away on every side. There wasn't a trace of the trail. Grimly, Victor pushed down the accelerator. We rushed blindly ahead, as if trying to outrace the grip of our kicked-up wake. After some time, a half-hour, perhaps even more, Victor groaned. "No, no. Look. I fear we are in deep trouble."

I ducked to see out the windscreen. My heart ducked, too. We were moving directly toward the cone of our own giant plume. "*Sometimes,*" I muttered, "*man who wants to go straight goes in circle.*"

"Wait!" Victor cried, not trying to lower his voice. "It's a car. Another car!"

I saw it, too. It came bucking and lurching across the sand. Victor swerved, steering so as to head it off. The other car slowed. It was a Buick. Whatever color it had once been—red or black, green or blue—it was now the buff and chalk of the desert. I watched as it swerved, making straight for us.

Then an amazing event occurred. A coincidence, perhaps. A miracle, that's what it seemed at the time. A balloon, or a ball, or the egg of an ostrich appeared out the left window of the approaching automobile. Another such sphere appeared at the window on the right. Could it be? Impossible! Improbable! But it was an actual fact. The Epsteins! Phil and Julie!

Both cars halted simultaneously, practically grille to grille. Julie got out of the passenger side. He waved and grinned. "Tennis, anyone?"

Phil stepped from behind the wheel. "We're a little late, but we can probably still get a court."

Victor and I jumped from the Packard. We actually did a little jig in the sand. "What are you doing here?" Victor shouted. "I thought you were on *Pandaemonium*."

"We are," said Julie.

"We were," said Phil.

"What do you mean? Are you off the picture?"

Julie: "Well, let's put it this way. We know we're off. Rudi hasn't found out yet."

"Actually, that's why we're in a bit of a hurry."

I said, "Do you mean you quit? Then who is writing the script?"

Phil said, "Oh, Rudi's got Flatow. His friend from Vienna."

"Flatow!" cried Victor. "How can a man like that do a picture about the American West?"

"Well, far be it from us to criticize a fellow Guild member—"

"But they won't be calling this a horse opera for nothing. These cowpokes could sing their lines."

Victor: "Nonsense! It's preposterous. Come back with us. We'll straighten this out."

"That wouldn't be a good idea," said Julie.

"Not good for our health, anyway."

"To tell the truth, we've got other plans."

"What other plans?" Victor demanded. "Aren't you on contract? Where *are* you two going?"

Phil: "I thought we told you. We're going to play a little tennis. And golf. I don't know how we could have ignored such a wonderful sport. The pleasant vistas. The gentile companions. And you only have to bend over once every mile."

"Don't forget hunting," said Julie. "And rod and tackle. Do you remember the time we got up at six in the morning for deep-sea fishing? On the *Ann and Lil*? By a quarter of seven we were so bored that—"

"All right, all right," said Victor. "I know it hasn't been a picnic out here. You aren't the only ones who wish they were at Hillcrest this minute."

"Hillcrest?" echoed Phil.

"We wouldn't dream of Hillcrest," said Julie.

Phil: "Not posh enough."

"Not enough class."

"As a matter of fact," said Phil, "I'm planning on joining the Jonathan Club."

Julie: "Me? I'm joining the California Club."

"But fellows," I objected, "you know that's not possible. We aren't welcome at those places. *Movie people,* they say. But they mean Jews."

"Oh, don't believe those stories about anti-Semitism," said Phil. "That's all a vicious canard."

Victor shook his head. "You're joking. You have to be. Even L. B. couldn't get in."

Julie: "What a terrible thing to say. I'll have you know that we have definitely been invited to join both those fine institutions."

"That's right," said Phil. "The California Club invited me to join the Jonathan Club."

"And the Jonathan Club," added Julie, "invited me to join the California Club."

At that we burst out in laughter. We howled, the four of us, like so many hyenas. Victor wiped his eyes. "Quiet. Quiet, boys. Don't wake Valentina. She has a fever. Doc Mosk—he's still on location?"

"Yes," Phil answered, "but you're not going to take her to him, are you?"

"Why not? He's the best doctor in the industry."

"Yeah," said Julie, passing his hand over his hairless and hatless head, "but he's—well, he's lost his sense of humor."

Phil: "That's become a common affliction out here. Listen, I think you'd better turn around. We'll be back in the city well before morning."

"No, no," said Victor. "We've got a job to do here. We're on assignment."

"Then let's move Valentina into our car. We'll drive straight to Cedars. There's nothing Mosk can do for her here."

Victor: "Wait. How far from the ghost town are we?"

"Maybe forty minutes. If you follow our tracks you come to where they've repaired the old road."

"Then that's what we'll do. I'd be afraid to let her drive through the night. I don't know if she'd make it."

The twins turned toward me. "All right," said Julie. "There's no dissuading Victor. For reasons best left unexplored. Peter, you come in our car. The truth is, we're going back to Warners. On a new project."

"Warners! Is it true?"

"Oh, it's not all that exciting. Just the usual crap, like *Algiers.*"

"But we've got Bogart and Greenstreet, and Bergman on loan from Selznick."

"Right, and there's a swell part for you. Jack said so himself."

"For me?" I echoed.

"Sure. Ugarte. A smuggler. A low-life."

"Ugarte? What kind of name is that?"

Julie: "I think it's an Italian racing car."

"Renault. Ferrari. We're naming all the characters after foreign automobiles."

I hesitated. "I don't know, fellows."

"Listen, Peter," said Julie, dead serious now. "Come with us. It's your chance to land with Warners. And you've got a hell of a death scene. It's better than driving to Pandaemonium. You don't, believe me, want to know what's going on there. If Rudi has his way, they won't be just playing the part of corpses."

Such temptation! I actually stumbled two or three steps after the twins, who were heading back to their car. Then I stopped. Why? Was I going to give up this opportunity? Just because Miss Hudson was waiting in the desert? I knew, at bottom, that was not my motive. It was true, of course, that as long as I remained on location I would not have to report to Manfred, who was waiting to start *Mr. Moto Meets the Sphinx*. But if I had a job at Warners—with Bogie, with Greenstreet; why, it was practically a *Maltese Falcon* reunion!—I could also continue to postpone the work at Fox. As for Magdalena, I'd rescued her once. That job was up to Victor.

"Wait, boys!" I shouted.

This time Julie was behind the wheel. He started the engine. Phil held open the opposite door. But my feet remained rooted. I could not lift them. It was as if every tissue in my body had been replaced by minerals. *Voilà!* Petrified wood. Now Julie honked the horn. Phil gave a shout.

"Don't be a fool," said Victor. "It's obvious they are exaggerating conditions on the set. They need an excuse to walk out so they can start the job at Warners."

But it was his daughter's words I heard, not Victor's. *Do something! You have to do something!* Cursed conscience! I had my photograph. With it I would confront Rudolph Von Beckmann. I had to be certain he would make a picture that would tell the story of Hitler and the Jews. My shoulders slumped. I shook my head.

Instantly the wheels of the Buick began to spin. The sand flew up underneath them. The car backed up five feet. Then, surprisingly, it came to a halt. I watched in amazement as both doors flew wide. The Epsteins leaped out and ran back toward our Packard as if chasing a skillfully placed lob. They fell to their knees in front of the grille, as if before an icon, a god. Then they reached for the canvas sack. They clutched it. They clawed it. They ripped at the spout. The water came pouring down into their gaping mouths. They did not stop drinking until the last drop of the tepid brew was gone.

Victor and I stared at each other without a word. Still wordless, we trudged back to our automobile. We got in and started the engine. Valentina, asleep in the rear, did not stir. The Epsteins went west. We followed their tracks to the east. No turning back now. As far as the eye could see there was nothing but sand, along with the ranks of the cacti, which stood like an army, Roman centurians at the salute.

ON LOCATION

On we drove, across the boundless desert. The sun sank behind us. The sky turned orange and blue, like a rugby jersey. Within minutes the temperature in the desert started to drop. Victor discarded the useless air cooler and rolled his front window down. That is why we were able to hear the settlement at Pandaemonium long before the town itself came into view. Over the rush of the wind, the engine's growl, floated a far-off hammering sound: a clang and a pause and another brassy clang.

"What's that? That noise?" asked Valentina. She had awakened with the flow of cooler air. She seemed quieter, calmer, and her eyes no longer stared like blank buttons. But I noted that she put her hands over her ears, as if the dull, distant clang were causing her pain.

"I hear it," I said. "But I don't have any idea of what's causing the sound."

"J. Arthur Rank," she said with a giggle.

Victor smiled—not, surely, because he was imagining the start of those British pictures, the man with the huge Chinese gong, but because if Valentina were up to making that little joke, she must be feeling better.

"Look," she said now, pointing to where, in the last of the light, a dust cloud rose high in the air. "Is that where we're going?"

Hard to believe that the people in the old ghost town, the picture crew, the many extras, could raise such a storm with their comings and goings. Yet when I glanced back, I saw that our Packard, rolling over the unpaved road, had by itself thrown up a funnel that stretched for miles.

Valentina rolled down her window in back and leaned into the indigo air. "I see it! The town! Over there!"

I stared as hard as I could. Then I realized that it wasn't the town she had seen but the ridge that encircled it. I could just make out the hump that reared out of the ground the way a wave hauls itself out of the sea.

"I know what that is," said Victor. "It is the edge of the crater. The town is inside it, where a comet hit the earth."

"You mean," said Valentina, "a meteor."

"Do you know, a thought just came into my mind—like a blazing comet, dear heart. The town is where the mine is; the mine is where the gold is; the gold is near the center of the crater. Do you think that element was brought to the earth by the meteor? That all of that precious metal came from outer space?" He broke off. His daughter was staring at him, or at any rate the back of his hatted head, as if he were the one from another planet.

"No, no," I countered. "I have a better explanation. Not so farfetched. Maybe the heat of the impact, you know, the force of it, made a kind of alchemy—maybe that's what fused the gold inside the veins of quartz."

Our Packard came to a halt at the base of the ridge. It looked to be no higher than a tall man, about six feet, but the incline was too steep for anything but a team of mules. Victor put the car back in gear. Our instructions were to follow the rise northward, to the left, until we came to a breach in the wall. We started along the perimeter.

"*In the desert*—" That from Valentina.

"Not now," said Victor.

It took twenty minutes more before we came to the gap in the bulwark. It was just wide enough to allow a single lane of traffic. I could see, in the naked cross-section, that beneath a layer of sand the ridge was solid rock. The passage must have been made with Manfred's expensive dynamite. As soon as we drove through, two men—it was still light enough to see that they had guns and holsters—stepped forward and motioned for Victor to pull the Packard parallel to the inside of the wall. Then they indicated that the three of us should get out of the car. Victor did so; so did I. Both men approached. First I saw, from the studio logo, a *G* inside a square, that was sewn onto their shirts, that they were Granite employees. Then I recognized them: Kuttner and Lydon, guards from the Olympic Boulevard gate.

"Good evening, gentlemen," said Victor. "We're in a hurry to get to town. My daughter is ill with fever. We have to get her to Dick Mosk as soon as we can."

Lydon, the taller of the two guards, stooped to peer through the rear window of the automobile. "Who's the girl?"

"I told you. This is my daughter, Valentina. I am Victor Granite."

The other guard, he had a paunch and a goatee, turned toward where I was standing. "And who's this?"

"Ha! Ha! You don't recognize me? *Chop-chop! So solly! Catchee thief!*"

"It's all right," said Victor. "That's Peter Lorre."

But the guard would not be mollified. "Still, we're going to need some identification. From both of you."

Victor, chuckling, took out his wallet. "The two of you are certainly on your toes."

I took out my wallet as well. Kuttner checked it, then gestured toward the car. "What about her?" he said.

"Look, my friends," said Victor. "I have been driving all this day. I am tired and thirsty; my daughter is ill. There is no time for this. I am going to drive on to find Dr. Mosk."

Lydon stepped into Victor's path. His partner said, with a nod toward Valentina, "We'll have to see something."

"Is it possible? Do you really not know the person you are speaking to? I am the head of production for the studio you work for. The G on your shirt stands for Granite. That's my name. It is her name as well."

"We work for Mr. Von Beckmann."

"It's all right." That was Valentina, from inside the car. She held up her pocketbook. "I've got something here."

We all watched silently while the girl dug through her purse. In the open air the clanking sound echoed more loudly, and at a higher pitch. I thought I could feel its vibrations through the soles of my shoes. Certainly the heat of the desert sand, so much more searing now than the lingering warmth of the air, penetrated the leather; it was as if, buried beneath us, the ancient meteorite were still shooting out sparks.

"This is my student pass from the Crestview School." Valentina held up the laminated card.

Kuttner reached through the window and took hold of her handbag. He said, "Let's see what you have in here."

Victor: "This is unacceptable. There is no need for such behavior. I have to warn you—you two are going to lose your jobs."

Lydon, the tall guard said, "We have to check for weapons."

"Weapons! This is a teenage girl."

"We can't be too careful," said Kuttner. "We've just had an escape."

"What do you mean?" I said. "*Escape?*"

Lydon, his gray eyes boring into me, said, "You didn't pass another car, did you? A Buick?"

"Oh, you mean—" But Victor gripped my arm, squeezing it tight.

Kuttner saw the gesture. He moved round to the back of the sedan. "Would you open the trunk, Mr. Granite?"

"For what reason? Do you think we have weapons there, too?"

"Weapons—or water."

Victor put the key to the lock in the trunk and lifted the metal door. "I wish we did. I think I must be half crazy with thirst myself. I can't think of any other reason why I am standing here talking with you. Look, at least be human. Why don't you, while we're waiting here, get my daughter something to drink?"

Lydon, meanwhile, came forward and lifted our luggage out of the trunk. The bags weren't locked. One by one he snapped them open and begin to go through the clothes.

Kuttner leaned over to watch. He said, "We can't get you something to drink. I'm not saying we wouldn't like to. We have a rationing system. No one's allowed more than anyone else. Not Mr. Laughton. Not Miss Mezaray. Not even Rudolph Von Beckmann."

"I don't understand you," I said. "What you said isn't logical. If there is a shortage of water, why should anyone mind if we bring more of it in?"

"What's important," said the guard who was squatting over the handsome valises, "is that we're self-sufficient. That's why we put up with that banging from the well."

"Is that what it is?" asked Valentina. "The well? It makes the clanging sound?"

"That's the pile driver. If we don't keep pushing deeper, we run dry. You'll get used to it. The only time you won't hear it is when they're shooting the picture."

Kuttner helped his partner close up our bags. "Maybe you've got used to it," he told him. "But not me. Bang, bang, bang, all night, all day."

Victor turned toward the looming Lydon. "You mentioned Mr. Laughton. Have you seen him? Is he all right? I mean his health. Has he been well enough to play the role of the sheriff?"

The guard turned his eyes away. "I can't," he muttered, "say anything about that."

Impatiently Victor reached down for the largest suitcase, but Kuttner pushed his arm aside. "No. These are going to town in another car."

"Another car?"

The guard: "There."

And in truth a second vehicle—not a car but a small truck, a Ford, black and battered—was just then pulling up nearby. The driver stepped out of the cab and started toward us. I was relieved to recognize the short, stout form of the chief grip, who had moved over from the B unit. Victor also smiled at the sight of Hoffman's sparse, crewcut hair. "George," he shouted, "will you tell these people who we are?"

Hoffman began to pluck up our luggage; he swung the pieces onto the bed of his truck. "Oh, they know who you are, Mr. Granite."

Valentina stepped out of the Packard. She leaned against her father. "Oh, that's George. Did you hear that I'm an actress now? I have a part in the picture."

"We know that, too," he said.

All of us walked over to the Ford and squeezed into the cab. Valentina sat on her father's lap; I took the middle. Hoffman ground the gears as we drove off toward the center of the crater.

It was now nearly night. A handful of stars stood out against the face of the sky, like marks on the negative of a photo. It didn't take long for us to make out a number of flickering lights, with the silhouettes of what looked like stones, squat boulders and taller rocks, scattered on the desert floor. Hoffman slowed. He turned on the headlights and rolled up his window. To Valentina, sitting on the outside, he said, "Better roll up yours."

But the girl was leaning into the breeze. "Oh!" she cried. "Indians!"

And so they were—men and women, some crouching, some standing, all with blankets thrown over their shoulders. They stirred to life as the truck drew near. Dogs ran about, excitedly yapping. Children grinned and waved. Old people, seemingly asleep, lifted their heads. It was clear that we were moving through the center of an encampment. All around us fires were burning inside scooped-out hollows or pits. I wondered what the fuel could be; there were no trees, nor was there any brush, for miles. The smell of roast meat wafted into the car. The flames leaped up to catch the dripping fat. By each fire women crouched, turning pieces of wire that served as skewers. The scorched meat was bunched like marshmallows, except that the tidbits had whiskers and shoestring tails. Mice! Field mice! It dawned on me: these people were starving.

"Stop! You have to stop!" cried Valentina.

"That would be a big mistake," Hoffman replied, and in fact he slightly increased our speed.

"But don't you see? Don't you see her? Just look!" Valentina was pointing at the closest fire. A woman was squatting there, no different, it seemed, from any of the others. I leaned across Victor and his daughter to get a better look. Then I saw how the heads of three children, bony and wide-eyed, poked from the folds of her blanket like marsupials from their mother's pouch.

Suddenly Hoffman stuck out his arm, knocking me back against the tattered fabric of the seat. "Don't do that!" he shouted.

It wasn't me he was addressing; it was Valentina. But he was too late. She had already dug into her purse and come up with a handful of change. She thrust her fist out the window. "Here! For you! Here!"

The flat-faced woman looked up from the fitful flames. The coins flew through the air, bouncing and rolling about her.

The response was immediate. From nowhere, from out of the ground it seemed, a group of Indians appeared before us. More of the tribe came running from every direction. Old men were shuffling forward, holding up their pants. Soon our vehicle was surrounded. Hoffman was forced to slow to a crawl. Determinedly we inched ahead, though the dark figures were draped over the fenders. Hands clung to the metal; faces pressed against the glass. It was like a scene, I couldn't help thinking, with other Indians, the ones in the newsreels of Calcutta. Hoffman struck the horn, he revved the engine; but the beggars hung on. They thrust trinkets through the open window: necklaces, punchboard games of chance, snakeskin belts.

"Get that window up!" Hoffman commanded.

Victor, cramped by Valentina, tried to turn the knob. But the long, thin arms waved like tendrils before our faces. The smell of the Indians, like bananas somehow, filled the cab. The bright teeth of the men flashed in their dark faces. They kept clacking together, like windup teeth from a novelty store. It took me a moment to realize that they were saying something, that the words I heard, the drone, the guttural growl, were in English.

Gimme two bits, half of them were shouting.

The other half: *Gimme dollar.*

"I'm going to fix them," Hoffman said. He had a length of pipe in his hand.

But no sooner did he raise it in order to smash the paperlike skin, the paper-thin bones, than Valentina let out a terrible scream.

"No! Oh, please! No!"

The white man wasn't intimidated in the least, but the score of Indians gaped in astonishment. What they saw was that the girl was jerking her head from side to side against her father's bony chest. Perhaps they thought she was possessed by a spirit. They all stepped aside.

Instantly Hoffman gunned the engine. The truck leaped forward, swerving away from the group of astounded natives. It roared off toward the brighter lights of the town ahead.

Pandaemonium, the ghost town, didn't seem that different from Hiko or any of the other places we had passed on our way: a main street, a handful of sidestreets, dust everywhere. The way people lived their lives clearly hadn't changed a great deal since gold-rush days. For that matter, if we had been riding into Thebes, the original location of the drama that Von Beckmann was filming, things might have looked very much the same—with lanterns and torches, perhaps, for the bare-bulbed electric lights. Civilization began in a Wild West town.

We came to a halt at what had once been the church. Hoffman said that was where Dr. Mosk had set up shop. Dick Mosk himself, a short, thin, deeply tanned man, was standing at the door when we drove up. Valentina was as tall as her father and weighed, in all likelihood, even more; but he insisted on carrying her up the steps to the dispensary. Without more than a glance at his patient, the doctor said, "Dehydration. Leave her with me."

Victor had no qualms in doing so. Mosk, after all, was part of our tennis crowd, too. In fact, the doctor was wearing the same hat he always sported on court: a duckbill visor in front and, at the back, a lightweight cloth that kept the sun off his neck. "I see," said Victor as they moved back to the steps, "that you've got your cap. What about your racquet? Can we put up a net?"

The little man stopped in his tracks. "Are you serious?"

"Why not?" said Victor, peering out over the flattened landscape. "It looks like one huge clay court to me."

I called out from the street. "Maybe John Payne could be our fourth. They say he's got a swell game."

"A clay court? A fourth? That kind of talk is dangerous. It demeans the nobility of our endeavor. It undermines morale. Or is that your intention? To distract us? We're not here to play games."

We stared at our friend in astonishment. Was it a joke? *The nobility of our endeavor?* But neither of us saw, on the physician's thin lips, any sign of a smile.

"Listen, Mosk," said the filmmaker. "What can you tell me about Laughton? We haven't a single shot of him in the rushes. He's practically disappeared from the production."

"Why are you asking me?"

"The rumor in town is he's sick. Louella's already put an item in her column. You're the doctor, are you not? Who else should I ask?"

"I can tell you this. He is under my care. You don't have to worry about his health."

"Then why—?" Victor broke off the question he had started to ask. Instead, he grasped his friend's hand. In his anxiety he wrung it between his own. "All right. Forget it. Tell me one thing. What about Magda? Have you seen her? Talked with her? How does she look? Jesus, just tell me how she's wearing her hair."

At that moment Hoffman, down in the pickup, started to lean on his horn. Mosk stepped backward. Then, without a further word, he turned on his heel and disappeared inside the former church.

Inside the cab of the truck, Hoffman drove the two of us through the rear of the town—so that we wouldn't leave tiretracks on Main Street, as the chief grip explained. Soon enough we came to what looked like a small tent city on the eastern outskirts. This was where the Granite crew and the non-Indian extras were housed, along with most of the studio's equipment. We didn't stop there, however, but continued further east to what Hoffman called the water station. This was a long, low shed made from corrugated iron. The grip led us both into the interior, where a counter stretched across the front part of the room. Here we each were given two empty canteens, with our own name stitched army-style into the canvas holders. Then we went round to the back of the same building. Perhaps a dozen people were waiting in line for their rations. I knew most of them; so did Victor. But no one came forward. On the contrary, they backed away, leaving a space around us. About thirty yards off was the clanking well itself. Puffs of steam came out of the derrick. No question now; the ground was shaking under our feet. Hoffman shouted, to make himself heard.

"I know you're thirsty. You're going to want to drink your fill. Don't. You get two canteens every twenty-four hours, plus what's served you at meals. There's water in the communal shower, but it's not potable. Every day Mosk has to treat somebody who got sick from trying. Maybe you think the two canteens are plenty, but believe me, it's hot here like you wouldn't believe. One of Maynes's men the other day drained the radiator from the truck. Now he's plenty sorry."

I shouted, too. "What happened? Was his stomach poisoned?"

"Poisoned? What from? A little rust? That's iron. Good for the blood. No, he's still in the lift. He's got one more day to go."

"And what is the lift?" asked Victor.

Hoffman shook his head. He passed his hand through his sparsely cut hair. "That's the elevator in the old mineshaft. It's like an animal cage once you padlock the door. Schotter—he's one of the gaffers—was the guy who stole the water. You can bet he wishes he never wet his lips."

I licked my own lips, on which a crust had formed. I was now only a few feet from the steps that led into the back of the shed. I could smell the water, the way, on Fontenelle, I could smell the ocean when the wind was strong enough from the west. I looked up; inside the building the surface of the tank was reflected crazily on the wrinkled metal walls. Why wouldn't the line move faster?

Victor was a few steps behind, with the chief grip. "What you are saying to me is that he is being punished. You've put him in jail."

Hoffman laughed. "We've got a jail. A real one. I'll take you so you can see where the old-time prisoners scratched their names and crossed off the days. It's genuine Americana. One guy who was a murderer even wrote a poem. No, what I'm talking about, the lift, is hanging a hundred feet down. The temperature, day and night, is a hundred and ten degrees."

"Jesus," said Victor. "This is not punishment. It is torture."

Hoffman: "That's not the worst of it. The worst is that they're using the original cable. How old is it? Sixty, seventy years? Sometimes there are three or four people hanging on the end of it at one time. You don't dare move in case it might snap."

"I am having trouble understanding this. Who makes these rules? Who enforces them? This country abolished slavery a long time ago. The studio can demote people. It can dismiss them. You have the authority to fire them, or to recommend firing them, yourself. But to put men in cages? Why didn't Schotter, if that's his name, simply quit?"

Hoffman gestured out toward the darkness, the surrounding desert. "How would he do that?"

Victor: "George, explain something to me, will you? I'm thirsty, all right. I'll tell you right now I intend to drink my canteen. Perhaps I'll drink them both. When I am done, what will happen if I ask for more?"

"You'll be refused."

"And if I take it myself?"

"I think you'll be restrained."

"Are you kidding? Victor Granite? The head of production? Who will do this? The people who work for me?"

"There is not enough water. Everybody accepts the situation. We have to ration."

"That is what I do not understand. Why? I see about the well. They told me on the coast that the reason Pandaemonium was abandoned wasn't because they ran out of gold but because they ran out of water. That's a familiar story in the West. There are settlements, Hopi settlements, not far from here; they were simply wiped out when the climate changed. But we're not living in a prehistoric culture. All you have to do is bring in a tank truck from Hiko or Las Vegas or Lake Mead. The idea must have occurred to someone, because I saw the scene in which the miners try the same solution. One truck a week would probably meet the needs of everyone here, including the Indian extras. You would not have to run this pump. I can see where it might drive a man out of his mind. You could shut the thing down once and for all."

Hoffman: "We tried to insulate the pile driver, the way we insulated the generators. You don't hear them because they're actually underground, in what was once a cistern for the town. But there was no way to muffle the well."

Suddenly, as I stood listening to this debate, everything went black before me. Victor disappeared. Hoffman disappeared. So did the zigs and zags of reflected light. Had I fainted? Was it a stroke? A weight, a heaviness, oppressed me from behind. But my other senses were in operation: I smelled the licorice of Black Jack gum and heard a familiar voice saying, "Guess who?" The Queen B! Miss Hudson! With her hands over my eyes!

Victor stepped toward us. "Ah, Rochelle. There's something I've wanted to tell you. I've seen your work in the dailies. I think you are doing a remarkable job. The nuance in your voice. The range of emotions. You have truly come into your own."

The hands dropped away. I wheeled. There she was: her freckles, like a handful of pennies, were spread across her tan bosom, and her hair, as usual, was falling off one side of her head. "Yes, yes," I said. "An excellent impersonation. It's Annie's sister, *n'est-ce pas?*"

The actress smiled. "Gee, I always get compliments from Petey, but they mean a lot coming from you, Mr. Granite."

My head, at the sight of her, had started to spin. Or was it the thirst? Yes! For her lips! "Miss Hudson," I whispered, leaning close, "come to my room. We're at the hotel. I have, you know, a surprise."

Immediately she put her hands on her hips and stamped her foot with its pretty pump. "Hey, I'm not here for funny business. What we are doing is much too important for that. I heard what Mr. G said about bringing water in on a truck. I wanted to tell him we could never do that. We wouldn't be self-sufficient."

What struck me was that she'd used the same phrase, and with something of the same reverential tone, as Lydon, the guard at the wall. No doubt Victor had noted the resemblance, too. He hugged one arm to his torso and put a finger under his chin. "What you said about being self-sufficient—I do not understand it. How can you achieve such a thing in the middle of a desert? And why should you want to? What is the purpose?"

The actress said, "We can't make the film our own way if we don't have our independence."

I, or the lunatic dwelling in Loewenstein, said, "You mean Von Beckmann's way."

Now someone else—it was Kleinbard, the sound man—pushed forward. "You'll find that there is no difference between his goals and what we're trying to do. Our minds are one and the same."

Or else, but this time I only thought the words, *you end up in the cage.*

Miss Hudson had more to say. "Just think how vulnerable we'd be if we had to depend on places a hundred miles away for water. We'd be at the mercy of anyone who wanted to attack."

"*Attack?*" Victor exclaimed. "I think you people have been affected by the sun."

The small crowd gathered closer. Nakhimovsky, the cameraman, looked to be in a fury; his hair, thick, matted, stood up like quills. He said, "Are you saying we're crazy? That we're paranoid? That's ironic, since we are the ones who see reality as it is."

John Payne, who played one of Annie's two brothers, was in the crowd as well. "Think of it this way," he said. "If the outer world is corrupted, it makes sense to keep it away. There's a purity of spirit in what we can do on our own."

Now Hoffman held up his hands, at which the others quickly fell silent. "It is no secret, Mr. Granite, that you haven't come here just to chaperone your daughter. We understand that it is your job to keep us on schedule and on budget. And if you decide you can't do that, you'll try to shut us down. So you mustn't be surprised if some people here don't regard you as exactly a friend."

"Don't be fools!" Victor burst out. "I am the only one who can keep this picture going!"

At just that point we stepped over the threshold and into the tin-topped structure. The sight inside struck me dumb. DC current was driving the electric lights. They played on the steaming surface of the cistern and swam, in currents and eddies, under the roof and across the walls. It was like being under water. Immediately I suffered an anguishing attack of thirst. Hands, that's what it felt like, were wringing the last drops of moisture from my throat. I couldn't have said a word now if I had wanted to. Silently I handed over both bottles, which a woman in a hairnet, like a cafeteria worker, submerged with a number of others in a rack. Air bubbles rose through the cistern, like the thoughts wobbling toward consciousness inside Mr. Moto's skull.

Here were the detective's deductions. First, it was obvious that there was no reason for the system of rationing or for the shortage of water in general. Therefore, it existed solely because Von Beckmann wished it to. The same held true for the absurd notion of self-sufficiency, of preparing the settlement for an attack. The question was, why had Von Beckmann created this artificial drought? Even an inferior thinker, like Boston Blackie, or an utter nincompoop like Charlie Chan, could see the answer: the conditions for everyone on location had been designed to resemble those that existed within the picture they were making—a state of siege and thirst. Nature was being held up to the mirror of art, instead of vice versa. It was just what Von Beckmann had said he would do at the Wilshire Ebell: make a film that was not based on illusion. Clearly the director had concluded that the anguish of a town like Pandaemonium could not be captured unless those portraying it suffered the same deprivations themselves.

Up came the streaming canteens. Rochelle handed both of Victor's to him. I took mine from the rack. Then we followed her past those waiting in line and moved outdoors.

The heat of the bottles went right through the canvas, singeing my fingers. I took off a cap. The water inside was hot enough to leach the flavor from a bag of tea. I saw that contrary to Hoffman's advice, the crowd of picture people, the extras and gaffers and grips, were drinking with abandon. They held their canteens in the air, the way Spaniards hold wineskins. The liquid bubbled in their mouths. Victor drank like the others. So did Kleinbard. So, in fact, did Miss Hudson. I saw her throat working. I saw water streaming on her chin. For a moment I alone forbore. I drew up beside her. "Remember, Miss Hudson, honey. The Fancy Free. I will be waiting. Room 204." Then I lifted my vessel and drank along with the rest.

The Fancy Free, which in old Pandaemonium had been the Halcyon, had been provided with a new false front, so that it matched the facade in the B-unit takes. The studio ran it as an actual hotel for the principal actors and the more highly paid members of the crew. Coco, Von B, and surely Magdalena all had rooms on the second floor. Now Victor climbed the main staircase and went down the hall to room 206. Fully clothed, he threw himself down on the bed. From the look of things, nothing had changed since gold rush days. The wood was not petrified, as rumor had had it, but the dry air had preserved it as carefully as a dealer his antiques. The headboard above him, for instance, was shiny enough for him to see the reflection of his features, as a violinist might see his brow in the grain of his violin. There wasn't enough moisture, he guessed, to support the bacteria, not to mention the termites, the weevils, that would otherwise have rotted the wood. For much the same reasons, one was not supposed to catch colds at the North Pole. Perhaps here, where it was as hot as the Arctic was frigid, they would be equally immune to such ills.

On the other hand, the vibrations from the pile driver had surely done more damage to the town of Pandaemonium in three or four months than the normal process of decay had wrought in all the years since it had been abandoned. Wherever the filmmaker cast his glance he was aware of a certain vagueness, a blurriness, though whether this was due to the shaking of the objects themselves or to the throbbing—like a case of chronic nystagmus— of his own eyeballs, he could not say.

He forced his eyes shut, but he knew, for all his exhaustion, he would not sleep. Where was Magda? Her room must be somewhere near. He thought—was it a hallucination?—that he could smell her perfume. Was Frauen Träumen. Perhaps she had been in this very room earlier in the day, or yesterday, or a week or two weeks ago. Perhaps a single molecule, that's all it would take, had lingered behind. He tried then to empty his mind—to think of nothing, like a yogi who empties himself of circumstance and desire. Impossible! A thousand memories flooded through him: an earlobe; an earring; a thread on a jacket; a hair on a comb. They circulated through his system like drops of medication from an intravenous tube.

Again he tried to force himself to sleep, but his body reacted to the slightest sensation: the clamp of his collar, the chill wind at the window. Even the individual hairs that grew on his chest, his shoulders, the small of his back pricked him like the points of innumerable pins. It was as if he were being marked by a thousand seismographic needles. Oh, how many times had he felt that sensation? Too many to count: those were her fingernails. Good God! The claws of the bloody bitch!

With a moan he swung out of bed and lit a cigarette. He paced back and forth in front of the open window. The floorboards, rubbing against their metal nails, made a high-pitched squeak, as if he were a western hero with spurs. His thoughts now were not of the imminent encounter with Magda but of the first time they'd met, shortly after she'd signed at Metro back in 1930. He had been having lunch with Mayer and some others when the glamorous European star, arm in arm with Thalberg, had swept into the room. Of course she'd made a beeline for L. B. and fussed over him in the usual manner. She even pretended to straighten his necktie from the back. Like a genie from a jug a photographer materialized to take their picture. All grins. All smiles. Then the actress had come round the table with a word for everyone. Victor had kept his eyes on the piece of meat that, with his long fingers and knobby wrists, he'd been cutting into precise cubes. The next thing he knew he felt the actress's warm breath, the touch of her lips, as she whispered something into his ear. What had she said? Was it in German? In English? No matter. He knew for a certainty that the real message was in the warm wash of her breath, the nibbling lips, and even—could he have imagined it?—the quick poke from the tip of her tongue.

Naturally enough he had called her that night. But she was cool. She was distant. She would not see him for dinner, nor lunch, not even a drink. Then what had that—what else to call it?—that caress been about? Or had she been making fun, for Thalberg's pleasure, of the stick of a man beneath the broad-brimmed hat? He'd had his share of teases. He didn't call back.

Not long afterward, when Von Beckmann backed out of his contract, Manfred and Mayer arranged for a joint showing of her tests in the Granite projection room. He sat alone in the back. Ten minutes into the screening, Magdalena came in and slipped into the seat on his right. He could make out the same scent—he didn't know then that it was What Women Dream— that had wafted over him at the Metro table. He was also aware that she was pressing the length of her thigh against his. He turned to her. There, lit by the varying beam of the projection lamp, was the very profile that was blown up to quadruple size at the front of the room. Not only that, around her neck were the same fake pearls that the smartly dressed woman wore in what he already recognized as a standard Metro test: a woman at a dressing table reacts to a knock on her door. Disaster—she pulled her leg away. But when he returned his gaze to the screen, her leg, in her creased slacks, resumed the pressure.

A quick learner, Victor—quick enough to realize that it was his distraction, the way his thoughts seemed to be elsewhere, that aroused her. He kept his eyes on the screen. As a result, she slipped her left hand into his. He put his arm over the back of her seat and stroked her neck beneath her hair. Like kids they leaned together in the dark. She slid her hand up his sleeve, raking, though gently, the skin of his forearm with her nails. He groped for her throat, and when, sighing, she tilted her head back, he extended his fingers beneath her blouse, scissoring open the first and second buttons. Straining, he reached under her brassiere. She mewed. She moaned. Her nipple, when he grazed it, rose quick, hard, and determined from its beaded bed. Victor appreciated the demonstration, which reminded him of a magician popping open a tiny collapsible hat.

Still he kept his eyes on her gigantic image, while his fingers propped her life-sized breast in his hand. Just for an instant he felt something of what she, and perhaps every star, did: the thrill of looking through a one-way mirror. She sighed, murmuring something. Once more the sound was meaningless, not intelligible. Only later, when the lights came on and they sat circumspectly apart, did he realize she had been saying, *Rudi. Ah, Rudi.* The sighs were for her missing mentor.

Victor stopped pacing. In moonlight, or starlight, he glimpsed himself in the hotel's full-length mirror. The way he stood there swaying slightly, with his hat swelling on top of his head—even to himself he looked like a snake, a cobra. And these thoughts filled him with venom. He threw himself back on the bed.

What he hadn't known after that screening was whether he'd see her again. There'd been no notes. They didn't call. She simply showed up at his Granite office one week after their encounter in the projection room. She walked in while he was on the line to New York. He motioned for her to take his chair, while he paced up and down, holding the receiver in one hand, pointing at his invisible interlocutor with the other. In the swiveling seat, Magda took off her hat. She took off her shoes. Then she began to pull on the stretched-out cord. Victor had enough wit to go on talking—about weekly grosses, about an advertising campaign, about anything he could dredge to mind. Slowly she reeled him in, until he stood beside her. She took the loose end of his belt in her teeth, tugging. He took hold of her hair. She began to kiss him through his pants. Still his voice, crossing the continent, did not waver. On that occasion she had been wearing a summer dress covered with black and white figures, as incomprehensible as hieroglyphics. It was cut low at the shoulders, so that he saw how, as she panted, her small, pointed breasts fell free at each exhalation. Still talking, he reached down and slid his hand under the lacy frill. She gasped, loud enough, apparently, for the party on the island of Manhattan to hear.

"No, Jerry. Not a thing," Victor said into the receiver. "It must have been something on the line."

Magda giggled, smothering the sound girlishly beneath her hands. Then she reached up for the handset and put the receiver by her ear. Jerry's voice came out like an insect's. They both laughed this time. Quickly she thrust the phone upward so that poor Victor could explain. While he did so—*No, of course I'm alone. Are you sure there's no one listening in on your end?*— she raised one of her legs, smooth-shaven, without nylons, and used it to separate both of his own. As soon as Jerry started to reply, she reached eagerly upward for the receiver and listened, showing her teeth in a grin. They were now in a three-way conversation. Whenever Victor spoke, she moved her shinbone, from ankle to knee, like a churn at his crotch. When she held the receiver, he strove to undress her. He slid the straps of her dress off her shoulders and worked it down past her diaphragm, over her belly. Then he hiked the material upward, off her thighs, around her hips. Finally the whole of the dress circled her waist in a band of black and white, like a wadded-up newspaper. Sweat pooled in her throat and ran over her breasts. Her kneecaps glistened. The silk of her underpants was dark with the stain. Her bent legs swung slowly out and in, the way a resting butterfly will work its wings. Here Victor leaned down to kiss her. His open mouth encircled her thin upper and full lower lip. She grasped his narrow hips with her knees. As it happened, Jerry in New York was just then telling a funny story. Victor, bending lower, licking her neck, her salty throat, heard him laughing at his own joke. Something about the moment chilled him. He glanced up, under his ubiquitous hat brim, toward Magda. Her head was thrown back, her eyes half closed, her mouth half open. She was as rapt as a medium at a séance. It was as if she had invited someone else, a ghost of a person, to join them at long distance. A pulse beat mightily in the flesh of her throat. The tinny voice, like that from a gramophone horn, barked at her ear. Was she, once more, hearing Von B?

In Pandaemonium, in the newly named Fancy Free, Victor let out an involuntary groan. By the time he had finished dwelling upon that scene he was spent and covered in sweat, as if, like one of those cultists—was it the Oneida community? The childless Shakers?—he had engaged in a long act of intercourse without a climax. Fitting, he thought. The perfect metaphor for his life with Magda. All those rumors, the innuendo in the "Merry Go Round," in Whistler and Hopper, the knowing glances from friends: false, specious to the core. Oh, he'd had every actress in town, including Greta and

235

Marlene; but the one woman he'd never been able to bed was the great star with whom the whole world assumed he was having—in the language of Louella's column—a torrid affair.

And the truth? Did anyone know? Only Lorre. He hadn't the least doubt in the world that Magda told her lamb everything. Victor fought back a sudden wave of bitterness toward the German actor. *He* was the one who should be writing a column. *Lorre-lies.* Like those women, those sirens, who lure us to our doom. *Loewenstein*: the stone lion. He, that fat little man, was the Sphinx who guarded their secrets. Then Victor relented. Behind that partition, on a bed identical to his own, poor Peter was also waiting for a woman who would never become his mistress.

Why had the story, the myth of Victor and Magda, constantly played in the papers? It was all based on the fact that he was the one man she had been willing to appear with in town. That should have been the clue, he thought with a bitter smile, that nothing occurred between them but unending foreplay. What a spectacle they had made! People used to take their meals at Chasen's just to catch a glimpse of the two of them at their table. They always sat side by side at the banquette. Over time they mastered the art of eating one-handed, the way the pianist Wittgenstein, who had lost his right arm in the Great War, made a career out of a commissioned repertoire. You didn't need much imagination to see that what was going on under the table wasn't footsie. A persistent story had it that one night the lovers became so carried away they threw themselves to the carpet and, in evening dress, began to copulate behind the protective curtain of their quickly assembled friends.

Another falsehood. Those culprits had been Chaplin and Goddard. The truth was that no matter how much he begged, cajoled, threatened, the actress never gave in. It was always the same: she only desired him when he was concentrating on something else—driving, or on the telephone, or when he had to meet a deadline and so could not take his eyes off a manuscript or the screen or a book. In a way he had known the truth from the start, that is, at the back of the screening room: his mind had to be elsewhere. And her mind? Was it constantly on Rudolph Von Beckmann?

In that ghost-town hotel, with the ghosts of old miners about him, Victor felt little more than a shade himself. He had never been allowed to look directly, undistractedly, upon her, which meant in turn that she did not have to return his gaze. He did not, at least in the flesh, truly exist. He understood that that was the key to how she managed simultaneously to conduct a public affair and create the reputation, as had Garbo, of a recluse. It was as if everyone's eyes glanced off her, as light does from a polished surface; as if, as

Tolstoy says of one of his countesses, the look of too many men—and Magda had been stared at by millions, from the anonymity of the dark—had left a kind of lacquer upon her features.

At that moment the clangor outside Victor's window came to a sudden halt. He sat bolt upright, listening to the molecules of air, like bees about flowers, bumbling against his large, papery ears. Then he leapt from the bed and in two strides ran through his door. A split second later and he was pounding on Loewenstein-Lorre's.

"*Entrée*," said the voice inside.

Victor burst into the room, which for some reason was drenched with the smell of Turkish delight. "Come on! Get up!" he commanded.

There sat I, cross-legged on the bedspread, drenched head to toe in perspiration. "I was," I said, "expecting someone else."

"Don't you hear? The pump! The pile driver! It's stopped!"

"What does that mean? Does it mean they are shooting the picture?"

With Victor in the lead the two of us raced to the double window at the end of the hall. We threw the shutters wide. Below were a series of lights: flashlight beams darting up, down, into the air. Behind them came a dozen running figures. Now, in the hotel, more people were coming out of their rooms. They ran along the corridors and down the stairs. The whole town was rushing toward where the next scene of *Pandaemonium* was about to be shot.

Without a flashlight of our own, Victor and I fell behind the stragglers as we rushed from the town. We made our way to the set by following the tangle of electrical cables—no wonder Manfred had been presented with such tremendous bills!—to the north. Long before arriving at the ridge, we saw where the arc lights had brightened the nighttime sky. I knew enough by then not to wonder why Von Beckmann hadn't ordered a mockup, in cardboard and plaster, of the crater's edge. Only the real thing, no illusion, would do.

The whole town, and most of the Indian extras, had arrived before us. They squatted on the ridge to either side of the segment that had been marked off for the shoot, like a crowd of spectators in the bleachers. We joined them and stared down at the active members of the crew, who were milling about on the flat ground below. I picked out Von Beckmann at once. He stood off to one side, dressed in black, his hair sliced over his forehead. There might have been a circle drawn around him; that's how careful, in the hustle and bustle of preparing the scene, everyone was to keep his distance. As I watched, the director brought his hand in a swatting motion to his face; then I realized he was sucking the stub of a cigarette.

Where were the stars? Laughton? Magdalena? Nowhere in view. The only actor I recognized was Leo Gorcey, one of the original Dead End Kids. He was, with his big head, his pint-sized body, rehearsing his role as Ethan. Holding a revolver at arm's length, he strode deliberately forward, taking aim as he went. It was an odd bit of casting—in the vernacular, a wise guy from Brooklyn as the cold-blooded boss of a mining town. It was as if at any moment he was going to say, *Stick 'em up, ya bum!*

"Kill the lights! Maynes! The lights!" That was Coco Goodheart. His voice, or the half-voice left him, had to be amplified by a megaphone. With a faint popping, like someone stamping on paper cups, the main bank of klieg lights went out. Only the torches continued to burn.

We prepared ourselves for the usual delays. Off to the right Nakhimovsky, the cinematographer, was measuring the distance between his lens and Gorcey's stand-in, a young man with shiny black hair and, remarkably, the same broad nose and wide Irish lip. Someone else held a light meter to his face. To our left a couple of bit players lay stretched on the ground. A woman, Ellie from costume, came over and began minute adjustments in the way they wore their ten-gallon hats. On top of the ridge two men from Hoffman's crew unfurled a sheet with the outline of a man drawn upon it. The target hung down in front of the embankment. Finally Mike Meltsner called out, "Places, everyone! Leo, we're ready for you. I'd like quiet on the set!"

Victor nudged me with his elbow. Just below our vantage point Reynaldo Flatow was peering down into the open pages of his script. Sampson Frank was looking over his shoulder. Something about the two men, in their physical appearance, struck me as odd, though it wasn't their dark clothing, their foreignness, or even the Mr. Mutt and Mr. Jeff disparity in their height.

"Flatow," Victor called quietly down to the writer, "is this a scene from the Epsteins? Or one of yours?"

Frank, in little more than a whisper, gave the answer. "Scene 86. By Reynaldo. Here Ethan prepares for combat with his brother."

"*Ethan.* But his real name is Eteocles. Am I right about that? That you have adapted *Antigone*?"

Now Flatow, the round dome of his skull shining in the torchlight, and his glasses shining too, answered for himself. "This is correct. We have here a scene in which Antigone—we call her Annie, still—arrives to plead with her brother to call off the duel. She finds him practicing with his revolver."

"Annie?" Victor interrupted, unable to hide the crack in his voice. "You mean that Magdalena is part of the scene?"

Frank: "Oh, yes. She begs Ethan. No killing! She begs also her uncle. When she knows she cannot persuade either one, she climbs on top of the ridge and calls to her other brother. There is no answer. Only the sounds the Indians make, imitating the animals and the birds."

Flatow: "You have to understand what I have written here. It has been agreed that each brother will have only one bullet in his gun and that as they approach one another from either side on the ridge, each will be free to fire that single shot whenever he wishes."

But Victor was no longer listening. He twisted about, searching for Magda. She remained, however, out of sight. Just then Liz, the slate girl, held her clapboard in front of the camera; Coco Goodheart in his raspy voice cried, "Action!" At once Gorcey started forward. At his side a camera was tracking; over his head the sound boom hung, ominous somehow, like a sword over Damocles.

Flatow looked up toward Victor. In a nasal half-whisper he said, "Do you see what is occurring? For Ethan it is a dilemma. With every step, each new second that he can force himself to withhold his fire, he increases by geometrical proportions his chances for success; he also increases to precisely the same degree the prospect of being shot through the heart by his brother. Now we see him attempt to determine the exact distance at which his opportunities are maximized and his risks made minimal."

Victor bent toward the round-faced little man. "The Greeks themselves would say that such calculations are beyond the human sphere. *Hubris* was their name for the attempt to make them."

Bang! The actor's revolver went off with a terrific report. The flash of powder lit up all our faces.

"Cease!" That was Von B.

"Cut!" Coco yelled a half-second after.

The director moved swiftly to where Gorcey stood. He reached out and, rather like an old-fashioned schoolmaster with a schoolboy, pinched the actor's ear. "Allow me," he said, "to make a suggestion."

The reaction was striking. All those who had been at work on the shot seemed to freeze on the spot, like figures in a *tableau vivant.* Above the scene, on the ridge where we sat, a wave of movement passed over the crowd. Everyone leaned forward, straining to hear what the director would say next.

Von B: "Is this how you intend to approach your enemy? I do not mean the image of your enemy drawn on a sheet. What will you do at dawn? When you face your brother?"

Gorcey smiled quickly. He shrugged. "I thought I was doing an okay job."

Von B: "You forgot one thing. Your opponent is armed. He has the same weapons—a gun with one bullet, a seven-inch knife—as you."

"I know that."

"Then tell me, why do you stand full-face? Like this?" Here Von Beckmann mimicked the actor's stance. It was true: the target he presented was as large, as looming, as what Americans call the side of a barn. "Do you see? Do you understand? After another ten paces, he is not likely to miss."

Gorcey hung his head. "It was dumb of me. I guess I was thinking—not of real life, you know, but the way I played scenes in pictures."

"And in real life? How do you propose to proceed?"

"What if I ran at him? A moving object is hardest to hit."

"That is certainly true. But how would you aim? Your goal is to kill, not merely to avoid being killed."

Gorcey dropped into a squat. "Then what if I inch along this way? Or even better, I could crawl on top of the ridge. I could use the ground to support the gun."

Von Beckmann considered this for a moment. "No. What if Paul adopts the same tactic? That would destroy your chief advantage, which is the fact that you are perhaps thirty centimeters shorter than he is. No, the change I suggest is subtle, but nonetheless crucial. Simply turn sidewise."

"Like this?" Gorcey held the gun toward the painted figure and took a series of short hopping steps.

Von Beckmann held up his hand. He shook his head. "No. Like this."

The director swung round and advanced, not toward the target but toward where Victor and I sat on the ridge. I was amazed at the transformation. A suppressed gasp went up, as well, from the crowd. Von Beckmann was a large man, with a heavyset torso upon thin, even spindly legs. But of a sudden he seemed to shrink, to suck himself in. The knees bent, the chest collapsed, and the big, square head sank into the shoulders. The effect was like that of a weathervane that is suddenly tossed from broadside to edgewise by a ninety-degree shift in the wind. All at once the body was perpendicular to the head and the outstretched arms. Taking crossover steps, like a man on a high wire, he came closer and closer, growing—and this was contrary to the laws of perspective, if not of physics—smaller with every footstep. Then, with a single puff on his cigarette—*poof!*—he disappeared. Gorcey gaped. Coco drew in his breath with a wheeze. Even Victor stared openmouthed. A murmur went up from the onlookers. How long would this hallucination—what else, after all, could it be? Some feat of mesmerization, a collective hypnosis: how long would the phenomenon last? A millisecond? A moment? Flatow looked toward us.

"Wake up, Mr. Granite. Also you, Herr Lorre. This is only a trick. A cheap one. Don't you see?"

Frank said, loud enough for anyone to hear, "Fools! It's so obvious. I have seen better in the music hall."

At last Meltsner, the assistant, cried out, "All right, everybody, let's try it again," and Von Beckmann, as big as life, reappeared.

Immediately Goodheart raised the megaphone to his lips. "Camera ready? Sound ready? And action!"

Liz brought the clapper down onto the slate. Gorcey, his weapon extended, moved forward again, darting, dashing, with the sidewinding motion of a reptile. Closer he came to the target, and closer still.

But I was looking down at the two Europeans. All at once, at the sight of their frowning faces, I had realized what it was that separated the refugees from everyone else at the set—and for that matter, from everyone else in the reinhabited town of Pandaemonium. The guards who had searched us, Hoffman, Mosk, all those on line at the water station—each one of them had skin that had been darkened by the desert sun. Even Miss Hudson, who had traded on her pale skin in every B picture, had become deeply tanned. But Flatow and Frank looked like ghosts.

"Can it be?" I cried, not attempting to muffle my words. "Have you both been punished inside the lift?"

There was at that instant a thunderous report, as Gorcey, or Ethan, pulled the trigger again.

This time no one called *Cut*. Instead, Nakhimovsky dollied in for a tight reaction shot of the actor's face. Even at a distance it was possible to see the look of shock upon it. Then Gorcey said, *What are you doing here? I almost killed you.*

Now the crew drew the camera back until the gunman and the embankment were both in the same frame. I looked toward the target. A woman was standing by the sheet. Magdalena! She was almost in front of the painted silhouette.

Why didn't you? she asked. *Since you are so eager to spill our family's blood.*

Ethan: *Move aside.*

Annie: *If you would kill a brother, you can just as well kill a sister. I will not move.*

Now Clayton, the sheriff, stepped into the space between the siblings. He turned first toward Annie. *How did you come here? I told Raymond to keep you with him until the duel was decided.*

Annie: *Nothing is easier than to deceive a man in love.*

Ethan: *Go back to him. A bed of shame is a better place for you than this battleground.*

Annie: *This is the place of shame. What else would you call the spot where two brothers conspire to murder each other? Ethan, look—do you see how I am on my knees? How the tears run from my eyes? Doesn't that move your cold heart? Do not kill Paul! Do not allow Paul to kill you! No! No! I will not permit the sun to rise on that dreadful dawn!*

All this while I sat in a state of stupefaction. Laughton had not appeared. Von B was the sheriff. There on his breast was the badge of office. How could I have not noticed before? It shone on the dark cloth of his vest as conspicuously as the shock of silver in the black strands of his hair. Now Annie turned to him. As she did so, I turned toward Victor. Here was the moment, the historical moment, that would save Granite Films: actress and impresario reunited in motion pictures. Unaccountably, he seemed unmoved. He frowned. He snorted. I heard him mutter Flatow's impossible lines—*Dreadful dawn! Bed of shame!*—under his breath. Annie, the Antigone, spoke again.

Uncle, the blood of these youths flows in your veins, too. Speak to Ethan. Make him see reason. It cannot be called cowardice to withdraw from folly.

Von Beckmann stood with arms folded. His thick lips were stretched downward in a scowl. *It is not for me to interfere in this contest. I carry out the law, I do not make it.*

Annie: *How can it be lawful that two dear brothers are allowed to murder one another?*

Clayton: *They are the owners of the mine. It was agreed between them.*

Annie: *And if in their crazed state they should decide—what? My mind fails me. To foul what remains of our water? Or that every fifth person should be sentenced to the loss of an arm or leg? Would you carry out that sentence, too?*

Ethan: *Sister, it is you who would sentence far more than one in five to a terrible fate, and deprive countless others of more than a single limb. Have you not seen the corpses on the battlefield? Have we not slaughtered enough already? Will you not be satisfied until there is no man—nor woman, nor child— left in Pandaemonium?*

Magdalena clutched her hair, long and wavy, and pulled on the roots. Victor looked as if he would clutch his as well, had he not been wearing his hat. He leaned toward me. "It's wrong," he whispered. "All wrong. This dialogue—it's like what Louella said, something out of Verdi: *La Forza del Destino* or *Don Carlos*. And Magdalena? Jesus! Peter, what has happened to her? Rochelle would do better with those lines."

It was all too true. I heard the false note even as the actress turned back to the officer of the law.

Do not let my brother's logic sway you from your duty. There are higher statutes than those which govern our little town or even the greatest of cities— and fratricide, from the time that Cain raised his hand against Abel, is a violation of them all.

Clayton: *Do you see this badge? The oath I took when I pinned it on was to enforce the laws of this town. Those are the only decrees that concern me.*

Annie, in tears: *If the laws of nature do not move you, then your duty to the family must. Act as our father's brother. Call on your conscience to make his children as precious as your own.*

Clayton: *Then heed a father's advice. Return to my son, your husband-to-be. You asked me to search my conscience; I ask the same of you. Why do you presume the welfare of a single family is worth more than that of the greater family of our town? Must an entire community groan because you would save those closest to you? Selfish girl, leave us. We have men's work to do.*

At that, Coco called for a stop. There was a brief pause while a second camera was brought forward to secure a closeup of the actress's reactions. In no time everyone heard the crack of the slate board that Liz held in front of the lens. In this shot, scene 87, Magda stared off—not at Leo Gorcey or Von Beckmann but above them, toward the nighttime sky. Her eyes seemed unfocused. Her lips moved tremblingly, inaudibly, as if she were repeating a message or a lesson to herself. At the same time she continued to tangle and twist her hair about her fingers. When she spoke, the words were in little more than a whisper. *I see. I see. What sadness. The terror! Poor brother, a painful end awaits you. Uncle, woe unto you: you shall suffer more than either of these children, whose deaths you refused to prevent. As for Annie, my fate—*

Clayton, off-camera: *Enough. Seize her. Take her away!*

Coco Goodheart cried, "Cut!"

There was a brief period of scurrying about. Von Beckmann lit a fresh cigarette. Then Nakhimovsky pulled his camera back from the closeup on Annie to a medium shot of the embankment. In less than a minute, Coco was crying *Action!* again.

When scene 88 began, four or five hatted men, Clayton's deputies, came rushing forward. Annie, seeing them, broke from her trance. As the men closed in she whirled around, grasping the sheet in both hands. She used it to haul herself to the top of the ridge. Then she drew it up after her and began to wave it like a banner over her head. *Paul!* she called. *Paul! Paul!*

Below, the men were leaping, attempting to seize her ankles. They struggled to boost each other to the top of the embankment. The actress dropped the flag. She put both hands to her mouth and cried out one last time, *Paul! Oh! Oh! Paul!*

"Cease! Stop that camera!" This time the command came from Von Beckmann. He strode toward the embankment. Before he arrived Magda held up her hand, as if to keep him away.

"Don't say anything. Not a word, I beg you. You don't have to tell me this was not a good performance."

"*Not a good performance?* Is that what you call it? Here is a young woman in ecstasy. The gods have whispered into her ear. She is a girl with the vision of the Maid of Orleans—yes, of Joan of Arc. And what do I see? Someone who is languishing. Someone who waits for Robert Taylor or Clark Gable or some other star with a moustache to kiss her on her trembling lips."

Magda: "Rudi, don't. I am embarrassed enough already."

"You are embarrassed. You are ashamed. What of me? Do you know what I have gone through to bring you here? The whole world has waited to see Magdalena Mezaray as Antigone. But is this the innocent child who lives only for her ideal? Or do you think you can play such a role the way you played next to Jannings? In your little Nazi farce? Ah! Have they sent you here to sabotage our film? Is that it? Are you under orders to kill me? Why don't you simply put poison in my food? Or plunge a dagger into my breast? Already I feel the pain in my heart, it is agony, when I watch you pull on your hair like this—you see, like this, as if you were an old woman knitting wool!"

"An old woman! Yes, that is what I am. And who cast this hag for the role? Do you think it is easy for a person my age to play a young girl? I am trying. I am doing my best. I am at my limit."

Von B turned, addressing the crowd. "Did you hear? She has done her best. She is at her limit. I have more faith in her than she has in herself. I know she has not begun to act. Ladies and gentlemen. My colleagues. My friends. Do not judge this actress by what you have seen these last days, or by what you have seen tonight. This is not Magdalena Mezaray. It is a puppet of wood. With a rubber squeeze-bottle for tears. When she was a girl, a schoolgirl, I directed her as Ophelia. That was a woman of flesh and blood! You could smell her at the back of the theater. The Berliners were wild! Yes, they were like beasts! Von Beckmann, better than anyone in the world, knows what she can do."

Magdalena: "And what about you? You think now you're an actor? That all you have to do is slick down your hair? Ha-ha-ha! And clip your moustache? You want to look like *him? Him?* What a joke! I don't see my master any longer. There's just this fat official. Good God! You look more like Mussolini!"

Von B raised his hand as if to strike her; indeed, Magda flinched. But he only said, "Is that it? Is it Hitler? Has he done this to you?"

She broke into a wail. "Yes! No! I don't know. Is it his fault? Or mine? Or is it you? I came back to learn from you. I feel as I always felt—devoted to my art. But something has happened between us. I am—how can I say it? Immune. To your gaze. Your magic. Your eyes. And these people! I used to love working in front of a crowd. Now I cannot bear it. To be watched. To be stared at. Oh, Rudi, please. Send them away."

"I cannot believe you mean what you say. These are our friends. Our coworkers. They make the same sacrifices that we do."

"I do mean it. I agree to make another take. I'll make as many as you like. I'll listen to you. How I'll listen! I've wanted nothing more than to hear your words. But these people have to leave us. All of them. The ones up there and everyone here who is standing, staring. The lighting people, the makeup people, and wardrobe. They have done their jobs. This Goodheart. This Meltsner. Herr Flatow, too. We don't even need the slate girl. Send them away, every person who is not absolutely necessary. We do not need Mr. Maynes for lights. *I will not be looked at.* The two of us, just the two of us— we'll do our work together."

"And if I refuse?"

"I shall have to leave the set."

"What? What? It's a threat!" With that shout Von Beckmann staggered backward with his hands at his throat. His eyes rolled up. He looked as if he had been poisoned, after all. Then he turned on his heel and stumbled backward. "Vincent!" he called in a hoarse, strangled voice, and fell in a heap to the ground.

Immediately Victor jumped down from the embankment and ran toward the crowd that was already gathering around the director. I trotted after. "What's happening?" he asked. "Who is Vincent?"

Flatow restrained him. "Vincent? Didn't you see him? He is the boy.

The stand-in for Ethan. Don't be alarmed. This isn't the first such attack. It is all part of the act."

I watched as the Gorcey look-alike went running up to Von Beckmann. Like Serge he carried a tank of oxygen. The crowd parted. Someone removed the director's cigarette and ground it out. Then the boy leaned forward to apply the mask to the stricken man's face. No one reacted with hysteria or panic. On the ridge some people stood up, but no one left his place. Everyone remained silent, with the single exception of one young woman. "Oh! Oh!" she cried in a high, piercing voice. "Poor man! We have to help him!"

Valentina! She ran forward from beyond the torchlights and threw herself down next to Von B. "Is he dying? What did she do to him?"

Victor hurried forward to join her. "Where have you been?" he demanded. "With Dick Mosk? All this time?"

"Look what has happened, Victor," she responded. She was beginning to weep. "I heard him say he had a pain in his heart."

Vincent was stroking Von Beckmann's forehead, above the edge of the mask. He smoothed his disheveled hair. "He doesn't need you," he said to Valentina. "I know what to do."

I peered down at the young actor. Was this Burton's replacement? He didn't look in the least effeminate. He looked, if anything, the tough young punk.

Valentina: "We need help. We need a doctor."

I looked right and left for a sign of Mosk. He was nowhere in sight. Instead I saw Magda striding toward us. Victor clamped my arm. There was more pain in his heart, I imagined, than in Von B's. He clamped his teeth on his lip in a wretched smile. "Magda—" he began. But the look the actress cast upon him, or through him, as if he were as transparent as a wisp of smoke, froze the words on his lips. Her own words were addressed to the tearful girl.

"What are you doing in my clothes?" She clutched the material at Valentina's shoulder. "I must inform you that I do not require a stand-in. Rudi knows this. I made it clear before we began."

Only then did I notice that the two women were identically dressed in what might have been a cross between a cowgirl outfit and a toga: rawhide vests that left their arms bare, and rawhide skirts, heavily pleated. But there was no way Victor's daughter, with her dark eyes, her swarthy complexion, could ever be used to adjust the lighting for the brunette from Berlin. The values would be incorrect. Coco, standing off to the side, confirmed the fact.

"Stand-in? She's not your stand-in," he said. "There's no resemblance."

"Then why is she here?" Now Magda whirled upon Victor. "And what are you doing here? Why have you brought your daughter?"

Here Von Beckmann opened his eyes. He pushed the oxygen away from his face. In a perfectly sound voice he said, "Victor will not be staying. He returns to the studio. But I am the one who asked the girl to join us."

Magda: "Why? For what?"

Von B, sitting upright, ignored the question. He turned toward Meltsner. "We will go back to the last closeup on Annie. In front of the sheet. Do you know your lines?"

"Of course I know my lines," Magda replied. "Would I forget them in fifteen minutes?"

Then an astounding thing happened. As if the actress hadn't spoken at all, Valentina said, "I think so. I've been studying and studying. I can try."

Von Beckmann nodded. "Vincent. Be so kind. Help me to my feet." The stand-in did so, brushing off his jacket and lighting him, in his own mouth, a new cigarette. The director turned on poor Coco. "Why are you standing there? We'll shoot the closeup. And you—" He beckoned to Valentina. "Come with me."

Von Beckmann took the girl by the arm and led her off into the shadows. Goodheart moved toward the camera. Meltsner, in his footsteps, started to shout: "Lower the sheet. Bring the camera for the closeup. Everyone, to your places. Maynes, we'll need the torches. Liz, scene 87, take two."

I watched as Von Beckmann stood facing the girl. He was blowing smoke from his nostrils and mouth. I knew perfectly well what Rudi was doing: he was hypnotizing her, just as he had everyone else on the set, including myself. How did the man do it? I'd always heard that a snake charmer's melodies had nothing to do with charming the snake. Cobras, possibly, were deaf. The enchantment was in the movement of the flute, not the music. It dawned on me that that was how Von Beckmann used his cigarette. Or if not the cigarette, then the hand that held it. No, no: it wasn't so much the hand but the face behind it—one moment hidden, the next moment—now!—exposed. *Ah, so!* That was his secret: those features, constantly covered and revealed, were like the image on the far side of a shutter. Valentina was giving herself to that face, we had all given ourselves to it, the way one gives oneself to a movie's flicker.

Now Victor shook himself from the trance. "But she's just a child. Her role—that was supposed to be a child's, too."

Von Beckmann blinked. He looked at the head of production for Granite

Films. "But Victor. You are a classicist. The daughter of Oedipus *is* only a child." Then, nodding toward Valentina, he pointed. Instantly the girl ran off to the spot by the wall. Ellie fussed for a moment with her gown. Gloria Umin dusted her skin with a powder puff. Then Liz approached the camera with the slate and Meltsner shouted for quiet. Coco gave the command for the camera to roll.

Slowly, silently, with all ten of her fingers, Valentina spread her hair out from the sides of her head. It wasn't like someone knitting this time. It was as if the dark-skinned girl were drawing her thoughts out from the center of her brain or, stranger still, as if she were stretching the dark strands of antenna wires so as to receive a message from parts unknown. She might have been one of the Fates, who hold the thread of life. What struck me most were her eyes, which were once more black, blank, lusterless. The button eyes of a doll. But her voice, when she spoke, wasn't that of a child.

I see. I see. What sadness. The terror.

Beneath my hair my scalp tightened, as if it had been seized by an Apache with a knife. Another person, or so it seemed, had entered Valentina's body and was speaking through her. Was this woman who was predicting the death of her brother and the suffering of her uncle the same little fortune-teller who had foretold the future? Who knew that her schoolmate would soon be dead?

I wasn't the only one to be thunderstruck. Everyone on the set seemed to be holding his breath. The flames on the torches barely dared flutter. Even Von Beckmann was unnerved. Clayton's line was *Enough. Seize her. Take her away!* But when he uttered it his voice was trembling, as if he believed that the fate which awaited him was indeed the worst of all. And you could tell that Coco, too, was shaken by the way he said, quaveringly, "Cut!"

Of the approximately one hundred people on the scene, perhaps only one remained unaffected. "Now I understand!" Magda cried, turning on Von Beckmann. "You accuse me of being part of a plot! But it is you who are the schemer. You used me—my name, my reputation, and my popularity with the public, the people who love me all over the world. You have exploited these things to get funding for your production. Your millions of dollars! You never would have gotten a penny without me! And now you want to drop me! To replace me with this child! Oh! And I was at the pinnacle of my fame. All of Europe was on its knees before me. The strongest men groveled at my feet. The screen between us, between me and my public—that was my sheet of glass."

No one dared interrupt the great star—not in the middle of her finest scene. The whole desert was silent. Now Mezaray laughed. "I am smarter than you are, Rudi. Your plan cannot succeed. I have a new contract. It is what you call ironclad. It will not allow you to substitute this little girl in my part."

"But Magda," said Von B, really quite sweetly, "it was you who threatened to walk out. You demanded impossible working conditions. A completely empty set. Oh, do not trouble to deny it. I have a hundred witnesses."

"Let's pay attention, everybody. We're doing the medium shot. Are the deputies in place? Is the lighting ready? How many torches do we need on the far side of the ridge? They're lit? Sound ready, too? All right, Coco. We're set for 88, take two."

That, of course, was Meltsner. There was a minute or two, not longer, during which the usual bustle filled the set. Only Victor thought to look after Magda as she walked off in the direction of the town. But even she stopped in her tracks at the sound of Coco's voice saying *Action!*

And there she remained, one of the crowd of spectators, as the deputies in their wide hats rushed forward to seize the girl. Valentina uttered a little shriek of fear, which must have been her own improvisation, and began to claw her way up the twisted sheet. Atop the embankment she did a dance, a sort of flamenco, to avoid the grasping hands of the men below. She waved the sheet back and forth. The sound boom dangled above her head, twitching this way and that in anticipation of her cry. She gave it, hallooing the words:

Paul! Paul! Oh, Paul-l-l-l-l!

There was a brief silence. Then a dog began to bark and another dog answered. A fox yawned and yapped. Something chattered; it had to be a squirrel. Then a nest of birds all began to chirp at once and an ominous owl answered with a long, chilling hoot.

We all stood, filled with astonishment. Were these the copycat cries of the Indians that Von Beckmann had scattered about on the far side of the ridge? Was it they who made that sound of a horse neighing? The warbles and whistlings of the birds? Each of us knew in his bones that whatever had been called for in the script, these were not merely men who were clucking and calling. I turned. Off to the right there was a faint streak of gray, a fainter streak of yellow, in the sky. Dawn. In a moment we would see the rosy red sun. No one yelled *Cut*. The camera rolled and rolled. The girl stood there, her shoulders slumped, the white banner limp in her hand. All about her, swelling from the earth, the sounds continued. There: a far-off rooster began to crow, like the one in the adage who puffed with pride at causing the sun to rise. But this was no fable. The girl had awakened the whole of the animal kingdom.

CHAPTER SEVEN

HOLLYWOOD MERRY GO ROUND

What a world we live in! One moment I'm at the center of the Merry Go Round—I'm thinking of the fabulous party that Mr. Hearst gave at his West Coast Camelot for Archduke Otto of Austria, where the guest list ranged from royalty all the way down to the "Bums Club" that Bob Stack and Glenn Ford have formed with some of their pals. Girls, you might as well know that Bums means Bachelors Union Matrimonial Sidesteppers, even though one of their members, Dick Denning, danced the whole night long with Pat Dane, so pretty now that she has lost weight. The conversation ranged just as far. The gals were all abuzz about the forthcoming addition to the Robert Young family, though Betty told me in confidence that it is only their horse which is expecting. The guys were nose to nose about Communistic activities in America. W. R. made no bones about the fact that there are plenty of Commies in the Roosevelt administration who are strangers to the American way. "You cannot handle pitch," said he, sounding just as wise to me as Confucius, "and keep your hands unsoiled." These days it's hard to avoid the sad thought that the burdens of office are becoming too much for our dog-doting leader. What we could all agree about was crossing our fingers and hoping that the rumors about the Warners forgetting the whole thing and ending their separation are true, for there are no more popular people in Lollywood than Ann and Jack. As I was saying, one minute I am in the middle of the social whirl, and the next minute I am all alone in the middle of nowhere. At least that's what I'd call the old gold-mining town of Pandaemonium, Nevada, where I landed this very morning.

They say this place was named by a young Ivy Leaguer, a Milton scholar, who'd come west in gold-rush days. That's John Milton, so famous for writing his tremendous poem *Paradise Lost* when he couldn't see his hand in front of his face, and for being married only two weeks before he sent his wife, you can't expect me to remember her name in this godforsaken spot, packing. Not to mention the scandal when people realized he wasn't divorced when he started courting again.

Well, I don't want you to get the impression that I'm completely alone in the wilderness. Right down the corridor are the rooms of Rudolph Von Beckmann, Chick Chandler, and Rochelle Hudson, not to mention such old friends as Victor Granite and the mysterious Magda Mezaray—now there's a combo that still might sizzle like a fried egg on the tin roof of this old hotel; and in the midst of pals like these you can't exactly complain that you've been abandoned on some desert island. Come to think of it, an island right now might be just the ticket. At least then I'd be surrounded by water. You don't know what it's like to be thirsty until you've been to a ghost town in the alkali flats.

Say what you want about your correspondent, and over the years some people—and *H. H.* doesn't stand for the director of our latest big hit, *Sergeant York*—have written things that make me out to be a regular Rasputin, there's one piece of chitchat not even my worst enemy would dare to spread, which is that I'm the type of girl who would waste a minute feeling sorry for herself. But I have to confess I'm feeling lonelier than Robinson Crusoe before he met Friday, and if it weren't for all these dear friends I might just break down and have a good boo-hoo. For the one and only occasion in my career I can't be absolutely certain that what I'm writing out in my infamous chicken scrawl is going to appear in so many of the nation's finest newspapers tomorrow. That's how cut off I am from my truest family—I mean my readers all over the world. George Hoffman, who is a whiz at these things, says that he'll do his best to repair the telegraph ticker, but even he can't give me any guarantees. So forgive me if this stiff upper lip of mine starts to quiver. I just can't believe that this is the first time ever that I might have to put a question mark instead of that cheery exclamation point—and doesn't it stand there atop its tiny globe like my own little Oscar!—after the words *See you tomorrow.*

How does a girl get herself into such a jam? I reckon it began with a little Merry Go Round item about how the entire *Pandaemonium* production seemed to have dropped off the face of the earth. Because no sooner had I wondered aloud about why we weren't seeing the work of either Miss Mezaray or Mr. Laughton than I got a call from Les Kahn, the publicist who singlehandedly made a glamour girl out of Barbara Stanwyck before he went to work for Granite. It seems that the latest rushes had just arrived, starring none other than the fickle fraulein. "Louella," Les told me, "it's Magdalena's big scene, the one where she pleads with her uncle to cancel the duel between her brothers." Did I want to come over to Olympic and La Brea that night to take a gander with all the top brass—excepting of course the thin-as-a-pinstripe Victor Granite, who I happened to know was already on location himself? Well, no one has to ask me twice to watch the Rhine maiden, who, even if she weren't an old friend, constantly amazes me because of the way she, like old wine, improves with age.

So there I was, breathless with excitement in the plush screening room. Truth to tell, this private event had all the flavor of a first-night premiere. Both Granite wives were there—Giselle, who was wearing the prettiest print I have seen this year, and Georgia, Mrs. Manfred Granite, whom Doc Mosk did such a swell job on last winter when he removed those crow's feet from around her eyes. I was sporting my "night" and "day" earrings that Billy DeMille gave me in the wee hours after one of those fabulous parties on his million-dollar yacht. They're diamonds on one side and sapphires on the other and can be worn with either side out. "Do they match the swift changes in your mood, Louella?" asked Manfred Granite, who was in one of his better moods himself. In fact he was grinning like the cat who has swallowed the canary. That was because the atmosphere of anticipation was so thick in that room you could have cut it with a knife. Who could have guessed that in such a short while our high hopes would be so thoroughly dashed? I don't think I have experienced any other occasion so filled with eager expectation and utter dismay, unless it was the hours I spent before I broke the sad story of Mrs. Ria Gable's divorce from Clark.

But I am getting ahead of myself. The fact is, either the projectionist was late or the promised canister of film had not yet arrived. We spent the time as Lollywoodians usually do, which means on all the latest that had just appeared in THE CHATTERBOX. A spirited debate broke out about Veronica Lake. Some thought she had a great future and some did not. I was saddened to hear that Gene Tierney's eye trouble is much more serious than the world knows. On a brighter note, everyone agreed that Sonja Henie, the little fancy figure skater, looked like a million dollars at Slapsie Maxie's the other night with hubbie Dan Topping. I wanted to get my two cents' worth in to Manfred Granite and was just telling him that I hoped he was not turning *Pandae-monium,* which had seemed like such a terrific western, into something depressing just to please a crowd of four-eyed professors, when the room went dark—after all these years I still get what we kids in Freeport used to call the heebie-jeebies when the beam of light from the projector darts through the air—and the first few feet from the dailies appeared on the screen.

It's no secret in Lollyland that your correspondent has the constitution of a horse. You won't catch me taking so much as an aspirin. I always maintain that laughter is the best cure for the blues. In my book there's no better pick-me-up than watching Joe E. Brown performing those somersaults and grimaces for which he is famous. If that doesn't work, a sip or two from the medicinal flask will make me fit as a fiddle. I guess I'm getting sidetracked with these thoughts because I sure have a doozy of a cranium-splitter this very minute. It feels like half of Der Fuhrer's army were jackbooting right across the top of my head. Doc Mosk, he's the one that saved Mickey Rooney's foot after the smashup of Jeffrey Lynn's car, is right here on location, but there's no need to call him. Ha! As if there were a telephone to do so! Do you suppose this pain is caused by being so cut off from my fans? Oh, the constant pounding! Rochelle Hudson, the buxom B, told me it's the machinery for digging the well. It sounds like the chorus from *Il Trovatore* to me! I reckon they have to do it, since that's where our water comes from, but do you suppose it's going to go on all night? Speaking of Mickey, he's done a lot of growing up—hard to believe he is now old enough to vote!— and is carrying a torch for Linda Darnell as big as the lamp in a lighthouse. I know the rule about dailies in filmland is Mum's the Word. Ordinarily I'd be the last one in town to spill those beans, but the fact is I'm pretty certain this headache, the feeling of coldness near my heart, is actually caused by the memory of what I saw projected inside the Granite screening room. Look, an ink blot. Even my trusty Waterman does not want to write the words.

Of course all of us were waiting for our first glimpse of Magdalena. But there was no sign of the lady with the au-lait locks. I can't say why but right from the start I got the willies. The screen was dark, not pitch black, but like a room where the curtains are drawn. At the same time you just knew you weren't indoors, but outside. Then, up high, way to the right, as though through a crack in those curtains, we saw a light. It was throbbing, and growing brighter. All of a sudden there was a closeup of a man, it was Leo Gorcey, who was such a meanie last year in *Pride of the Bowery*. His face filled the whole screen. It was upside down and his eyes were closed. I didn't know if he was breathing. I leaned over to Les, who was sucking away for all he was worth on a Life Saver, and said, "Is that Magda's brother? I hope she comes soon to save him. It looks to me like it might already be too late." But the publicist didn't answer, he just kept making these smacking noises, and meanwhile the camera pulled back so that it became apparent that Leo, you'll remember him as the Dead End Kid who always was talking out of the side of his mouth, was lying on his back with his head hanging over the edge of some kind of embankment and when the light hit him his eyes sprang open and he gave us a terrible look. Someone right behind me, it was Burton Granite, said, "I get it. It's the sun. It's the dawn."

The next thing I knew I was clutching the sides of my chair as if it were the loop-the-loop at Ocean Park Pier. The screen in front of me was whirling like a hepcat doing the jitterbug. Then I realized that the man played by Gorcey had gotten to his feet and was seeing the world right side up. Now the rising sun was at the lower left where it belonged. Already the camera was pulling back at what must have been a hundred miles an hour. I hung on to my armrests. I don't know what was making me such a nervous Nellie. My heart was beating faster than the hooves of Man o' War. I didn't even dare pinch myself, the way I used to do at the President Lincoln Theater in Freeport and say, *Now, Lolly, this is nothing more than a movie.* Up on the screen, Leo Gorcey had become no bigger than an ant. Facing him was another man, not an inch larger than he. They began to walk toward each other with what looked like pistols in their hands. A duel! The very one that Magda Mezaray was supposed to prevent! The funny thing was, though we were looking at them through the wrong end of a telescope, we were hearing them—not their words, but the sounds they made, their footsteps and their breathing and the swish of their pants—through what sounded for all the world like a stethoscope. The thump of their heartbeats was like the tom-tom—a tom thumb, Mike Curtiz always calls it—in *Tarzan and His Mate.* Only a movie? In all my days I had never seen one like this!

Oh, my head is just splitting! I can't seem to catch my breath. Maybe it's because that old Ford trimotor I flew out here in didn't have a pressurized cabin. Not that I was worried one bit. You wouldn't be either, if you had the pilot that I did. Well, I won't keep this light under a bushel. The moment the screening was done I simply marched up to Manfred and told him that unless he personally flew me to Nevada that very moment I was going to spread the story in over four hundred papers that the news about Magdalena Mezaray appearing in that Granite picture was nothing more than a hoax. Well, butter wouldn't have melted in that mighty executive's mouth. To make a short story even shorter, I was going to get my flight into the wild blue yonder! I trust no one will be shocked to hear that this aeronautical acrobat has a bit of the ladies' man about him. There we were, chatting away in the cockpit, when all of a sudden he took off his sky-blue flying scarf—he said it was his lucky charm and he had been wearing it ever since he did his high-wire act as a child—and put it round the neck of yours truly! He looked at me in such a strange way that I couldn't tell whether he was going to strangle me or draw me even closer. Even my oldest friends wouldn't have recognized me at that moment because I was speechless! The only thing I could think of was a romantic moment during the on-again-off-again courtship between Alice Faye and Phil Harris. It seems that just before Alice boarded her transcontinental flight Phil gave her a record and a wind-up Victrola. When she gave it a spin at fifteen thousand feet, there was Phil's voice chanting over and over, "Will you marry me?"

Bang! When both men fired their revolvers at once I almost jumped out of my seat. One of the marksmen—the camera had now come up close enough for me to see that it was John Payne, who simply ran away with last year's *Kid Nightingale*—was hit in the shoulder, while the other, Leo Gorcey, was struck in a place Mr. Hearst will not allow me to mention in this paper. Would you believe it? The two of them continued to stagger forward, each with a knife in his hand. How could I watch? In fact, I had my pocketbook, a gift from Alex Korda, in front of my eyes when the blades of the knives sank into their targets with a sickening thud. "Manfred!" I cried. I was shaking like a leaf. "Stop the picture! This is inhuman! It is not the scene you promised I would see!" I didn't dare tell him the thought that had popped into my head: if there is a hell for us bright, gay folk of Lollywoodland, it will surely consist of our having to sit chained in our chairs while just such a feature goes on for eternity.

Whenever I was frightened at the President Lincoln I had only to remind myself that the other people in the dark were my friends and neighbors, the fine, upstanding people of the great Midwest. When the show was over I could step into the afternoon sunlight of Main Street: there was the banker, the baker, the friendly policeman, and the barber standing next to his barber pole. So many of these dear people, whom the touch of time has only made gentler, the way the tides will smooth a jagged rock, were there to greet me at the wonderful parade the Freeport Civic Association gave me just last year. Stretched across that same street was a banner that said, "Louella, we love you!" But in the screening room at Olympic and La Brea I saw no such Christian faces. Among this crowd of swarthy sophisticates where could a girl turn for help? My stomach was heaving. My hair was coming undone. I felt as sick as poor Rin Tin Tin in *Jaws of Steel*. Before my eyes the battle between the brothers was still going on. Not with knives now. With fingernails! As God is my witness, with teeth! Gorcey had his jaw clamped on the neck of

John Payne, who also made an agreeable impression recently in *Weekend in Havana,* and John was clawing at Leo's jugular! I know what you are thinking, America: *Why on earth, Louella, did you sit in that seat one moment longer?* The answer is that it was a matter of duty. I knew that the disgusting scenes unfolding before me would never be shown in a single theater in our nation— not if the power of the Hearst papers had anything to say about it. I alone would have to endure this screening to the end, because I knew that I might very well have stumbled onto the story of the century. Yes, the tip of my sharp little nose had started to twitch. HAD SOMETHING TERRIBLE HAP- PENED TO MAGDALENA MEZARAY?

And that is why I soon found myself sitting practically shoulder to shoul- der if not cheek to cheek with Manny Granite: I was hell-bent, if you'll excuse my French, on getting an exclusive interview with that beauteous Berliner. Try to imagine my feelings when that supposed grim Granite suddenly asked if I would like to sit with him in the pilot's seat and actually take the wheel. For a moment I thought I might faint. The next thing I knew, Manfred had pulled me onto his lap. Of course everybody knows that the elder of the Granite brothers is no spring chicken, but what no one could guess is that he has muscles like Victor Mature. The legs underneath me were like iron rods!

We hit a "rough patch" above the Sierra Nevadas and began to pitch and roll like a tiny rowboat in a typhoon. But how could I be anxious? Wasn't Manfred's lucky scarf around my neck? Weren't his strong, manly hands around my waist? When I asked him if everything was going to be all right, he whispered directly into my ear, "Louella, in this life you never know what is going to happen." That is one thing I know already! Everybody was so sure that after Ruby Keeler and Al Jolson parted she was going to marry John Lowe, the young and quite wealthy Pasadena socialite, that even I was knocked for a loop to hear that romance has chilled. I almost swallowed my grapefruit whole and choked on my coffee when Ruby called me first thing in the morning and said, "Louella, I have decided that I must concentrate solely on my career."

Another inkblot! There's nothing wrong with my pen. These are tears that are falling on the paper. I've really got to get hold of myself. After all, here I am on good old terra firma and none the worse for wear. Soon the mystery of Magdalena will be solved. I would have sat down for a heart-to- heart with my friend already, if only Rudolph Von Beckmann hadn't told me personally that the preparations for the big scene where she recovers her brother's body were taking all of Magda's time. Yes, his body, for the result of that terrible struggle was that each man was killed by his brother's hand. Leo Gorcey fell on one side of the embankment and John Payne rolled down the other. Why does the Hays Office ban sweaters (which doesn't bother Miss Carole Landis: she's wearing peek-a-boo blouses this year) when such bloody sights are allowed on the screen? By the way, Rudi, whom I never really chatted with before, is an imposing man with a striking streak of white hair in his full black mane. I couldn't help thinking of the hair of the late Sergei Diaghilev, whom he resembles in other ways, when the master of the ballet came to the Lollywood Bowl. It was difficult not to stare into the director's mournful and riveting eyes. Of course I've heard all the stories about how hypnotic the great man can be, and I was on guard lest he ask me to gaze at his pocket watch or neigh like a pony. The truth is I found him charming. As soon as I stepped out of the airplane he greeted me with a bouquet of dried flowers. The whole cast—except of course for Magdalena and the equally busy Charles Laughton—had lined up to shake my hand. Then we went for a tour of the bustling streets of the set, which was like an industrious western town with everybody cheerfully at his task. I didn't see Peter Lorre or Victor Granite, but Victor's daughter, Valentina, was there to greet me with the others. She's a dream of a girl with dark skin and luxurious raven locks, and I thought to myself that someday she could play the kind of parts now taken by Dolores Del Rio. When I said I was tired from the heat and the flight, Manny himself brought me my own personal water canteen and escorted me to my room in the Fancy Free Hotel. Even though it was only nine in the PM, he practically tucked me into bed. For one exciting moment I thought he was going to kiss me good night. To make sure everything remained good and proper, this happily married middle-aged woman asked that happily married man—oh, I don't doubt that, even though Georgia and he have certainly had their ups and downs and she hasn't aged as well as her sister-in-law, Giselle—to run along, which he did, though he promised to look in later on to make sure that everything was all right. I put that blue bandana, which I'm sure I'll treasure for the rest of my days, under my pillow.

Of course, what with all the excitement and the hammering of that drill, there was no question of sleep. I've been up now for hours. I've really got to catch forty winks or I'm going to look a fright. Sure, a gal gets lonely. But the only thing to do is remember what Mr. Hearst says about keeping your chin up and hoping for the best. That's what I'm going to do with dear Lana Turner. It's true that she was seen doing the highstep with Bob Stack at the Palladium the other night. When I asked her if that meant she and Tony

Martin were through, she said, "Louella, do I have to draw you a picture?" Call me a cockeyed optimist, but I'd be willing to bet that when Tony flies back tomorrow, Lana, who has always kissed and made up with him in the past, will be at the airport to meet him. Oh, before I forget, Clarence Brown says I hurt his feelings and that his bike is a real one and not electrically controlled. He pedals twenty miles every day and that's how he lost his tummy. Goodness, I see I've written enough already for three whole columns. I'll end by saying that's all for today. Will I see you tomorrow?

UNDER THE HAT

Louella landed in Pandaemonium on November third, five days after Valentina's debut. In all that time Victor had not been able to see his daughter, who was constantly at work on her new lines, or Magdalena, who was—supposedly on doctor's orders—forbidden contact with anyone. Miss Hudson, I am sorry to say, remained aloof; rather, whenever I approached her, Chick Chandler, so tall and so wiry, intervened. Off she went on his arm, with one hand in the pocket of his Levi-style jeans. Thus in impotence and languor did one day pass into another, until the arrival of Manfred and Louella took us all by surprise.

What happened was that late one afternoon the pump suddenly stopped. Like the trained dogs of Pavlov, everyone ran to Main Street, expecting that an unscheduled scene was about to be shot. Instead, Von Beckmann, in his regular cape, not his sheriff's outfit, appeared on the balcony of the court-house. Mike Meltsner stood by him, and when the last of the stragglers had come up at the rear, the production assistant lifted a megaphone to his lips.

"Ladies and gentlemen, we are confronted by an emergency. A crisis. Even as I speak to you an airplane is flying here with an unwelcome passenger on board. It's Louella Parsons, the columnist. She thinks she has an exclusive. She wants to expose a scandal. Or maybe create one. She'll do that by saying that we're full of strife and dissension. Today we must do everything we can to prove that she's wrong."

Now Von Beckmann moved to the railing. Meltsner offered him the megaphone, but he waved it away. Though he spoke without effort, his voice rolled over the entire crowd. "Let us be clear about the situation. This woman is our enemy. She is employed by Hearst. He is a supporter of the Third

Reich and has launched a campaign to keep America out of the European war. She is hoping on his behalf to discredit what we have accomplished here—our joy in work, the beauty of our vision, the urgency of our warning to the world. She will be flown here by Manfred Granite. He has hated me from the days of our youth. He seeks any excuse to terminate our picture. He wants to destroy me! He wants to destroy my life!"

Hemmed in on all sides, I thought I could see tears well in the director's eyes. Others saw the same shine and glint. A murmur of sympathy ran through the crowd. From behind me some person cried out, "Don't worry, Rudi! We won't let anyone stop us!"

To this there was a growl of assent, then applause.

Von Beckmann: "Why do you think I am suffering? Because you see tears? Don't trust them. They mean nothing. The truth is, it is you I weep for. My dear colleagues! All your sacrifice: the thirst, the heat, the endless hours of toil. When I think that your pain and effort, the magnificent contributions you have made to the art of film, might never be seen—yes, then the tears start to fall."

Now more voices rang from the crowd.

"We'll finish no matter what!"

"Why don't we block the runway? Then she can't land."

"We'll shoot her plane down!"

The people about me gave a roar. They shook their fists in the air. Upon one such hand I saw a flash and a gleam. A diamond. It was Miss Hudson's ring! She was shouting louder than any of the others: "The witch! I hate her! All she writes about is Veronica Lake!" How cute her lips, curled in anger. The wisps of her hair, like bees around the beehive, were excitedly dancing about. I then saw, just behind her, the tall form of Chick Chandler. At the sight of that jutting cleft jaw, spots and wavy lines, a filigree of fury, rose before my eyes. Heedless of everything, I started to shout along with the rest: "Kill him! I am going to kill him! Yes, with my bare hands! I shall crush his windpipe! His Adam's apple!"

But these words were lost in the surrounding tumult. The crowd was also calling for a life—not Chandler's but that of the columnist. The director, caught in the beams of the declining sun, held up his hands. Benignly he smiled.

"No, no, no—this will not be our way. Who is this person? A magnate? A tycoon? A senator? A judge? None of these. Where, then, does she derive her power? Listen to what I tell you: it is from the frustrations and the resentments of all those who hate our art. What do they call these people?

Gossip columnists? Is that correct, Mr. Meltsner? Yes? Who is kissing whom. Which one suffers from an illness, an infection of the gallbladder, and which one undergoes a fall from fortune. Who is engaged to be married. Who will soon be divorced. What clothes this young lady wears to the theater, what is her coiffure at the charity ball. Thus do the newspapers pull back to earth those we have set in the heavens. They make human those we have turned into gods."

You could not hear at that moment a single sound. To the crowd it was he, high on the balcony, with the sun playing upon him, who was the divinity.

Von B continued. "Why should we help her in her task? She expects us to oppose her. To come sneaking to her, whispering secrets in the dead of night. She will be disappointed. We shall not be disagreeable. On the contrary, we must show her every courtesy. All of us must greet her at the airstrip. I shall hand her flowers. Our dry desert daisies. Whatever she asks we will grant her. Wherever she looks she shall see how our work uplifts us, unites us, and gives us joy."

From among the spectators an anonymous but accented voice asked, "What if she wants to see Laughton? Or Miss Mezaray? What do you tell her?"

"Unfortunately, our dear friends are now indisposed. Dr. Mosk has informed me, as he will inform the columnist, that the malady may be contagious. There is no way that she will be able to see them in the course of her brief overnight stay. I mean, there is no way she will be able to see them in the flesh. Luckily we possess three scenes of Magdalena—86, 87, 88." He paused, grinning. *"Take one."*

Laughter rang out down the length of the street. Even I had to smile at the success of Rudi's trick. He had shot just enough footage of Magda to fool everyone at Olympic and La Brea. With a smirk he leaned over the balcony. "Perhaps Miss Parsons will do us the favor of taking these rushes back to the studio. That will satisfy the gentlemen at Granite Films."

There was another burst of laughter, which was interrupted by a second accented shout. "What if this woman and Mr. Granite become thirsty? The way we are now?"

"Ah, yes, that is something I neglected to mention," the director replied. "Until dawn tomorrow, when our guests are scheduled to leave, the water ration will be increased to three canteens. Whoever asked that question can drink his fill. So can the rest of us. We'll have a holiday."

A cheer went up from the assembled crowd. But the smile faded from the director's features. "Now you understand how we shall turn this visit to our advantage. Our enemies will arrive in a mood of skepticism and distrust. But I have no doubt that when they depart they will be our allies. Unless—"

The director broke off; the crowd hung on his words. "*Unless*—?" came the echo.

"Unless someone should poison their stay among us with lies."

"Impossible!"

"Who would dare such a thing?"

Sadly Von B shook his massive head. "Alas, I must tell you there are far more dangerous threats to our work than this silly woman, threats that will not be so easily overcome. In our midst there is a man who with a single word could shut down our production. No paychecks—"

"We'll work for free!" someone shouted, to another burst of applause.

"Yes, but this person could cut off supplies, or refuse to replace our raw stock of film. He could halt distribution even if our last scene has been completed. Against this far more powerful foe we must be vigilant. He is not, like Miss Parsons, naive. Nor is he, like Manfred Granite, in the pay of New York bankers and motivated solely by the love of money. No, he pretends to be a lover of art, yet he cannot understand what true art, our art, can achieve. If this person should be allowed to come in contact with the columnist, everything we have done and hope yet to do could be destroyed. This individual and his accomplice must be isolated. Quarantined. Punished. We know, do we not, how to deal with saboteurs."

As if at some signal, the familiar sound of the pump resumed. In the crowd there was a stir. People were pulling away from the center of Main Street. In their place two lonely figures stood exposed.

The pity is, I was one of them. The other, his arms crossed, legs crossed, standing at the angle of the Tower of Pisa, was Victor Granite. In less than a week the desert sun, burning through the brim of his hat, had turned him the precise shade of an American football. A cigarette, lit and sparkling, hung from his lips. For a moment the crowd stood stock-still, undecided. I smiled as widely as I could. I clacked my teeth together. "Accomplice? Ha-ha-ha! It's a misunderstanding. Everybody is invited to Fontenelle Way for chop suey!"

No one responded. No one spoke or moved. The vast throng stood irresolute. Then a dark figure darted forward and pointed a finger at Victor Granite. "There he is," cried Valentina. "That's him! The spy!"

At once the extras surged by her. They closed in on Victor.

"Grab him!"

"Don't let him get away!"

"Catch the other one, too!"

Victor turned and dashed down Main Street, past the church and the livery stable and the wooden gallery in front of the saloon. I ran as fast as I could to keep up. But the mob was gaining. I could hear them behind me, snorting like horses; I could feel their hot breath on the back of my neck. Would they seize me? Beat me? Throw me into the lift? Then, of a sudden, their shouts, their angry cries, ceased. Rather, they were drowned out by the drone of the silver airplane that at that moment buzzed low over the town. It banked left. It banked right. Its wings waggled in greeting. Even the sound of the pile driver was muffled by the roar of its triple engines. Then it dipped, turned, and floated down toward the airstrip—that is, toward the parallelogram of basalt that had been cleared just outside the northern edge of the crater. The columnist for the *Examiner*, along with the president of Granite Films, had landed. The crowd—there must have been nearly a hundred people in it—rushed off to extend the warmest of welcomes.

Victor and I stood alone on the walkway. Then we heard our names being called from inside the saloon.

"Attention, Herr Granite."

"Psst, Herr Lorre."

We turned. Sampson Frank and Reynaldo Flatow were gesturing from between the Swallow's—only then did it occur to me that the name of the saloon was meant to be a boomtown pun—batwing doors. Said the tall actor, crooking a finger, "We wish a word with you."

We marched across the planks of the gallery and pushed through the swinging portal. The interior was unlit. The late afternoon light that came through the streetside windows didn't quite reach the long bar with its rows of bottles lined up like so many toy soldiers, each with its own round metal helmet. Everything looked as if it might have come from the Granite prop room: the long mirror, the painting of a nearly nude woman floating in air with her hands behind her head, the round tables, the bar stools, an upright piano, spittoons. Even the motes of dust that danced in the weak shafts of light might have been cast into the air by a grip. Herr Frank now retreated to a corner table in the darkest part of the room. Flatow, I noticed, had already pulled up a chair. We moved toward the two refugees.

"I thought it was you," Victor declared.

"How so?" said Frank, who sat down next to his companion.

"We heard two embarrassing questions. Who else could have asked them?"

"We should have asked sooner," said Flatow.

Frank said, "And we should have contacted you sooner, as well. We did not think you would believe what we wanted to say."

I settled onto the third chair. Victor took the fourth. He leaned forward, propping his chin on his hands. "You mean," he said, "that you thought we were under Rudi's spell."

Flatow: "We saw you at the crater's rim. We saw your face during the shooting. What else could we suppose?"

Victor remained in his gargoyle's pose. "Rudolph Von Beckmann is a very great director."

"This the world acknowledges."

"But I was not mesmerized. Certainly not completely. Nor was Peter."

I chimed in at the cue, "We also saw your faces. How pale they were. Deduction: that you had been punished."

"Is that true?" asked Victor. "In the lift?"

The two older men looked at each other, the one through the thin glass of his spectacles, the other through his thick lenses. "Best not to speak of it," Flatow said.

Victor pushed on. "There was much I wanted to ask you that day. Why had we been searched? Why those guards? Why was it that everyone was willing to tolerate this unbearable thirst? And then there was talk of putting people in cages. Like animals! It seemed to me there was as much suffering off-camera as there was on the screen."

"On this location," said Flatow, "Dr. Mosk is a busy man."

Frank: "I will tell you a small secret, a detail that may have escaped your notice. Perhaps you saw the rushes of the water wagon? The ambush by Indians? The attack? You may not have noticed that I played the part of a man with a rifle. A man who soon was shot through the heart. This scene was not done in one take. It was necessary to lie many hours beneath the sun. No water for us, though a sea of water was inside the wooden wagon. No shade. Not even the pleasure of shifting our limbs. Do you know, I think I lost consciousness for a time. It was as if I were truly a dead man, without thought or feeling. And it was not I alone, an aged man, who suffered. Many of the others fainted as well."

I gave a start. Here was the same phenomenon I'd noticed before. Von Beckmann was forcing his actors to experience the very thing they were portraying—up to, including, the miming of death.

Flatow nodded toward his fellow refugee. "You were not so pale then."

Victor: "But how can you bear it? This inhuman treatment? Why don't you leave?"

"Best to answer that," said Sampson Frank, "by asking, why don't you?"

"But we're going to. I hope this very night."

Flatow: "And how, please, will you make this escape?"

"Why, in my car."

Both men chuckled. Frank said, "Do you think they will simply hand it over to you? As if you were a chauffeur? A valet? It is without doubt carefully guarded."

"If you had attempted to drive it earlier, even the morning after your arrival, you would have found it inoperable—under repairs, perhaps, or drained of gasoline."

"The Epsteins," Frank concluded, "were the last to get out. Von B has made sure no one else will follow."

"Are you saying we're all prisoners? Has no one tried to escape on foot?"

Flatow: "Without a map? Without water? Are we to drink, perhaps, our own urine? No, no. This is not a practical scheme."

Uneasily I glanced through the exhaust of Victor's cigarette to the reaches of the saloon. At the bar the rows of bottles, the whiskey, the gin, chimed a bit, rubbing shoulders from the impact of the far-off pump. On the opposite wall hung a painting of a bird, surely the eponymous swallow. It soared between the treetops and a layer of puffy clouds. "Wait! I have it!" I cried. "The airplane!"

"That," said Frank, "was our thought precisely."

Flatow beamed, so that little lines, like those for latitude and longitude, broke out all over the world of his face. "It is an opportunity literally from heaven. We must not fail to seize it."

Victor looked from one man to the other. "But how can you? And how can we? Peter and I are marked men. The minute we show ourselves we'll be captured. And I know Manfred—he'll never allow you onto his plane."

"Ah-ha!" Flatow exclaimed, and in this moment of pleasure he twirled his bow tie—as if he, himself, were capable of starting one of the aircraft's propellers. "But what if we were *already aboard*!"

"All of us!" chortled Sampson Frank, pulling, in *his* excitement, at various pieces of his beard. "All four!"

Victor gave one of his downturned smiles. "Well, you will have to explain to me how this can be accomplished."

"We shall require," said Flatow, "a small proportion of luck."

"That is," said Frank, "the airship itself must be unwatched. Here I think circumstances are in our favor. How could Von Beckmann post a guard? Would Manfred Granite allow it? And how could such an action be explained to the ever-alert Miss Parsons?"

Flatow: "Moreover, an aircraft is not an automobile. Rudi will not be in fear that anyone here will attempt to fly it."

"Very well," said Victor. "Let us say luck is with us. The plane is un-guarded. What then?"

Frank: "There are two opportunities to approach it. Scene 94 will be shot shortly, at sundown. In it Sheriff Clayton addresses the town. As usual, every-one will gather here to witness the great man's performance. The rest of the crater will be deserted. At such a moment, might it not be possible to depart through the back of the saloon? There is risk, of course. But there is also the chance we could reach the rim undetected. From there the airship should be only two hundred meters away."

Flatow: "The second possibility would be to escape under the cover of darkness. In my opinion, this is the way of less danger. We could leave at some time after midnight. However, we must be secreted within the aircraft before first light. Scene 95 is at the northern rim. Annie is scheduled to bury the corpse of her brother, the disgraced Paul, just after dawn."

The two refugees fell silent. Both stared eagerly, first at Victor, then at me. I shook my head. "But what will happen when Louella and Manfred board the airplane? They will see you. They will throw you off."

"Not," said Sampson Frank, "if we can offer her something she wishes."

"What?" asked Victor.

Flatow reached under his chair and pulled out a flat cylindrical disk. "This!"

"And what," demanded Victor, "is that?"

"A canister. A reel. Film from *Pandaemonium.*"

"I see that. But why should Louella—or Manfred, for that matter—want to have it?"

Once more Frank had begun to pluck away at the scattered pieces of his beard. "Because we have here scene 87. You see?" He snatched the canister from his comrade and held it aloft. "And scene 88!"

"You're too late," I told him. "Either Rudi has given her that footage already, or he soon will."

"No, no," cried Flatow. "Not this footage! You do not understand!"

Frank: "These scenes are *take two*!"

I gasped. So did Victor. Flatow almost shouted the next words. "Now do you grasp it? Our cleverness? Our daring? Here is the evidence that Louella requires."

"The girl! The adolescent! Definite proof that Magdalena Mezaray has been removed from the film!"

"We stole it!" shouted Flatow. "We stole it from the portable lab!"

Now it was our turn to stare from one man to the other. "It's an idea," I declared. "A good one. It might even work."

But Victor was frowning. "I don't know. Oh, I don't mean your plan. It might certainly succeed. Louella would kill for that strip of celluloid. But that's just the trouble. Without Magdalena, the production will be shut down. My God, I *will* be a saboteur. I'll have destroyed a masterpiece."

"I don't understand," said Flatow. "Isn't that what you want?"

"Yes!" I declared. "Victor, have you lost your senses? After everything we've seen? I wanted Rudi to denounce Hitler! But he's becoming Hitler. Right in front of our eyes! Yes, it *is* what we want."

But Victor did not respond. Instead, he took out a fresh cigarette and lit it from the stub in his mouth. Then he sat pulling on the flesh of an earlobe. "Perhaps so," he said at last. "But perhaps not. It depends on Magdalena. If, as I fear, she has been mistreated, if she's in danger, yes. I would end this picture myself. But if there's hope, any hope at all, that she could continue—"

"*Magdalena?*" Frank exclaimed. "*Continue?* But she is in the lift."

Victor: "Very well. Then take me to her."

"To *that place*? It's not possible."

"Why not? All I want is to see her. To talk to her."

Frank: "Don't think of it! Don't speak of it! It's madness!"

Flatow: "There is a guard. Maybe more than one. Nighttime and daytime. Please. You must not ask such a thing."

Victor leaned toward the two frightened men. "Herr Frank. Herr Flatow. I do not ask much of you. And in return I am prepared to assist you with your plan. Take me to the mine at midnight. If there is a guard, he can be bribed. Or distracted. Or even disabled. I will not spend more than ten minutes in the shaft. Five minutes. Or one! Just one! I must see her. I must know if she is alive. Then we can leave for the aircraft. In the morning, perhaps even in the air, we can decide which canister to give Louella. Take two or take one. We have the night before us. Hours and hours of darkness. You said you wanted to seize this chance. Will you agree?"

Sampson Frank stood up abruptly. He towered over our table. "Many years ago, at Stettin Bay, I played the part of Moses. In that role I killed the cruel taskmaster who was smiting my people. Before this, in another lifetime, upon another planet, I was a yeshiva student. Thus I knew that our script was Exodus and read as follows: *And he looked this way and that way, and when he saw that there was no man, he slew the Egyptian.* Was I looking about for another Egyptian, to make certain that I would not be seen? That is how Rudi wished me to play the part. But I knew that the prophets wrote that Moses was looking about for another Jew, a rebel, a man—a *mensch, ja?*—who would act so that he would not have to. From that former life, I remember, too, the words of Hillel: *Where there is no man, try to be one.* When a crime is being committed by Pharaoh, what choice have we but to act?"

Flatow got to his feet as well. "We shall return at midnight. No one will do this if we do not."

"But why not?" I asked. "This is what bothers me. Why does no one else stop these crimes? How is it that everyone here has become a confederate? These good people, picture people—it is as if there is some charm upon them. How is it you two have managed to avoid it?"

"We have," said Flatow, "worked with Rudi before. We know his tricks."

"In my case," said Frank, "for forty years. That was an inoculation."

I remembered Magda's word: *immunized.* Was what was occurring here a disease? Had everyone become infected? "Wait. Tell me. This crime. This terrible thing that is happening. How is it going to end?"

The two refugees were on their way to the door. When they turned about their faces were, if anything, even paler than before. But Frank only shrugged. "Who knows? Who can say?"

Flatow: "How will *he* end? The pharaoh of Europe? Does anyone know that?"

Frank: "Not even Hitler himself. Then how can Rudi, who is only playing his part?"

The two men had reached the batwing doors. For a moment I thought that Flatow would crawl under and Frank vault over the top. But they pushed through together, so that both sides swung back and forth on their rusted hinges.

There were six or seven hours to kill. Victor and I moved round to the back of the bar, where we could not be seen should anyone step into the saloon. And someone did come in, almost before we had settled down behind the rows of empty bottles, the ranks of tinkling glass. I peeked over the top. Valentina! Victor stood upright. "Dear heart," he announced, "we are here."

She ran to the bar and, like a drinker, leaned her elbows on the surface and her foot on the rail. She talked excitedly, not pausing for breath. "Victor, I know you're mad at me. I bet you are too, Uncle Peter. I don't know what came over me. I think I was in a trance. But at least when I saw you go into the bar I didn't tell. And I'm sorry I haven't come to see you. I wish I could talk to you now. Golly, I'm late for wardrobe already. We're shooting my big scene first thing in the morning. I am going to bury my brother. Not with dirt. Not with sand. Guess with what. My hair! You don't mind? If I cut it off?"

Victor forced his way into the flow of words. "Yes. I certainly do."

She went on, unheeding. "Anyhow, I hate it this way! Long hair doesn't suit me. It's the style for a little girl. I'm going to cut it with pieces of glass. So I have to get to sleep early. Rudi said so. The wakeup call is at four-thirty A.M."

Victor said, "Val. Sweetheart. We have to talk. There's something I want to tell you."

"But I said I have to go. I have an appointment at wardrobe. First, though, I'm having an interview with Louella Parsons. She doesn't know it yet, ha-ha-ha! She's looking for Magdalena. That's because she still thinks Magdalena is the star. Oh, Victor, what should I tell her? *Louella, I have always dreamed of being a leading actress.* Don't laugh! Don't laugh! It's true in a way. You don't know it, but when all the beautiful stars came to the house for a party—Joan Crawford and Jean Arthur and Hedy Lamarr—I used to spy down on them from the staircase. When I was supposed to be in bed. I saw Greta Garbo. I saw a lot more than you know. *Louella, not once did I think that my dreams could come true. The only part I ever played was one of the Magi. Oh, that was a fiasco. I have to laugh when I think of it now. My beard itched. And I spilled my myrrh! All over the floor! Isn't that a scream! I was simply mortified. The whole audience laughed. And all the time I knew, I really knew, that they only cast me because the Magi were from the East, from Asia, from Africa, and I had the dark skin of a gypsy. Between you and me, Louella, I confess I made a vow: never to step on the stage again. I thought I'd be a college professor. That was my ambition. Or maybe a historian or a philosopher. You know, just an old fuddy-duddy with my nose in books! Well, look at the bookworm now! He who laughs last laughs best, don't you think?"*

Victor—it was a rare action—removed the Chesterfield from his mouth and ground it out. He leaned over the bar and grasped the twig of his daughter's arm. "You are right, dear heart. Louella has no idea that you have become the leading actress. Rudi is determined to hide this fact from her. That means it is not safe for you. You'll stay with me until we go."

But the girl wrenched herself free. "Oh, no. You can't fool me. I know who's hiding! You are! Rudi told us all about it. You're here to spy. You want to stop *Pandaemonium* from being made. You never wanted me to act in the picture. You made fun of me when I was in school. You don't think I can be an artist. I'll never, ever leave with you."

I stared at her, amazed. Her lips had curled away from her teeth. Her nostrils were flared. Was this the same girl who, it seemed only hours ago, had shouted so gleefully, *Marmalade! Coconuts! Burma Shave!*?

Victor lunged forward again, reaching for her arm. Valentina eluded him and backed toward the door. It was then that I noticed that the glassware behind us was no longer chiming. "Listen," I said. "The pump! It's stopped!"

Valentina ignored me, just as she had her father. But it was toward him that, as she reached the threshold, she leveled a finger. "Don't think I don't know about you and Magdalena! You're just jealous. You want her to be the star!"

From outside, from Main Street, came Mike Meltsner's voice. He was calling for quiet. Valentina stood on tiptoe to see over the swinging doors. Victor hurried round from one side of the bar, I from the other. We joined the girl and stared, no less rapt, toward the second level of the courthouse. As he had earlier that afternoon, Von Beckmann stood on the balcony—only now the badge of office glittered on his chest. His hair was combed over half of his forehead. When Coco called for action, he leaned over the railing. He raised his arm over the crowd of extras.

> *Do we have water to spare? To bathe in? To sprinkle on flowers? Are there birdbaths in gardens? No! We haven't enough to swallow our food. It sticks in our throats. Our children, when they cry, have no tears. There's not even a drop to wash our dead who fall in battle. They're buried with the dirt of the field, with the dried blood caked on their cheeks.*

None of us could take his eyes off Von B. There was something about the way he thrust his hands under his armpits that made it seem he was holding himself together, as if otherwise he would burst from the sheer pleasure of power. His voice, low at the start, was rising higher and higher. The spittle flew from his mouth, onto the hats and heads of his followers below.

> *How could anyone dare to think of using our water to wash the body of the traitor? Anyone who honors that corpse would be a traitor himself. We shall bury any such sentimental fool alive in the mine! Remember: that unworthy brother knew full well what he was doing when he turned against us. Now he must rot. Ah! Do you smell what I do? It is like perfume from France! Rare spice from the Orient! The stink of the dead man's flesh! No one may wash him! No one will bury him! No one may utter a prayer. Not on pain of death. The birds are his only friend. Let them carry off his flesh to the winds. Let the wild dogs of the desert chew on his bones!*

Valentina turned toward the two of us. Her cheeks were covered with tears. "Have you ever heard anything like it? Ever in your life? There is no one like him. I feel like his slave. Oh, Daddy! Uncle Peter! It's so exciting!"

The main shaft of the Pandaemonium mine was located at the opposite end of Main Street from the pile driver and pump. The entrance was built into the side of a small mountain of dirt and spent quartz that had been hauled up from under ground. At the top was a derrick, with its jumble of broken machinery. True enough, a guard was squatting against that pile of rusted metal. We heard him whistling. It looked, in the darkness, as if he were whittling a piece of wood. Sampson Frank knew what to do. His shoes kicked up a cloud of quartz dust as he marched toward him over the tailings. Then the actor engaged the guard in a muted conversation. Once it was clear that the latter's view was effectively blocked, Flatow led us across the open space toward the boarded-up mine. We halted at what had once been a stout wooden door. Now it was merely a group of haphazard slats, through which we slipped with ease.

What struck us at once was the difference in temperature; the inside of the mine was hotter than the alkali plain had been by day. But this heat was as moist, as humid, as the desert had been dry. Sweat poured down our faces, our bodies, soaking our clothes. Flatow lit a match. His face, round and wet, was glistening too. His glasses were completely steamed over. The match went out. The darkness, however, was not total. A faint aura seemed to come out of the very earth we stood on.

"That's the shaft," Flatow whispered. "Take care."

I had done my homework. The original vein of ore that that Ivy Leaguer—Riggs was his name—had discovered plunged directly down to a depth of more than four hundred feet. The main shaft had chased it all the way to the bottom. Every fifty feet horizontal drifts struck out from this timbered chasm. Through these small tunnels the miners had crawled on hands and knees to the wall of quartz in which the gold itself was embedded. Back in the 1880s the mine, much like Lang's Metropolis, had been as busy as an underground city—or at least as a single great skyscraper that had been buried upside down in the earth. And just as the recent invention of the elevator had made it possible for those tall buildings to soar into the sky, the same machinery had allowed the great mines of the West to plunge no less far into the depths. A cable hung down the center of the shaft. One end must be wound around the metal drums in the derrick above; the other was attached to the cage somewhere below. Was that where Magda dangled? Over the steaming sump?

By now our eyes had become accustomed enough to the dark to make out the lip of the shaft. If it had ever been guarded by a railing, the wood had long since turned to dust. Cautiously we moved forward. A dank smell of putrefaction rose from the bottomless pit. I shuddered, thinking of stories of how mules, and even men, had tumbled into the scalding cauldron. The three of us lay flat on our bellies and peered into the abyss. There was little to see: stray beams of light struggled upward, like lightning bugs, around the dark box that choked off the rectangular shaft. I heard Victor gasp—not, surely, at the sight of the distant lift but at the closeup view, so near that we could practically touch the taut steel, of the cable. Steel? The cord looked as if it were made of frayed rope. Rusted strands, brittle strings of metal, stuck out everywhere like the unkempt hair of a woman's braid. What held it together? With our bare hands we could snap it in two. "Oh, Peter," Victor moaned. "Magda hangs by that thread!"

I turned to Flatow. "The elevator! We have to raise it!"

The playwright shook his round head. "You forget, there is no power for this machinery. The lift has been stranded there, halfway down, for more than forty years."

"But Magda—?"

"You must go to her."

"But Herr Flatow—dear Reynaldo," I said, "what about you?"

"Never will I go in that shaft again. Here—" He produced the flat can of film. "This is for you. It is past midnight. Time for Herr Frank and me to attempt to board the airship." So saying, he turned on his heel and headed back toward the loose boards at the exit.

I stood with the metal container in my hands. Déjà vu! Was I really about to rescue Magdalena once again from a suspended lift? So it seemed. Victor had already moved to the iron ladder that was clamped to the side of the shaft. The next moment he completely disappeared. What choice had I? I tucked the container inside my shirt, next to the photo of Jew-free Lemberg, and went after. Rung by rung, handhold after foothold, the two of us started down the shaft.

After a few minutes, though it did not seem like minutes, we reached the first level. By then the arches of my feet, both of them, were cramping; my hands slipped on the damp, flaking iron. We stepped off the ladder onto the platform. Quartz dust ground under the leather of our shoes. Quartz powder circulated in the air. I glanced over my shoulder. The drift, no more than a yard in height, stretched off to the right. The remains of railway tracks ran side by side into the narrow tunnel. It was not hard to imagine the men, bent double, pushing the ore carts along the rusted rails.

"Hurry," said Victor, who had remained near the edge of the shaft. We both stared down into the void. The tin roof of the elevator cage was still far below us. We had come only one fourth of the way. Victor swung himself back onto the ladder and resumed the descent. I followed. We came to the second level, paused but a moment to rest, then continued on to the third. Now the lift was only fifty feet below us. Was it my imagination? Mixed with the smell of festering, of organic decay, and no less with our own acrid perspiration, I thought I detected the distinct odor of Was Frauen Träumen.

Victor must have smelled it, too. Eagerly he grasped the iron bars and descended to level four, where the elevator had been hanging for decades. The stew of the sump was still well below us, yet wisps of steam swirled in the saturated air. The illumination that had guided us came from somewhere inside this fourth-level drift. By that light I could make out the droplets of water gleaming on the cylindrical bars of the cage; and inside that cell, in a half-buttoned blouse, long as a nightshirt, sat the great star. She was huddled in a corner, the cloth of her garment clinging to her sickly white skin. It was like a sarong. The mat of her hair, like moss, hung over her features. Victor dashed forward.

"Magda!" he called. "What have they done to you?"

The actress lifted her head. From ten feet away I could see the irises of her eyes coming into focus. "Victor," she murmured. Then she gave a little cry and got to her feet. She stumbled forward and thrust her arms through the bars. "Help me! Take me away!"

For an instant both the filmmaker and I stood frozen in horror: that was because with each movement she made, the entire cage bobbed up and down, as if it were tethered by an enormous rubber band. But the look of panic, the slug-white pallor, on the face of the woman brought me back to my senses.

"Ha-ha!" I laughed as lightly as I could. "I see they have cast you in *The Perils of Pauline*."

"My God! Oh, God! He's making a joke!" She grasped the bars and began to shake them. The whole lift jerked in response.

Victor flung himself onto the cage. "Don't! Don't do that! We'll get you out!" Now he began to pull on the bars that separated him from the star. But the door of the cage would not budge.

"Please, oh, please," Magda begged. She was now close enough to touch him. She did, grasping the damp cuff of his sleeve. "You don't know what it is like in here!"

I stepped toward the cage. "It's no good," I said, pointing at the padlock that held the bars. "She is locked inside."

Victor looked wildly about. "Where is the key?" he asked. "Who has it?"

"I do." The speaker, George Hoffman, came stooping out of the nearby drift.

"George!" cried Victor. "Thank God it's you! Do you really have the key? Open the lock. Let Magda out."

Hoffman's breasts showed like a woman's through his wet tank top. "Oh, I couldn't do that," he said. "We have to keep her here until tomorrow morning."

Magda groaned. "I shall be dead by tomorrow morning."

"I can't accept such a thing," Victor objected. "I want you to open the lock now."

Hoffman looked genuinely distressed. "I would like to. The thing is, I can't. It's only another eight hours. Not even that."

"And why can't you?"

"Because Von B gave us orders. That's why we're down here. To make sure they're carried out."

Victor: "Von B! Do you know what you're saying? For whom do you work? For Von Beckmann? How many years has my family signed your paycheck? I am head of production. I want that door unlocked at once."

"I'll take her up at eight-thirty. I'll carry her in my arms if I have to. Look—you see the canteens. She has all the water she wants to drink. The only one in the whole town!"

I glanced toward the cage, where a pile of the metal bottles was heaped in the corner. But Victor hadn't taken his eyes from the buckle of Hoffman's belt. I looked, too. The key ring! The key! Suddenly the slight filmmaker threw himself at the larger man's waist. The sliver of metal went flying. It fell with a clink onto the quartzite surface of the platform. Both men dove for it. They groped in the dust. "Help!" cried the sturdy chief grip. "For God's sake help me!"

"I'm coming! Here I am!"

And out of the drift came, of all the people on earth, Chick Chandler. He threw himself upon Victor Granite. The next instant, with a curtain of blood before my eyes, I raised my arms above him.

"Watch out!" cried Hoffman, from his knees. Too late. With a hollow clang I brought the metal container of film straight down upon the head of the leading man. The hated hero froze, then rose half upward. I had a better weapon this time, a jagged fragment of quartz. With both hands I raised it, and, just as Magda let out a terrible scream, with both hands I hurled it down. Chandler ducked. The sharp glittering stone struck George Hoffman, splitting open his skull.

"Excuse, please," I told the hapless victim. "Explain later."

Victor, meanwhile, was scrabbling in the dust. "I have it!" he cried in triumph. Then he stood, holding the key.

There was a groan. Not from Hoffman. It was Chick Chandler. He was on his feet, blinking, swaying, looking around. I seized another rock, as sharp as the first one. *I am doing this*—such was my thought: *Loewenstein-Lorre, not Allen Fox.* Then, just as I raised my weapon, the stunned cowboy—the star, ironically, of *Time Out for Murder*—dropped downward, striking his head on a blunt piece of ore. Magda gasped, pointing to where a stream of blood trickled from his ear.

Instantly Victor was at the cage. He thrust the key into the lock and the door sprang wide. Magda, sobbing, fell into his arms. He clasped her close, so that she did not sink to the hardened earth. "Oh, Victor! Oh, Victor!" she sobbed.

A reply of sorts came from far above:

Yoo-hoo! Oh, yoo-hoo! Are you there? Yoo-hoo, Magdalena!

"*Gott im Himmel!*" cried the former Laszlo Loewenstein. "Frau Parsons!"

Victor took command. "Quick, take Magda that way. To the drift." He handed the half-fainting actress into my arms, then bent to seize Hoffman's ankles. He dragged him out of sight and returned for Chandler.

Pausing with Magda, I looked gloomily at my friend. "The Rubicon," I said, "has been crossed."

"Don't stand there! Hurry!"

The three of us, dragging Chandler behind, entered the tunnel. In only seconds we reached the cavern, where three candles, in black candleholders, burned in the sweating white wall of quartz. At the base of that wall, with a gag in his mouth and his hands tied behind him, lay Charles Laughton. Victor and Magda crouched beside him. I lay flat on the ground. We all listened fearfully to the footfalls descending the rungs of the ladder. What sounds came next? Voices: a murmur, a whisper, a laugh.

Curiosity, as Louella herself might have said, *killed the cat.* Thus thought the impersonator of that other marked man, the murderer of *M.* Nonetheless I crawled ahead on my knees and elbows so that I might see what was occurring at level four. I inched to within a foot or so of the end of the drift. A man and a woman were just stepping off the ladder. The *he*: Manfred, holder of Mr. Moto's lifetime contract. The *she*: Louella. Over her shoulders she wore a scarf of perfect azure.

Manfred said, "Just what I suspected. A wild goose chase. That lift is empty."

Louella took three steps toward the cage, whose door gaped wide on its hinges. "Oh, this is awful. I know she was here. I can practically smell it." Here the columnist raised her beak of a nose, as sharp as Woody Woodpecker's, to sniff at the fetid air.

The Granite president turned back toward the ladder. "I like to fly above the earth, not crawl around underneath it. Let's get out of here."

But Louella was pacing the platform. "Shouldn't we look for her? She must be here somewhere. I've been over every inch of the location. Look: a tunnel—"

The columnist had seen the drift; she began to move toward it. Inside, I held my breath. I picked up a rock. Behind me, I could hear Victor do likewise. Luckily, we did not have to use the weapons. Louella took Manfred's arm and clutched it to her bosom. "Manny," she said, "have you realized we're completely alone?"

Was I the one who was about to have a scoop? No. Manfred stepped backward. He thrust off her arm. "Come on, Louella. Let's get some shuteye. First thing tomorrow I'm going to give you your flying lessons." Laughing like lovers, the two of them made for the ladder and started the long climb to the top.

I backtracked to the illuminated cavern, from which none of us dared stir for a full quarter of an hour. Then Victor removed the cloth from Laughton's mouth. "I'll untie you. We have to hurry."

The fat face of the Englishman was twitching. It crawled with twinges and tics. "What are you doing? Where are you taking me?" he asked.

"To the surface," I said. "It's our chance to escape."

Laughton's eyes grew wide. "No, no. Please. Don't untie me."

Victor stared at the actor. "Have you gone mad?"

"I can't leave. What would Von Beckmann say?"

"What does it matter? We'll get you back to the coast."

"No. I beg you. They need me. Not for a big part. For a small one. I won't say a word. I swear it. Let me be part of the production."

Magda said, "It's hopeless. We have to leave him."

Crouching, dragging our victims behind us, we started back through the drift. We paused at the ladder. Magda went first. I came after. But Victor signaled us to halt. Quickly he stooped and turned out Hoffman's pockets. Then he stood, brandishing his find before us. "Look! You see? The keys to his truck." Then the three of us continued our climb toward the cool night air.

At the exit we discovered that both Flatow and Frank had disappeared. We could hear the guard whistling in the dark. I said, "You go. I'll distract him. We shall meet at the plane."

"No, Peter. You can't." Victor put his hand on my arm. "What if Hoffman or Chandler revives? What if Laughton cries out? You'll be caught."

I shrugged. "Mr. Moto never gets the girl."

At that, Magda put her fingers to her lips; then she touched them to mine. Tears full of salt welled in my eyes. I started forward, toward the distant guard.

Victor said, "Peter, wait. There's bound to be an alarm. You won't get away."

Fade out on gleaming white linen. Shiny round spectacles vanish. Last look at highlights of Wildroot Cream. "Just so. But honorable gentleman and beautiful madame will."

Victor and Magda fled back through the center of town. Everyone, it seemed, was sleeping. Victor knew that Hoffman kept the truck near the subterranean generators. The couple moved as quickly as they could along the road that led to the old cistern. The pile driver, nearby, shook the ground beneath their feet. The buried machines made the air hum. The little black truck was where Victor had remembered. They clambered inside. Magda sat shivering on the worn cloth seat. Why hadn't they risked stopping for warmer clothes? But Victor found a thin wool blanket behind the seat and draped it over the actress's shoulders. He hesitated an instant before depressing the starter. Would there be gas? It wouldn't surprise him if Rudi kept all the tanks empty, to stop anyone who thought of driving away. But the engine turned over and the tank read three quarters full. Without any lights, they drove in a wide arc around the town.

They continued in darkness through the Navaho encampment. Victor steered by the light of the tribe's half-banked fires. As they approached the opening in the western wall, Victor reached across Magda's body and pushed down the button to lock the door. He gunned the engine and turned on the headlamps. They were not going to stop. What if Hoffman and Chandler—dead, for all he knew, or in a coma—had already been found? That's why it was folly to think of boarding the plane in the morning. He pointed the Ford at the unmanned gate and pushed the accelerator to the floor.

The truck shot forward; the steering wheel shook in his hand. He knew that beneath a thin layer of earth and sand, the wall before him was made of solid rock. He aimed the headlights at the center of the narrow gap. At the last moment he saw, first, his Packard, and then a man, who was waving his arms. It was Lydon, the taller of the guards. Victor remembered that his eyes had been gray. Then he shot by him, careening through the passage into the open desert.

He and Magda laughed together. They might have been actors in a B-unit feature, the kind of adventure that Coco or Sumner would have made in six days. *Desert Fury.* Victor looked over at his companion. She was smiling, her teeth almost glowing in the dark. She held the ends of the blanket in one hand, but her blouse was unbuttoned beneath it. The skin of her breasts gleamed as white as her teeth.

He returned his eyes to the plain before them. The only danger now was of getting lost, or turning in a vast blind circle back to the town. There was nothing to steer by; the desert was lit only by moonlight, and by a crazy quilt of stars. Victor believed he was heading more or less in a straight line, toward where he thought he and Peter and Valentina had left the paved road, but he knew that without a compass he might just as well let the Ford take him where it would, as if it were animate—a horse, a homing pigeon, a dog.

Call it luck, then: they made the highway. It showed first in their headlights. Then they felt it under their rubber wheels. Almost on the instant that luck ran out. A wind sprang up, and the sand began to drift over the road. It rattled against the truck, striking in handfuls against the doors and windows. The alkali dust was like a pea-soup fog. The black macadam ahead had been turned into a buttery syrup by their incandescent lights. Slowly they slid along it.

Magda moved closer. Victor thought that with his long, fine nose he could smell two separate layers of sweat: that from the subterranean heat, which had long since dried into a crust over her skin, and that from fear. But he was wrong: it was not fear that made her reach across his body and undo the buttons of his shirt. She was wearing a pair of double bracelets that he had given her years before. He heard them tinkle faintly and felt the cold metal against his flesh. With her fingertips she circled the shallow depression at the center of his breastbone. Then, with a little nip of her teeth, she sucked on the flat gristle of his paper-thin ear. Up ahead the road suddenly fell away as the two right tires slipped from the asphalt and dug into the sand. The headlights hung in midair, in a cross-eyed glare. He swung the wheel hard, veering back to the paved surface. "*Gott!*" he said, a word from childhood. "We almost went over."

Magda did not reply. The smell of her sweat, acrid, bitter, was giving way to the familiar aroma of perfume. When had she last applied it? It was as if the continental scent were like those tiny animals that remained suspended in the form of cysts, melting only in certain states of desire. Craning his head, with his chin above the steering wheel rim, Victor peered at the four or five feet of illuminated roadway. It was like oozing though the phosphorescent wake of some invisible vessel that churned the waves ahead—except that as the dust storm grew more intense, even that path became obscured. There was nothing to do but plunge into the golden haze, like a cloud of frantic fireflies, of their own headlight beams.

This was the moment that Magda chose to grasp the zipper of his trousers and work it down. Her hot breath as she labored blew onto his cheek, into the cavern of his ear. Eagerly she parted the clothing and freed his member, long and curving, from the elastic of his underwear. This was, of course, nothing new. The difference was that instead of moving at this snail's pace, they were usually barreling at eighty miles an hour along the Pacific Coast Highway. She would slide her palm under his buttocks to tickle his anus when they were hurtling down San Vicente. The crucial thing, which was the danger, the demands upon his attention, remained the same. In the middle of the desert he tried to keep to the center of the road, paying no heed to any car foolish enough to be coming from the opposite direction in this storm. Even so he wavered from one edge of the pavement to the other, twisting the wheel from left to right.

Magda was attached to him like a sea anemone to a rock. Her lips sucked hard at his right nipple. Her left arm was curled round his neck so that her fingertips could flick at the nipple on the left. With her free hand she reached into his crotch. The underside of his penis strained against her wrist and forearm. She cradled his testicles, manipulating one against the other.

It was more than he could bear. He wrenched the wheel and pulled off the road. They tipped onto the soft, blowing sand. He killed the engine and turned toward her. "Magda, my darling. Magda, my love. This is killing me. You are killing me. I have been waiting for years. Not just since you left for Salzburg. Since the day I met you. Do you remember? At Metro? And then again, in my office at Granite?"

To his dismay, she released him. She was beginning to inch away. A little desperately, he went on. "Do you think we will just resume? Just resume that craziness? That we would go on, the laughingstock of the industry? Is that what you want? All that was madness! It's over! My God, Magda! Not to be able to look at each other—it's making me bleed inside. The taste of blood is in my mouth."

Magda had drawn fully across the cab of the truck and was huddled against the door. She looked as if she meant to open it. Lillian Gish, Victor thought. *Way Down East*: into the howling storm. From force of habit he struck a match for a cigarette. In the flare he saw her face, with the eyes wide, the mouth pulled back in fear. The tendons stood out on her throat. The sight so shook him that the match went out. Was she acting? This was the Gish of *Broken Blossoms*. It was as if she expected to be attacked in her hiding place. Or had she seen his own face in the puny flame? Was it so frightening? He said he tasted blood. That was only talk. Except he did feel the heat of it in his cheeks, pounding through his head.

"Magda, listen. Do not, please, misunderstand me. This is different. Everything is different between us. I am not even the person who beats around the bush. So listen carefully. This is what I am thinking. Valentina is now grown. Not only that—I don't always like what I see on her face. Better for her if I am out of her life. And you know everything is over between me and Giselle. Do you understand what I am saying? I am saying that I am going to leave her. We start a life together. Two steps forward. Okay? No steps back."

Magda laughed. The sound astonished him. She was chortling into her hands.

"So now tell me what is funny. Do you think I said something absurd?"

She kept her hands in front of her face, speaking through her fingers. "Start the engine. Victor, turn around. Go back the way we came."

"Go back? Don't you understand? That's over, too. Finished. I am going to shut the picture down. Everyone on location has lost his mind. They're performing for a madman. Can't you see that something terrible, something unimaginable, is going to happen? We have to stop it. We'll stop it together. You'll see. You'll see, Magda darling. I'll give you everything you wanted."

"What is it you think I want? For you to leave Giselle? And Valentina? You are always too late. Years too late. I too am not the same person."

"It *is* Rudi, isn't it? Rudi! My God! You are like Laughton and the rest of them. All the good Germans. You are still in the cage."

Magda wailed. "I wanted you to save me! Victor, I wanted you to take me away. I thought I could do it. I can't. Do you want me to say it? He is lost without me. That's what I see. Oh, so clearly! If only I'd seen it in Vienna. No. I won't leave him again."

"You mean," said Victor, "that you are lost without him." But he stretched out his foot and depressed the starter. The engine, choked with dust, sputtered; then it turned over and came to life.

"Yes!" said Magda. "Take me back!"

Victor made no move to do so. The headlights, which had come on with the engine, were refracted off each grain of sand, every particle of alkali dust. They shifted in the air like searchlights. The cabin of the truck, shaken by wind gusts, was illuminated. He saw Magda's bare arm holding the blanket beneath her chin. But in the open fold one breast was exposed to the nipple. Beneath the wool her long legs were extended. The knees were parted. He thought he saw an inner muscle twitch high on her loin.

"What is it, Magda? About Von B? Is he a genius? Does he have a sexual hold upon you? Just tell me. God in heaven! This is a scene from Dostoevski! Does he do to you what he does to the little boys?"

Magda, gasping: "Don't. Stop. Don't do this, Victor."

What she meant was that he had climbed onto her, with his legs straddling her lap. He held her head to the seat by the strands of her hair. He leaned toward her face, without missing a beat of a word.

"I know it is hypnotism. My God, I've seen him do it to horses. Even they come under his spell. Are you his horse? His little pony?"

"No. Oh, no. This can't be. Victor, do you want to force me?"

He did not hear her. Perhaps he did not know what she was talking about. All he heard were his own words. But he held her head immobilized. He reached under the blanket, under her shirttail, and pulled at her panties. They gave way without a sound.

"All right, Magda. All right. I'll tell you the most astounding thing: I, too, have stood gaping at his genius. It is true! It is as if I have never seen a film being made, never dealt with an actor, never had a thought of my own in my head. I am like a tourist in my own industry. Do you know what's horrible? The most horrible thing? I still want this film to be made! In spite of everything! Oh, it's humbling. It's humiliating."

The actress did not answer. She was twisting her shoulders left and right to escape his grasp. At last he fell silent, while pressing himself against her legs. With a quick wrenching movement she lashed out with her elbows. At the same time she managed to knock him askew with her knee. Off-balance, he toppled back to the driver's side of the cab. At once she lurched up and around, as if she meant to climb over the seat and force herself through the hopelessly small window in the back. He caught her. He thrust the blanket up and over her head, as if it were a dress. He wound his arms around her hips. He started to mount her from behind. Lucky for Magda she weighed almost as much as he did. By pushing against the fabric of the seat she managed to ride him backward, against the dash. Once more she moved to escape, this time grappling with the handle on the door, but in her frenzy she forgot to pull up the lock. Deliberately he drew her the length of the seat and spread his body over hers. He hooked one arm under her leg, hauling it upward until her foot scraped the battered roof of the cab; he stretched out her other leg, entangling it in the hollow of the steering wheel. She was pinned. Still she struggled, using her teeth, her nails. She beat at him with her fists. Hopeless. All the while the shaft of his member rubbed against her belly, her thighs, and into the curls of her pubic hair, as tight as a pickaninny's.

"What have you done?" he suddenly cried, releasing the pressure. "You have knocked off my hat!"

He rolled away. He was groping over the tin-covered floor. She could just make out the narrow wedge of his skull, with its carpet of fine black hair. It bobbed, it jerked, as he searched left and right. Silently she pointed. The hat, as wide, almost, as a ten-gallon, was upside-down in the dashboard corner. He snatched it up. He settled it upon his head.

"Ha-ha-ha!" Magda laughed.

Sheepishly, he grinned. Magda laughed on, louder still.

"Shhhh," he said, to calm her. "I have some idea of what happened. I'm not completely certain. Was I about to rape you?"

At that the actress whooped uproariously. Her bare shoulders shook. Rather, they went up and down as if jointed like a puppet's. Victor reached out—there was no question he meant this tenderly—and adjusted the collar of her blouse. He pulled the twisted blanket over her knees. "It is all right. It's over. Something came over me. A fit of some kind. I am myself again. Magda. Please. Don't cry."

He was right: if the sounds she made had ever been laughter, they were not anymore. She sobbed. She moaned. He moved to comfort her. Her body was stiff, unmoving. It was as if she had been flash-frozen. "You see," he said, "I could not do it. I suppose it is against my principles. They are stronger than I am. You know better than anyone that I would fire any writer who said it, but it's your spell I am under. The same way you are under his. We'll just go on, Magda darling. Shall we? Believing the lie? Our whole industry is built upon it: that love conquers all."

Magdalena was sitting upright. She seemed to be listening. So he continued. "Sometimes I think everything is fated. Do you ever feel that? We're in a tide, like a swimmer at the beach. What's the most we can do? Thrash, that's all. And curse the day we ever met." He said that, and what followed, with a smile. "Ah, you are a bloody bitch."

But her head was not tilted to catch his words. She held up her hand. "Listen. Listen. I think I hear them. Yes. No. Yes. Yes. Yes. *Die Grillen!*"

Victor moved back behind the wheel. He adjusted his clothing. "What is it? I can't hear anything. It's the wind. Like a whirlwind."

There was light enough to make out the look she cast upon him: one of disgust, of scorn. "Wind!" she echoed. "You fool. Don't you hear them? *Die Grillen!*"

He knew the German word. He shrugged. It didn't make sense. Meanwhile, Magda had begun to roll down the window. "Don't do that," he admonished. "We'll choke on that dust."

She paused. "But I want to hear."

Victor hesitated. Should he stop her? The whole world was filled with alkali powder. Sand swirled through the air. For some reason he thought of the trip they had taken together to Yosemite, years before. He remembered the time both of them had been locked in the car when two grizzlies were prowling. One leaned, rather like a bored mechanic, on the hood. But the other cuffed the frame of the sedan. This, the dust storm, the sandstorm, was the way it had been then—like looking out the window at the mass of matted fur.

"Now," said Magda, as she rolled down the glass. "Listen."

"Magda. There's nothing to hear."

"Shhhh!" she hissed fiercely. She thrust her head out into the mist.

He sat back. He finally lit his cigarette. Sure enough, tendrils of dust began to filter inside the car, like a hairy paw. It even smelled vaguely of fur. Wherever he looked, forward, back, up toward the sky, everything was erased. It was like being in a special classroom—no, in a great university, where every blackboard was smeared.

Magda pulled her head back in. She rolled up the window. He took that as his cue to put the truck in gear. But she stopped him.

"When I was a girl of nine, very ugly and freckle-faced, with teeth like this, horse teeth, buckteeth you say—at this age we spent a month of the summer on Hiddensee. That is a Baltic island, you know. I learned to swim. I made fortresses in the sand. I imagined animals and monsters and hump-backed men in the clouds. My skin turned dark, the color of tobacco, and my hair was as white as—yes, the paper of your cigarette. As blazing as that tip. Ha-ha-ha—you could have smoked me! That little girl!"

Victor might have been one of Von B's enchanted horses: not a muscle moved. Her voice was like a nine-year-old's! It chilled him through. There was no way on earth—not even if she were Bernhardt, Duse—that this could be an act.

"One day, a hot day, I was playing—not at the edge of the sea, but behind our cabin. The grass there was taller than my head. The game was to trample it. To make circles in it, and boxes and x's. Then you could look at your work—foot painting, we called it—from up on the roof. The first thing I noticed was that I had started to shiver. The grass was waving. A cold wind had sprung up. Next I heard a rustling sound. A flapping. I thought that Mama must have put her linens on the line. But the ropes were bare. The noise came from that direction—" Here Magda pointed out the window, toward far-off California and the invisible Pacific. "From the west. From the sea. Do you know what I did? I ran indoors and up the staircase and up the ladder and onto the roof. There they were—birds! Thousands and millions of birds! The darlings! They were trying to outrun the shadow that was rolling up behind them. You know, don't you, that it was a hopeless task? Later, that fall, no, that winter, the schoolmistress explained. In an hour the moon travels more than three thousand kilometers. That's almost a kilometer every second. Poor birds! For just an instant it seemed that the flock was carrying a great black blanket in their beaks. Off it billowed to the rear! But do you know what happened? In an instant? All of them were swallowed by the penumbra, and then the umbra, of the moon. The white wings all turned to black. It was as if these seabirds—the thousands of gulls, the pelicans, the terns—had been transformed into crows."

"An eclipse," Victor murmured. He thought vaguely of one of poor Coco's South Sea adventures: *Tropical Midnight,* in which the white explorers, about to be hurled into a steaming kettle, had been saved by just such sudden shadows.

"Yes, a total eclipse. But I didn't know. I was only a girl! My heart—how it beat and beat! From excitement! From fear! Up above, the edge of the moon was cutting like a scythe through the circle of the sun. Everything around me was divided into darkness and day. The sea was half gleaming glass, half sticky tar. Even the sky was cracked: alight in the east, black in the west. And oh, there was a roaring sound. Like angry people. Like the turning of the ferryboat screws. It was the sound of the shadow drawing near. It was trampling everything before it. It was a giant. A giant! He was making a foot painting out of all of the world. I wanted to run. To hide. But it was like a dream. My feet would not move. I tried to cover my eyes. But something made me look up. What did I see? At noontime? High noon? Don't you know? Can't you guess? The whole sky was filled with stars."

The actress paused. Her head was thrown back, as if she could look through the roof of the little truck, through the sand-strewn mist, to the heavens. Her chest, beneath the stuff of her shirtfront, was heaving. When she spoke again it was in a whisper.

"What could I think? I thought I had gone mad. And that is when I heard it. From behind the cabin. In the grass. In the woods further off. From all over the island. It was like singing. *Die Grillen.*"

"Crickets," said Victor.

"Yes," said Magda. Again she started to sob. "The poor darlings! They thought it was night."

A moment passed. Victor blew cigarette smoke from his mouth and nose. "It's funny how they do it. They don't sing with their mouths. They rub their legs together."

"Oh, yes!" she said, in a high-pitched girlish squeal. "I know that!"

Resolute, he pushed in the clutch. He put the gear in first. Sure, he said to himself, maybe Hitler had given her a private showing of *Pinocchio.* Maybe that's how she knew. But his thoughts were interrupted by the voice of the mature woman.

"I wish I heard them now. They saved me from going insane."

Victor spun the wheels, then skidded back onto the highway. Was it his imagination, or was the road somewhat clearer? He started slowly along the asphalt, the way they had come. In an instant, from nowhere, a wave of cynicism had gripped him. Not from nowhere, this despair: he was intelligent enough to recognize that such bitterness deflected his thoughts, and his judgment, away from himself. Nonetheless, he calculated the odds. No better than fifty-fifty. He'd be willing to take the bet himself—that there had been no eclipse of the sun on the island of Hiddensee, on the Baltic, or anywhere in northern Europe, when Magdalena Mezaray was a girl.

At eight the next morning Valentina crouched on the same section of the ridge she had danced on a week before. The wind blew her hair about her shoulders and over her eyes. She glanced back. The entire company, even the poor, bedraggled Indians, was standing below, inside the crater. The corpse of her dead brother lay on the other side of the rim. It was covered by birds—not vultures but black birds, like trained crows. They crawled over the remains of his clothes. They seemed to be picking at his skin. She could not control the shudder that ran the length of her body.

"So, Valentina," said Von Beckmann. "We now are ready."

The director stood beside her on the ridge. Coco Goodheart was beside him. Behind them both Nakhimovsky, the cameraman, was peering into the viewfinder of his camera. Then he stood up and for the third time moved forward to measure the distance between his lens and the veil of her blowing hair. Through those dark strands she took a last glance at Von B; his own hair, with the white streak blazing in it, like the flash of Arthur the chauffeur's smile, alternately flattened and rose upon his enormous head. His cape snapped out behind him on the breeze. Valentina took comfort in that; the cloth was owl-shaped, or like a great bat, and would surely keep the flock of scavengers away.

Now, from among the crowd, Mike Meltsner said, "We need to have quiet. We're ready to begin."

Liz, the script girl, held her slate in front of the camera. Coco Goodheart looked toward Von Beckmann, who nodded. "Action," Coco said.

For an instant the actress did not move. She raised her hand to brush the hair from her eyes. There was no sound boom, no sound man. That is why Von B was able to give his instructions aloud: "Now, Valentina. Call to them."

He meant the birds. She raised her hands to her mouth. She pretended to utter a cry. On some hidden cue the whole flock rose into the air. She saw how they carried flesh in their beaks, and more flesh in their talons. "Go to him," Von Beckmann said.

Once more she obeyed. As she made her way down the crater's rim, the camera followed, gliding along its hidden track. The voice of the director floated down from the top of the ridge, as if it too were on a well-oiled dolly. "Continue. Continue. Keep moving. You dare not look at the corpse. You hide your eyes behind your hair. You have tried to prepare for this sight. You have imagined it. Still, you are frightened. Will this be your brother? The person you loved? Or have the birds picked him clean?"

The voice, so calm, so clear, seemed to be whispering at her ear. All of her attention was focused on his words.

"Closer. Closer. Still you dare not look. How will you find him? Is it by the smell? Like a blind person, you put your hands before you. Yes. Like that. Almost. Almost. So! Your feet have touched him. You are there."

It was just as he said. Her feet bumped against her brother's remains. Now she dropped to her knees. She began to grope with her hands.

"That's right. You touch him. You feel his body. You recognize him—yes, by the shape of the buckle on his belt. Excellent. You tremble. A terrible trembling. It is because you must now part your hair. Wait! Not yet! Remember, the audience will not see the dead man. There will not be the vulgarity of a closeup. The only way they can form an image of his face is by what they shall see on yours."

Valentina pulled aside the curtain of hair. She thought she heard the cameraman gasp—not at the corpse, but at her own reaction. Was her face such a fright? She felt that little hooks were embedded in her skin, dragging the mouth agape, pulling the eyeballs outward from her eyes, pinching lines of anguish onto her brow.

Von B: "Yes. The horror. You feel it. But already it is changing. It gives way to sorrow, to pity. Poor Paul! You want to wash him. To clean the dirt. To bathe that face that is now no more than a bloody pulp. You reach for the water bottle, even though you know it holds no more than a teaspoon. Hold it up. Please, a little higher. Now it is empty. The last drops are gone. Now you lean over the corpse. Yes, closer still; at least you will be able to wash your dear brother with your tears."

As Von Beckmann spoke, the hundreds of fishhooks continued to pull the skin of her face, making minute adjustments. The corners of her mouth were twisted into a wail. A sob was yanked from her throat. At the same time her nostrils were drawn wide with a sudden feeling of dread: was there enough moisture left in her body to produce a single tear? Dry-eyed, she stared down at the corpse of the brother she had loved. The sap would not come.

"A thought now occurs to you. That bottle. If the glass were a knife, you would plunge it into your heart. Fit punishment for a weak and unworthy woman. Yes, smash it down. Upon that rock. Perfect. Now you have a hundred knives to choose from. Pick any one you wish. Yes, Annie. My Annie: look. That piece has a point like a dagger."

Valentina picked up the sliver. She held it up before her. Then, surprisingly, and for just an instant, the spell was broken. That is, a stray thought brushed by from her former life. She recognized it at once. It came from two years before, when she and Victor had gone downtown to see the visiting opera. The little Japanese lady, no older than she was, had held up such a knife and then plunged it into her belly. In her orchestra seat, she had clung to Victor's brown hand. Now she dismissed the thought, along with the whole of her previous life. The Annie inside Valentina took over. She leaned forward and cut through a lock of her hair. It fell onto her brother. She raised her hand again, to resume the slashing. But before she could do so, Rudolph Von Beckmann said, "Cease."

Valentina dropped the make-believe blade, which had been designed to look like a shard of glass. Why had the scene been interrupted? Why had they stopped? She got to her feet. At that moment she saw a man walking alone through the desert. Instantly she recognized the leaning stick figure. It was her father.

Von Beckmann had seen him, too. "How dare anyone interfere with our shooting? This scene is not complete. What must we put up with *für den Scheisskerl? Ja,* from that little shit."

Rooted to the spot where she stood, Valentina stared intently. Victor continued to walk across the plain—not aimlessly, but in a straight line. She shifted her gaze along the trajectory and saw, parked at the far end of what had to be a runway, the silvery shape of the company plane. The moment her eyes fell upon it, the aircraft came to life. The engines coughed. Smoke came out of them. All three propellers started to turn. Victor did not hesitate. He had almost reached the long, sand-free strip on the desert floor. The plane taxied toward him, so as to be able to take off into the wind. Victor, if anything, quickened his pace. It was obvious to Valentina that this was a rendezvous. He was going to fly away. But where was he going? Back home? Without her? Wasn't he going to stay for her scene? She strained to see more exactly, pulling the black bunches of hair away from her eyes. The airplane, trundling along the runway, went by her father and came to a halt only a few feet away. The whirling propellers were only a blur. She waved to him. "Victor!" she cried. Of course he could not hear her. "Daddy! Daddy!" she called, like a little girl.

Now another figure dashed down from the top of the embankment. He was shouting. With one hand he held something aloft in the air. It was as round and flat as a plate; it gleamed in the early morning light like the discus of a Greek. It was, she realized, a canister of film.

Uncle Peter! Valentina put her hands to her mouth to stifle a giggle. Down fell Peter Lorre. Then, like a jack-in-the-box, he popped up again. With his knees high and his elbows jerking, he galloped forward, even faster than before.

Even if Victor had looked back, it is not likely he could have seen either the running man or the waving girl. That was because the wash from the turning propellers had kicked up dust all around. He could barely sense the thrust-up nose of the plane as it turned above him. The crisscrossing winds whipped at his hat, which he held tightly atop his head. The blades at the center of the vortex were thrashing the air. *A Caucasian sword dance,* he thought, and glanced upward, toward the cockpit. There he made out a flash of blue, the same sky-blue he had seen when watching the daring Manfred walk the wire above the crowd. Then that memory, and all his other perceptions, were lost in the deafening roar.

HOLLYWOOD MERRY GO ROUND

As all the great philosophers say, how fickle is fate. Just this morning I was feeling down in the mouth when Manfred Granite and I left the Fancy Free Hotel and boarded our silver skinned plane. Come heck or high water I'd been determined to interview Magdalena Mezaray. But after Manfred and I had literally searched heaven and earth—that is, after we'd sailed high in the air and explored deep in the ground (we had a tip she was sequestered in a romantic old mineshaft)—we hadn't turned up hide nor hair of the tousle-haired Teuton. Even LOP has on occasion to admit defeat. So it was with my tail between my legs that I climbed into the trimotor's cockpit and flicked all the switches that Manny—he hadn't given up trying to teach me to fly!—pointed out. The powerful engines started to turn—and so did my luck! One minute I thought all my efforts had been in vain, and the next thing I knew I had the story of the decade. And an exclusive to boot! Even though the tale I have to tell is a sad one, and involves the loss of a dear friend, I have no choice but to reveal the sensational news.

Victor Granite is dead. The chief of production for Granite Films, who brought such high artistic standards to our industry, was struck down in a tragic accident not far from the goldmining town that was the site of his company's latest picture. I was probably the first person in the world to view his remains. People think I'm a tough hombre, but I can tell you that I uttered an ear-splitting shriek when I saw that his head had been cut off by the propellers from his body. It lay feet away, still inside its hat. Manfred reached across me to shut off the engines and put on the brake. The whole crew from the *Pandaemonium* production, who had been shooting a scene only a few hundred yards away, came running toward us. I was speechless at the sight of the blood on the wing. No one could console me. Even hours later, when we were once more revving our engines for our flight into the firmament, I was still sobbing gently into my beautiful blue scarf. It may knock my readers cold—and heaven only knows what Mr. Hearst will say—but I am ready to confess now that my emotions were overwrought because I felt myself to be personally responsible for the awful mishap.

I know that all my friends will rally around me. "How can that be, Louella?" That's what the dwellers in Lollyland are going to say. "After all, it wasn't you who was flying the plane." That is one hundred percent correct! If I had a Bible with me I would swear upon it. All those knobs! So many levers! How was I, who was already busier than a one-armed paperhanger, supposed to know which one to pull? Besides, once we started to taxi down the runway, there was more dust in the air than powder on the face of La Swanson. I couldn't see poor Victor, who always was as thin as a thistle. He was practically invisible. Must I be the one to wear sackcloth and ashes?

The story of the decade, I wrote. But why will this encounter between man and machine still intrigue the readers of the "Merry Go Round" ten years from now? Well, it's been twenty years since Fatty Arbuckle did or did not do in the raven-haired beauty Virginia Rappe, and nineteen since somebody shot William Desmond Taylor—and no one in all of Tinseltown has stopped tattling about either event. I might just as well add the case of the delectable Thelma Todd. The grand jury may have ruled "death by carbon monoxide," but lots of us are still scratching our heads as to how inhaling a deadly gas could have ripped the clothes off that ice-cream blonde or left her with so much blood on her delicate features.

The oxygen up here where I'm penning today's column is as thin as the bean soup at Dave Chasen's is thick (that's an old line of Groucho's), or maybe it's just heights that have made me as dizzy as Rita Hayworth claimed to be after her dance scenes with Fred Astaire. In any case, readers won't fail to notice that my list of scandals does not include the ridiculous rumor that at the time of my first visit to Hollywood, Mr. Hearst caused the death of picture pioneer Thomas H. Ince. Some people who ought to know better actually describe yours truly as an eyewitness on the yacht *Oneida,* formerly the floating palace of the Kaiser; that's where W. R. supposedly caught the irrepressible Charlie Chaplin *in flagrante* on the lower deck with the breathtaking Marion Davies and by accident put a bullet, not through the forehead of the little tramp, but into the brain of the "Father of the Western," who happened to be standing nearby. It hasn't been beneath the dignity of some columnists—you can tell who one of them is because she always elbows her way up to the *hedda* the line—to claim that it was no coincidence that shortly afterward I was given a lifetime contract and worldwide syndication in Hearst publications. Let's set the record straight. In the first place, your correspondent was not on the 280-foot yacht on November 15, 1924. In the second place, there has never been anything between Chaplin and Marion, who has never wavered in her devotion to Mr. Hearst. If that weren't enough, W. R. is a wonderful marksman, whom I have seen with my own eyes bring down a seagull with a quick shot from the hip. If he shot at somebody he wouldn't miss. Besides, as everyone knows, Thomas Ince died, as Dr. Daniel Carson Goodman testified, from acute indigestion.

What do all these cases that have rightly or wrongly captured the public imagination have in common? The answer is, *mystery*. No one to this day knows how Virginia Rappe got her ruptured bladder, or who shot William Desmond Taylor, or whether or not Thelma Todd killed herself or was beaten to death by her lover, thriller director Roland West, or was murdered by the thwarted Lucky Luciano. For that matter, as I sometimes have to remind W. R. when the old boy gets on his high horse and criticizes a perfectly good column, a dose of lead might give *anybody* indigestion! The real question is, what intrigue is there in the death of Victor Granite? Surely the proper authorities will take into account the conditions on the runway—a man running about in a dust storm, the noise of the engine, a novice pilot—and rule that this was an unfortunate mishap.

Then why is Lolly's nose twitching? It can't be from the ether at ten thousand feet. I may not have been present on the *Oneida* when Mr. Ince overindulged himself at dinner, but I was Johnny-on-the-spot at Pandaemonium. Here are the facts I have gathered. On the night before the "accident" at the ghost town, a truck owned by Granite Films was stolen from the location. Minutes later a guard at the rock wall that surrounds the town attempted to stop a vehicle as it sped through the gate. He swears that this was the missing truck and that in spite of the blinding headlights, he recognized the occupants: they were Magda Mezaray and Victor Granite. Obviously the two old friends had driven off to the desert to hold their tryst and, as lovebirds will, had a quarrel. I won't be telling tales out of school if I reveal that the honey-haired Hun and the swarthy-skinned Victor had once upon a time been an item. No one guards her privacy more than Magda. But one afternoon some years ago—I remember that in her light chiffon blouse and her big sun hat, she was a poem of beauty—my friend said to me, "Louella, I love him desperately, with all my heart. But I cannot bring such pain to his wife, Giselle, and to his pretty little girl." Even in the desert, it seems, she stuck to her guns. That's why Magda threw him out of the studio truck. Victor had to walk all the way back and, disoriented by the shifting desert sands, crossed the path of our departing plane.

But if that's all there is to it, why does my nose still need a good scratch? Perhaps there is more than meets the eye to this sad desert encounter. Could it not be that, heartbroken and in despair, Victor Granite paid little attention to the danger of the whirling propellers? Indeed, in his anguish might he not have actually welcomed their sharp embrace? He would not be the first Lollywoodian to end his life because of unhappiness in love. I do not have to remind my readers of how Paul Bern, whom many of us thought of as filmdom's Father Confessor, turned a gun on himself because of his tortured marriage to Jean Harlow. He was found drenched in Mitsouko, Jean's favorite perfume. Beside him, a note to his "Dearest Dear" contained his last words: *I love you.* You may have forgotten John Bowers, the handsome leading man in so many silent movies, but everyone remembers Norman Maine—can't you still hear Janet Gaynor saying, "This is *Mrs.* Norman Maine!"?—for whom Bowers served as the model. After he was divorced by Marguerite De La Motte—remember *her,* opposite Doug Fairbanks?—and his career went into a tailspin, he drowned himself in the Pacific, just like Fredric March. I wouldn't be surprised if works of art like *A Star Is Born* are based on Victor Granite, once he takes his place among those legends who found they could not live without love.

An accident. Suicide. Hard though it is, I have to gird my loins and put the third possibility on paper: FOUL PLAY! Could it be that Victor Granite lost his skull to, no pun intended, skulduggery? Let's examine a few more facts. Last night, at about the same time that Victor and Magda drove off for their assignation, George Hoffman, the well-liked key grip of what had been the Granite B unit, together with Chick Chandler, whose career I have been following ever since his terrific debut in *Melody Cruise,* were found together at the bottom of the mineshaft, unconscious and in critical condition. They might have slipped and fallen, it's true. But then why was a blood-covered rock found near the scene? And why was Peter Lorre so eager to give me the prints of Magda Mezaray's last scene that he too ran onto the runway? His role in all this—it's no secret that Chick's friendship with Rochelle Hudson made Peter see green—will be looked into by our boys in blue and by our crack coroner's office. Only Hoffman and Chick himself know the truth, and unfortunately both are deep in a coma. But it certainly would be one heck of a coincidence if two such terrible accidents—the one to Victor and the one in the mineshaft—occurred at practically the same moment. Do you know what we used to say in Illinois? Tell it to the Marines!

As my old pal Bill Powell always says at such moments, *look for the motive*. Faithful fans of this column know that *Pandaemonium* has had its share of troubles. Herr Von Beckmann drove the production over schedule and over budget, and even though two canisters of Magda's latest rushes sit here on the seat beside me, the mystery of her role in the picture has yet to be solved. With such difficulties, and all the tension between those on location and the studio on La Brea, is it any wonder that the great director should have looked on the arrival of Victor Granite as a threat? I have it on good authority that at the moment our plane was about to land, which was only twenty hours ago, Von B, as he is affectionately called by his loyal associates, made a speech in which he offered me a heartfelt welcome but called the emissary from Granite Films a spy. *We know how to deal with him,* were his very words. How could those hearing that speech not feel that Victor's presence on the set put the completion of their film in jeopardy? Did one of them, fearing for his job perhaps, or under the sway of the forceful director, feel compelled to act?

What's more, Manfred Granite, who just might not be the great flier I had thought, has long been aware that *Pandaemonium* has been draining his stockholders' finances at the very time the studio was attempting to recover from the fire on its lot. From the moment he felt he was losing control of what had once been a simple shoot-'em-up, the elder Granite brother has wanted to end production. The only person standing in his way, the one man who believed in what Rudolph Von Beckmann was doing, was Victor Granite. When you think of it, it's so ironic: Victor was endangered from one side because he threatened the completion of the picture and from the other because he wished to save it. The question that must be asked is, which of these two sides proved his undoing?

The one person who can provide the final answer sits behind that dark green curtain at the front of our plane. I never dreamed that Manfred Granite was so jealous of his younger brother that he might stoop to the curse of Cain. Yet all he had to do to avoid the tragedy was say to his nervous copilot, *Don't touch that lever! No! Pull that one! That one over there!* I do not like to speak ill of anyone, but I did notice that he was not always completely respectful of the fact that LOP is a happily married woman. I am afraid I am going to have to return his lucky scarf.

Away with such morbid thoughts! The truth always comes out. Either

Hoffman or Chick Chandler is bound to wake and tell his tale. Magda, too, will have a good deal to say. And soon we shall see how she performs on these precious reels of film. Meanwhile, I can't wait to put my nose back to the grindstone. In this town, if you're away for a single day you miss so much! Still, there might be a few scraps left in THE CHATTERBOX. For instance, I know for a fact that Al Jolson flew out here to huddle with Ruby Keeler's mother and that can only mean one thing: Al wants Ruby back. In true Jolson fashion, he brought along a diamond as big as a cube of Domino sugar. All their friends hope there will be a reconciliation, for Al is a good guy and Ruby is a swell gal. Mrs. Irving Berlin was seen lunching at Romanoff's with of all people Binnie Barnes. And of course I'm as excited as a schoolgirl in anticipation of the big news. Did Lana Turner show up at the airport to greet Tony Martin, and did romance blossom for the two of them once again? Or does she still, in spite of everything, hold the torch for Artie Shaw? That's all for today. See you tomorrow!

METEOR

November 1941

CHAPTER

O N E

A MIX-UP

The line of limousines, all with their lights on, stretched out forever. Here and there I could make out a sedan, a convertible, a coupe—even a bright yellow taxi or two. We turned right on Van Ness Avenue and continued south across Sunset, then Fernwood, then Fountain. One car ahead, just behind the hearse that carried Victor's remains, Giselle and Valentina rode in the Cadillac De Ville. Burton drove Georgia and Manfred in a rented Lincoln. I was in that vehicle, too: Moto in the motorcade. I sat low in the seat so as to avoid the gaze of the mounted policemen, who, as we rolled slowly by, touched their white gloves to their caps. Still, I couldn't help seeing the crowds that lined the sidewalks. Anyone would have thought a Harlow had died, or a star like Valentino. But Victor? He'd been responsible for a million feet of film; it had spun from his brain like thread from a spider. Yet that sad, sallow face had never appeared on so much as a single frame. A thought, out of—as my fellow countrymen say—the blue: was that the reason he never took off that horrible hat? So as not to appear in even a still photograph? He used that broad brim the way a gangster, confronted by the press, used his overcoat or his hands.

The press had been waiting, just minutes before, when our cortege, then on Hollywood Boulevard, stopped in front of Grauman's Chinese. Sid Grauman himself had opened the door of the De Ville. Valentina stepped out, followed by Giselle, all in black. Off went the flash lamps, like milk splashed from a bucket. Newsreel cameramen shot their film. The crowd surged forward against the line of police. One car back, I watched as Les Kahn came up to the widow. He held a cushion from the Granite prop department, plump and red, with yellow braid, like a pasha's pillow from a scene in the harem. When Giselle saw it, or what was on it, she put the back of her hand to her mouth. She sagged against Valentina.

"I'll be right back," Manfred told us, before he climbed out of our Lincoln. I glanced up: *Suspicion,* that was the feature on the marquee. With Joan Fontaine. Manfred hurried over to where Kahn was standing. "What the hell is going on?" he yelled at the publicist.

On the silk threads of the cushion sat Victor's hat—rather, a facsimile of that ten-gallon, in brown felt with the famous floppy brim. Where was the original? In the desert? Impounded by the police? For all any of us knew, it was inside the coffin. At the sight of that headgear, a hundred women broke into a wail. They were like Arabs with their hullabaloo. The uniformed cops pressed back against the crush of their bodies. Kahn grinned; for him it was like a premiere.

"Give that to me," Manfred growled. He plucked up the hat and strode over to where Grauman was waiting by the square of sidewalk. Without further ceremony, he bent onto both knees and, rather like a praying Arab himself, leaned forward in order to force the impression of the profile, crown and brim, into the wet cement.

Our rubber wheels thumped over the trolley tracks at Santa Monica. Burton, behind the wheel, pointed through the opposite window: there was the cemetery. White Christian crosses rose over the edge of the plaster wall. We didn't turn in, however. Instead, we drove down the long block to Melrose, keeping the buildings of the Paramount lot on our right. Then we turned, so that Bronson, Irving, and Windsor passed by on our left. Manfred snorted. He was glowering toward where, out the window, the crowd had grown even thicker. Almost all of the people in it were women. They stood two and three deep, waving their handkerchiefs like the foamy caps on an unending wave. "That bastard Victor," Manfred muttered, just low enough so as not to wake the dozing Georgia. "Did he fuck them all?"

On the rear seat, between Manfred and his wife, lay a round metal canister. Louella had forced her way through the crowd at Grauman's and thrust the reel at Manfred. "You have to see this!" she exclaimed. "It's sensational! The future of the studio depends upon it." Manfred took the container and ducked back into the limousine. Louella attempted to follow. "Aren't you going to let me in?" she cried. "Manny! Manny! After everything I've done for you?"

"Burton! Get moving!" said the Granite president, pushing down the button that locked the door.

The odds were that what lay on the seat before me was the footage of Annie at the crater's rim. But there was no way to tell, merely by looking at the tin container, which of the two actresses, the newcomer or the star, had played the scene.

We came at last to Gower. The procession turned right and, only a moment later, moved under the arch of Beth Olam. Georgia woke up; but from what she saw out of the curtained windows, she might very well have thought she was still having a dream. Green lawns surrounded us, and hills and dales, and trees from another climate—what were they in the English tongue? Like women washing their hair: weeping willows! Easy to imagine that the entire scene, with these bluebirds chirping and the little pebble-strewn walkways, was nothing more than a fixture on the neighboring studio's lot.

The limousines pulled over to the right, with their wheels against the curb of the drive. The doors opened and the mourners got out. Jews with armbands directed the crowd down the long, sweeping slope to where, near a pretty patch of pansies, a pile of fresh earth marked the grave. Irene Selznick stepped from a maroon La Salle and took Giselle by one arm. Selznick himself emerged from the same car and held the widow by the other. Georgia walked over and bent to give Valentina a hug. But the girl slipped aside and called through the Cadillac window. "You take me, Arthur. Please, Arthur. You."

The colored chauffeur slid from the driver's seat. He wore his usual uniform, with the stiff white collar that pressed against the dark flesh beneath his chin. His skin, I saw, was shiny from shaving. He said, "I'll do that, Miss Valentina." The two of them started down the swath of high-grown lawn. Now, from the same car that had carried Victor's daughter and widow, three more figures stepped out. From the front, Charles Laughton, who stood hunched, hands behind him, as if wearing handcuffs; and from the rear, Magdalena Mezaray and Rudolph Von Beckmann. At the sight of that couple, a gasp went up from those who had lingered on the hill. Magda moved off, after the other mourners; but the director, with his monocle and cape, a flower at his lapel, turned up the drive toward the hearse.

Manfred and Burton got out of our Lincoln and blinked in the sunshiny air. The Goldwyns, Sam and Frances, came up to them. "I'm worried about your father," Goldwyn said as he shook Manfred's hand.

"Why do you say that? No one in Germany is going to touch him. That would create a big international incident."

Frances said, "What Sam means is, we're worried because of what's happened. No one, no parent, should have to hear such terrible news. The death of a son! But to be so far away. And by himself. Who will tell him? Oh, Manny—what will he think? His darling Victor!"

Burton tossed his head. He gave a rueful laugh. "Don't worry about Alex. He wanted to stay. To find his wife. Drahomira."

At that the Goldwyns went side by side down the pathway toward where two or three hundred people, that's what it looked like, had gathered round the Granite plot. A few more stragglers hurried over the lawn, between the handsome headstones. Manfred and Burton, however, walked up the drive; they joined a much smaller group near the hearse. The Epstein brothers were there, along with Wilder and Ernie Glickman. They all clutched their skull-caps, against the westerly breeze.

Manfred, who had put on his yarmulke too, called back to me, "Come on. They're waiting."

I got out of the Lincoln and walked toward the pallbearers. Ernie said, "Hey, where's Dick Mosk? Didn't Giselle put him on the list?"

Von Beckmann shook his head. "Poor Chandler. He's just come out of his coma. He must not be moved. Dr. Mosk has volunteered to remain on location."

Chandler! Not dead! Not in a coma! The news struck me like a thunder-bolt. It felt as if the pin of my own yarmulke, which an usher was just then attaching, had driven straight into my skull. *Dead man,* as Mr. Moto was fond of saying, *tell many tale.* Imagine, then, the stories to be told by the living! No wonder that at such a moment my hand found my jacket pocket and dug inside for what I hoped would be taken for a pinch of snuff.

Just then the last of our group, Arnie Schoenberg, came breathlessly up the drive to join us. With both hands he pressed down on his yarmulke. "Windy!" he said.

Now a tall man, the only one in an overcoat, called out to us from the rear of the hearse. "Gentlemen, please. Will the family and friends gather here? We must prepare ourselves for our task." It was the rabbi, Magnin.

"What sparkling dialogue," said Julie, *sotto voce.*

"Don't blame the poor man," said Phil. "This is his third funeral since Tuesday."

"I know," said Julie. "It's been a slow week."

Wilder giggled behind his hand. Glickman grinned.

Manfred whirled on them all. "All right. We don't need this today."

I walked to the hearse. The rear door was open, the smooth brown wood of the casket in view. Engraved on the lid was a six-pointed star. Burton came up, too. "Where do I stand?"

The rabbi's glasses flashed and dimmed, like the light in a lighthouse. "Here. And Manfred, here. Mr. Von Beckmann, if you'll stand with the family. Now, Billy, Arnold, Ernest—on this side, here."

We sorted ourselves into two lines and crouched to receive the burden. There must have been rollers inside the hearse, because the box slid smoothly onto our shoulders. Victor, alive, couldn't have weighed more than a hundred and twenty or twenty-five pounds; between us, he should have been as light as a feather. But the casket's beveled edge dug into my neck and shoulder. Was it lined with lead? Or was the box filled, like the tomb of an Egyptian mummy, with necessities for the afterlife? I tried to think of what Victor would require. Chesterfields. A hundred cartons. Or enough cash, in bullion it felt like, to buy an endless supply. I kept my eyes on Schoenberg's pant cuffs, his shoes, just ahead. Our route wasn't across the wildflowers and grass. We took the zigzag path, which wasn't covered by pebbles after all. These were seashells, the shells of scallops and oysters, crunching under our feet.

It didn't take long to reach the newly dug grave. The diggers themselves were standing a little off to the side. They were chatting, in their longshoremen's caps, and trying to cup their cigarettes. Like the gravediggers in Shakespeare. Magnin pointed us toward a stand on wheels, a sort of hospital gurney; onto this portable bier we deposited Victor's casket. The mourners surrounded us, above the grave and below, and to either side. I thought I knew all the women, in spite of their blowing veils: Dietrich and Garson, Colbert and Crawford, Rogers, that skater Sonja Henie, Lombard, Loy, Bette Davis and Alice Faye. I hadn't the least doubt that Victor—oh, they rubbed like cats against his bony legs—had, as Manfred put it, fucked every one. As for the others, the men, it was as if someone had drawn a list of the top ten stars for '39, '40, and '41. Throw out the kids, Rooney and Garland and Temple, and count up the others: Gable, Power, Tracy, Cooper, Cagney, Taylor, and Flynn, plus Hope and Crosby and—I glanced round the crowd of sad faces—take your pick: Autrey, the western star, or one of the clowns, Abbott or Costello. If only Victor had known! Singing cowboys! Vaudevillians! He'd have had his ashes thrown to the winds.

Nor were the cast and crew of *Pandaemonium* missing. Poor Coco Goodheart! Poor Eugene! His yarmulke had long since blown off the white wisps of his hair; his breath, always labored, came out in sobs. Liz, the script girl, and Ellie, from wardrobe, were also dabbing their eyes. John Payne and

Gorcey stood stone-faced in a group of husky grips. But where was Rochelle? Where her beehived hair and beestung lips? Absent. Not present. Had she, too, remained in Nevada, to nurse Chick Chandler back to health? Instead of my paramour I saw the palomino: Miss Umin, from makeup, was determinedly edging toward me. Did she intend, in front of this multitude, to Motoize me? To buck my teeth and slick my hair and stain my skin the color of weakly brewed tea?

The cantor, an old Jew, strode to the coffin and started to sing. He had a thin voice, which came out of a thinner body. While he performed, Manfred crossed over to join the group of his peers. I saw Cohn. I saw Zanuck. There were the Warners, and L. B., and Frances and Sam. The foreign contingent was present from A to Z: Alton, the Hungarian cinematographer, to Zinneman, the director—no, there was old Zuckor, also Hungarian, poking at the grass with his cane. All in all, there hadn't been such a gathering—not at any of the Academy Awards, not even at the Wilshire Ebell benefit—since Thalberg had gone into the ground.

The cantor stopped on a high note. Now Magnin uttered some gobbledygook in Hebrew. I saw Miss Umin, still plowing forward. And there was Basserman, in a cutaway and black-on-black four-in-hand, trying to catch my eye. I slunk back into the crowd. Nearby, Manfred was standing next to an old man, conspicuously bareheaded, with a flushed, lined face. Hearst. The great W. R. He had buttonholed the surviving Granite brother.

"You're not going to resume the Nevada production, are you, Manfred? I don't like the look of things out there. This Von Beckmann—he's out to drag us into war."

"No, no," Manfred replied. "I don't care about that war business. Or what he thinks about Hitler. He's bankrupting us. Either we shut him down or it's the end of Granite Films."

"I want your word on this, Manfred. The interruption in filming has got to be permanent. Don't forget, there's plenty that's fishy about what happened to Victor. We can go after Granite in a big way. Even if you finish the picture, I can make sure it never opens."

"I told you, *we'll* be finished, not the picture. It's over. Kaput."

The prayer that the rabbi was chanting came to an end. All around me people were saying amen.

Magnin: "I ask you to join me in the twenty-third psalm. *The Lord is my shepherd—*"

I shall not want. Out of the hundreds in the crowd, only a dozen people joined in. That was because we all saw how the gravediggers sauntered over and seized the black straps that hung down on either side of the bier. With these aids, the workers—thank God they'd dropped their cigarettes—lifted the casket and, two on each side, suspended it over the hole. A sigh went up from the mourners. Somebody—to my surprise I saw it was both the Epsteins—let out an audible groan. Half the women were gulping, gasping. Magnin, however, did not miss a beat. While he intoned the words about the rod and the staff, the oil and the cup, the four burly men let the straps slide through their gloves; the milk-chocolate coffin disappeared into the ground.

Valentina was the first person to step from the crowd. She moved to the foot of the grave and knelt down. Then she gathered a handful of earth and threw it onto the coffin. Giselle came next, clinging to Irene Selznick's arm. With one hand she held her handkerchief to her mouth; with the other she threw the dirt and stones rattling down.

"If anyone in the family, or any friends of the family, should wish to participate," said Rabbi Magnin, "they are very welcome to do so."

That was the start of an endless parade. Burton was next. Then Manfred. His whole head had turned magenta. He marched to the grave, crouched, and scooped up the earth. "Goddammit, Victor," he muttered, and hurled it down. The pallbearers followed, one by one. Except for Loewenstein, Laszlo. I hung back. The soil I snatched came from my pocket. It dribbled across the cummerbund of the dapper detective like a trail of confectioner's sugar. For a moment everything went out of focus, as if Nakhimovsky—there he was, tossing his own handful of pebbles—had given a twist to his lens. The world was spinning. It was upside down. Then I heard a voice, courteous and polite, saying, "Forgive me. Excuse, please. So solly." With that, the agent of the International Police pushed his way through the crowd. He was about to risk shame, ridicule, humiliation. Perhaps even arrest. And why not? Was he not already a dead man? Deader than Victor? Even worse, was not that death sentence to be pronounced by his number-one enemy and rival in love? Very well. Let this dead man tell his tale!

Such were the last pallbearer's thoughts as he burst through the mourners and knelt down before the astonished Rabbi to the Stars.

"Listen, rabbi! Listen, everybody! Don't laugh! Don't turn your backs! I'm on my knees! I beg you to listen!"

There was, throughout the far reaches of Beth Olam, a sudden silence. Everyone stared as I sat pulling the coattails of the man of the cloth. "You are a great human being! A man of vision! Forgive me. I'm only a worm. All I ask is that you listen! A minute, rabbi! A minute of your time!"

The reply came not from the clergyman but from the ranks of the crowd. Basserman: "Peter! What are you doing? Come back!"

"No! There is no going back! I've tried everyone! No one will listen! They laugh at me! They think I'm a madman!"

But no one was laughing now. There must have been something about me, my hollow voice, my hollow Hungarian eyes, that struck the crowd dumb. I might have been the Ancient Mariner, doomed to walk the earth with his tale; even Manfred, I saw, stood with his mouth gaping wide.

There was no time to lose. I had to seize the silence that hung over the cemetery. Thus did I thrust my hand deep into my formal jacket, toward my abdominal zone. The onlookers gasped. Did they think the sleuth was suicidal? That he was about to commit hara-kiri? If so, they were mistaken. Instead of plunging a knife into my bowels, I pulled out an enlargement of a black-and-white photograph.

"Look! Look, friends! This is the main square of Lemberg! Lemberg, in Poland! Do you see? No Jews! Not one! I have been there myself! I have seen with my own eyes. There has been a massacre in the city! Dear Jews! They are killing us! They are deporting us to the east! It's the crime of the century! But no one will listen! No one will act!"

The silence lasted but a split second longer. Then a confused mumbling, part protest, part lamentation, rose from the crowd. Soon people were sobbing. Here and there someone started to wail.

"Can it be true?"

"What is he saying?"

"Does he mean Hitler? Hitler killing the Jews?"

Then one voice, already familiar, cut through the clangor. "Don't get taken in by these stories. These people want to force America into war. It's just propaganda." It was William Randolph Hearst.

No sooner had he finished than someone else—it was the suave Adolphe Menjou—said, "Let's get on with the service. It's a disgrace the way these Communists will use any occasion for their ends."

Robert Taylor, the star of *Waterloo Bridge,* added, "Even a funeral for one of their own. It's macabre."

That seemed to turn the tide. A growl rose from the mourners. There were angry shouts. A call went up for the police.

I hardly knew where I was or what I was saying. I flung myself upon the mortified Magnin. Like a beggar, I clutched him about the knees. "Wait! Wait! Rabbi! You must believe me! The Jews of Europe are being sent to their graves. For them there will be no prayers! Who will throw earth upon their graves? Only you can raise the alarm! Only you can stop the slaughter! This is their one chance! I beg you—save our brothers!"

Magnin's glasses flashed, as the brain behind them turned over its options. Then he said, "Naturally you are upset at the death of your friend. At such a time, it's easy to exaggerate. Things seem worse than they are."

Victor! Oh, oh! Victor!

That cry did not come from my throat. It was a woman's call. Now a figure swathed in mourning broke from the crowd and ran toward the grave. She did not kneel for a handful of earth. Instead, with hardly a break in stride, she hurled herself into the dark, damp hole. The earlier uproar was dwarfed by the tumult that now swept over the hundreds of mourners. In one great wave they rushed forward to the lip of the excavation. Everybody wanted to see what would happen next. From the depths of the pit came a high-pitched keening. Who was this grief-stricken person? Was it Giselle? No, she had collapsed in the arms of both Selznicks. They were lowering her onto what was left of the trampled flowers. Valentina? The girl stood to one side, next to her family's colored chauffeur. Of course! It must be the lover! The mistress! The grief-stricken Magdalena Mezaray! But everyone noticed that the actress was standing apart, upright and stalwart, though it was clear to me that she was ashen beneath the net of her veil.

"Stop her!"

"It's a disgrace!"

"Do something!"

At the bottom of the pit the woman in black was scraping the earth from the top of the coffin. In a wild, accented voice, she kept up the cry: *Victor! Don't leave me! Victor!* The little stones, the clods of dirt, flew off in every direction. Now the wood reemerged. There was the Star of David. At the sight, the woman, still weeping unrestrainedly, hurled herself onto the convex lid. Above, the directors, the producers, the many great stars, held out their hands to her. Magnin, on his knees, begged her to come to her senses. But she grew only more crazed. Pushing herself upright, she ripped off her hat and veil. Then she threw back her head, revealing what had once been the most famous face in the world.

Simultaneously, from a hundred throats, came a single word:

"Greta!"

Manfred stepped forward. With his fists he seemed to be hammering at the sky. "Lester!" he shouted. "Why didn't you think of a stunt like this?"

No one paid the least attention. That was because the solitary Swede, as Louella had always called her, did something now that filled every man and woman with anguish and dismay. With her gloved hands she gripped the lid of the coffin and—only the Lord who is our shepherd knows where she got the strength—hurled it back on its hinges. Then she let out a scream that could not have been coached, even by the publicity department at MGM.

"Ahhhhhh!"

The outcry from all the others in Beth Olam was no less deafening. For lying on the interior plush of the coffin was not the dark, narrow head of Victor Granite but the cropped and dented skull of George Hoffman, the key grip.

"Son-of-a-bitch!" blurted Manfred.

"Hoffman!" cried I. "Why couldn't it be Mr. Chick Chandler?"

Now everybody was running every which way at once. The *Pandaemonium* people—Von Beckmann, Goodheart, Nakhimovsky, and Liz the script girl, too—were all dashing up the slope toward the Cadillac De Ville. With dismay I saw that Valentina was running after them. Manfred had seen her, too. "Arthur!" he commanded the Negro. "Stop her!"

The servant attempted to do so, though Valentina scratched at him and pounded his chest with her fists. A stranger, just a boy, sharp-featured and blond, came up. Was this Gerhardt? Her classmate? "Let her go. I tell you, release her." Then, of all people, Laughton came up to join the chauffeur. Together they managed to restrain her.

Von Beckmann thrust his head from the rear window of the De Ville. "A driver!" he shouted. "We need a driver!"

"Here! I'm coming!"

The person who shouted those words was none other than Burton Granite. Seeing this, his father let out a howl. "No. No-o-o-o! Burton! Come back!"

Too late. The young man clambered behind the wheel. The engine turned over. Exhaust came from the tailpipe. The big black automobile, spinning its wheels, made a U-turn and fishtailed down the drive.

Now the whole mass of mourners began to run up the grassy slope. They looked like a charging army in a battle scene—or, it occurred to me, like reporters running for their phones.

"Come on!" yelled Manfred, heading for his own limousine. "Come on, Lorre! We'll catch them in the Lincoln!"

But before I could follow, another car came to life. With a thrill of amazement I saw that it was a green Plymouth coupe. Gorcey and Meltsner jumped into it. Maynes, the gaffer, Ellie from costume, and what looked like a half-dozen others squeezed in as well. The doors slammed and the engine roared.

Just as the coupe wheeled round in a tight circle and started down the drive, I came cantering up the incline. "Wait! Miss Hudson! Stop! I know it's you!"

Astonishing that the car in fact came to a screeching halt. The front door flew open and Rochelle darted out. I ran toward her. With her arms wide she ran toward me. I opened mine as well. "Miss Hudson! Honey! Ha! Ha! Are you going for a spin?"

She threw herself upon me. She beat at my chest with her balled-up hands. "You bastard! You lousy bastard! I know it was you! What a jealous creep! He tried to kill Chick. My Chickie!"

The next moment the other door of the Plymouth sprang open and Gorcey, the tough guy, and Maynes got out. They ran right by me and seized Valentina, who had broken loose from her protectors. They hauled her to the driveway and, before a dozen paralyzed onlookers, threw her straight into the open trunk of the car. Kidnapped! Abducted! Already Miss Hudson was back behind the wheel. She gunned the engine. She slipped the clutch. The little Plymouth sped out of sight.

By now the rest of the excited crowd had reached the hilltop and were rushing for their cars. I trotted toward the Lincoln. Opening the door in the back, I was surprised to see that the whole rear section was filled with scraps of yellow paper. In the midst of this haystack sat Manfred Granite. He seemed, by this phenomenon, as befuddled as I. In the front seat sat Lester Kahn, sucking a peppermint lozenge.

"What is this?" I asked.

Without a word the studio president handed me one of the rectangular slips.

RESERVING ENTIRE MONTH OF DECEMBER STOP
INCLUDING CHRISTMAS NEW YEAR SEASON STOP
WILLING TO MAKE 40/60 PANDAEMONIUM SPLIT
CARLO AXELROD, MGR. RKO PANTAGES

It was a telegram! Western Union! I snatched up a second cable on my own.

WANT OPENING DATE BECKMANN-MEZARAY
FEATURE STOP UNLIMITED BOOKING STOP
WILL TAKE ROAD SHOW SINGLE BILLING BOTH
THEATERS STOP YOUR TERMS
H. WEINER, ROSEMARY AND DOME

They were all telegrams! A hundred! Five hundred! More than a thousand! They seemed to come from every theater—I saw Sid Grauman's name at the bottom of one wire and A. J. Balaban's on another—in America. Now Manfred burrowed through these wires the way a miner in Pandaemonium might have dug after a vein of gold. He held up one and then another of the golden nuggets. "You tell me: what the hell are these telegrams about? It's crazy. They all want the premiere of a picture we aren't even going to make."

Kahn, from the front seat, gave the reply. "We're the ones who are crazy if we don't finish *Pandaemonium.* All this, these wires, they're only the tip of the iceberg. You should see what's back at the office. Five thousand more! And not just from our chain. Not just the indies. We've got offers from Loew's. From Fox. From all over America. And not just America. I heard from London. I heard from Rome. Look, look at this." Here Kahn seized one of the telegrams; his eyeballs darted back and forth behind the pink framed lenses as he read the text: "*Urge you consider Majestic world premiere* Pandaemonium *Stop Extreme discretion required Stop Will take any Granite product second feature.* Do you know who that's from? Bobby Pinsky! The head of the whole Paramount operation! Do you see? Do you see what it means? Christ, Manfred! It's the end of states' rights! It's the breakup of the system!"

Manfred took his beet-red head in his hands. "Because of Victor? You're telling me all this is happening because he was killed?"

"Killed? *Murdered,* if we're lucky! And this is *before* Greta threw herself in the grave! That wasn't spontaneous, believe me. L. B. called. He wants into the action. It's illegal. Boy, is it illegal. He could get into big trouble. Are you following me? Mayer wants a piece of the picture! So does Dick Sherman, the biggest distributor on the other side of the Mississippi. And Freedman. Jeff Freedman! The king of South America! By tomorrow morning, when the papers break, we'll have to hold them back with tanks! With cannons! We've got financing! In the millions! This is going to be bigger than *Gone With the Wind*! Bigger than *Birth of a Nation*!"

Manfred balled up his fist and thrust it with sledgehammer force into the roof of the Lincoln. "To hell with them! Yesterday they were waiting for us to go under. They were going to chew us up like sharks. Get me to the studio! Step on it, goddammit! Do you see this container? It's our future! I've got to see these rushes!"

Kahn slid over and started the engine. Next he released the brake and forced our left fender into the close-packed stream of automobiles. Behind him, Manfred and I, like two badly behaved children, continued to dive into the cables. We threw them about the close confines of the cabin.

"My God," said the surviving Granite brother. "Will you look at this?" He held up more sheets. He waved their glued-on messages. I strained to see, but now that we had moved off the hilltop, the light that spilled through the curtains had become faint indeed. Manfred stared at the text. He started to laugh. "Do you remember how Alexander would always talk about our theaters in—I don't know, in the middle of the desert and the jungle and Timbuktu? *You Are Never More than a Day's Walk*—that was his motto—*from a Granite Picture.* Well, look at this—a cable from Fiji! A cable from Greenland! Oh, Jesus! Christ, Jesus! A cable from Borneo!"

Behind us, and ahead, all the automobiles had once again turned on their headlights—not because they were still in a procession but because at the twilight hour the streets of the city, the avenues of Highland, Melrose, and finally La Brea, had been cast entirely in shadow. Curtains drawn, our limousine sped by the tar pits, where the tigers of another age, the Pleistocene, had been caught with their claws as long as hunting knives and fangs as sharp as sabers.

At Granite Films, the projection room was deserted. Kahn trudged up the steps to the booth, with the canister under his arm. It took him, inexpert as he was, a quarter of an hour to thread the film. Manfred waited alone in the dark. Finally the beam of light slashed through the room, filled as usual with motes, like bacteria or animalcules in the murky water of a pond. On the screen a slate board appeared:

> *Pandaemonium*
> *Scene 87*
> *Take 2*

In the front row Manfred hunched forward, elbows on knees, fists under chin. He heard what was left of Coco's voice telling the camera to roll. There was a closeup. It was not of the world-famous star. It was of his niece, Valentina. She was holding her black hair out from her dark-skinned head. Her eyes, also black, stared straight into the lens of the camera.

"What's this shit?" said her uncle. "Where's Magda?"

From the dark and empty room there came no reply. Rather, the only answer came from the adolescent, who said,

I see. I see. What sadness. The terror.

For a moment Manfred sat as if his entire body had been turned into the igneous rock for which, upon his arrival in America, he had been named. Above him, in front of him, the girl was chanting in a voice utterly unlike her own:

Poor Brother, a painful end awaits you. Uncle, woe unto you:
you shall suffer more than either of these children—

That was enough for the president of Granite Films. You would have thought from the way he jumped up, calling for lights, that those words of prophecy had been directed at him. High in the booth Kahn threw a switch, and the hundred-watt bulbs in the auditorium came on. Manfred, on his feet, was shaking his fist at the booth's glassed-over window, as if the man behind it were responsible for shooting and developing and editing the film.

"We've been tricked! Goddammit to hell! That bastard Rudi pulled a fast one! It's not Magda! That bitch! It's Valentina! Burn that stock! Do you hear me? If anyone sees it, we're ruined!"

"Too late, Manfred. I've got my scoop."

"Louella!"

The gossip columnist rose from her seat in the very back row. "I'm as shocked as you are. Who would have dreamed it? It's certainly a day of surprises. No sooner do we have one story than it's topped by another."

"You can't do this to us, Louella. There are millions of dollars at stake. Do you understand what I'm saying? Millions!"

Louella started to walk down the steps that divided the rows. "I hope I haven't understood you. What I hear when people talk about money is a bribe."

"No, no, no. This whole thing is a mistake. These must be outtakes. Or maybe test shots. How did they get into the can? How do we know they were shot on location?"

"There's been no mistake. You flew these rushes back from Nevada on your very own plane."

Manfred put his hands out in entreaty. He started to climb up the aisle. "Louella, you can't print this. You've got to help us."

Louella: "Well, I need your help, too."

"Anything!"

At that the columnist's face, with its nose even sharper than Manfred's, suddenly collapsed. Tears came from her round blue eyes. "I didn't mean to do it! It was an accident! But people are saying the most awful things. Hedda's putting them up to it. You have to believe me. How did I know which levers to touch? You should have told me. Oh, and the propellers! They threw up so much sand!"

Manfred climbed the steps that remained between them. "There, there," he said. "There, there, there."

Louella threw herself into his open arms. Almost at once she drew back, laughing lightly through her tears. "Why, Manny!" she exclaimed. "Are we both going to have our own little secret?"

Roughly, he reached for her. He put his hands around her plump hips, her plump waist.

"Lester!" he shouted, while on the screen Valentina listened to all the desert creatures—the birds, the coyotes, and even the supposedly silent reptiles. "Lights!"

MISSION TO MANCHURIA

The Ford trimotor was clearly overloaded. Almost every seat was taken by the federal marshals, who, because the live Valentina Granite had been transported over state lines in one direction and the dead George Hoffman in the other, were taking over the investigation at the Nevada location. In addition, Manfred had arranged for his own sentry force, a handful of men under the direction of old Blowen, the guard from the La Brea gate. With a racing form on his lap, he lay dozing at the rear of the passenger compartment. Les Kahn sat near him, turning a wintergreen lozenge round and round in his cheek. Magdalena sat a few rows ahead, staring out over the wing. I too looked out my little window. What I saw was the range of the Sierra Nevada looming ahead in the morning mist. It seemed obvious to me that our laboring aircraft would never clear the white-topped peaks. That is one reason why my jacket pockets, like those formidable mountains, were full of snow.

Another reason was the queasiness created by yet another attack of déjà vu. Everything I experienced seemed to be a repetition of something I had lived through before, whether it was rescuing Magda from a lift or joining her on yet another perilous flight. What was it Rudi had said? About persistence of vision? That the medium of film was based on memory, the images that lingered from what had already been spooled into the past. And life—? Was it too a matter of persisting scenes, repeated images, a dim recollection of what had been undergone in youth, or childhood, or perhaps even before, in a different realm of existence? I glanced across the aisle and saw what might have been my own mirror image: round face, brilliantined hair, wire spectacles, skin the color of cedar. Was the pressure of the past being speeded up to the present? The film spilled from the sprockets? No. Upon boarding, the almond-eyed Asian had introduced himself: "So pleased to meet you. I am Takashima. Dr. Takashima. Coroner, City of Los Angeles." There, as predicted, was the white-coated angel of doom. From the *crack coroner's office*. No wonder that I carried my magic dust: only a pinch of that powder, one to each nostril, removed the past to the realm of oblivion.

The engines, in their struggle for lift, for loft, whined at a higher pitch. Up front, behind the bottle-green curtain, Manfred must have seen the mountains, too. Poor Manfred! Unhappy man! He had kept his promise to Louella, never once mentioning her role in Victor's death. And she had kept her part of the bargain; no hint that Magdalena had been replaced in the *Pandaemonium* feature appeared in her column. What both bargainers had overlooked, however, was that there was a witness to that scene of double blackmail: the clever Kahn. It was he, surely, who had leaked the scoop to Louella's chief rival. Thus it was that the whole world had read the news of Valentina's starring role not in the feared *Examiner* but in the no-less-dreaded *Times*:

EXECUTIVE'S DAUGHTER TO APPEAR IN HIS FILM
Valentina Granite Replaces Magdalena Mezaray
Multi-Million-Dollar Gamble
Exclusive by
Hedda Hopper

Kahn's motive was, in retrospect, perfectly plain. Unlike Manfred, who had assumed that the loss of Magdalena would be a disaster, Lester realized that her replacement by the brilliant young actress he had seen on the projection room screen, an actress who was also the daughter of the man who had been killed on location, would be a tremendous boon. In this the publicist's instincts had proved correct. Great as the interest in *Pandaemonium* had been before, the response now was beyond belief. Not only had theaters all over the world agreed to book the feature sight unseen, a bidding war had broken out for the rights to the world premiere. In the end Sid Grauman signed a contract that guaranteed an advance of three hundred and sixty thousand dollars—an unheard-of take of twenty thousand dollars a day for each of the eighteen days the picture would play before general release on Christmas Eve.

Nonetheless, Manfred's troubles, not to mention the difficulties for Granite Films, were far from over. Not only were the mysterious deaths of Victor Granite and George Hoffman still unexplained, but too many people had seen the way Valentina had apparently been bundled into Rochelle Hudson's little coupe. How could the girl act in a film if, in fact, she'd been kidnapped?

It was to address just these issues, and the uproar that continued about them, that the studio and the coroner's office had held a joint conference for the press. Takashima—he was no stranger, even before he had climbed the airplane ramp—spoke first. His finding was that the key grip had expired some forty-eight hours before the debacle at the Jewish cemetery. The cause of death, the coroner had declared, was a single sharp blow to the top of the head. The fact that the victim had appeared in the wrong man's coffin, and had almost been buried in the wrong man's grave, might well lead to the conclusion that there had been an attempt at concealment. The case was not closed.

Hurriedly, Les Kahn rushed to the podium and told what must have been a hundred and fifty journalists that the mix-up in bodies had been an understandable oversight, given the state of shock and grief into which everyone in the town of Pandaemonium had been thrown. As for Hoffman's wound, and those of Chick Chandler, they had been occasioned by a fall down the old mining shaft, at the top of which the wooden railing had long since rotted. It was an unfortunate accident, one that Granite Films not only regretted but was taking steps to make certain would never happen again. "Ladies and gentlemen," the publicist concluded, "you might be interested to know that in gold-rush days, this kind of accident was almost commonplace. Dozens of miners, and their mules too, perished in that shaft. We've got the evidence in the sheriff's records. After filming, when we invite you all out to the location, you'll be able to see their bones in the sump."

The last to mount the podium was Manfred himself. He had announced that at Giselle Granite's request, he was personally flying to the location—both to take charge of Victor's remains and, if not to bring home his daughter, then at least to determine once and for all whether she was in Pandaemonium of her own free will. If not, then Magdalena Mezaray, the original star of the picture, had graciously consented to replace her. The truth, of course, was that Manfred had no intention of either bringing Valentina back to Los Angeles or allowing Magda her former role. The real reason for the flight, aside from quieting the controversy that still raged about the picture, was to deal with yet another problem that threatened the production. It turned out that the unit on location, cut off as it had been from the outside world and obsessed by the need for perfection in every take, had nearly run out of unexposed film. Von Beckmann's plan, which had been to take a fresh supply to the desert by car, had been disrupted by the fiasco at Beth Olam. Manfred's role aboard the silvery trimotor was to make certain that nothing, most particularly the federal officials, got in the way of distributing the raw stock that was stored in the cargo compartment.

Those officials remained a problem. They were armed, every one of them, with rifles and handguns and, it was rumored, heavier weapons—also stored in the cargo bay below. The great obstacle for Manfred was that if they should decide that a crime had been committed, whether kidnapping or murder, they had the means to close down the production for good. That determination would almost certainly be made by the man now leaning toward me from his seat on the aisle: Dr. Takashima, my dark-skinned double.

"Would you permit me to offer my sincere condolences?"

That gave me a start. "Condolences? But for what?"

The coroner leaned yet closer. I saw that even the pencil strokes of his tiny moustache were more substantial than either of his eyebrows, which were practically invisible, as if singed away in a fire. "Of course I saw you at the back of the press room. It is unfortunate that, taken up by the baubles of the day, a single death, two such deaths—and perhaps after all they shall prove to be nothing more than accidents, coincidence, an act of fate—no one would listen to your tale, even though you have evidence of the death of thousands."

"They laughed. They always laugh. No one wants to hear."

"In time the laughter will stop. But perhaps, for your people, not soon enough. I sincerely regret it."

"You believe me? You don't think I'm a madman? A clown?"

"You will not, I hope, take offense if I say that I wish you were. But I have heard similar stories—from other sources."

"Then you might help me. You have an important position. You could make a finding. You could hold a press conference of your own. It would be as if you were the coroner of the world!"

Dr. Takashima laughed. "I fear it is too late for me as well. I will not be even the coroner of the city for long. Maybe weeks. Maybe days."

"How can that be? Everyone knows your work. You have a reputation. Surely you will be in office long enough to help me. Why should you be removed?"

"Perhaps it would be best not to speak so loudly." The Lorre look-alike lowered his own voice and leaned almost all the way across the aisle. "America will soon be at war. And not only against Germany. Also, alas, against Japan. These two nations, you know, are bound by a treaty for mutual defense."

Japan! My heart leaped like a gazelle, gaily, within me. Of course I saw why Takashima's position was in danger. If war broke out in the Pacific, no one would allow a Japanese to hold the office of coroner. But was not my own role threatened as well? Who would pay to see a picture with a Japanese hero? No one! Freedom! Freedom from the Pharaoh! So long, Sphinx!

"Yes," Takashima said, with a sigh. "It seems my days, along with those of a certain world-famous detective, are surely numbered."

In my excitement, I paid little heed to that reference to myself. "Days? You said days?"

"Or weeks. Perhaps a month. Perhaps a little longer. I shall have time to attempt to solve the mystery of the blow to the head of Mr. Hoffman. It may be that Mr. Chick Chandler, since he is no longer in a coma, can provide much information. But might I humbly ask if that master of deduction, I. A. Moto, has an opinion about the cause of the contusion and the crack in the skull?"

That word, *Moto*, could not be ignored. I barely managed to check the movement of my hand to my pocket. A stinging sweat broke out on my brow. As I had done countless times upon the screen, I played for time. "Contusion? That's a bump, isn't it? Or is it a bruise? Isn't that just what you'd expect if a man fell down a mineshaft?"

"Ha-ha! I have always admired your sense of humor. Do you truly think the death of Mr. Hoffman an accident?"

"Hoffman? Accident? Sure! You bet! Didn't Kahn say there was no railing? No doubt about it, he fell down the shaft."

The coroner threw up his hands. "Please, I beg you—enough tomfoolery. You know better than anyone that no such fall occurred."

"I do? But what about the contusion? The fractured skull? It's obvious he fell headfirst."

"How long, please, is this shaft for mining? It is not more than two hundred feet?"

"Yes, yes. More than enough to kill a man. Or an elephant, ha-ha!"

"But you must then explain: how can a man fall such a distance, upon a hard platform of stone, and suffer only a single wound? No, no—you are playing a game with me. My dear friend and colleague is surely aware that if there had been such a fall, there would be multiple traumas. Not a single bone would remain unbroken."

"Then how—? Then who—?"

"Mr. Laszlo Loewenstein, those were precisely the questions I was about to ask you."

My heart no longer leaped like a graceful gazelle. It lurched from side to side in my chest like a prisoner in a cell. I had, in order to peer out the window, to blink the streaming sweat from my eyes. Ahead, filling the space of the porthole, I saw a vast sheet of ice. Black trees, pines and firs, stuck out of it, like cloves in the fat of a ham. Impossible, even with the efforts of all three panting engines, to climb over. I shivered, less from the prospect of an imminent crash than from the strange sensation that I was being accused by my own image, or my Siamese twin, much as, in *Last Laugh, Mr. Moto,* the great detective had been implicated in murder through a series of clues planted by a man made up to be his double.

"But why would you ask me such questions? I wasn't there. How could I know?"

Takashima smiled, wrinkling his hairless brows. "Let us first examine the *how.* You are aware, are you not, that a bloodstained stone was found at the scene?"

"Yes. A piece of quartz. I mean, I read that in Louella's column."

"Could this not be the murder weapon?"

"*Murder?* That's, you know, a harsh word."

"Let us continue. We have a certain weapon. We have a certain wound. What do these two things together tell us about the nature of the deed?"

Through sheer force of habit, I found myself turning these clues this way and that, the same way that Agent 673 had so often held a piece of evidence—the heel of a shoe, the mouthpiece of a trumpet, a single playing card—up to the light of a lampshade. "Perhaps," I declared, "we should consider the region of the blows. You said the wound was on top of the head. Wouldn't that rule out a murder? Why, to strike such a blow the killer would have had to be a giant." *And,* I could barely restrain myself from adding, *I am only five feet four inches.*

"Not necessarily," said my Oriental interlocutor. "The actual position was here—" Takashima bowed his head, indicating the knob at the back of his skull. "At the occiput. That means either that the rock was hurled or that the victim—"

"*Was on his knees!*" In spite of myself I blurted out that crucial piece of information.

"Ah! Excellent! First-rate deduction. And why on his knees? Can you tell me that?"

Alas! Alack! I could indeed. In my mind's eye I saw only too clearly how Hoffman and Victor had fought each other on the platform floor. I could hear the grip cry for help and then, his last words on earth, shout out a warning to the leading man. "Maybe," I said weakly, "he was pleading for his life?"

"Or struggling for it," Takashima replied. "That would mean that while he was wrestling on the ground with his antagonist, a second man—"

"An accomplice!"

"Just so. An accomplice. This man struck him with—what did you say? A piece of quartz? Struck him a blow that smashed in his skull. Thus have we, dear Mr. Lorre, acting together, discovered the *how*."

"*Two heads*," I said, echoing my mentor's motto, "*often better than one.*"

"Now we must discover the *who*."

Again I glanced out the window. The sheet of glacial ice was closer than ever, but our plane, though the engines whined shrilly, had risen no higher. "The who?"

"The name," said Takashima, stretching out his arm and gripping my wrist with the force of a manacle, "of the murderer."

From my body there rose, as from the corpse of a poisoned man, the sharp, bittersweet smell of cyanide. My mind, locked in place, could only repeat the words that had last made a sensation upon it: "*Murderer?*"

"Or murderers. We must not forget that there were two victims in the town of Pandaemonium."

"*Two victims?*"

"Honorable Hoffman. Honorable Victor Granite."

"*Victor Granite?*"

"Would you be so kind as to tell me whether there is, in your opinion, a connection between the death of one man and the other?"

"No! Absolutely not! Even if Hoffman's death turns out to be murder, Victor's was definitely an accident. He was killed on the runway. He was never inside the mine. The whole thing is nothing more than coincidence."

"*Coincidence is sometimes only lack of imagination.*"

Was I hearing things? "That's *my* line," I protested. "From *Mr. Moto Takes a Vacation*."

"I have memorized," said Takashima, "all your lines. *Man with crutch*, for instance, *better not attack man with cane*."

"Attack? What do you mean? I never attacked anyone."

"Hmmm. Then why this nervousness? Eh? The working of sweat glands? The rolling of eyes?"

Those eyes, I knew, were bulging practically from their sockets. Why? Because my worst fears had been confirmed. I was a suspect!

Takashima: "You said, sir, that there was no connection between the death of Mr. Hoffman and that of Mr. Granite, and that the latter gentleman had never been in the Pandaemonium mine."

I was without power of speech. I only nodded.

"Of course, it is possible that Honorable Hoffman was killed elsewhere and afterward moved under ground. However, such a theoretical possibility has been disposed of by the findings of my office: on the clothes of this man, in his hair, under the nails of his fingers—quartz dust. Here is the proof that indeed he struggled for his life in the depths of the mine. Now, Mr. Peter Lorre, tell me: would it not be most interesting if, when I examine the corpse of Victor Granite, I should discover—upon his clothing, in his hair, and under his nails—"

"Quartz dust!" I shouted. "Yes! Yes! I see it! I see it! *Ah, so!*" At that instant there had occurred to me, just as it occurred to Mr. Moto in each of his features, a blinding revelation. "That would mean that Victor was in the mine! That he was the murderer! Yes! The perfect explanation! Victor's death was no accident! But it was not murder, either. *He killed himself!* Out of a guilty conscience! From contrition! Takashima, you are a genius! Both deaths are solved! Case closed!"

Just then the trimotor gave a shudder from tail to nose and dropped alarmingly—sixty feet, eighty feet, before the pilot regained control. I risked a quick glimpse through the frosted glass. The mountains were no longer ahead of us. Instead, the peak, with its evergreens, was towering *above* our craft. I strained to see through the window on the opposite side of the fuselage. No blue sky: nothing but sheer cliffs of white. Could it be? Were we about to crash? A sorrowful groan escaped my lips.

"Is it possible," said the calm coroner, "that the agent of the International Police has a fear of flying?"

"Takashima! Farewell! It is the end of us!"

"I do not think so. Mr. Granite merely flies through the pass."

"No! No! Look! There's ice on every side!"

"This phobia is most unfortunate. Your next feature, I believe, will be *Your Turn, Mr. Moto.* In it you will be required to undertake a mission to Manchuria."

"What? What are you saying? There is no such picture. I haven't even finished *Mr. Moto Meets the Sphinx.* And then Manfred's loaning me to Warner Brothers."

"I see you are in ignorance. Let me be the first to inform you that in this film you will be required to fly over peaks far higher than these. Of course, these aerial episodes might be performed by another person. Mr. Allen Fox. Eh? Is he not the daredevil who flies and swims and throws all your punches?"

I shook my head. I stared in disbelief. Was there anything this Takashima did not know? Grinning, he continued. "With what pleasure do I look forward to seeing how you and your costar—by the way, at her request, Miss Hudson will no longer be available for Moto features; the part of the statuesque Sonya, and all future heroines, will be played by Miss Hillary Brooke, also a blonde. Yes, how entertaining to see how you and Hillary will fly through the air in order to save the oil formula for"—and here the Asian's accent took on a note of scorn—"good old U.S. of A."

Could it be? Had I been double-crossed? Was I never to escape this Far Eastern epic? Monotonous Moto! Once more I looked through the window. The ice was closer than ever. It seemed to me that I could see the individual needles upon the branches of the trees. But now a fiery crash, whether it be in the Nevadas or the Greater Khingan Range, was a fate to be welcomed. "How," I asked, in a voice that was shaking, "can you know these things? What is your connection to Mr. Moto?"

Takashima gave a light, careless laugh. "Oh, do not be fooled by my profession, or allow this white jacket from my lab to mislead you. Underneath such offices and garments I remain a man of Nippon. Naturally, Moto is a hero to me. And not just to me! All of Japan worships your name. I have made many visits to Tokyo, where my honorable parents now reside. With my own eyes I have seen the line at the cinema as it twines like a dragon around the block and around. Little children, sir, dress themselves in mock cutaways and fashion spectacles from wire, even though their eyesight is, as we say, twenty-twenty."

"Yes," I replied. "I have heard of my many fans in Japan. But how, from these children, could you learn so many studio secrets?"

"I do not speak only of children. Everyone from the sweeper of streets to the divine emperor follows from caper to caper, as with wits and jujitsu you fend off your many foes. I have some contacts at the court. And in the corridors of power. In such places there is much to be learned. The prime minister, for example, is such an admirer that he ordered twenty copies of his personal favorite."

"Twenty copies? The prime minister? Which picture is that?"

"*Mr. Moto's Last Warning.*"

I felt, at that title, the familiar fingers of ice as they began to close round my heart. "But why that film? It was not a top grosser."

"Mr. Tojo Hideki is fascinated by the scenes in which enemy agents plot to blow up the fleet in the harbor. He told me himself that if you—or was it

Mr. Fox?—had not, in that exciting undersea struggle, overcome Mr. Sanders, the French sailors in Port Said would have had quite a surprise."

"Tojo! The general!"

"Yes, Tojo. And Yamamoto, the admiral, who has also seen the motion picture many times. Both men agree that the sneak attack was a brilliant conception. They are not without hope that perhaps next time Mr. Moto will be on the other side—?"

Suddenly everything crystallized in the suave sleuth's mind. This man, this Takashima, the urbane Oriental, with his access to secrets, his connections to power—he was no coroner. Surely he must be in real life what I had only pretended to be on the screen. A spy! But for whom? America? Japan? MGM?

"Well, Mr. Laszlo Loewenstein-Lorre: has the light of wisdom finally dawned?"

Yes! It had! There was going to be a war with Japan! Heavens! In mere weeks! Or days! Or hours! Only I, of all the people in America, with the possible exception of this fifth-column coroner, knew how it was to come about: the Japanese were going to blow up a harbor! From me they had learned how to destroy the American fleet!

Not, however, if I could stop them. I jumped to my feet—that is, I attempted to do so. But with an iron grip Takashima held down my wrist. Not only that: he had by now stretched clear across the aisle and, through his round wire glasses—for all I knew the lenses were made for magnification—was examining the nails of my fingers for quartz!

No sooner did I realize what my interrogator was doing than, with a supreme effort, employing the subtle counterforce of the art of judo, I wrenched my arm free and stood upright.

"My friend, where are you going?"

No need to answer. Stumbling, staggering, I made my way down the aisle toward the jade-colored curtain that separated the passenger compartment from the pilot's cabin. "Wait!" cried Takashima. "There is nothing to fear. The danger is behind us."

It was true. I did not have to glance out the windows to see that the interior of the aircraft was now flooded with light. We had broken from the Sierra Nevada into the blue. The smooth sandy floor of the desert lay stretched out below. Yet I knew that a greater danger, far from being behind us, loomed ahead of the entire nation: war with Japan!

With a trembling hand I swept the partition aside. Manfred, glaring, twisted about. I opened my mouth, but no words came out. Did I, after all, really wish to speak? Nothing more was required of me than to keep silent and I would be released from my bondage forever. But the soldiers! The brave sailors! Could I put personal advantage before so many lives?

"Well," Manfred demanded, "what the hell are you doing here?"

"I must ask a favor. It's tremendously important. Everything depends upon it. The fate of thousands!"

"Oh, the Jews again. Christ, aren't you ever going to give it a rest?"

"No, no! It's not about Lemberg. Not about Jews. I've made a terrible discovery. America is about to be attacked by Japan. They're going to blow up our fleet!"

"Ha-ha-ha! You'd say anything to get out of your contract!"

"Don't laugh! You must not laugh! Think of the suffering. There will be fighting everywhere. In the Atlantic. In the Pacific. Another World War!"

Manfred shook his helmeted head. "What a lot of crap! Even if it were true, what could I do?"

"Turn back! Change the course of the airship! I swear to you: there isn't a moment to lose!"

"Goddammit! I know what you want. You want to get back to your pals. Those Epsteins. Don't think I don't know they've got a new part for you."

To that there was no reply. The boys had indeed started their script for Warners. Just the previous Sunday, over at Phil's new pool, they'd showed me the description of my role:

> *He is a small, thin man with a nervous air.*
> *If he were an American, he would look like a tout.*

I'd even tried one line aloud: *You despise me, don't you Rick?*

To Manfred I said, "Why don't you let me go? I can shoot every scene in only three days. Three days! I swear it!"

"You're too late. Look. That's the crater."

I followed Manfred's gaze out the cockpit window. There, just as he said, was the circular bulge in the desert floor, as if someone had thrown a huge lasso onto the earth.

"But you promised! You said if I came back on location you'd release me to Warners."

"What choice did I have? Magdalena wouldn't get on board unless you were with us, and Giselle thinks you're going to bring Valentina back to the coast."

"Turn back! Turn around! It's not just the part! It's war and peace!"

"Hold on," said Manfred, and banked the plane so steeply that I was forced into the seat beside him. We were circling! We were returning!

"Manny, God bless you! You will not regret this. All mankind will thank you. And I thank you, too. It's such an opportunity. A wonderful character. Named for a race car."

Manfred banked the plane even further. "There," he said. "Look there."

I did so. Plain as day, the ghost town appeared through the windscreen. It revolved beneath us as we passed in a tightening circle. I could see the entire set: the roads and the houses; the details of the jail, the stable, the saloon, the hotel. Just beyond was the encampment of Navahos. Smoke rose from their little fires. Back at the center was the mound of earth and quartz at the entrance to the mine, and at the far end of Main Street, the canvas huts for the grips, the gaffers, the wardrobe people and extras. As I watched, the entire crew, hundreds of people, emerged from these tents and from the nearby buildings, and began to dash crazily about.

Beside me Manfred worked feverishly. He lowered the flaps. He cut back the throttle. We sank lower, and lower still.

"What are you doing? You aren't going to land? What about the war? What about Ugarte?"

"Not a chance," answered Manfred. "When are you going to get it through your head that you aren't ever going to stop playing Moto? First we're finishing *Sphinx*. Then we've got a great new property, *Your Turn, Mr. Moto*. You fly an airplane in Manchuria. And that's not the end. Hell, it's only the beginning. We're negotiating with Marquand. We're going to buy the rights to every Moto book he's ever written. Then we'll commission him to write ten more after that."

In my ears there was a metallic ringing. It was the sound of prison doors clanging shut. With a shriek I hurled myself from the copilot's seat and clamped my hands around the neck of the pilot himself.

Manfred shook me off, as if I were a bug. "Wait," he said. "What's that?" He too had heard the clang, clang, clang. Could it be the far-off pump? We both looked down. There was the derrick. A plume of steam came out of it. But more steam puffs arose from above the heads of the many men on the ground.

"What the hell?" cried Manfred.

The clanging—actually, it was more a pattering, like the sound made by a tap dancer's shoes—was now all around us. It struck the wings. It struck the fuselage just below.

"The bastards! They're shooting!"

Such, in fact, was the case. It was apparent now that those puffs of smoke came from everywhere in town—from the streets, from the tents, from the rooftops. The people of Pandaemonium were shooting at us with guns!

"Strap yourself in!" But even as the pilot issued that command, the plane suddenly lurched to the right and dropped, faster than the fastest elevator, toward the ground.

"We're hit!" cried Manfred as he wrestled with the controls.

Behind us came a metallic swish. I turned around. Someone had opened the curtain and stepped into the cockpit.

"I'm Captain James. Dave James. Head of the force of marshals. I'm also a pilot. Can I help?"

"Just hang on!" yelled Manfred.

The marshal, a thin man with a blue-shadowed jaw, braced himself against the bulkhead. "Looks bad," he said.

With horror I watched as the needles spun in their dials. Then I glanced toward the wing. Smoke, thick, black, and oily, was pouring out of the engine that was attached to it. A strange, Motoesque calm came over me. I might, with such steady nerves, have flown my own plane over the Manchurian mountains. "Right-hand engine on fire," I reported.

"Feather it," said Captain James.

"Feathering," Manfred reported. "I've shut her down."

No sooner had the pilot made that announcement than the fire, denied its flow of fuel, burned itself out. Our downward spiral ceased, too. Instead we slipped sideways, away from the town, over the outer rim of the crater, and toward the landing strip that had been cleared on the basalt surface below. The engine at the nose continued to roar. The engine on the far wing gave an answering growl. The airplane shuddered. It bucked. But the president of Granite Films had it under control.

"Gear going down," he declared.

It was I, not my double, who said, "Check."

"Ready for touchdown."

The runway, covered with snaking sand, rushed up at us. Alkali dust swirled by the windows. Then the rubber wheels rumbled, sprang upward a second, and settled upon the ground.

Said Captain Dave James, "Perfect landing."

For the length of a football field our momentum carried us forward. Then we slowed to little more than a crawl.

"Open the doors," James ordered. "I'll order the marshals out."

Manfred shook his head. "I wish I could."

I said, "But what can you mean?"

He pointed out the window on the right. More puffs of smoke had appeared at the rim of the crater. Bullets, making a pizzicato noise, whizzed closely by.

"Take off! Take off!" cried James.

Again the pilot shook his head. "Not on two engines. I know this plane. Not enough lift. Oh, shit: look. They've shredded the aileron."

Suddenly, from within the cabin, there was a scream—high, piercing, and ending in a sob.

"Damn!" shouted Manfred. "Somebody's hit!"

I knew who had uttered that terrible cry. I clawed at the buckle and straps that held me to my seat. With a click they fell open. Instantly I sprang from the cushion and dashed back through the fuselage. Once again a tattoo of bullets danced along the aluminum shell. I heard a window shatter. But it was not the one to which the woman who had been one of the world's great beauties was pressing her face. That glass, I saw, ran with her tears.

"Oh, lambie," she cried, throwing herself into my arms. Her body shook and trembled. I looked through the smeared portal. There was a dark shape on the basalt. The limbs were spread-eagled. The head and hat were at a peculiar angle.

"It's Victor!" Magda screamed. "Darling Victor!"

I shut my eyes. I clung to the actress. I remained that way, in self-imposed darkness, until, only a few seconds later, the two working engines began once more to roar. Then I looked about.

Inside the cabin Takashima had ducked down in his seat. The lawmen were standing, with their pistols in their hands. There was no one, however, to shoot at. The engines were howling. The trimotor, or bimotor, started to roll.

"We're taking off!" shouted Kahn.

But I knew there was no chance of that. The plane swerved to the left and rolled off the runway. It bounced along the unswept desert floor. Our pursuers, if indeed there were any, were soon left in a huge cloud of alkali dust. Onward we plowed, careening left, careening right, cutting a channel in the sand. After some minutes the engines sputtered, as if they were choking in the very dust storm they had created. Then they stopped. There was a pause. Impossible to see out the windows. Impossible to hear any sound from without. For a minute, for two minutes, we remained lost in our own cloudy cocoon. Then the captain of the marshals threw the latch on the fuselage door. It swung open, and, one after the other, each of the passengers dropped down onto the dry, inhospitable ground.

CHAPTER

THREE

SCENE 101

As soon as the federal marshals dropped to the ankle-deep sand, they threw up a semicircular line of defense midway between the rim of the crater and our crippled aircraft. Its perimeter was anchored on either side by two machine guns that the officers hauled down from the belly of the plane. Those weapons were aimed at the top of the ridge, as were the rifles of the score of marshals who lay prone on the desert floor. If Von Beckmann's troops—how else could we think of them?—charged over the edge of the crater, the defenders would be able to repulse them with a killing crossfire. But no attack came. There was no movement, no sign of life on the far side of the ridge— only the incessant clank and chug and clang of the distant pump.

A half-hour, a full hour, went by. The midmorning sun beat down upon us. Its rays were worse than a hail of bullets. Those of us from Granite, the civilians, sat at the center of the defensive arc. Takashima had long since removed his lab coat. I slipped out of my camel hair. Manfred peeled off his flying helmet and covered his head with his hands. The sun rose still higher, doubling and redoubling its strength. Eventually Captain James, the chief marshal, called for his men to pull back the machine guns and draw in the curve of defense. This operation was repeated two more times, until all of us who had undertaken the perilous trip on the airplane sat huddled beneath its shade. There we remained, until high noon and after.

What assaulted us now was not so much the heat as our thirst. Les Kahn boarded the aircraft, which was hotter inside than the open desert, and brought out whatever there was to drink in the tiny galley. The marshals devoured their portion and asked for more. Blowen, on their behalf and that of his own three men, hauled himself aboard and ransacked Manfred's private closet. By the time he emerged he had changed color, like a lobster thrust into a pot of boiling water; but his arms were loaded with wine, with whiskey, and bottles of soda. James thrust his thin frame between the old man and his marshals. "That alcohol could kill you in twenty minutes," he told them. He locked the liquor in the baggage compartment and pocketed the key. The soda was shared out, with a full bottle to Magda, and the rest, which came to a third of a bottle each, to the men. We drank it down in a gulp.

Then James and Takashima moved from the shaded spot under the wings. The lawman walked to the engine on the right, which was still leaking oil onto the black puddle that had already formed on the silken sand. The coroner peered up at the opposite engine, the one on the left, whose sharp propellers had severed the head of Victor Granite. Stretching upward, he ran a finger along the blades.

Les Kahn leaned toward me. "Do you remember?" he asked. "The screening room?"

I knew on the instant what he meant. "The ambush. The Indians. That water tank."

Manfred overheard us. "Don't remind me, goddammit. That scene needed thirty-eight takes."

Kahn took off his pink plastic glasses and pinched the pads of his nose. "It's eerie. It's as if this were take thirty-nine. Except we have to live through it. You know, in real life."

We fell silent. Each of us was thinking of how the band of white men had gathered under the cylinder of the water wagon just as we were crouched now under the fuselage of the plane. Impossible not to recall the slaughter, the blood in the pools of water. Suddenly Kahn burst out: "They're going to kill us! Not with bullets! They're going to let us die of thirst!"

"No, no," said Manfred. "They can't do that. We've got their raw stock. They can't finish the picture without us."

Blowen, the aged gate man, raised his head from his knees. "Maybe the heat's getting to you, Mr. Granite. What's to stop them from letting us die and taking the film when they wish? I'd bet that's their plan."

At that Kahn scrambled to his feet. He turned on Manfred. "Manny! The radio! Can't you use it? Can't you call for help?"

Manfred shook his head. "Not if we're on the ground. We're out of range. There's no one to hear us."

Then the publicist called out to the head of the marshals, "You! James! You've got to get us out of here! Tell us, can you make the repairs?"

James turned around. His hands were covered with engine oil; his shirt was smeared with it, too. "Not a prayer."

A groan went up from everyone. Magdalena stifled a sob. It was I who said, "If only I had learned the secret of the pharaohs. Then we would have poison to drink."

More time passed. The sun began to move down the far side of the sky. Cruelly it sought each of us hidden beneath the plane. It nosed us out like a police dog, licking at our skin with its hot, rough tongue. We moved away, out from under the protection of the aluminum wings, but the sun came anyway, following relentlessly—the way burning flames oozed under doorways in so many B-unit films.

But these flames were cool ones. Everyone felt it: a breeze! Through our parched throats we sent up a halfhearted cheer. We turned, each one of us, to the west. There the sun was going down like a flaming hot-air balloon. All about it the clouds, like scraps of canvas envelope, had caught fire. But in the east the pale blue sky was turning navy. The wakened wind sent loose sand, like drifting snow, about our calves. Magda wrapped her arms around her shoulders. The men pulled down their hats. First one, then two or three, and then all the stars came popping out, like the paper in the Navaho punchboard games. Thus did the night take us by surprise. But we had no time to celebrate having survived the day. Now our enemies were the blackness, the cold, the wind. Our only option was to reboard the plane. We lay huddled in groups while the sand, like pebbles thrown by an impatient lover, rattled at the double-paned windows.

The heat, descending at dawn, drove us outside once more. Again we were tortured by thirst. Dave James siphoned the nonpotable water from the galley and the sinks. Blowen fashioned a pit in the sand and made a fire out of the half-dozen books, the stacks of old magazines, scattered throughout the plane. The blaze lasted only half an hour, but that was time enough to boil the water, which we drank with the bubbles still rising in it.

The same pattern was repeated over the next twenty-four hours. The cold of the night sent us into the airship for shelter; when the heat of the day turned our refuge into an oven, we gathered beneath it, panting like hyenas. At midmorning Captain James climbed aboard the trimotor and drained both toilets in the lavatories. Blowen made another fire, this time from the foam in the seatbacks, which rose in coils of oily black smoke. We drank what otherwise would have been contaminated waste as if it were champagne.

By afternoon, however, we were as desperate as ever. Our tongues were swollen. Our throats felt as if they had been slipped into nooses, upon which the hangmen were pulling. Some of the marshals began to talk of breaking into the cargo bay, or of loosening the valves to get at the hydraulic fluid. That was, as Takashima told me, the first sign of delirium.

It was then, at the hottest part of the day, that Kahn cried out, "Does anybody see what I see? Am I crazy? Is it a mirage?"

He was pointing toward the ridge. A white flag was waving there. It was no mirage; a minute later a group of armed men, dozens and dozens of them, marched over the rim of the crater and headed toward the landing strip that lay between us. A shout went up from the marshals. Then our whole band of castaways sent up a cheer; for in the midst of the approaching crew—the actors and extras, the grips and gaffers—was a small band in dungarees. Everyone saw at once that these were Navahos and that they had poles slung over their shoulders. In a reflex we all started licking our lips. What we had realized was that these Indians from America were carrying large vats of water, the way Indians from Bombay or Delhi carried rajas about in a chair.

Now the marshals bolted forward. James ran ahead, shouting commands. It was all he could do to get his men under control. He ordered the machine gunners to bring up their weapons. The rest of the lawmen formed a wedge, behind which our contingent from Granite moved forward. Across from us the army from Pandaemonium came to a halt at the far side of the runway. We stopped at our side of the strip. James shouted across the cleared basalt, "Who's in charge there?"

"I suppose I am."

At the sound of that voice, Manfred staggered. Weakly, his voice breaking, he called out, "Burton!"

His smiling son moved onto the open runway. He wore a blousy white shirt and was, for all the heat of the sun, bareheaded.

The captain stepped onto the strip as well. "My name is Dave James. I'm in charge of the United States marshals. We have reason to believe that a number of serious crimes have been committed here."

"We know you feel that way. It's understandable. But you must be thirsty. We've brought water. Why don't you drink first? Then we'll have our discussion." Even before he'd finished speaking, Burton motioned with his arm. Two of the Indians came forward, carrying one of the steaming vats. They set it down at the center of the coal-black surface. The sight was too much for the marshals. With a hoarse yelp they broke ranks and dashed across the volcanic stone.

"Take care!" Burton shouted. "It's hot."

But the men dove at the vat. They scooped up the scalding water with their hands. They put their faces into it, like children bobbing for apples. Blowen had to force a path through them so that Magdalena, Kahn, and I could drink. Burton shook his head. He turned to his father. "The deeper the drill goes into the ground, the hotter the water gets. You'd think we were drawing it out of molten rock." But Manfred, like everyone else, was stretched over the rim of the vat, his head plunged into the bath-hot brew.

There was, for the moment, a general melee. The captain looked about. Most of his men had dropped their guns. Two of them were vomiting onto the runway. The rest were intermingled with the *Pandaemonium* crew, many of whom had come forward, rifles in hand. Even the Indians had started moving about the white men, selling their trinkets or begging outright: *Gimme dollar. Gimme two bits.* Only the machine gunners held their position; then, at a signal from their commander, they trotted in to have their fill.

When at last I lifted my own head, and the water streamed from my eyes, I saw a man, tall and bespectacled, standing a little apart from the crowd. It was Sampson Frank, the actor. Plucking at his piecemeal beard, the former Moses, the ex–yeshiva student, said, "In the Bible the doomed drink with their heads in the water. Only those who drink from their hands are saved."

Finally the marshals moved back. They were burping. Their bellies bulged over their belts. Burton stepped through their ranks and approached the captain. "Perhaps now we can talk about these serious crimes."

"Yes," said James. "Now that my men are disarmed."

"Oh, you'll have no need of weapons. We're prepared to cooperate in every way."

"You can start by explaining why you fired on our aircraft. Mr. Granite barely managed to avoid a tragedy."

"So?" I recognized the man who said that. It was Leo Gorcey. "Nobody got hurt, right?"

James: "Impeding a federal officer while carrying out his duties. That's a felony. So is attempted murder. I could arrest you all on the spot."

Gorcey threw back his head and laughed. "That wouldn't be a good idea. You're outnumbered seven to one." All those standing about, the heavyset grips and gaffers, laughed with him, making a braying sound.

Captain James said, "Who ordered that attack? Was it you? Was it Mr. Von Beckmann?"

"There was no order," Burton replied. "The shooting was spontaneous. You have to understand, there has been a tremendous amount of tension on the set. All of us are under pressure to finish the picture. Some of our people, I'm afraid, are at the end of their rope. We regret what happened to your flight. Yes, we agree it was a criminal act—but one caused by a few hotheads. There is no need for an investigation. We've caught them. We have them here."

With that, three men were dragged forward from the midst of the crew. Their hands were tied behind them. I knew that one was Schotter, the gaffer who had been in the lift. The other two, in miners' outfits, must have been extras. They all seemed to have been beaten. They stood in a daze.

"Three men?" Blowen exclaimed. "You must think we're fools, all right. Those shots came from all over the town."

Burton: "We don't claim to have everyone, not yet. But we will. We're going to turn them over."

Blowen turned to his employer. "I don't like it, Mr. Granite. I think we ought to make our own investigation."

"No, no, Mike," said Manfred. "We'll let it go for now. We can't go in and search every building."

Burton addressed the chief marshal. "What about you, captain? Are you satisfied with our efforts?"

"I'm here on more serious business than your attempt to scare us off. There is, to start with, the fact that you have kidnapped Mr. Granite's niece."

Gorcey gave a high-pitched laugh. "I like that! The *fact*! There's been no kidnapping. All you have to do is ask Valentina."

Those words must have been a signal, because no sooner were they uttered than a tight group of the Navahos parted. The girl, her hair as dark as theirs, and her skin no less swarthy, stood in her rawhide costume.

Takashima strode toward her. "So, miss, can you tell us? Many people claim they saw you abducted."

Valentina answered without the least hesitation. "*He's* the one who tried to abduct me." It was Manfred she pointed at. "He tried to keep me from returning to my work. And that is what I came here, of my own free will, to do: to work and to learn and to become an actress. Oh, and I *have* worked. I *have* learned. Since I've come back I've shot ten different scenes. I won't let you stop me. I have to finish."

"It's true," said Burton. "We've reshot all the B-unit scenes. We've done the matches with Magda. We'd still be shooting if we hadn't run out of stock."

Takashima said, "Very well. We must in that case drop the accusation of kidnapping."

James: "That leaves the gravest charge. Of murder. Perhaps murders."

"Oh, we don't deny that there has been a murder. We freely admit it."

Manfred turned on his son. "What the hell are you talking about? Do you want to ruin us?"

Les Kahn said, "He's mistaken, that's all. He wasn't here when the accident occurred. He's never been in the mine to see the missing rail."

Takashima: "Perhaps it might be possible to speak with someone who has? Am I correct when I say that one of the victims has recovered from his wounds? That he is no longer in a coma?"

At those words the gallon of liquid I had sucked into my belly began to churn, as if I had swallowed a pail of acid. Stealthily I moved backward, toward the edge of the runway. But I stopped in my tracks when I heard a familiar voice say, "You are. I'm doing fine." Chick Chandler! He was standing on his own two feet. There was a bandage on his head and Dick Mosk had hold of his arm.

"Ah," Takashima exclaimed. "This is good news. Is it also the case that on the night of Mr. George Hoffman's death, you were inside the mineshaft?"

"Yes, that's true."

"And you were also with him when he was killed?"

"I was. Yes."

How to describe, at such a moment, my sensations? The hair on my head felt as if each strand were standing upright and waving, like the tentacles of some sea creature that senses the approach of food. But *I* was the prey! The detective was about to be detected. But I would never give my old rival the pleasure of identifying the criminal—no, before that happened I would serve myself up on a platter.

Takashima: "So. Take, please, your time. No need to rush. Tell us kindly what occurred."

"Well, George and I were in the drift together when we heard voices."

Yes! My voice! Victor's! Magdalena's!

"George went out to take a look, and the next thing I knew—"

"Yes. Very good. The next thing you knew—?"

"I heard George calling for help."

Help! For God's sake help me!

"And then, sir?"

"Naturally I came running out and saw George rolling on the platform with another man, and, and—"

"That's all right," said Dr. Mosk. "You don't have to talk now."

"No. I want to."

Takashima: "And who was that man?"

"I didn't stop to look. I just jumped on top of him."

"Aha! What then occurred?"

"Something, somebody, hit me on the head."

"And the name of this person?"

Loewenstein, Laszlo! Lorre, Peter!

"His name?"

"Yes, please: the name."

I provided it, by screaming out loud. "I! It was I! I. A. Moto!"

Chick Chandler said, "I don't remember. After that, everything is a blank."

But everyone, even the red-skinned savages, had already turned toward me.

Manfred: "What? Lorre! What are you talking about?"

"I did it. Don't you remember? *Thank You, Mr. Moto.* I stabbed the knife-wielding assassin three times. I buried him in the dirt. Ha-ha. Just reminiscing."

The others turned away in disgust. Doc Mosk held up his hand. "I am sorry to say Chick doesn't remember anything from that moment on. Somebody hit him, but he doesn't know who."

"But we have learned much. Very much. This was no accident. This is a case of murder." Takashima happily grinned, making his teeth stick out as far as mine. "The man who struck Mr. Chandler is obviously the person who killed Mr. Hoffman."

Captain James: "And transported him across the state line."

Manfred: "What? Are you going to take Chandler's word? He's a sick man. He's suffering from amnesia."

"That's right," added Kahn. "His testimony won't hold up in court."

"But you needn't depend on his word," interrupted Burton Granite. "We know who the killer is. And we're more than willing to produce him."

My heart came to a full stop inside my body. If it were not for the steady beat of the pile driver, the pump, my blood might have stopped circulating altogether. Should I step forward? Or attempt to flee? Flee where? Into the burning sands?

"Is this some kind of trick?" demanded James. "How do you know the name of the killer?"

"Because," said Burton, "he has confessed."

Manfred stared at his son. "What? A confession? Impossible!"

Burton gave a wave, after which there was a ripple in the crowd of burly grips and gaffers. Then Reynaldo Flatow, the Viennese writer, was thrust to the fore. He already had his hands out, squirrel-like, as if he expected hand-cuffs to be put upon them. One of the marshals—the name *Blake* was stitched to his shirtfront—quickly obliged him.

The captain stepped up to the prisoner. "What is your name?"

The writer's head drooped until it seemed that it must slip like a ball from the shelf of his shoulders. His spectacles hung to the tip of his nose. "Flatow," he declared.

"Flatow? F-L-A-T-O-W?"

Still staring at his feet, the little man nodded.

"You heard what Mr. Granite just said. Is it true?"

Another nod.

"You killed Hoffman?"

"I did."

"How? With what weapon?"

Everyone strained to hear the answer. "A rock. I struck him once. I struck him again."

Takashima stepped in. "Alone? Without accomplices?"

"Yes, alone."

Manfred, at this admission, was almost as flabbergasted as I. "What is this? A put-up job? This is no murderer. Look at him. He's shorter than Lorre. And he's as old as I am. How could he take on a man like Hoffman? Not to mention a six-footer like Chandler? He's been hypnotized. He's been brainwashed. This confession is a phony!"

Suddenly, from the crowd, a figure in a thin foamy dress, rose red, and with her purse over her shoulder, came running. It was the Queen B! She held her arms out and loped toward the spot where Mosk was propping up her Chickie, her Chandler. "Oh! Oh!" she cried and, to my amazement, swept right by her lover and headed toward me. So swift was she, so lithe, that the material of her gown—was it silk? Was it cotton? It was something I could almost see through—clung to her body and stretched out behind her, so that the tips of her breasts and the bulge of her abdomen and the pillars of her thighs all stood markedly out. She was like the Greek statue of Nike. Yes! Yes! *Victory!*

"Oh! Oh! Petey!" she cried, throwing her arms around me. "How could I ever doubt you? How can I make it up to you? Will you forgive me?"

"Ha-ha! Miss Hudson. How are you, honey?"

The head of the marshals stepped forward. He motioned to his men. "Take this suspect, and take those three, too. Secure them underneath the plane."

"You mean," said Manfred, "you believe him? You really think there's been a murder?"

"Hold on, Manny." That was Lester Kahn. "This might not be so bad. There was no kidnapping, right? Plus, we've got the men who shot at the plane: And on top of that, the murderer of Hoffman has confessed. All these crimes—either they never happened or they've been solved. Everything's perfect. We give Von B the unexposed film and Von B finishes the picture."

"One moment, if you please." That was Takashima. He paused to polish his lenses with a handkerchief. "There is still one piece of business yet to be concluded. I have not yet determined how Mr. Victor Granite met his death."

Gorcey said, "That's no problem. We've got plenty of witnesses. Including the victim's very own daughter. Valentina—" And here the former Dead End Kid glanced toward the young actress. "You tell them. It was an accident."

Now everyone turned to stare at the girl. It was clear to all that she had made up her mind not to give way to tears. "Yes. All right. I can tell you. We were there, over there—just on top of that mound. We were in the middle of shooting. I climbed down to bury my brother Paul. Then I looked up. I saw him. He was walking on the runway. He was waiting for the airplane. I was afraid he was going to fly away. That he would leave me behind. I waved to him. I called. But he couldn't hear. That was because of the roar of the engines. He couldn't see. Because of the dust. The sand."

Captain James: "I don't know. We can't just accept the word of a child."

Gorcey: "But there are plenty of others. Coco and Nakhimovsky and Von Beckmann, too. And what about Peter Lorre?"

What about him? He stood, stupidly grinning, while both of Miss Hudson's hands crawled like spiders into his trouser pockets.

Manfred: "Never mind all that. I'm the closest adult relative here. The next of kin. I'm satisfied this was a terrible accident. The family won't be pressing charges."

Takashima, however, was not to be deterred. "My office requires me to examine the body of Victor Granite. Dr. Mosk, would you accompany me to the corpse?"

Here everyone, even the heavily breathing Miss Hudson, and even I, looked down the runway. Victor lay where he had fallen, except that his head and hat were mere inches, not feet, from his body. I saw that in the heat of the desert the filmmaker had been instantly preserved; the muscles were like the taut ropes you might expect to see when the bandages are removed from a mummy. The skin was at once dark and pale, like an old chocolate bar.

"I'm sorry," Dick Mosk responded. "I'm afraid I can't allow that."

"Why not?" asked Captain James. "That's his job. He's obliged to examine the remains."

Burton broke into the conversation. "That won't be possible. We can't let anyone near the body. Not until shooting is completed."

"Excuse, please. How long will that be?"

"We've got only three scenes of principal photography left. There's the sheriff's speech, where he calls for the final battle against the Indians. That's scene 100. We have just enough stock, maybe, to film that now. Then there's the battle itself, scene 101. That's the miners' revenge for the attack on the water wagon, and it will take just as long to shoot. Probably even longer. With multiple cameras, we'll need three or four thousand feet. And of course there is the last great scene in the mine."

James: "I don't understand. Just how long, in hours, will those three scenes take?"

"Well, we've matched all the shots with Valentina. We've completed all our rehearsals. I'd say that once we have the raw stock in the cameras, it will take no more than an hour for the first scene. And two days, all told, for each of the other two."

"Days? Days and not hours?" Takashima was frowning. "This is irregular. I cannot permit it."

Gorcey: "Well, captain, what do you say?"

"This is a murder case and stays a murder case until the coroner makes his ruling. The film you want is in the cargo compartment. I'm not going to give you a foot of it until he examines the body of Victor Granite."

Burton: "And until we complete our picture, you can't have access to his corpse. It seems we're at an impasse."

"So be it," said Captain James.

Burton shrugged. "By this time tomorrow you will have changed your minds."

"What makes you say such a thing?" asked Takashima.

Burton didn't answer. He simply motioned to the Navahos. They moved quickly to the three remaining vats and, before anyone could think to interfere, spilled their contents onto the sand. More laughter, like the cawing of crows, broke out from Von Beckmann's crew. Each one of us who had been a passenger on the disabled airplane stood mute with horror. Then the lawmen ran for their weapons. The workers on the *Pandaemonium* production shouldered theirs.

It seemed, at that moment, that there might be an armed confrontation.

But the captain, sensing catastrophe, waved his men away. "Get back to the airplane. All of you." The marshals, the riflemen, and the machine gunners too, were eager enough to obey. Magdalena and Kahn, Takashima and James, followed in their wake. Blowen and his men made up the rear guard. Manfred remained behind, fists balled at his side. "No, no!" he shouted. "Come back, goddammit! Give them the film! Who cares about Victor?"

But the others were already trudging across the desert. Manfred whirled to address his son. "Burton! Be reasonable! Let the Jap look at Victor. What difference can it make?"

The whole of the entourage from the ghost town had already moved off to the ridge. Burton paused. "Believe me, Manfred, it's not my decision. There's nothing I can do. Go back. Go back, Papa. And be careful."

"Burton, listen. You don't know him. You don't know what happened. We used to travel in a wagon. Of course, I know you know that. But the rest! The way we traveled! From village to village. At night. All through the night. Alexander was outside, humming to the horse. Inside, I'd watch until Drahomira, our mother, would rise from her place over the right rear wheel and move—oh, her breasts would sway to the same rhythm as the black pots strung on the overhead rails: she moved to where Rudi was sleeping over the right wheel in front. A minute would go by. Hardly more than a minute. Then Rudi would rise—that mark in his hair! Like a lamp in the night!—and move back to the rear wheel on the left. That's where I was. Not sleeping. Not breathing. Waiting. Do you understand? Do I have to spell it out?"

Did Burton hear, much less understand? No way to tell. His back was turned. He was walking to the crater's rim, over the top of which he soon disappeared.

Manfred, shoulders sagging, dragged himself over the plate of basalt toward the silvery glare of the airplane.

Only two living people were left on the runway. "Oh, Petey," said Miss Hudson. "I feel something. Do you?"

"Not yet. Try more. A little more. Just another inch."

"Never mind. I'll come back with you. Wait 'til tonight. I'm the one who's going to give you a surprise."

The water we drank went through us like rain through a drainpipe. We pissed it into the crystals of sand. The sun sucked it out of our pores. By midafternoon we were thirstier than we had been in the morning. What was

Burton's boast? That we'd change our minds in twenty-four hours? The marshals were ready for mutiny before the sun went down. As soon as it was dark, James returned to the trimotor cockpit, where he spent the nights stretched across the pilot and copilot's seats. An hour later his men crept through the aisle of the fuselage and fell upon him. They grappled him round the neck and kicked at him with the soles of their shoes. He fought back, two-fisted, until someone struck him across the forehead with the butt of a government-issue rifle. Then they clawed at him, ripping open his pockets. They seized the key to the cargo compartment.

The captain had told his men that the alcohol there would kill them. It didn't. However, they all became drunk as sailors in five minutes flat. Howling, hallooing, they reeled over the desert. They sang "Over the Rainbow" and "Chattanooga Choo-Choo" and "Beer Barrel Polka." They fought one another. They kissed and made up. Like prairie dogs they burrowed into the sand. It would have taken inhuman strength for the rest of us, the civilians, to hold out. Kahn knocked the top from a bottle of wine and, cutting his lips a little, joined in the debauch. Takashima drank himself silly and, to demonstrate his surgical skills, kept tying and untying his shoes. Flatow and the other prisoners drank up the beer, and even Manfred sat down with a bottle of gin in his lap.

Finally, as the night deepened, all of the shipwrecked passengers fell into a stupor; they lay helter-skelter upon the desert floor. Inside the trimotor Miss Hudson and I lay side by side. Each night I had put on my pajamas: white cotton with red fire engines and red firemen's hats pointing up, sideways, and down. Rochelle had nothing but her filmy, rosy gown. She didn't reach into my pockets; she groped through the fly, behind which my male member crouched. "It's ten o'clock," she whispered. "Where's the cuckoo?" Then she took me—it was indeed a surprise—between a finger and thumb. I lay back on her pillowy bosom. Perspiration, thick as toothpaste, squeezed through the ducts of my glands. It cemented my legs together. It sealed up my lips. It stung my eyes.

"Hey," said the Queen B. "Is it Passover or something? I smell macaroons."

I said not a word. I hardly breathed. I watched as, from my paramour's gown, both breasts fell forward like loaves of Langendorf bread. I also saw something not allowed by the Hays Office: a glimpse of the flesh of her thighs—dimpled, dappled, and white as the wax on the side of a candle.

"Petey! My goodness!" Miss Hudson exclaimed. And for the first time in our long relationship she added two more fingers.

There was a thump. A curse. A bang. Someone was coming down the airplane aisle. "Goddammit, Lorre. Where are you?"

Rochelle sprang away. "Here we are, Mr. Granite. Back here."

Somebody struck a match. It was indeed Manfred Granite. "Lorre, get out of here. Magda's waiting. She's got the film. Four thousand feet of it. Hurry up. They're drunk. They're sleeping. It's our only chance. You've got to help her."

I rose. Over my pajamas I pulled up my trousers. I bent down to Miss Hudson. "Wait for me," I whispered. "I'll be back in, you know, a jiffy."

Magdalena was waiting underneath the fuselage, next to the quartet of prisoners. The tin canisters were heaped in a pile by her feet. We each took an armful and started off toward the town of Pandaemonium. We climbed up one side of the ridge and stumbled down the other. Inside the crater the alkali-covered floor stretched out before us like the sawdust-strewn planks of the Swallow Saloon. Which way to go in this circle? How to find our bearings? There was no light ahead from the ghost town. The clanging of the bit, the blow of metal against rock, was no help; the curve of the crater, the bowl we were in, bent the sound around us, so that it seemed to come from every direction.

But Magda hurried on, eager and breathless. She seemed to skip, so that the heels of her shoes clicked almost gaily against the hard-packed surface. In her arms the reels of film rattled like castanets. In the starlight, the moonlight, I saw that her illustrious lips, the upper rather thin, the lower full and meaty, were set in a grin. I knew why: she was going to see Rudolph Von Beckmann. On she went, navigating by sixth sense or second sight. She might have been following a magnetic compass or, stretched out before her, a painted line, white dashes on an asphalt highway: the white streak in Rudi's jet hair.

Soon enough we came to the outskirts of the old mining town. Everything there was dark and, save for the unending beat of the pile driver and pump, still. I motioned for a halt. "Magda. There are guards. They'll shoot if we come up in the dark. It's only a few hours to dawn. We have to wait."

She sank down beside me on the cracked floor of the basin. We huddled together against the cold. I could smell, behind her ears, on her wrists, What Women Dream. The moon, I saw, was sliding down the left-hand side of the sky. Very quietly, she started to speak.

"I know what you are thinking, lambie. *Why is Magda returning to Rudi?*

I believe I am going to tell you. Not just why I am going now. Or after Munich. But why I left Granite and Victor, the whole of my career, for Salzburg. You remember. Salzburg. Nineteen thirty-eight. When all our troubles began." I didn't say a word. I didn't move a muscle. "This is hard for me. It's my biggest secret. It is humbling. Humiliating. I never told Victor. I never told Rudi. Oh, it hurts more than my time with Hitler."

She was trembling. I put my arm around her. She took a deep breath, sucking in the air the way a condemned man might draw upon his last cigarette. "In the summer of nineteen thirty-seven—no, don't interrupt me. I *want* to tell you. Little lambie, only you. That summer I joined Max Reinhardt. You know he has a small workshop on Sunset. It's very modest. It's a scandal how a man like that must earn a living in America. The dust! The cobwebs! But I adored the nights in that room. I don't deny that part of my pleasure was that I knew that with Max I was in touch with Rudi—with the tradition: Salzburg, Vienna, Berlin. But I swear to you that wasn't the main reason I went back week after week; or if it was, it soon ceased to be. What I loved was watching those talented young people at work. There was a chamber production of Maeterlinck. Of Brecht. There was Pirandello. For all those months I only watched. I didn't take any parts. Believe it or not, from shyness—from the embarrassment of being a star.

"But then, that winter, in November, Max announced he was going to stage *Hamlet,* and before I knew what I was doing, I had volunteered. Of course I *did* know what I was doing, and I'll say it, lambkins, before you do: yes, this was an attempt to reenact, with this first part with Reinhardt, my first part for Rudi."

"Of course. Ophelia. I saw you in Berlin: nineteen eighteen. What a sensation! So erotic. My God, you were beautiful!"

"And young. Rudi had just pulled me out of Altschuler's. I was a shopgirl. I modeled hats. The next thing I knew I was onstage, singing those songs, Elizabethan songs, in a torn dress."

I remembered every word. She looked as if she were just out of puberty. The crowd of war-weary Berliners had roared when she milked her own breast:

> *Then up he rose and donn'd his clothes*
> *And dupp'd the chamber door—*

What had Rudi said? That you could smell her at the back of the room. It was true!

Let in the maid, that out a maid
Never departed more.

"I cringe," said Magda, "when I think how Max must have heard the eagerness in my voice: *Mr. Reinhardt, it would mean so much to me.* That note of begging. But he laughed; he was gracious. He said what an honor it would be for him and his students if I would join the production. We set a date for first rehearsal, on the Tuesday to come.

"*Just four days!* I was terrified. Those young students, so ambitious: they'd know their lines. They wouldn't need scripts. But what about me? I hadn't done Ophelia in twenty years! So, lambie, I called in sick to Granite and learned my part in a day and a half. Again and again I turned in my mind how I would play the scene—two scenes, really—of madness. I had to capture the girl's spiritual nature—oh, it's there, in her pity for Hamlet, for his distraction and suffering: but I wanted the sensuousness, yes, the sexiness I'd had in Berlin. A hundred times I went over that moment when she gives each person the appropriate flower—fennel, yes? For Claudius? And columbine. The sadness of that girl breaks your heart.

"How I feared that fourth day! But how I yearned for the other three to pass! I was completely alone. No calls from you, lamb, none from Victor—no calls from anyone. I locked myself in my study. The only other being in my life was the image in my mirror. I tell you I became that girl all over again. I could not stop weeping for her father and her lover. What horror at realizing the one has killed the other. Did I eat, those days? Did I drink? I honestly don't remember. All I saw was my own face growing thin, growing gaunt. In that mirror, nothing but cheekbones and hollows.

"How did I get to the street, to my car, to the workshop on Sunset? I don't remember that, either. I wore white, like some bride. I let down my hair. The nervousness! Like an ingenue. The same as Berlin, only there was no Rudi to hold me, to kiss me, to whisper in my ear. All Max could do when I arrived at the workshop was squeeze my hand.

"The chairs in the room were in a circle. Everyone else, all the men and women, were already there. No stars, no names. I did see that the Claudius was going to be the writer John Huston. He sat there scratching a day's growth of beard. The Hamlet was Henry Fonda, whom I had seen in small parts in one or two pictures—*Way Down East,* I think, and *That Certain Woman.* The rest were just young folk, my fellow students; even the Polonius was a boy hardly twenty, who wore clear spectacles to put himself into the mood. Do you hear, lambie, how I am rattling on? It's from the same nervousness I felt then. Also, my own dear, my lamb, I believe I am trying to put off telling you what happened next."

The moon, I saw, was nearly down. But there wasn't a hint of the dawn. Magda's eyes, as she spoke, were tightly closed. "Did I mention there was a circle of chairs? With one place open? I felt every eye upon me as I took that last seat. Max said something about how there was no reason for speeches, we were about to read the greatest play in the world, and why didn't we just begin? The next thing I knew, he, Max, spoke the stage directions: *Enter Bernardo,* isn't that right? *And Francisco?* Right away a young man across from me, Ken Brecher I think his name was, says *Who's there?* And another fellow with curly hair, very Jewish, Aaron Fogel, says *Nay, answer me,* and so off we go. I didn't bother to open the play. I didn't even bring it with me. I knew every line. Horatio comes in, another adolescent, failing in his attempt to start a moustache. With Marcellus. I closed my eyes for a moment. I listened to all four of them exclaiming about the ghost and trying to work up the courage to challenge it to stand. Their voices trembled from the excitement. *But soft, behold! Lo where it comes again!* When Horatio said that, I couldn't resist taking a peek. Max was standing there, in his not very clean and not very well pressed suit. Yet that poor ghost looked so sad and—what does Marcellus say?—so *majestical!* Then the famous Reinhardt, he put his hand to his lips and—*Cock-cock-a roo!*—crowed like a cock, and then we were ready for scene two."

I had to suppress a gasp at that sound. It was, that imitation of crowing, what Jannings had done at the end of *Der Blaue Engel.* I thought, too, of how the animals in this desert had answered Valentina's call. Would that the cock crowed now, to bring on the dawn.

Magda continued. "Now, then. Now, lamb. Scene two. Again my eyes dropped shut. It was Claudius's turn. I heard Huston say how he mourns his brother and delights in his queen and how he intends to deal with the threat of Fortinbras. What a good king! Next he gives permission to Laertes to return to France, but not before dutifully asking his father's leave. The good family man! Everything smooth and orderly and proper. Lucky Denmark! Nothing remains undone—except the problem, off in the corner, of this gloomy young man. *But now, my cousin Hamlet, and my son.* And Hamlet rudely answers, *A little more than kin, and less than kind.* And the king says, *How is it that the clouds still hang on you?* The quick-witted prince says, *Not so, my lord, I am too much in the sun.* What was I thinking? I was thinking to myself with pride how much better my English had become, because now I saw how clever this is. It is a pun. On *son*. And I wondered whether or not everything he said had just such a meaning, and then—and then—"

"And then?" I echoed.

Magdalena remained motionless, her eyes screwed tight. She replied in a whisper. "Then there was just this silence. No one said anything. I think a full moment passed. I opened my eyes to see what was the matter and—" She broke off again. When she resumed, it was not in a whisper but a wail. "Everyone was looking at me! I couldn't understand it. I smiled. I gave a shrug. And then Max, Mr. Reinhardt, he prompted me: *Good Hamlet, cast thy nighted color off!* And in one instant, the way a magician will pass his hand over a glass of inky water and make it clear: in that instant I understood! How horrible! I can't explain it to you! I can't explain the humiliation!"

Yes, and in that instant the wool was pulled from the eyes of her sheep, her lamb. "The part you were to play: it was Gertrude, not Ophelia."

"Oh, God! Oh, yes! Gertrude! The boy's mother! That old woman!"

"Oh, my. My Magdalena."

"Do you know what I saw, in that moment of clarity? That lightning flash? I said there was a circle of chairs with men and women: not true! There was only one other woman—a girl, a beauty, with gray eyes and black hair. The child star. Nanette. Nanette Fabray. *She* was Ophelia! Not a day older than I had been in Berlin! She wouldn't look at me. She was blushing. I wanted to die!"

"I am so sorry," I offered.

"*Sorry!* You're *sorry*! Do you know what was the worst of it? I had brought a bouquet! From my garden! To hand out to the actors! *There's rosemary, that's for remembrance.* Oh, God! The shame of it! *There's pansies, that's for thoughts.*"

"I see. That's why you left us. But you shouldn't have. Who would know?"

"Who? Everyone! I was going to be a laughingstock. Louella! That Hopper woman! Winchell! The whole town would know."

"And you thought—what? What were you thinking? That Rudi would restore you? That he would make you Ophelia? That teenage girl?"

I felt for her. Poor Magda! Surely that *had* been her fantasy. And what had happened? Once again she had been replaced by a girl half her age.

But before I could say anything more, the pump suddenly stopped and the sky grew lighter. Not from dawn. From the bank of arc lights that Maynes and his men had switched on at the center of Pandaemonium. Magda stood. She clutched her reels of film.

"You said the wrong thing, lambie," she told me as she started off toward the lights. "Stupid Magda! Fool that I am! Oh, my little lamb. I had a fantasy. A simple human wish. I allowed myself to hope you would say, *That Max! How could he make such a silly mistake?*"

By the time we arrived at Main Street, the company was already shooting the hundredth scene of the film. I saw the number chalked on the slate board that Liz held under her arm. Rudi, in black, with his Hitler hair, his Hitler moustache, was already on the balcony. Nakhimovsky was shooting from below, from the point of view of the fifty or sixty miners who had gathered in the street. The camera was soundlessly rolling.

> *How long are we to tolerate the actions of this tribe? They were warned that if by their cunning and intrigue they should plunge our two nations into war, it is they who would be annihilated. Yet they made so bold as to attack us not once but repeatedly. Now it is time to remove our foe not just from our midst but from the face of the earth. Let no one question our resolve. Let no one be moved by pity. This is not a fully human race. Alone of all people they failed to develop a system of writing. Alone of all people they failed to discover a thing as rudimentary as the wheel. As a result they literally drag their wretched belongings behind them on sticks, spreading disease, pestilence, discord wherever they go. Who among us, when facing such filth, dressed in rags, or in savage paint, the feathers of birds in their hair and the bones of animals upon their bodies, has not asked himself:* is this a man?

I stood, as chilled by these words as if my legs, like a bottle of Rhine wine, had been plunged into a bucket of ice. What was it that frightened me so? I knew it was not the brilliance of Rudi's acting; that wasn't so much a performance as an impersonation, or a reincarnation perhaps. Was it his terrible words? Dreadful to say, even in a motion picture, that Indians were not human beings. I had to beat down the urge to interrupt the tirade. Luckily someone in the crowd cried out instead.

I am such a one.

I followed the swinging camera lens until I came to the speaker. It was Chick Chandler, cast in the role of Raymond. His bandages, if they were still on his head, were tucked into the crown of his cream-colored hat. He stood his ground against his father's wrath:

All men are equally human in the eyes of God.

The camera swung back to Von Beckmann. His eyes narrowed. His hands crashed onto the railing.

Then these are the creatures of another god! They spring from a different root of the human family. And that root must now be pulled from the ground!

This time I kept my eyes fixed on the crowd. It was their reaction, not Rudi's speech, that filled me with dismay. They were not acting, either. For all their costumes, the slouch hats and bandanas, the look of rapt attention on their faces was not assumed. These men had been ravished.

I pulled Magda by the arm. "Come. We must go back. Can't you feel it? Didn't you hear his words? Something terrible is going to happen."

But she only stared up at the balcony. Her eyes were glistening. Her throat, bare in the electrical light, was arched in surrender. I stepped away from the street, in the hope that she would follow. "Come. Magdalena, come. We must not give them the film."

She turned toward me, but to my astonishment, her lips curled back and her voice, when she spoke, was in far from a whisper. "Look! Do you see him? That man! It's the saboteur! *Ja! Ja!* The spy!"

The whole crowd turned toward us. Coco Goodheart yelled, "Cut!"

I clutched my share of the canisters to my chest and ran into the night. The extras came after. In my anxiousness, my haste, I could not prevent the reels of blank film from slipping out of my arms. One after the other they fell to the ground and spun there, like gigantic coins. A cry, an exclamation, went up from my pursuers. They halted at the sight of their prize.

It took me the better part of an hour to reach the runway and, beyond it, the aircraft mired in the sand. By then a strip of pink, no wider than sewing thread, lay along the eastern horizon. In that light I could make out the logo, the *G* in a square, upon the upright rudder. The lawmen, like felled cacti, lay stiffly in the drifting sand. I ran to one, then another. They could not be roused from their stupor. So too the studio contingent and the four prisoners; all were deep in their drugged repose. I made for the aircraft and hauled myself up through the open door. Had the chief of the marshals recovered? He alone might be able to respond to Rudi's speech, with all of its frightening fervor. I turned right, toward the cockpit. But the words I heard came from the left, at the tail.

"Cuckoo! Cuckoo! Is birdy out of the clock?"

I whirled. There, in the half-light of dawn, I saw Miss Hudson, with her hair, unpinned, tumbling off the side of her head to the bare flesh of her shoulder. I attempted then two things at once: to dash down the aisle and pull off my trousers. Hipping and hopping, I drew up to where she waited on her knees. Her eyes, I saw, grew wide, and then even wider. Her mouth opened in a red-rimmed O. No double required for this performance. No stunt man needed for this natural act. Above all, no stand-in: I was standing all by myself. Rochelle's jaw dropped in amazement as, like one of the ladders from my fire trucks, I extended myself even further. The last thing the Queen B said was, "Let's make it snappy," before she found it impossible to speak anymore. Time seemed, as this most ancient of mind-body problems was about to be solved, to suspend its tick and its tock. I heard only a soft sound of choking, and then a cough. This was followed by a hacking, as if some person were clearing his throat.

"Ah, Miss Hudson! Ah, honey! What bliss! It almost feels as if we are moving."

"You jerk! We *are* moving!"

It was true. Quite slowly, but quite perceptibly, the heavy airplane had begun to plod over the sand. And that sound I'd heard? It hadn't come from Rochelle but from the engines! The left one was spinning and spinning. And a whine, a whirring, came from the one on the nose.

"Let me out of here!" My co-star stood. She pushed by me and dashed down the aisle toward the door.

"No, no!" I cried. "Do not do anything desperate!" But the poor frightened creature, clutching her handbag, leaped from the cabin and disappeared from view.

We were moving faster now, bouncing over the desert's miniature white-caps and troughs. I hadn't a moment to lose. As fast as I could, like one of my firemen on his way to a fire, I rushed down the aisle to the curved rectangle of the door. The ground raced by below me. Pinching my nose, I hurled myself outward and landed foursquare upon the cushion of sand.

Already people were stirring. The marshals were up on their hands and knees. Kahn came running forward. "What's happening? What's happening?" he cried.

Manfred stomped angrily toward us. "It's that fucking captain! That James! He's going to bring reinforcements!"

Blowen came hobbling over. "Impossible! The aileron's broken! The engine's out!"

But the impossible was happening in front of our eyes. On two engines the plane nosed across the desert, sending up a huge plume of dust that, even as we motionless castaways watched, began to rain down upon us. Kahn turned to his employer.

"What can we do? Is there any way to stop him?"

Manfred shook his head. James had already taken the crippled plane to the end of the runway. For a full moment it remained there, engines roaring, straining forward like a great dog on a leash. Then it bounded ahead.

Rochelle buried her bouncing curls against my shoulder. "I can't look," she said. "He'll never make it off the ground."

For what might have been a full minute it appeared that she must be right. The airplane rushed ahead, across half the runway, across three quarters, without its wheels once leaving the basalt.

"Up. Up. Pull up!" cried Blowen, lifting his hands, as if that gesture could help the five tons of aluminum into the air.

Perhaps it did. With no more than a few feet to spare, the aircraft rose upward some inches, and then a few inches more. It cleared the end of the runway and then lumbered low over the alkali flats; a tall man, an athlete, might have jumped high enough still to touch the wing.

In spite of everything, all of us left behind burst into applause.

All, that is, except Manfred Granite and Lester Kahn. They watched, the one in fury, the other glum, as the airplane, all aglitter in the first rays of sunlight, rose from the surface of the earth.

Oddly enough, those of us who had been abandoned did not recognize the peril we were in. The marshals reasoned thusly: the picture people had got the film they wanted, now we'd get our water. Moreover, the daring pilot would soon be back at the head of an avenging fleet of planes. But no water came. It began to dawn on everyone that once Von Beckmann and his men had received their raw stock of film, they no longer had any motive to render assistance.

Thus did the morning go by. High noon arrived. Still many pairs of eyes peered into the watercolor blue of the sky. Where was the hero? Where were the paratroopers, the bombers, the aircraft filled to the brim with troops? Alas, there wasn't even a hawk in the heavens.

Now, despairing, we began to dig foxholes, both to keep off the heat of the day and to provide some degree of shelter for the night to come. We used our hands, our shoes, the empty bottles from the debauch of the night before. All too soon we struck impenetrable basalt. Then we piled up the sand into a series of saucers and, with more ambition, cups. Two by two we lay suffering inside. The hot coils of the overhead sun grew even hotter. If it were not for the undying faith in Captain James and his airborne armada, I believe we might have approached the point of ending our own lives. Anything was preferable to the heat that we bore now and the cold that was to come.

That terrible day—there was some comfort in knowing that it was the last we would have to endure—came to an end. The merciless sun sank into the alkali plain. The stars came out. In time the moon, nearly as full as the one I'd seen drop over the ghost town, rose high overhead. At three minutes to ten on my Gruen, a coyote—though for all I knew it might have been a hyena or a wild dog or even a wolf—started to howl. Then all was silent. The pump, which had been busy all day, came to a stop.

Inside our dimple Rochelle and I lay shivering. My teeth chattered and clacked in spite of the fact that, like a boy at the beach, I had buried myself up to my neck in sand. My companion was the first to notice that the sky was growing brighter.

"Psst, Petey," she said. "Will you look at that?"

I sat up, spilling my silicon blanket. To my amazement, I saw that the sky was filled with beams of light.

Within their shallow shelters, others had now taken note of the phenomenon. A murmur went up. Then a shout. And finally a cheer. I heard Kahn say, from his hole nearby, "Listen, everybody. They've built us a fire. A bonfire. They don't want us to freeze from the cold!"

That was followed by Manfred's voice. "You're blind as a bat. Those aren't flames. That isn't a fire."

I rose to my knees to get a better view. What I saw was that the rays of light seemed to be shooting out of the earth. A glow came from the center of the crater, the whole of whose rim seemed to be frosted with light, the way the edge of a cocktail glass is sometimes encrusted with salt.

"What's that?" came Blowen's voice. "That noise?"

"I do not know." That was Takashima.

"Petey," said Rochelle. "What is it?"

I did my best to hear. From far off—it must have been from well inside the crater—I could make out a number of sharp, snapping sounds, like the cracking whip of Lash La Rue.

The inhabitants of all the nearby pockmarks fell silent. We all listened as the sounds grew louder. They came more frequently, too. There was a banging, a clatter, almost as if someone in a kitchen were rattling the pots and pans.

"I think," said Blowen, "that those are gunshots."

There was no mistaking now the bark of the distant rifles, the crack of revolvers, six-shooters, pistols. They made a regular tattoo. In addition a new sound, that of human voices—faint cries, shouting, and faraway screams— was borne in on the steady breeze.

"Good, good, good," said Manfred. "They're shooting the next scene. It's about time!"

He was the first to jump from his little dish onto the level plain. The rest of us came pouring from our shelters. We all stood together on the dun-colored sand. The shooting went on, sometimes in a fusillade, sometimes in scattered, random shots. The cries of the wounded—a woman's shriek, the wail of a child—came drifting over the crater's rim.

"Explain, please," said Takashima. "Is this part of your motion picture?"

Les Kahn answered. "It's scene 101. The night attack. Where the miners wipe out the Indians."

Blake, one of the marshals, shook his head. "I don't like it. I don't like the sound of it."

Takashima raised his head and sniffed the air, as if he didn't like the smell of it, either.

Reynaldo Flatow, still in handcuffs, and still in a daze as well, muttered, "Why is it taking so long?"

The prisoners, Schotter and the two others, exchanged glances. One of them said, "It's going to take even longer."

That observation was soon confirmed. Minute after minute went by: a full five, then almost ten. Blowen stamped his boots on the desert floor. "Jesus," he said. "My toes are frozen."

So were mine, not to mention those parts of the body barely covered by my thin cotton pajamas. I, too, might have been concerned by the length of this shot, had I not recalled that the scene I had watched at Granite, when it had been the Indians who were springing the ambush, had also been filmed in a single endless take.

"Look," said the Queen B. "They're coming toward us."

At first I didn't see what she meant. Then, taking a second look, I realized that the crown of light—that's how I thought of it, with a circle of spikes shooting into the air—was actually moving closer to our segment of the crater. I could see what must have been gunsmoke drifting through the corona, like milk swirling through a glass of iced coffee. There was no question the din of the scene—the howls of the victims, their weeping, the screams of the women—was drawing nearer, too. The reports of the guns were loud enough now to make my eyelids reflexively flutter in response. The next moment, as if the pile driver had resumed battering the drill bit against the buried stone, the ground beneath our feet started to shake.

"What's going on?"

"You feel that?"

"It's like an earthquake!"

Everyone could feel the waves of force moving through the desert soil. Then we heard a distant roar, like thunder. "I know!" Miss Hudson shouted. "It's like during the stampede, remember? It's the cattle! The steers!"

"Not cattle," said Lester Kahn. "Horses!"

Blowen shouted, "Here they come!"

In the next instant everyone saw the same thing: an Indian, a brave, in what looked like dungarees, appeared at the top of the embankment. For a moment he paused, looking back at what must have been a scene of carnage. Then a shot rang out and the Navaho threw up his arms and, as skillfully as any trained stunt man, tumbled over and over down the length of the slope.

Even before the victim had reached the bottom of the ridge, more of his fellow tribesmen had gained the top. First two of them, then three of them, and then in numbers impossible to count, they swarmed over the rim of the crater. Some were in workclothes, the dungarees and denims they had slept in, while others were wrapped in blankets or stark naked. There were women among them, and children, and babes in arms. None made the mistake of pausing to look back the way they had come. They clawed their way over the hump of earth, and, some on their feet, running pell-mell, and others rolling or somersaulting, they swept down the incline.

Atop the rim a row of miners appeared, firing their six-shooters and rifles. With each shot, it seemed, a Navaho fell, whirling realistically about, or throwing up his arms, or, in a simulation of death, lying spread-eagled on the ground. Those of us looking on, the lawmen and their prisoners, us Granite people, the coroner, stood openmouthed. The smell of gunsmoke was in our nostrils. The tumult of the massacre—the cries of fear and pain, the gunshots as loud as thunderclaps, the hoofbeats of the hidden horses—assaulted our ears.

Suddenly a bank of portable lights appeared at the crest of the ridge. They picked out the dark forms, clothed and unclothed, that lay on the sand. The survivors, some seventy or eighty souls, ran across the bodies of those who had already fallen. Those in the lead had drawn out of range of the rifles. They were approaching the hard rock of the landing strip. It was clear to all of us—who, much as if we were watching the completed film in a theater, could not help from rooting—that those desperate Indians were going to make good their escape.

"Hurrah!" shouted old Blowen. "Run for it, fellows!"

But Flatow shook his round head. "Look," he said, pointing to the ridge.

There we saw the horsemen, atop their horses. A score of the steeds, their flanks spattered with the foam that flew from their mouths, struggled up and over the rise. Once on the desert floor they chewed up the ground that lay between them and their prey. The sand flew from under their hard, sharp hoofs. In their blood lust, like carnivores, the animals whinnied and neighed. Already those in the van were on top of the slowest squaws, scattering them to either side. Without pause they galloped onward. None of the riders fired his weapon. None veered to chase down any of the natives. Instead the squad came hurtling on in formation. It soon became clear that their goal was to ride through the ranks of the Indians, herding them together before they could escape into the vast reaches of the alkali plain.

There was a tremendous clatter when the posse reached the runway. With that hard rock beneath them, the horses leaped ahead. Now their hoofs, or perhaps it was the metal shoes upon them, struck sparks against the basalt. To the Indians they were pursuing, it must have seemed that a vengeful god was scattering thunder and lightning in his wrath. However fearful this apparition, the few fleet braves who had not yet been overcome continued their flight. More's the pity for them: at that moment an even more terrible phantom came bearing down upon them out of the north. Casting a huge cloud behind it, shooting rays of light out the front, and with what looked like a winged spirit sitting atop, this chariot descended at three and four times the velocity of the swiftest stallion. At the sight, even the most courageous of the natives halted, as if bewitched. We spectators, white men, sophisticated people, also stood appalled. It was Manfred Granite who broke the spell.

"Son-of-a-bitch! It's Von B!"

The director, for indeed it was he, was perched behind the cab of the studio's black Ford truck. His cape flew out behind him like the wings of a bat, and the silvery patch in his hair was like lightning in a cloud-darkened sky. Beside him, manning the camera, was Nakhimovsky. A scaffold with four rows of lights had been set up in the bed of the truck. Their beams seemed to set the very night afire. Gears grinding, engine roaring, the vehicle bounded across the desert, bearing down on the remnants of the Navaho tribe.

A piteous wail broke from the redskins. They turned about in despair. Then they began to walk back over the basalt, until the soles of their feet became caked with the blood of those who littered their path. The horsemen had lined up in formation behind them. Their mere presence prodded the braves to move steadily ahead. If it had occurred to any of these survivors to dash forward and once more scale the crater's rim, the miners who remained perched upon it, weapons drawn, must surely have dissuaded them. Instead they walked without a sound until they came to the base of that wall. There they spread out in a line. The truck moved forward, so that the glare of its lights fell full upon them. Some of the savages wore no clothing, not even a breechcloth; they covered their genitals with their hands.

Now the horses deployed in a line before the row of prisoners. The riders shouldered their rifles. They aimed them at the Indians' hearts and the Indians' heads. The men atop the embankment pointed their weapons downward. There was a brief moment of silence. Even the horses, who had been so agitated, so full of fury, made no sound. Then, from my mouth, spontaneously, came a cry: the single word *No!*

In unison all the weapons erupted. A sheet of flame passed along the line of horsemen. Briefly, a cloud of gunsmoke obscured the whole scene from view. When it lifted all the Indians were on the ground. For a moment it seemed they were alive; but that was because the flies, moving across their bodies, gave the illusion of motion. In the moonlight they glittered like glass, like blue-and-green sea glass. They were already at their feast.

The horsemen, looking on, got off their mounts. They walked along the line of execution, occasionally firing. Now the miners atop the ridge moved down to the desert floor. They fanned out among the Indians. Now and then there was a flash from their guns, a single report, as they administered to the last moaning victims the coup de grace.

Among our group in the desert, someone had started to sob. It was the refugee Flatow. With his handcuffed hands he attempted to wipe the tears from his eyes.

"Quiet," hissed Manfred. "The cameras are rolling."

But the elderly Viennese only sobbed the more. With a wail he cried, "They've killed them!"

Blowen said, "What do you mean?"

Now Takashima, troubled, once more sniffed the air. He narrowed his almond-shaped eyes. "Yes, yes. I should have known it. There! There again! Can't you detect the smell?"

We all raised our heads. The coroner was right: the unmistakable stench of gore came floating toward us on the steady breeze.

"Oh, no! Oh, my God! Can it be?" That was Lester Kahn. Pleadingly, he addressed those words to Manfred Granite. But the president of the studio stood stunned. His head, instead of turning its usual red, had gone ghastly pale, as if all the blood had drained from it in a single stroke.

"Lord Jesus, they've done it!" said Schotter. "They've slaughtered them all."

Blowen turned to the shaken marshals. "Fellows, we've got a job to do. Get the machine guns. We've got to save who we can."

However, before any of the lawmen could respond, Rochelle Hudson said, "Don't move! Any of you. If you do, I'll shoot."

To the astonishment of all, she had a gun in her hand. Its barrel poked out from under the lip of her open purse.

"What the devil—?" said Blowen.

But she had him covered, too. "You heard what Manfred said. The cameras are rolling. We're going to wait here. Understand? We're not going to say anything or do anything until Rudolph Von Beckmann says the word *Cut!*"

Instinctively we all turned toward the great director. He was still in the bed of the Ford, which had been moved up to the near edge of the landing strip. With both elbows he leaned on the roof of the cab. He was staring intently at the crater's rim. Of course our little band, no less captives now, followed his gaze. Yet another white man was coming over the top. No. Not a white man. This person had long dark hair and was wearing a full-length pleated skirt.

"Valentina," I whispered.

Miss Hudson frowned. "Annie," she said.

The girl made her way down the incline. Looking neither left nor right, she began to walk through the scene of carnage. The lights from the Ford fell full upon her. The lens of the camera, subtly altering, kept her in constant focus. On she came, the sand shedding from her sandals. She reached the runway and moved across it, so that those same slippers made a slapping noise. She did not pause until she reached the body of her father. There she knelt. From the folds of her gown she removed what at the distance appeared to be a clear glass bottle. She upended it over the dead man. A few drops of water came out, spilling ineffectually over the dried-out corpse. Then, with a crashing sound, more startling to us than any of the gunshots, she hurled the empty vessel to the basalt. It shattered. With one hand she parted the black hair that had hidden her features. With the other she cut it, using a shard of glass. The locks came raining down.

What could we think but that the girl had gone mad? She cut and methodically cut. I could not imagine what she was thinking. Was it of the drive she had taken with her father? Of the game they had played or the conversation they'd had? *Burma Shave!* That's what they had cried out together. Then we had rolled over a snake. It was she who had told us how the Roman soldiers had made a desert and called it peace.

Now the last of her tresses were gone. They lay lightly upon Victor's form. With her bald poll she leaned forward and embraced him, his poor hat, his poor head, his shriveled body.

Von Beckman did not say the word *Cut!* He said the word *Cease.*

SHOOTING STARS

"My heroes! My darlings! How I feel for you! On the verge of victory, to be stricken by dire calamity. How you suffer! Poor creatures. Poor wretches. After all our sacrifice, the days and nights we have spent in the desert: like the Hebrews wandering the wilderness for forty years. Yet are we to have no promised land? No milk and honey? Where are the fruits of our labor? The rewards for our toil? Is the prize to be snatched from us just when it lies within our grasp? I can hardly speak; that is how deeply your anguish—oh, I hear your labored breath, I see your pale faces: yes, how it pierces my heart.

"My audience! My army! Let us think of the worst torture that can be inflicted on man. The rack? Wooden splinters driven under the nails? They say the Germans hang people on hooks, like sausages. Jews, probably. Inverts. Also gypsies. In Berlin, in Bavaria, they like their sausages. They eat them with steins of beer. Think of England. Merry old England, ha-ha-ha! There they tied people between horses, which they whipped off to the four points of the compass. And what of Arabian horses? In those deserts they bury a man up to his neck and then charge upon him with their foamy-mouthed steeds. They want to see who, with his shining sword, can cut off the head. Or was that the pampas? In Argentina? Or the fierce Apaches in our own desert sands? No, no, forgive an old man his error. The tricks in his mind. These are fierce Berber tribesmen. Close your eyes. Can you see it? They are playing a game, a game like polo, with that scrap of a ball."

Rudolph Von Beckmann was seated atop the manmade mountain, the pile of earth and quartz that loomed above the entrance to the Pandaemonium mine. All the actors and extras, the members of the crew, were sprawled out beneath him. Even in the predawn darkness it was possible to see how they were spattered, the lot of them, with blood. The cuffs of their pants were soaked through with it, as if they had waded through a sticky stream. They did not remove their eyes from the director, who suddenly started to laugh.

"How loyal you are, my sweet soldiers! Ha-ha-ha! Devoted as dogs. The look of adoration on your faces! Forgive me: I do not mean to laugh. How can you worship Von Beckmann when he suffers, my darlings, no less than you? Did you think I was a god? I am just a poor old man. My tongue, it's like your tongues. Swollen. Blackened. A thick rag on which I choke. I know only what you do—that the worst torture is thirst.

"Now I will tell you a story, a bedtime story for my loyal little children. It is about a man who suffered, and they say suffers still, from the worst thirst of all. Do you know who this is? What? Not one of you? Ignorant! Ignorant fools! This is Tantalus. King of Lydia. What a terrible punishment he had to endure. And all because he wanted to test the gods. He could not stand the fact that they were omniscient. Know-it-alls! Intolerable! Unbearable! A man can hardly think in their presence. *Then let them guess*—this is what King Tantalus said to himself—*what I shall serve them for dinner.*

"Do you believe in miracles? Do you, my dears? Perhaps one shall occur. Then we shall live to work together another day. This is the scene we shall stage: *The Banquet of Tantalus!* Enter the gods, naked males, naked females. Look, they seat themselves at a single long table. They laugh. They boast. They tell their silly jokes. A touch of vulgarity, of drunkenness even, as they slosh down their goblets of wine. From stage right, enter four servants; see how they stagger under the weight of their sizzling pot. Two more servants, stage left: they are the ones who remove the iron lid. Sudden silence. Absolute silence. Not a sigh. Not a snicker. Not a word. The gods lean forward. They stare at the tender white pieces of meat. Well, after all, there is one wee sound. It is the smack-smack-smack of a pair of greasy lips. Women's lips. Demeter is chewing absentmindedly upon the bone, the gristle, the flesh. With what horror does she realize—too late! Too late!—that she has eaten the shoulder of Pelops, her host's dismembered son."

A murmur, a moan, went up from the assemblage below. Von Beckmann held up his hand. "*It's an outrage! A disgrace! How could such a thing happen?* Oh, Von Beckmann knows your thoughts. Every little fear. Each puny desire. He lives inside your heads. Maybe *he* is the one who is omniscient, ha-ha-ha! No need to worry: the great god Zeus demands that every such deed be punished and that the good always triumph. He is as powerful as Mr. Breen, ha-ha-ha! In the office of Mr. Hays! Thus in his fury he condemns Tantalus to the realm of Hades. If the gods smile upon us, perhaps we shall be allowed to stage that scene as well. The place is Tartaros, in the furthest region of hell. As far from earth, some say, as the earth itself is from the heavens. Overhead is a cloud that makes the spot three times darker than darkest night. Black rays come out of it, as in the etchings of Rembrandt; here is darkness made visible, the very goal we seek in our art of film.

"Now, at the very center of those dismal shades, we find the dethroned king. Woe to the man who would deceive the gods! He stands in a pool of water that comes up to his chin. But whenever he attempts to relieve his excruciating thirst, a thirst greater even than ours, the water recedes below the lapping level of his blistered tongue. Poor Tantalus! Look above him! Just above! There are fruit trees, pear, plum, and peach, yet each time he strains upward to seize the branches, they are tossed out of reach by the wind."

Another moan went up from the gathering below. At the sound a sad smile, a smile's shadow, crossed the impresario's lips. "Hush, children. I know what you want to say. *Thirstier than we? That's not possible! A spot lonelier and darker than this? That's impossible, too. No one suffers the way we do.* But remember: Tantalus must undergo his punishment not for a year, or ten years, or even a lifetime. Torture without end! An eternity! Longer even than *Gone With the Wind!* Selznick! They call him an artist! And Goldwyn! The glovemaker! Those Warner brothers! That Harry! The ridiculous Jack! Well, you must forgive my own tiny torments. Everything will be over soon, so very soon. How much longer can we survive without water? Another day, dear ones? A half-day? Look up! That black sky will soon grow bright. The sun will rise in less than an hour. Where are our enemies of the air? Where those winged legions? They are only waiting for enough light to land. Before we know it, they will descend upon us. They will rip us to pieces, the way vultures tore at the entrails of Tityus, the giant, or the way eagles pecked at the liver of Prometheus for thirty thousand years.

"Look. A tear is running from my eye. It is upon my cheek. Can you see it, in the light of this moon? I believe it is the last tear left in that dried-up pool. *Why is he weeping? For Tantalus? For Prometheus? What do we care for the Greeks?* Are those your thoughts? My foolish warriors, don't you know that I weep only for you? For you are right. You have been right all along. Your sufferings *are* greater than those of the ancients. These gods and demigods, and those exalted humans—all have become immortal in legend and drama and myth. Prometheus is honored by all mankind. Did he not bring us fire? Did he not teach us the use of plants? How to tame horses and cultivate the soil? For all his sufferings, there is sweetness in being revered as the benefactor of the race of man.

"And we? We little band of artists? We too have bestowed a gift on our people. We have attacked the German tyrant. We have exposed him for all the world to see. Millions will be saved from his yoke through our efforts. And what is our reward? Rebuke, misunderstanding, and the rage of the very folk we wished to save. Small minds! Incapable of gratitude! That is why the tears—oh, see, they come now in a torrent—spring to my eyes. To labor in vain! Without appreciation. Without acknowledgment from the world. That takes toughness! Toughness! Greatness, even. Yes, that is the worst suffering that can be inflicted upon a man!"

Indeed the tears were streaming across Von B's sallow, faded cheeks. His shoulders shook. From side to side he swayed. In the crowd someone stood. It was Vincent, the youthful stand-in. The oxygen tank was in his arms. "No, no," the director declared. "Von Beckmann does not need oxygen. He does not breathe ordinary air. And neither shall his children. Come, friends! Come, colleagues! Let us go under ground. There we shall inhale flame and sulfur. We shall finish our task beneath the crust of the earth!"

In the exhausted army, no one stirred. With their empty, unblinking eyes and the caked blood on their clothing, they looked like nothing so much as corpses after a battle.

"Up!" shouted Von Beckmann. "Awake! Arise! We must complete our work!"

Again, not a soul stirred. The impresario's mouth twisted in a ghastly grin. "So," he said, but not loudly; these words were for himself. "My power is at an end. I am to be betrayed after all."

Was it true? Had the great Von B lost his iron grip on his men? The truth was, what he faced from his followers was not rebellion so much as sheer weariness and all-consuming thirst. Both were the result of that night's exertions. As soon as the attack, scene 101, had been completed, everyone— the parched actors, the drained crew members, even the trembling Dr. Mosk—had straggled back to the silent pump. The thrill of the chase was over. Now they held up their empty canteens.

"All right," Mike Meltsner had shouted to the mechanics. "Start the machinery."

Almost at once they'd heard the usual hiss, the rumble from the rising weights, and then the welcome clang as the pile driver released the drill into the ground. But those familiar sounds were not repeated. Instead there was a loud crack, as if Liz's clapboard had been amplified a hundredfold. The bit, when it was hauled from its shaft, proved to have melted; the rod above it had split in two. The heat radiating from the jagged iron kept the stunned men at bay. From the empty well a reddish light played up into the pitch-black sky, as if a piece of the hot metal had broken off and lodged in the earth—or, more frighteningly, as if the meteor, still molten at its core, were about to be exposed.

The actors in their blood-soaked boots, the grips and gaffers, then made a dash for the tin-topped shed. The cistern inside was practically empty. Nonetheless the men, and the women among them, too, tumbled into it. They gripped each other by the throat. They thrust their knees into one another's groin. They fought for the last hot drops of water.

"Stop it!" That was a woman's cry. "Stop!"

Stop they did. They turned to watch as a figure materialized out of the night. With her lipstick smeared, her hair in a tangle, Rochelle Hudson strode toward them.

Chick Chandler stood. He started forward to greet her. But he soon came to a halt. "What's that, Rochelle?" he asked. "Is it a gun?"

The actress nodded. "And I know how to use it."

Just then Burton Granite came running from the center of the town. "Hurry, everyone!" he shouted. "Rudi's waiting at the mine. He wants us. We're behind schedule. Where's Coco? Where's Meltsner? Come on, people! To the shaft! We have to start 102!"

Rochelle held her weapon threateningly at the end of her outstretched arm. "You heard him. That's my big scene. No one can take it away from me."

But not one of her coworkers responded. They sat or they stood, blinking their lusterless eyes. Then, at the edge of the crowd, a thin, dark-skinned boy began to sneak off in the direction of the mine. His shoulders were narrow and his skull, bent low on his chest, was shaven. From that bald scalp only a few black hairs stuck out. "Look!" cried Ellie, the costume maker. "It's an Indian!"

"He escaped!"

"Get him!"

"It's a witness!"

The lone survivor of the tribe halted. He turned to face his pursuers. "Didn't you hear?" said the brave. "Rudi wants us."

It wasn't a Navaho. It was Valentina. Once more the child turned and made her way slowly down Main Street. Without a sound, as if they were following what the girl had mistakenly called the Pied Piper of Harlem, they trudged along in her wake.

High on the mound of tailings, Von Beckmann continued to stare down at his disciples. It was not their faintheartedness, their failure to respond, that had made him pause. It was, coursing unexpectedly through his veins like a shot of alcohol, a sudden surge of pity. They lay before him, these men and women, like a pile of broken sticks. They had proven unworthy. For all their suffering, they would not enter *Das Gelobtes Land.* Then why not release them? He knew he had only to say, *You are free, my darlings,* and they would wake at once from their trance. *Run!* That's what they needed to hear. *Run for your lives!* In an instant they would scatter to the winds. Should he do it? Did he dare? He snorted, perplexed by his own indecision. Was he himself suffering from the lack of water? His head, usually so large and heavy, felt as detached from his broad shoulders as Victor's was from his narrow ones.

Then, at the eastern horizon, Von Beckmann saw that dawn was about to arrive. A pale streak of light hung horizontally in the sky, like the cylinder of a cigarette wreathed by the dark clouds of its smoke. That, not water, not oxygen, was what he needed. From beneath his cape the director withdrew his Virginias. Only one left in the gleaming gold case. He replaced it as, a hundred million miles away, the sun flared like the useless tip of a match.

"My dears," said Von Beckmann, "do you see how the sun struggles to rise? There are scholars who say that Tantalus was not a real person but merely a symbol of that heavenly orb. Do you remember those fruits, the plums, the pears, that perpetually escaped his grasp? Supposedly these are the stars that fade as the sun rises toward them. Think of that pool of water, which never failed to ebb as he stooped to drink it. Could this be the sea, which that same sun, licking with the hot rays of its tongue, shrinks through evaporation?"

He paused, not for rhetorical effect but because it was becoming more difficult to speak. His mouth felt as if it were padded with surgical cotton. "Anthropologists! Big thinkers! But even though they scorn the gods—and they, too, must beware of retribution—they have stumbled upon a greater truth than they ever dreamed. For it is not only Tantalus who rises into the sky. The heavens are filled with his descendants."

Was Von B mistaken? Or were his tired troops more alert? They seemed, in their attentiveness, hardly to breathe. The only sound he could hear was the faint rattle of Coco's respiration. "You have heard, my dears, the fate of poor Pelops, slain by Tantalus, his cruel father. But there is more to our story. At the command of Zeus, this child was reborn. Hermes collected the pieces of his body and boiled them once more in the bronze dinner pot. Clotho sewed them together, as if she were making one of her dolls. Rhea, consort of Kronos, gave him the breath of life. How splendid now, the living boy! So splendid that Poseidon, wild with desire, brought him back to Olympus in a chariot drawn by golden horses. The gap in his back, where Demeter had eaten his shoulder, was filled by a new blade of ivory. To Poseidon, and indeed to all who saw him, this gleaming prosthesis made him even lovelier. Not only that, but it possessed magical powers. How it dazzled the eye! All who saw it came under its spell. One had only to touch it and one was healed of every complaint. Such witchcraft! Such wizardry! And it is said that this single white mark, the magic talisman, was passed on to each of Pelops's twenty-three children—to Atreus, Thyestes, and to poor Chrysippos, who was so beautiful that like his father, he was abducted by a houseguest with a fondness for just such youths. This guest was Laius, father of Oedipus, grandfather of Antigone. Yes. Our own Antigone. Now we know why the maiden must die. Distantly, it was because of the crime of Tantalus, who served a feast of his own son's parts. More nearly, it was because of the curse which that son, Pelops, placed on Laius, because the head of that unhappy family had stolen his most beautiful child. That is why we, too, have no choice. We must, we will, bring the drama to its end today.

"What? Do you lack courage? Do you lack faith? Are your limbs weak? But nothing can stop us. Remember, the mark of ivory was passed on not only to the children of Pelops but to their children as well—and yet on, from descendant to descendant, to Iphigenia and Electra and Orestes; and further still, from generation to generation, until the present day. Look to the east. Do you see the bar of light in the clouds? Now look here: is it not reflected in the hair of Von Beckmann?"

There was, at this sacrilege, a gasp from the crowd. Their leader had just declared himself to be a god.

"Perhaps you doubt? You do not believe my power exists? The sky is filled with the descendants of Pelops. Do you see? I am calling them down upon you. There! There! Look! See!"

Everyone stared up to where Von Beckmann was pointing. In the west, which was the darkest part of the firmament, the sky was suddenly filled with shooting stars. Down they came in a series of dazzling lights. There could be no doubt: these meteors, dancing in the sky, spiraling and whirling, were moving toward Pandaemonium. It was almost as if the rock that still sizzled beneath them, the piece of the buried star, were pulling, through some force of affinity, or the invisible waves of gravitation, those heavenly bodies to earth.

The ragged army got to its feet. Each one gazed upward in awe. Von Beckmann remained unmoving, unblinking, without a further word. He seemed to be petrified, as if the proof of his own prophecy had turned him, like a figure in ancient mythology, to stone.

At that moment someone moved from the edge of the workers and started to climb the mound of quartz. Everyone saw it was Magdalena Mezaray. She turned to address them.

"Why do you stand here? Von B is speaking to you. Don't you hear him? *Are you men? Or are you nigger zombies? To work! To work! The time has come to act!*"

Still the crowd stood mute. They continued to stare upward like so many dumbstruck children.

"Fools!" shouted Magda. "Do you think those are heavenly lights? A shower of stars? It's the enemy! Those are the lamps of airplanes! The fires from their engines! Each one is filled with the squadrons of our foe. Quick! Under ground! We haven't a moment to lose!"

At last a movement, a ripple of attention, went through the actors. The grips, the gaffers, began to stir. Burton ran toward the entrance of the mine. He kicked through the broken slats. "Maynes! Start up the lights! Coco! You're head of the second unit. Get down the shaft. Set up next to the cage. Where's Valentina? Are you sure of your lines? Chick! Hurry! Get into costume. Rochelle! Comb out your hair! Gloria! Do something with her face— and Ellie, Ellie! Get her out of that dress! Meltsner! Meltsner! Nakhimovsky! Lizzie! Everybody, to your places!"

The spell was broken, indeed. All the filmworkers took one last look at where the lights, already lower, were describing a vast semicircle over the town; then, like bees funneling into the door of their hive, they flew off to the mine of Pandaemonium.

Von Beckmann remained alone atop his little mountain. Magdalena called to him. "Rudi. Come. They can't begin without you." When the director paid no heed, she continued up the incline; she set off little avalanches of quartzite, white rocks and white pebbles, beneath her heels. Finally she squatted beside him on the jagged crest. For a moment they sat together, looking toward where the sun was bulging upward in the east. In this first light everything cast a shade: the machinery atop the mine, the hill they sat on, their own huddled bodies. Every stone had its shadow attached, like—it was the ex-shopgirl who had this thought—a price tag. Von B gazed at where the band of light had turned a dull gray, shot through with scarlet threads. It looked—this was his thought—like a tourniquet over a wound.

Magda leaned against him. She said, "Do you know why I returned? Rudi, do you? No, no, I don't mean to America. And I don't mean to Salzburg. I mean Vienna. After the interview. To the bridal suite."

Von Beckmann took a breath, a deep one. But he did not say a word.

"Oh, I know what you told me. And I don't doubt you believed it. It would only be for an hour. And then we would have our permits. We would fly to Paris that night. But I was smarter than you were. I assumed they had tricked you. Do you remember that staircase, Rudi? Do you? I counted on my way up. Sixty-five steps. Each of them creamy marble. So pretty. So smooth. I knew I would not walk down them that night—or any night soon. Oh, not for years!"

Again, all that Von Beckmann produced was a sigh.

"Don't be sad, darling. I had my reward. That kiss—a poisoned kiss, you called it. And I knew what awaited me. Remember, I'd met Herr Hitler before I first left for Hollywood. He flirted. He fawned. His eyes, that's what struck me. They were pale, and he would narrow them and expand them, forcing them toward me, the way some animals protrude their eyes at the end of a stalk. I thought then of testicles, with that crude peasant's nose hanging down. I knew he would be at the Metropol. I knew all along he was waiting upstairs. Why did I go? Why shouldn't I? Without you, I was only the silly little model you found in Berlin. With not a scrap of talent. But if you could escape, I knew you would make a film. Oh, not any film, but a great and important work of art. The greatest since the invention of motion pictures. I even knew it would be the *Antigone.* And you have! You have! I was a prophetess. A Greek! I could foresee it!"

A sound, a rumble, came from Von Beckmann's chest. His lips, vertically split, caked with dried blood, stretched in a smile. Was he laughing? So Magda assumed. "I know," she said, "why you laugh. You think you made the picture not to save the Jews or expose Herr Hitler. No, with all of its cost, in dollars, in suffering, in human lives, it was to win my freedom. I appreciate the gesture, my darling. I also appreciate the joke. When you finally succeeded, and when at last I arrived, it turned out I could no longer act. Yes: not a good goddamn! Amusing. Quite amusing. But, my dearest Rudi, my darling Rudi, my only love: I will show you that you are mistaken."

Gaily, girlishly, she reached out and snatched, from her mentor's buttonhole, his dried-out flower. Then she stood, holding up the ragged bouquet. *"There's rosemary,"* she said. *"That's for remembrance; pray, love, remember.* She took a step downward, toward the entrance to the mine. When she turned, her eyes were wide. A flush was on her cheeks. Her upper lip was as full, as puffed, as the lower. *"And there is pansies, that's for thoughts."* She beckoned toward the impresario. Her nostrils were flared. One of her small breasts had spilled from the front of her blouse. *"There's fennel for you, and columbines."*

Von Beckmann rose. He staggered after her. She retreated toward the front of the mine. When she spoke again, holding out the bedraggled nettle, her words were in the lilting voice of a girl:

> *There's rue for you, and here's some for me; we may call it herb of grace o' Sundays. O, you must wear your rue with a difference. There's a daisy. I would give you some violets, but they wither'd all when my father died. They say he made a good end—*

She halted at the low portal to the underground works. Then, with a last, lascivious laugh—*"For bonny sweet Robin is all my joy"*—she disappeared inside.

Sliding and stumbling, Von B went after; but he did not enter the mine. Instead, he halted. He looked about, first at the half-risen sun, then toward every point of the compass. Dots of light were dancing before his eyes. He blinked, as if that action might make them go away. But the lights drew still nearer. He counted two of them, then four, then six. Even as he watched, the dots took on shape; they sprouted wings. The sunlight darted off them as if from silver. Then he heard a distant drone. He knew what that was: the relentless buzz of the Furies. The vultures, with their shining claws, were about to descend.

CHAPTER
F I V E

LAST CIGARETTE

Inside the Pandaemonium mine the temperature did not drop at night, the way it did at the surface. The air, in which the quartz dust swayed, remained as thick as that in a jungle. Saplike dew coated every surface. From the depths of the shaft yellowish rays came shooting upward, the way phosphorescence might from a beaker of radium. The cables for those lights slithered across the ground, then plunged into the maw of the pit. Magda and Von Beckmann followed them until they arrived at the open chasm. The blaze of light, they saw, came from two levels down. They could just make out, even further below, the shadow of the lift. For all the damp heat, Magda shivered.

"Thank God you replaced me. Valentina will have to go into the cage."

Von B did not reply. He, too, was staring into the shaft, leaning well over the edge so as to listen to the general hullabaloo—the hammering, the amplified thud of men's boots, a constant high-pitched squeaking—that rose from the depths. When he straightened, the lens of his monocle was slick with condensation. Then he swirled the ends of his cape and, still without a word, gripped the iron ladder. He took the first of a hundred steps down the side of the shaft.

On the second level, the cast and crew were racing to complete their tasks. The gaffers were adjusting their filters. Rochelle Hudson stood motionless while Nakhimovsky's assistant ran a tape measure to her nose. She kept repeating to herself the lines of Annie's sister: *Now, uncle, bury me beside my sister.* At the same time the tomb of her father, old Harwood, was being stuffed with the fuses that were to light the scene. They hung down from the wall of quartz like threads on the wrong side of a carpet. Valentina sat off to one side. Gloria Umin, with a pair of scissors, was snipping away at the few clumps of hair that remained on her head.

Deeper down, at the fourth level, Coco Goodheart was at work with the second unit. His men shouted back and forth across the square chasm. Most of the actors, the nameless extras, faceless townsfolk and miners, had deployed themselves either on the rungs of the ladder or on the special boards that had been set horizontally into the timbered sides of the shaft. Even at that late moment the grips were hammering the last of these planks into place. Amazing how all these men and women, so limp and lethargic aboveground, had thrown themselves into their myriad tasks. It was almost as if the humidity of the atmosphere had revived them, the way only a little water, or the spray from an atomizer, will cause dried-out plants to spring back to life.

"Quiet! Quiet, everybody." That was Mike Meltsner, shouting through his hands. "Pass the word to Coco."

The anonymous extra near the top of the human chain that led from level two to level four bent toward the man below him. But there was no need to repeat the command. That actor—in point of fact, not an actor but Kuttner, the guard from the gate in the crater's rim—had fallen silent on his own. All along the line the chatter ceased. So did the hammering. On top of the lift a man with an oil can squirted its contents onto the hook and hasp, so that the cage, in its elastic movements, would not creak. Then he too raised his eyes to where Von Beckmann, with his cape unfurled from the updraft, was making his batlike way down the ladder's rungs.

Even before the director reached the second level, Nakhimovsky stood up from the viewfinder. He ran his hand through his thick mop of hair and nodded toward his assistant. That man flipped open a lighter and started to ignite the rattail fuses. The ropes twisted about like snakes, they hissed like snakes, too. Now Von Beckmann strode forward. He stood with his arms crossed over his chest. Quickly Rochelle and Valentina moved to their marks. Liz stepped in front of the camera lens. She held up the chalkboard. Meltsner called out, "Is everyone ready? Sound ready?" Deep in the tunnel, Kleinbard took off his earphones and raised his thumbs.

Gloria Umin ran over to Von B. Quickly she combed a shock of hair over half of his forehead. Ellie removed his cape and pinned on his badge. Now the impresario opened his mouth. He pointed toward his throat.

Meltsner: "Where's the doctor? Somebody call Mosk."

Leo Gorcey said, "These are half-hour fuses. We don't have time for dry throats."

But already Dick Mosk was trotting along the railway tracks that emerged from the rear of the tunnel. Everyone saw that he was holding a canvas-covered canteen.

Burton called to him, "Hurry. Hurry. Give him what he needs."

Mosk unscrewed the top to the vessel and poured the water—it could not have been more than a thimbleful—into it. Von B seized the cap and upended its contents into his mouth. For a moment he held the liquid there, as if it were ambrosia. Then he swallowed it down in a gulp.

Meltsner: "Quiet! Quiet on both sets! We're ready to shoot. And action!"

Lizzie brought the clapper down on the slate that read *Scene 102*. Then she stared through her fogged glasses at Von Beckmann. Everyone else stared at him, too. He did not utter a word. The only sound was the hiss of the writhing fuses.

Then Magdalena stepped forward. This time it was she who shouted *Action*.

Once again Von Beckmann opened his mouth to speak. But it wasn't his voice that came out. It was that of the sheriff.

No more tears.

At once Annie responded: *You've seen none from me.*

Clayton: *Better for you if you covered your brother with those drops instead of forbidden water. Better, too, for all those who suffer in our town.*

The miners, offscreen: *She caused the drought! The horses are dying. The mine has come to a stop. We have nothing to drink.*

Clayton: *Well, my niece, do you hear the judgment of our people?*

Annie: *I spilled only a cup of water. You have drenched our land in blood.*

Clayton: *Enough! Since you are so eager to perform rites of burial, you can exercise them on yourself. Deputies! Take her to the cage!*

Before anyone could react, Rochelle Hudson stepped forward for her big scene. She seized her uncle's outstretched arm and, with her free hand, held up an unsheathed knife.

Irene: *Have no fear. It is not your throat I will cut. Look at my sister. This night she was to wed your son. Now, without her locks and curls, she is more beautiful than she would be on her bridal bed. I too wish to see, in my looking glass, the beauty that comes from courage.*

Clayton: *You are as mad as your sister!*

Irene: *Now I shall be as beautiful.*

With one downward slash of the knife, the Queen B cut through her trademark tresses. *Now, uncle, bury me beside my sister.*

Clayton: *Your fate, Irene, will be to live without her. Take only the criminal away.*

At that, four deputies came forward and dragged Annie toward the lip of the shaft. The camera, using the old mining rails, dollied behind her.

No one said *Cut.* This scene, too, would be done in one long, unbroken take. Now Coco's camera started to roll, along with that of Nakhimovsky. The klieg lights shone up at Annie from a hundred feet below. There was no double; it was Victor's daughter who was being passed hand to hand down the length of the shaft. *Lock her up!* cried the miners. *Put her away!* In the dim light it looked as if she were in the grasp of some mythical creature, an arachnid of enormous proportions, which was turning a still-living insect this way and that in its many arms. At the bottom the men thrust her into the lift. The door clanged shut, like the bars on a cell.

Annie, in a muffled cry: *Is this my home? Neither on the earth nor beneath it? Poor Annie! No longer living but not yet dead.*

That tiny voice floated upward a hundred feet to where Chick Chandler stood, shining with mica. The fool's gold made him look like a knight in armor. He confronted the sheriff.

Raymond: *What have you done, my foolish father? A brave man will not fight against a helpless girl.*

Clayton: *And an obedient son does not question his father. I would rather give up my power than be ruled by a woman.*

Raymond: *No woman caused the calamities that afflict us. It is you and your stubbornness who have brought war and drought.*

Clayton: *By curbing our enemies? By making the laws that are the only hope for our town? That allow it to live?*

Raymond: *No town can live by your laws. You are fit only to be monarch of the desert.*

The sheriff turned toward his deputies. He screamed out his next command: *Guards! Take him away. Let the bridegroom die with the bride.*

Raymond: *You cannot punish me. You will never, in this world, see my face again.*

With that, Chick Chandler whirled about and flew by the men who stood near the hissing fuses. They pursued him between the old iron rails. Nakhimovsky panned in a semicircle to keep the chase in frame.

Clayton: *Stop him! Block the ladder!*

It was not the ladder his son sought now. Dashing ahead, leaping over the ties, he made straight for the shaft, out of which hands, in pairs, like the disembodied limbs of a magician, rose to block the way. At that obstruction the young man neither swerved nor slacked his pace. If anything he sped along even faster, until, gathering the force of his own momentum beneath him, he hurtled into the air, over those who sought to restrain him, and down the endless chasm.

Ah! He's killed himself!

But for the moment that was not his goal, either. The handsome male lead caught the steel cable that ran down the center of the shaft. It whined. It made a terrible twang. As beautiful, with his gold-flecked hair, as the legendary Chrysippos, he slid down the well. The sharp threads of metal that protruded from the loosely woven strand ripped the skin from his hands and flayed the flesh from his body. There was a distinct sound, like the patter of rain. Even the grips, the technicians standing about, raised their heads to listen. On the fourth level Coco zoomed in for a closeup of the blood that splashed down on the tin top of the cage. Then Raymond himself collapsed upon the roof. Annie's hand reached upward, through the bars. Her bridegroom stretched his hand down. In that closeup their fingers did not, and never would, meet. The steam from the sump below them swirled through the pitiful gap.

Above, on the second level, Nakhimovsky's camera ground on without a halt. The sheriff, eyes wide with apprehension, looked toward the tunnel, from which two figures were emerging.

Clayton: *Who is this old man? And who the boy?*

No one responded. Vincent, the teenager, led a blind man to where the sheriff was standing. Clayton said, *Ah, it is you.*

This was Sampson Frank, without spectacles and with a full fake beard. He was recreating the role of Tiresias, which he had first played at Salzburg.

Old Man: *Prepare yourself, sheriff, for painful words.*

Clayton: *I do not fear an old man's prattle. You have one foot in the grave already.*

Old Man: *And when both feet are in, it were better for you to honor my corpse than to slay so many living.*

Clayton: *Who put you up to this? The girl? Or my wretched son?*

Old Man: *Not so wretched, in but one minute, as his unhappy father.*

At these words, the sheriff seemed shaken. Even Von Beckmann, the actor, appeared taken aback. His eyes seemed to pierce the ancient seer. Was it possible that he saw, beneath the beard and the palsied shaking of the head, the youthful yeshiva student who had challenged him—*by whose authority?*—so long ago; or the embodiment of Moses who had held his hands over the waters of Stettin Bay; or the skinny lad who had starred in the role of Jesus? The prophetic power of all those figures, and of Tiresias too, seemed to be confirmed as the old man put a hand to his ear.

There. I hear it. Your minute is up.

Instantly a horrible cry rang out from the depths of the timbered shaft.

Raymond: *No! No-o-o-o!*

It was answered at once by the chorus of miners: *Ah-h-h-h!*

Clayton: *Heavens! Only fear, not blood, flows in my veins.*

The old man leaned his arm on the shoulder of the boy. *Your trial is only beginning.*

The sheriff now hurried along the same tracks his son had flown across only moments before.

Clayton: *Deputies! Miners! Save them from this fool! Save them from themselves!*

Everyone stepped back to allow the crazed man access to the shaft. Nakhimovsky tracked behind him. Coco aimed his camera up from below. Clayton had reached the ladder. He called out to the bottom of the well:

Tell me! What do you see? I must know.

Miners: *Do not ask! It is a sight for no man's eyes, least of all a father's.*

The anguished man leaned over the chasm.

Clayton: *I beg you! Do not spare me!*

Miners: *Dead!*

She is hanged!

He is stabbed!

And each by his own hand!

What happened next—a thing not written into Flatow's script—made all the men and women under ground gasp aloud. There was a thump, a resounding thud. It didn't seem to come from anywhere inside the mine. Nor did it appear to originate from the surface. If anything—and here the pounding was repeated, louder than before—the sound seem to be traveling through the ground itself. And now a third blow, a boom, came fast upon the others. People held their ears. The earth around them began to throb. It was as if they were trapped inside an enormous drum upon which a drummer was steadily beating.

"What is it?" the extras cried. "What's happening?"

Now, with each blow, clouds of dust, a quartzite wind, rose into the already saturated air. Small pebbles bounded across the various levels, and larger stones, jagged rocks, squirted between the loose timbers and tumbled through the shaft. The stricken actors called out in pain. One man lost his grip upon his trembling wooden plank and fell to the top of the cage below. The others held on for dear life.

Now a figure appeared—not on the second level but even higher, at the very top of the shaft. He was exophthalmic, brachycephalic, and at least 450 upon the Sheldon scale. *En court,* Loewenstein-Lorre. I leaned over the edge of the pit and shouted as forcefully as I could.

"It's the pump! The marshals, the airmen—they have started the pump! You must get out! Get out! They have broken through to the meteor!"

Below me, on the second platform, all was confusion. I picked out, from among the mass of those running here, there, helter-skelter, the ruined curls of Miss Hudson. My next words were directed at her. "It's hopeless, honey! Run for the ladder! Come to me! Come to your Petey!"

I saw her hesitate, stop, look upward. Impossible, at such an angle, to ignore the twin breasts that bubbled like hot-spring geysers beneath her Grecian gown. Then, in obedience to my instructions, she came running toward the ladder. At the same time another woman, it was Miss Umin, was making for the same spot. "Yes! I heard you! I am coming to my man, my Moto!"

Luck was with me! The Queen B arrived first at the rungs and swung herself onto them. "Chickie! Oh, Chickie!" she shouted; then, to my inexpressible horror, she started to climb not up but down. Miss Umin paused only to snatch up the reel of that day's exposed film. Then she too leaped onto the ladder and began to climb toward the upper air.

Those left behind were now frozen with terror. Only Burton seemed to have retained his senses. "Up! Everyone up!" he cried. "We've got to get to the surface!"

Alas, his voice was drowned out by the bedlam within the shaft. A series of fierce shrieks—*Eeeee! Eeeee! Eeeee!*—rose from the timbers, which were being tortured out of plumb. In addition, an ominous hollow clanking came from the elevator cage as, like a tin can being kicked in a game by boys, it banged against alternate sides of the shaft. The whole of that concatenation, still punctuated by the steady reverberations from the distant pump, made it impossible for anyone left on the second level to hear Von Beckman's cry as his legs went out from under him and he sank to the earth.

Magda saw him first. "Rudi!" she cried, running toward him.

Von B, straining, tried to push himself upright. But there seemed to be no strength in his arms. With the back of his hands, he brushed first at his eyes, as if he were still seeing the winged dots swirling in air; and then, more frantically, at his clothing, as if that were where the plague, whether of birds or locusts, had landed. Magda leaned over him. She put her arms under his broad shoulders, his heavy head.

His lips moved. By putting her ear to them she could hear his voice.

"Cigarette," he said.

She groped until, in an inner pocket, she found the case with its sole Virginia. Then she produced a match. "I have it, darling. I've found it."

His thick lips broke into a smile. She placed the white cylinder between them and brought the flame to the tip.

Just then there was a tremendous moan, as if all those caught in the shaft had exhaled together. But this lamentation came from no human voice. Before the astounded eyes of all those at the fourth level, the entire sump drained away, as if a hidden monster had swallowed it in a gulp. What was left—this was worse than any nightmare—was a pit of bones.

Two levels up, Rudi was exhaling a stream of smoke. His lips continued to move around the stick of his cigarette. The words he spoke were not of demons and monsters. They had nothing to do with the Greeks or their gods. Magda, leaning close, could make no sense of the names *Dicker, Frau Dicker,* or *Jungermann,* or the commands, like an admiral's on a ship, that came next: *Northward! Southward! Coolies! Commence!*

In despair she rocked back on her heels. "Help! Help me! He's having an attack!"

From out of the tunnel, Vincent came running. He held the tank filled with oxygen in both of his arms.

In the days to come, no one was able to say precisely what happened next. The only surviving witnesses, Miss Umin and I, got no more than a glimpse of the cataclysm as we went dashing from the top of the mine. All I can report is that there was a tremendous explosion, and that the whole of the shaft was filled by a ball of fire. How could such a thing happen? It is not inconceivable that a tongue of flame or molten metal had traveled underground from the site of the pump and into the open crevice at the bottom of the mine. It is also possible that the tubes of fake dynamite attached to the sputtering fuses had been mistakenly filled with genuine powder. Such accidents, in Granite productions, had been known to happen. We cannot even rule out sabotage on the part of the Axis or its powerful ally, W. R. Hearst. But it seems most likely that Vincent, in his anxiety, came running forward and, without thinking, set down his oxygen tank. Magda's eyes would have been fixed on the full face, with its drooping eyes, its trimmed moustache, of the only man she had ever loved.

Rudi himself was concentrating on the face of a sleeping old man. He takes a step toward him. He takes another. Underneath his feet the floor-boards creak. Behind him the little devils giggle and cover their mouths. Blitzer, the rabbi, continues to doze with his chin on his hand. The daring boy strikes a match and lights the candle. Drop after drop of the hot wax falls onto the old man's beard. Rudi, recalling this, laughed aloud. What fun when the rabbi woke up! His beard was going to be stuck to the table.

It was at that instant that Vincent, hardly more than a boy himself, opened the metal cock and forgetfully sent a rush of oxygen toward the great man's glowing cigarette.

PART FIVE

DAYS OF INFAMY

December 1941–June 1942

CHAPTER ONE

HOLLYWOOD MERRY GO ROUND

Mea culpa, as our friends in the Roman Catholic Church say when confessing their sins to a priest. That's how yours truly feels at missing her column these last two weeks. I want to say to the thousands and thousands of readers whose letters have been pouring in from sea to shining sea don't you worry, I'm fit as a fiddle. Just last night George Raft asked me for a fox-trot at Slapsie Maxie's, and we didn't get off the dance floor for almost an hour. George is going out strictly solo these days, proving that he's true to Betty Grable. The truth is that since that terrible accident at the *Pandaemonium* location I have been in a state of shock. Every time I remember that I was down in that very mineshaft—that was when the call of duty sent LOP to the center of the earth in search of the mysterious Magdalena Mezaray—my body starts to tremble so much I can't hold pen to paper. And to think that was the very spot where the great actress lost her life. Many people wonder what the investigators meant when they said that the dust in the mine simply exploded, but I'm an old farm girl from Illinois and know how the same thing can happen in our grain elevators from only the tiniest spark. Yes, the hearts of all Lollywoodians are heavy when they remember the dear friends they lost in this tragedy, but it is the Granite family that has really suffered the afflictions of Job—what with Victor gone and the vibrant Valentina now lost as well. I've heard that in spite of everything Giselle Granite, you'll remember her as Giselle Fontenay, that jade-eyed lovely, is holding up well. I can't imagine what it must be like to lose a child so soon after the death of your husband. It's enough to drive even a teetotaler to drink! The only consolation is that I have it on very good authority that like the tragic heroes they so often brought to life, Magdalena and Rudi Von Beckmann died in each other's arms.

In times like these the best pick-me-up, even better than those delicious manhattans that Dave Chasen always insists on personally delivering to my table at his famous chow house, is to think of the other dear children of dreamtown. For instance, you wouldn't believe how Shirley Temple, only a few years ago a chubby, golden-haired little thing, has lost all that baby fat and grown into a young girl who is lovely, slender, chestnut-haired, and so intelligent. Her mother told me that Shirley, who will be fourteen next April and is a top student at the Crestview School, never has a book out of her hand. I had to rub my eyes when I realized—how tempus does fugit!—that the little girl who used to sit in my lap and talk about the Oz books is now studying French and algebra and history. Those same eyes held a tear or two when, with that famous Temple dimple still in evidence, she told me, "Louella, did you know that whenever I sang 'The Good Ship Lollypop' I never failed to think of my own Lolly?" Now that little lady who only yesterday was hugging a woolly bear to her bosom is deep into the life of Madame Curie!

Burton Granite may have been "one of the boys," but he was also a real whiz with his studio's numbers: gone! Rochelle Hudson, she used to have a pound of platinum in her gorgeous curls: gone too! And Dick Mosk, who had personally given me his famous treatment for hangovers: gone, gone, gone! On a pleasanter note, another former child star, Judy Garland, also has a good head on her shoulders. If you don't believe me, read the *Cosmopolitan* magazine that will come out in February. Judy's got a story there called "My Pal Mickey," which is so good that the managing editor told me she is not changing a word, a comma or a period. It is a wow. What's this I hear about Ginger Rogers being beaued by Lew Ayres? Milton Berle gifted his bride with a diamond bracelet that wide for a wedding present. In a ball of fire! Burned alive! Horrible! Terrible! But there was no way to save them. They say that the new troops who had just arrived at the ghost town location tried to put out the fire with that same studio pump that had kept me tossing all through the night. Too late! Even if they'd managed to pump out all the water in Lake Mead they could not have helped. A hundred human souls, including the fascinating Rudi Von Beckmann, whom I was just starting to call a good friend, had already been burned to a crisp.

If I want to chase these blues I may have to get over to Dave Chasen's after all. I wouldn't mind the sight of one of those toothpicks stacked up with cherries and a slice of orange. I'd do it, too, if tonight I didn't have to attend a really special premiere. By the way, Rex Bell and Clara Bow were in town the other day to do some Christmas shopping at Bullock's. I never believed the "It" girl when she told me she was giving up her career to live on a ranch with Rex, which goes to show how cynical columnists can become. Clara looked so thin and attractive in spite of her greenish makeup. Now that I think of it, how are you doing with your bundles for Santa? Only eighteen days to go! I sure wish Doc Mosk were around to give me some sleeping pills. I keep waking up from horrible dreams. The worst is when I'm back in the mine and all my clothes, including that cute Gibson Girl number I got as a gift from Mervyn Le Roy, are on fire! The way the flames leap around me! It's a nightmare! That motorized torpedo which is such an important "actor" supporting Bud Abbott and Lou Costello in *Keep 'Em Flying* is the brainchild of a former lumberjack, Carl Lee, originally from Fond du Lac, Wis. Carl has designed some of the funniest gadgets in many of our favorite film successes. And my hair is on fire too! Mischa Auer was a legal bachelor for just three minutes between the time he obtained his divorce degree and a license to wed Joyce Hunter. I could see my face melting! Like wax! I looked like Bela Lugosi! Mischa and Joyce were married by Mayor Fiorello La Guardia. Prince Troubetsky was one of the attendants. I screamed loud enough to wake up half Beverly Hills!

I can't decide which of the following two items is the biggest surprise. The first is that married men are starting to hate Merle Oberon, even though she's one of the prettiest gals in town. Seems that ever since the story broke that Merle's best-looking suit was "cut down" from one of Alex Korda's, wives all over the country have been raiding the closets of their lords and masters. The second surprise, maybe "miracle" would be the better word for it, is that the doomed desert production is going to have a second life after all. Gloria Umin, the mistress of makeup, managed to take Rudolph Von Beckmann's last shots out of the inferno. Since then everyone at Granite Films has thrown themselves into the herculean effort of getting the picture ready on time. Les Kahn, who pretty much runs the studio these days, told me that everybody—from the musicians to the boys doing the looping and the titles and the thousand and one other tasks that go into turning a hunk of exposed film into a major motion picture—has been working around the clock to get *Pandaemonium* ready for its world premiere.

It's not just for the fun of it that Bill Powell and his bride go bowling every night, although Mr. P's enthusiasm for the game has inspired him to start a team with Spencer Tracy, George Murphy, and several other M-G-M'ers. Bowling will be a big part of Bill's next opus, *That Was No Lady,* and the star is getting himself in shape to make all his own strikes. In case you haven't guessed it, tonight's eight-o'clock premiere at Grauman's is that same tragic picture that was rescued from the flames. Of course all of filmdom will be there. I'm going to be the date of Manfred Granite, because, as any wardrobe lady will tell you, it's never too late to patch things up. Yes, I'm going to get a grip on the old girl and force myself out of doors. No sense being a fraidy cat and sitting around the house just because of these silly dreams. Those Gabor sisters are sure in a rut. No sooner did word arrive about Eva's separation from Dr. Erich Drimmer than I hear that her redheaded sister Georgia, she's supposed to be the real looker in the family, is estranged from her husband in Budapest. Sometimes I don't even have to wait for night: in broad daylight a ball of fire comes hurtling up the staircase right for me like the wrath of God. I guess every gal goes through a time when she just wishes she was dead. There won't be a single woo-woo from Hugh Herbert when he checks in at Para for his next feature, *Mrs. Wiggs of the Cabbage Patch.* Hugh is definitely through with his comic chortle from here on in because, he says, it typed him—so it's bye-bye to woo-woo as far as he's concerned. I can't be a prisoner inside my own house. Even though these bags under my eyes would scare a redcap, as Georgie Jessel used to joke, I'm going to throw on some rags and get to the premiere, even if I do look a fright. You can bet I'll take my hankie for the tears. Saw Loretta Young snatching a peek at the baby shoes at Orbach's the other day. What do you suppose that means? That's all for today. See you tomorrow!

BLACKOUT

The red carpet was out at Grauman's Chinese. Powerful searchlights beamed up into the December night. Attendants stood by the velvet ropes. Sid Grauman himself, his curly hair spilling from under his top hat, paced below the marquee. He checked his watch: a quarter to eight. Where the hell were they? The showman was not thinking of the crowds, although the hordes of people who lined the streets at every premiere were indeed strangely absent. Only about a dozen people stood about on the sidewalk, and most of them—Manfred Granite in a wheelchair, Giselle Granite on the arm of her colored chauffeur, the solicitous Rabbi Magnin—had invitations. But where was the press? The newspapermen with their pads? The radio correspondent with his microphone on a pole? Even the Sunday night traffic was practically nonexistent: just the odd car moving silently along the boulevard. Grauman, however, had an even larger concern. Here it was fifteen minutes to showtime, and of his major feature—for which he'd paid such unbelievable sums—he hadn't received a foot of film.

Louella—and she was there, in a mink stole and a cherry-colored hat—had been right. It had taken a herculean effort to get *Pandaemonium* ready. Kahn and his crew, along with the marketing and distribution people from Granite, had not had between them a wink of sleep in the last thirty-six hours. All that day, and the previous night, they had been holed up at the Granite offices, trying to arrange the pieces of film into a finished picture. At nineteen minutes to eight they had piled into the studio limousine and taken off for Hollywood and Highland. Luckily, as Grauman had noted, there wasn't another car on the road. Amazing how they could fly up La Brea. Flatow, the rewrite man, hung on to the strap above the back seat. Bernie Fields, the head of marketing, clutched all five reels of the feature in his sinewy arms. At the wheel, the agent Ernie Glickman steered for the spot where the three separate lights crisscrossed the sky with their thousands of candlepower. He skidded to a stop in front of the marquee.

"Sid! Sid!" cried Lester Kahn, leaning out the open window.

Fields got out the side door of the limousine. He handed over the reels to the owner of the theater.

"Where is everybody?" asked Glickman.

But Grauman, the tails of his tuxedo flapping behind him, was already dashing past the rows of plaster dragons into his lobby.

Kahn walked over to where Gloria Umin was pushing her employer back and forth in his wheelchair. "Manny, we did it," said the younger man. "With five minutes to spare."

Manfred looked up into the face of his publicist. He opened his mouth, but instead of words spittle came out. The makeup artist leaned forward and wiped the liquid away. She used the same handkerchief to dab at her eyes. "Now, now, Mr. Granite. We're grownups, aren't we? We don't want to drool like a baby."

Lester, turning, said, "Look, there's Louella." With a big smile he strode toward the columnist.

At the curb a new car pulled up and Albert Basserman, wearing a black ribbon, stepped out. Flatow, who had a black armband, went up to him. "So, we have at last completed our picture."

Basserman shook his head. "Poor Rudi. Poor Sampson Frank."

"Who would have thought," said Flatow, "when it all started that it would end this way?"

"You mean back when the waters first parted? And I was covered with eels? Back in the days when locomotives seemed to come out of the screen? Not me."

Flatow nodded. "And not me."

Just then Les Kahn reached the spot, in front of the glass billboard, where Louella was standing. "Hi, sweetheart," he said by way of greeting.

The columnist turned on him. "You tell him," she said, her breath a mixture of whiskey, bitters, and sweet vermouth. "You tell him how rotten it is to stand a gal up."

"But Manny's here," said Lester. "He came just for you."

"Malarkey!" She glared across unrolled carpet to where the Granite president sat, head lolling, in his wheelchair. "He won't give me the time of day."

"But Lolly, you know he had a stroke."

"Don't kid me, buster," said the columnist. "I know an act when I see it."

Now a large man in a topcoat and tuxedo turned from the billboards. It was the rabbi, Edgar Magnin. "Never mind, Miss Parsons. God works in mysterious ways. Perhaps you would like to see the picture with me?"

On the other side of the marquee a man on crutches approached Victor Granite's widow. "Mrs. Granite? I'm Steve Bernow. At one time I was with the picture. Back when it was called *Mr. Moto Wins His Spurs.* I just wanted to say how sorry I am about how things turned out."

Giselle was leaning on Arthur's arm. She managed a smile. "Thank you, Mr. Bernow. I'm sorry, too, for what happened to you."

A short distance down the street two well-known actors were standing in whatever shadows the giant reflectors allowed. Basserman walked over, making a trio. Laughton nodded. Loewenstein-Lorre sneezed. Look closely: you will see that a trail of white powder crisscrossed his shirtfront.

Nearby, a young man stood with one foot in the roadway, one on the curb. He was a good-looking boy, about seventeen, clean-cut and blond. To Lorre he looked familiar, but he was unable to remember where he had seen him before. For a moment the boy stood, as if trying to come to a decision. Then he moved onto the carpet and followed it under the overhang of the marquee. That's when Arthur, the chauffeur, saw him too. He had no trouble recognizing him. This was the boy who had tried to help Miss Valentina at the funeral. Gerhardt stepped to the box office window. In the whole city of Los Angeles, he was the only person to buy a ticket for the show.

In the shadows, Lorre reached into his pocket for another pinch. He was working up courage to move under the overhead lights to where a tall blonde—the word *statuesque* has been applied to her on another occasion— was standing. Here was his new co-star in *Mr. Moto Meets the Sphinx.* And after that, his co-pilot over Manchuria. *Ah, Miss Brooke. Hillary, honey.* Thus did the actor rehearse a greeting in his mind. *Would you step over here for a moment? Into the shadows?* What ankles she had! What wrists! And the breasts—like the balls that Bill Powell was going to roll for a strike. But just as he made up his mind to approach her, Sid Grauman came out of his theater. He looked over the ten or twelve people on the sidewalk. Seeing Glickman, he said, "Ernie, do you know what I paid for this thing? Where are the people?"

Glickman: "I don't know. It sure looks like a bust."

At that moment another car, a cream-colored Buick, pulled up to the curb. The Epstein boys were in the front seat; they stuck their heads out of their windows.

"Listen, fellows," Julie called. "You've got to turn off those lights."

Phil said, "Don't you know there's a blackout? No lights allowed."

Grauman said, "What are you talking about? This is a premiere."

Julie: "Sid, where have you been?"

Phil: "You mean you haven't heard the news?"

"What news? I've been inside the theater all day."

"It's war," Julie said. "The Japanese have bombed Hawaii."

Phil said, "We're air-raid wardens. You've got to put out those searchlights."

"Ha-ha-ha!" That was Les Kahn. "You guys never stop. Never mind, Sid. It's just one of their gags."

"I should have known. War! Ha! Ha! Ha! You boys could persuade me that night is day. Remember the time you got Adolphe Menjou to save his hair with turpentine and cold cream? He had to rub it on every two hours. Not on his head! Ha! Ha! Ha! On his balls!"

Phil said, "This is no gag. The bombs started falling this morning. You've got to believe us."

"Bombs!" That was Glickman. "This is even better than the time you fooled Jack Warner into hiring your fraternity brother. Do you remember that?"

"Sure," said Kahn. "Jack was desperate for new talent. You guys dressed your Penn State pal in a tweed jacket and said he was this hot new British playwright."

"Right, right! I remember," said Grauman. "He worked on the lot for a month. You told Jack his name was Sherwood Forest!"

Now everybody, including Giselle and Gloria Umin, was laughing. Flatow and Basserman and even black Arthur chortled along with the rest. Only Manfred, from his wheelchair, scowled and glared at the twins.

Julie looked at Phil. "We've got a problem," he said.

His brother said, "And how."

Then Lorre spoke up. "Wait a minute. Wait a minute. You said the Japanese. You said they bombed Hawaii. Is that right?"

"Yes. It was dawn at Pearl Harbor."

"Pearl Harbor! It was the harbor?"

"They came out of the sun. It was a sneak attack!"

Lorre began to sway back and forth. His eyes bugged from his head. "Sneak attack? Sneak attack? On the ships? The ships in the harbor?"

"They sank half the fleet."

"It's true then! My God, it's true! War with Japan!"

Magnin: "Peter! What are you saying? Are you saying that it really happened?"

"Jesus!" Grauman exclaimed. "That explains it. Why there are no crowds. Why there are no cars in the street."

But there was a crowd, after all. From the beginning of this encounter, a number of people had begun to cross the street in the direction of the theater. By now there must have been two or three score of them. Cautiously the two wardens pulled away in their Buick, which allowed the crowd to converge at the curb. They surged forward. They pushed against the plush-covered ropes.

"Are you people crazy, lighting up the sky?"

"You want them Japs to drop one on top of us?"

"Whose side are you on?"

Now the whole crowd was yelling. From out of their midst a stone, or perhaps it was a bottle, crashed against the lit-up marquee.

At that the film people, the guests, moved toward the safety of the lobby. Manfred was wheeled in. Bernow hobbled on his sticks. Hillary Brooke, the new Queen B, took up the rear, casting a last look at Lorre. Only that actor, together with the columnist, remained outside to face the mob. Louella looked into the angry faces. "You mean," she asked, "that a war has broken out and I'm the only one who didn't know?" With that, she broke into tears.

Loewenstein-Lorre, Laszlo, was crying too, but the tears he shed were ones of joy. "Free!" he screamed and jumped so high that the white dust spilled from his pockets into the air. Suddenly, with a hiss, the first of the searchlights went out. More hissing, sizzling, and the others went out as well. Then the hundreds of bulbs winked off inside the marquee. Finally even the lobby fell dark, and the crowd, well satisfied, dispersed. Everything on Hollywood Boulevard was still. Except, that is, for Mr. Peter Lorre. He continued to dance down the middle of the thoroughfare. Like the sandman he scattered his dust in all directions. In a high happy voice he shouted, "At last! At last!"

DECLARATION OF WAR

Four days later, on December 11, the Minister of Propaganda and Public Enlightenment slipped into his chair at the front of the Reichstag. The seating arrangements were almost as they had been at Salzburg during the command performance. Dr. Goebbels looked around, nodding to Bormann and Himmler and Goering and the rest. This time, however, there would be no delay. Briskly the Führer walked through the door on the right and strode to the podium. He stood unsmiling and stern while the deputies, and the minister too, in his special shoes, rose to cheer him. And then, in the hushed hall, he started to speak about America and its leader.

> "Permit me to define my attitude to that other world and its representative, a man who, while our soldiers are fighting in snow and ice, very tactfully likes to make his chats from the fireside.
>
> "This Roosevelt comes from a rich family and belongs to the class whose path is smoothed in the democracies. I was only the child of a small, poor family and had to fight my way upward by industry and work.
>
> "National Socialism came to power in Germany in the same year that Roosevelt was elected president. He took over a state in very poor economic condition, and I, thanks to democracy, took over a Reich faced with ruin.
>
> "While an unheard-of revival of economic life, culture, and art took place in Germany under National Socialist

leadership, Roosevelt did not succeed in bringing about even the slightest degree of betterment in his own country.

"This is not surprising if one bears in mind that the men he had called on for support—rather, the men who had called on him—belonged to the Jewish element, whose interests are always aligned to disintegration and conflict. From the moment he stretched out his hands to the diabolical cleverness of international Jewry, the American president has labored with only one goal in mind: to create the war that will only destroy him and his countrymen. The last thing he wants is peace. Should peace come to Europe, his squandering of millions on armaments will be seen as the plain fraud it is. Thus he had no choice but to provoke an attack upon his country.

"The fact that the Japanese government, which had been negotiating for years with this man, has at last become tired of being mocked by him fills all the German people, and, I think, all other decent people in the world, with deep satisfaction.

"As for the German nation, it wants only its rights! It will secure for itself this right to live even if thousands of Churchills and Roosevelts conspire against it!"

Here Goebbels completely lost his head and, along with every one of his colleagues, jumped up and started to yell. He screamed so long, so loudly that his voice, like that of all those about him, emerged in a strangled hiss. In that din the Führer held up his hands.

"The Reich government therefore breaks off all diplomatic relations with the American government and declares that under the circumstances brought about by President Roosevelt, Germany considers herself as of today to be at war with the United States."

THE FOREST

On that same day, a fine one, with bright streaming sunshine, Alexander Granite, the Great Granach of old, entered the little town of Zhmerinka, well behind the eastern front. Upon making inquiries, he walked the length of the main street, turned left at the road by the livery stable, and entered a quarter that was separated from the rest of the hamlet by a series of wooden barricades. He stepped by them unimpeded and made his way to what had once been a tavern. A number of families, he discovered, were living inside. He climbed the stairs and knocked on the second door of the second floor.

An old woman in a kerchief responded. Although she was wrinkled all over and shrunken to little more than half her youthful size, he at once recognized Drahomira, his wife. Her eyes, however, were filled with cataracts like crystals of salt; even if she had been able to see, she would never have recognized the bald man with the fringe of snowy hair who stood before her. However, her mind, which had once been clouded, was now quite clear; when Alexander told her who he was, she embraced him.

Not long afterward, perhaps an hour, as they were enjoying a second cup of tea, they heard a disturbance below and then a loud knock on the door. Three German soldiers, in gray and green, ordered them to gather their belongings and join some twenty or twenty-five other people in the back of an open truck. Everyone, they explained, was going to be taken to the open country, where there were fresh air and vegetables and eggs, and where everyone would be able to do productive work on a farm. After making several more stops, the truck drove from Zhmerinka eastward, in the direction of Vinnitsa. But before they got to that city, they turned off the road and soon found themselves traveling in a lonely forest.

By then the sun had dropped well down in the sky and the shadows of the trees fell over the road. The people in the truck started to shiver. Drahomira asked her companion where they were going. "We're in a woods," he answered. "There are trees on every side." Then the road ended and the truck came to a stop. The Jews—for that, of course, is who they were—got out. Carrying their bundles, they followed the men in uniforms to a little clearing. Then they had to take off their clothes.

"Don't worry," explained one of the Germans. "We have clean clothing and blankets on the farm. It's not far. It's just ahead."

Granach-Granite took off his pants and his coat and his shirt. He took off his underthings. Then he looked at his naked wife. The little clearing, with the last of the sun upon it, was like the meadows they used to travel through in their youth, in the previous century. He was easily able to remember how full Drahomira's breasts had been then, and how smooth and pale all of her skin. He took her hand and began to walk with her after the others. They did not cross the clearing. They walked once again into the forest. Drahomira asked, "Is this where the clothes are? And the chickens? Is this where we'll plant the potatoes and beets?"

Alexander peered as best he could between the trunks of the trees. He looked through the bare branches. "Yes," he said. "I can see a farmhouse. There's a goat. There are chickens. Can you hear them? Cluck, cluck, cluck. That's where we're going."

Who can say? Perhaps it was a farm they were going to—or would have been, if, as he had so often done in the past, the legend of film had been able to arrange a happy ending.

CHAPTER FIVE

WARNERS

Here are the headlines from today's *Examiner*: GERMAN FORCES SMASH RUSSIAN DEFENSES, ADVANCE ON ROSTOV. Does that sound like a happy ending? ROMMEL'S TANKS ROLL TOWARD EL-ALAMEIN. What it looks like is the beginning of the end. There goes the fog machine. What a joke! A half-million cubic feet of vaporized oil. It's like pea soup. I can hardly see Ernie Glickman, a three-hundred-pounder. And there's Greenstreet, no beanpole, as thin in this stuff as a wraith. That would be fine if the scene were Waterloo Bridge or Santa Monica Pier. But we're supposed to be in Morocco. South of Gibraltar. North of Timbuktu. They haven't had fog in one thousand years.

This picture—it's an experiment in moviemaking, like the music of our tennis pal, Schoenberg. Throw the notes up in the air! Here we are, on the last day of shooting, and until an hour ago no one knew whether the hero would get the girl. Of course my own little scenes have been done for ages. Greenstreet, and M. et Mme. Dalio, and Cuddles—all of their work is also in the can. But they're here and so's Dooley Wilson, though Sam has long since sung his last song. Believe it or not, even the Epsteins showed up on the soundstage by nine. And why? The official story was that we all had new lines to loop, but the real reason was that everybody wanted to find out how the picture was going to end.

This morning's shooting, however, was crazier than ever. New dialogue, new lighting; Mike Curtiz screaming, Ingrid in a pout. Everyone running around like—what is the word for it? Hellzapoppin? The Katzenjammer kids. A Chinese fire drill. Ten o'clock. Eleven o'clock. Twelve. Poor Mike. He was in a rage. He's a Hungarian, too, from Budapest. Né Kertész. There the resemblance between us ends. All day I have wanted to speak to Madeleine Le Beau—*the beautiful*, it means in French. But each time I approach her, I break into a sweat. Not Mike! What a way he has with women! Three in an hour. All the pretty little extras on the set. Of course, he cannot speak English the way I can. At the end of this morning's shooting he shouted, "Lunge!" to the awkward Major Strasser. He was trying to show him how to fall after he'd been shot. "Lunge! Lunge!"

"Okay," said Julie.

"If you insist," said Phil.

And the whole company broke for lunch.

Now we are almost done. I can see the plane on the runway. Of course it isn't a real one. It is a cutout, to scale. Those mechanics are midgets. But you'd swear you were looking through the hangar at a Lockheed Electra. It has—and for me this is disturbing, disorienting—the Air France insignia, the familiar winged horse, on the nose. Nor can we say that this is precisely a happy ending. As it turns out, only the leading lady, and not the leading man, is on board.

If the morning had been chaos, the afternoon soon came to resemble the desert around El-Alamein. The trouble was that the Epsteins still hadn't thought of a finish. Is it possible that this was on purpose? *Go on, tell it,* that's what Rick says to Ilse when she admits that her own tale has no ending. *Maybe one will come to you as you go along.*

And maybe one won't. Everyone—the actors, the camera people, the grips and gaffers—was standing around long after the break for lunch was done. Veidt and Rains were having a game of chess. Henreid was circling horse after horse on the Santa Anita form. And Madeleine, with a mother-of-pearl hairbrush, was combing the curls from her hair. What hair! What a cupid-bow mouth! *"Vive la France,"* I sighed, echoing her last line in the picture. *"Vive la democracie!"* I'd read in Louella's column that she and Dalio were about to get a divorce. Could such a thing be true?

RENAULT: *How extravagant you are—throwing away women like that. Someday they may be rationed.*

That's what Rains tells Bogart after Rick sends Yvonne home in a taxi. But no one will ever hear the lines. Joe Breen crossed them out. That Hays Office is worse about sex than I am.

CROUPIER: *Another visa problem, Captain.*

RENAULT: *Show her in.*

More dialogue for oblivion. Our very own colonel—Jack Warner is in the
army now—didn't wait for the censor. He Xed out the lines himself.

Speaking of Warner, he finally stormed onto the set and—he was wearing
a uniform tailored in wardrobe and a peaked cap—made a beeline for the
Epsteins. He struck a pose, his hands on his hips, glaring from one to the
other. "This time you bastards have gone too far."

"What is it, Jack?"

"Did we forget to salute?"

The snorts, the snickers, floated down from the grid, where the electri-
cians were fiddling with the lights. Veidt began to choke on something. Rains
jumped up from the game and beat the actor on the back, as if he'd been
eating a fish with bones. Even Bergman hid her face in her hands.

"Salute? I don't want you to salute. I want you to come up with the lines
you've been paid for. It's not too late to take you off this picture."

Now Ernie Glickman, his lips inside out, came ambling forward. "Come
on, Jack. You know you don't mean it. We can't do a thing without the boys."

"Oh, yeah? That's what you think. And don't call me *Jack*. There's a war
on, in case you didn't know. I'm a lieutenant-colonel."

Ernie grinned even more broadly. He took hold of Warner's beribboned
lapel. "Excuse me, colonel. I only wanted to say this is no time for a court-
martial. Ha-ha! The boys will have an ending in just a minute."

"Don't try to con me, Glickman. This has been going on since day one
of the picture. One last-second rescue after another. Why else have we been
sitting on our hands—and at twelve thousand dollars an hour!—the whole
afternoon? These guys"—and here the officer waved contemptuously at the
twins—"haven't a clue about what happens next."

"Not a clue?" echoed Julie. "What a terrible thing to say."

"Scandalous," said his brother.

"Libelous."

"You'll be lucky if we don't sue you for a statement like that."

"Yeah?" said the lieutenant-colonel. He slapped his olive-colored trousers as if there were an invisible swagger stick in his hand. "Go ahead. Tell
me. Tell us all. Your minute's up."

There was a pause. One of the twins looked up toward the grillwork.

The other looked down at the ground. Then they looked at each other. *"Round up the usual suspects!"* they simultaneously declared.

It was as if a lightning bolt had struck all the occupants of Soundstage 1. Thirty-five people took in a breath. "Huh?" said Jack Warner. "For what? Round them up for what?" But everyone else had started shouting at once. Finally the director stood up on the canvas seat of his chair. He put both hands in the air. "Anybody who has some talking to do, please shut up!"

As if he were the officer, the set obeyed. You could hear an American pin drop. "Set up 278. We make it 278a. Medium shot. Again we put the bullet into Herr Strasser's heart. We make excitement. We make our ending!"

The rest of the afternoon sped by. The Epsteins scribbled out notes. Bogart and Rains memorized their handful of lines. This time, when Rick pulled the trigger, the German dropped with conviction. A police car raced up and screeched to a halt near Renault.

GENDARME: *Mon Capitaine!*

RENAULT: *Major Strasser has been shot.*

As the camera rolled I drew up with stealth to where Madeleine Le Beau stood, her hips thrust sideways against the door of the hangar. "Guess what?" I whispered, almost in her ear. "My life is a comedy. Ha! Ha! A comedy in disguise."

She whirled about. "Oh, hello, Peter."

I blinked the perspiration from my eyes. I plucked the damp shirt from where it clung to my skin. "I have heard the unfortunate news. About the divorce. Do not be sad, *chérie*. I have something for you. A little treat. *Un petit bonbon.* Look. It's here, in my pocket."

A little light shone in the irises of her pale blue eyes. She took a step closer. Then she lifted her head and sniffed at the air. *"Qu'est-ce que c'est cette odeur?"* she demanded. "That smell? *Mon Dieu! Quelle horreur! Une frangipane!"*

RENAULT: *Round up the usual suspects.*

GENDARME: *Oui, mon Capitaine.*

So Laszlo gets the girl—Laszlo, Victor; not Laszlo Loewenstein. They are on the plane now. The fog from the fog machine billows over the runway.

Rick and Renault stare out at the taxiing aircraft. Then Curtiz, to our astonishment, starts once more to shout.

"Cut! Cut! Goddammit, cut!"

"Now what?" That from Jack L. Warner. "I don't believe it."

Curtiz: "Where is the poodle? I asked for a poodle."

Up comes Kaplan, one of the production assistants, at the trot. "What do you mean, Mike? There's nothing like that in the script."

The Budapester glowers down at him. What fury on his purple brow. What scorn on his twisted lips. "You dumdum. Big bastard dumdum. I'm getting crazy! Where is the poodle?"

Warner: "For Christ's sake, don't stand there, Freddie. Go get him a dog."

"Dog? What dog? Idiot! Fool idiot! I want a *poodle*! On the runway! A poodle of water! Mr. Rick! Mr. Renault! They must go splash-splash-splash when they walk."

It is easy enough to arrange. A bucket. Another bucket. Now the two men take their stroll through the fog, the darkness, the damp. Each footstep, just as Mike wanted, sends up a little spray. They speak of the future. A new life. A new friendship. Brazzaville.

Over their heads, through the dark of the night, the twin-motored airplane wends its way west. Not a real plane. A job for the miniature department. Look close. Try to see the thread, treated with iodized salt, that holds it aloft. There were no such strings attached to the aircraft on which—through far thicker clouds, through bright lightning flashes—we'd circled Salzburg. We hung only by the thread of fate and luck, as all men must do when they are not in a movie but take their chances on life.

CHAPTER
S I X

WILD MAN OF BORNEO

In that same year, 1942, as the world war continued to rage, the sun came up over the Pacific and shooed the stars away. It hauled itself over the treetops; it set to lapping the dew from the leafy huts. From one such dwelling, still in blue shadow, a man emerged. He was quite tall, with reddish-brown skin and a very high forehead that had been purposely deformed in his youth. Except for the bone driven through the end of his penis and the betal pouch slung over his waist, he was clothed in nothing but a swirl of paisley tattoos. He stretched and yawned, revealing two perfect rows of sharply filed teeth.

Carefully, so as not to wake his fellow tribesmen, he moved away from his hut, past a line of posts, each of which was topped by a human skull. One of these he rubbed for luck. Then he crossed to where a pool of rainwater half filled a hollowed-out log. He bent and quite delicately scooped a handful, and then another handful, to his lips. At the edge of the jungle beneath an ironwood tree, he defecated and urinated, squatting for each. Then he set out, heading north-northwest through the towering *tapans*, the sago and sugar palms, the wild tobacco and wild pepper trees of the jungle.

The sun rose higher and higher. Beneath the shutters of the fronds, the vines, it remained perpetually twilight. On and on the native moved, at not quite a trot. He clasped his hands behind him, the way a skater will as he moves on ice. More hours went by. The sun began to slip down the opposite side of the sky. On the move, the traveler gnawed at a yam, half charred, half raw, that he held in his hand. Far away, he heard a sound like thunder, but no raindrops fell on the canopy. What he heard was the echo of warships and their iron guns. It grew dark. A wahwah, a long-armed ape, swung overhead, speaking gibberish. Off the trail, amidst the tree stumps, a honey bear made a fuss. In the growing blackness, squirrels leapt from branch to branch, and innumerable insects started to buzz.

Finally the native reached a small clearing. Members of various tribes, including a few fellow Dayaks, were seated upon the thistles. The lobes of their ears went to their shoulders. They were staring at a cloth, an old white sheet, that had been stretched between two cabbage palms. Already shadows were playing upon it. These were the forms of men and women. Some of them were clothed, some almost as naked as any of the aborigines. One man—he must have been a spirit—had a streak of silver in his hair. The shades of horses galloped this way and that. Sounds, making little more sense than the chattering gibbon, came out of a box on the ground. Grinning, the dark-skinned native crossed his legs and settled onto a spot. His unblinking eyes never left the phantasmagoria that played out before him. Sometimes he laughed, going huff-huff. On occasion, for no reason at all, a tear would drop out of his eye. Every now and then he would reach into his pouch and take out a betal nut, which he chewed into a pulp. The evening went by, full of warfare between these men and gods. Once a breeze came up, so that the sheet flapped gently, full of ripples. It was a soul in flight to another form of existence.

ABOUT THE AUTHOR

Leslie Epstein was born in 1938, in the same year Germans began sending Jews to Dachau, and filmmakers in Hollywood were at work on *Gone With the Wind* and *The Wizard of Oz*. His father and uncle were, respectively, Philip G. and Julius J. Epstein, legendary wits and the writers of dozens of films, including *The Strawberry Blonde, The Man Who Came to Dinner, Mr. Skeffington, Yankee Doodle Dandy, The Bride Came C.O.D.,* and, of course, two of the most famous films with Peter Lorre: *Arsenic and Old Lace* and *Casablanca*. This book is dedicated to them and in a sense to the author's childhood in California, which he left for an undergraduate degree at Yale and a Rhodes scholarship at Oxford. He has published six books of fiction, most notably *King of the Jews*, which has become a classic of Holocaust literature, and *Pinto and Sons*. His articles and stories have appeared in such places as *Esquire, The Atlantic Monthly, Playboy, Harper's,* the *Yale Review, Triquarterly, Tikkun, Partisan Review,* the *Nation,* the *New York Times Book Review,* the *Washington Post,* and the *Boston Globe*. In addition to the Rhodes scholarship, he has received many fellowships and awards, including a Fulbright and a Guggenheim fellowship, an award for Distinction in Literature from the American Academy and Institute of Arts and Letters, a residency at the Rockefeller Institute at Bellagio, and various grants from the National Endowment for the Arts. For many years he has been the director of the creative writing program at Boston University. Having sent his own three children off to college, he lives with his wife, Ilene, in what is now a very neat condominium in Brookline, Massachusetts.